Hybrid Aria

Jessica Hall

Avalon City
Copyright © 2021 by Jessica Hall

Hybrid Aria

Introduction

EAR. PURE FEAR, THE sort of fear that makes your skin itch. When you can feel every hair on your body rise, when you feel like your skin is crawling. Fear that makes your body freeze, paralysing you on the spot, that's the sort of fear I felt when I heard her blood-curdling scream.

The only thing was I was her big sister, so I couldn't run away. I had no choice but to move, to go to her. I forced my legs up the front porch of the Pack house, running in the direction I could hear her screaming my name. My feet pound on the floorboards in panic. I'm moving so fast, I felt myself slipping on the hallway rug, making me skid along the floor and into the wall. My head and shoulder twist at an awkward angle into the kitchen door frame, with enough force that black dots danced in front of my vision. My collarbone and shoulder send shooting pain through my body as I feel my shoulder dislocate on impact.

"Aria! Aria!" Her petrified scream echoed through the house. Jumping to my feet, my head spun. I turned the corner into the kitchen to see the Alpha dragging my sister by her hair into the basement with a whip in his other hand. I start running to her, grabbing the basement door frame just in time for him to slam the door shut on my fingers. My own scream escapes my lips in agony. I reach for the door handle, only to find it's been locked. I start trying to yank my hand free. I could hear her crying and screaming for me on the other side of the door.

"LEAVE HER ALONE!" I screamed at him, slamming my body into the door, trying to free my fingers and get in. Not being able to get a run-up, I threw my body with all my might towards the side where my fingers were stuck, the door moving just enough for me to free my injured bloody mangled hand. My fingers were definitely broken as they twisted and jutted out at unnatural angles. Backing up into the kitchen, I ran full force into the door and bounced off, knocking the air out of my lungs. I stood up, backing up again and running harder. I dropped my shoulder hitting the door with so much force it burst open, my feet hitting air as my body was thrown down the stairs landing at a weird angle. My head smashing into the basement's concrete floor.

Chapter 1

Aria's POV

"COME ON, LILY, TIME to get up," I whispered to my six-year-old sister. She rolled on the mattress stretching and yawning, her beautiful sapphire blue eyes fluttering open to look back at me. Our room was the smallest in the Packhouse and at the back of the house away from everyone. The room consisted of a double bed mattress, a window, and a few toys for Lily. All our possessions easily fit in the duffle bag that was also our wardrobe.

"You've been jogging, Ari,," she said, sleepily looking down at my outfit.

"No, they are just comfy now. Come on you have to get ready for school," I sat next to her on the mattress on the floor. Lily sat up frowning at me. I pulled her pyjamas top off before pulling her school shirt over her head.

"Quick, hop up and put your pants on while I get ready," I told her.

I quickly got up, walked over to the duffle bag next to the mattress, and pulled my work uniform out my bag before quickly undressing and slipping it on. I reached for my brush, pulling my hair into a high ponytail before doing the same to Lily's hair while sitting next to her on the bed. I reached over, grabbing her joggers and socks, placing them on her feet and tying the laces. We could hear people moving about in the house. Lily froze, staring towards the door.

"He's up, Ari," Lily whispered.

I quickly threw my shoes on and grabbed the duffle bag, throwing her pyjamas in it and the clothes I had on earlier. Throwing the bag over my shoulder, I walked over to the window, knowing we wouldn't be able to sneak out of the house using the front door. Slowly opening the window, I dropped the bag out before reaching for Lily. She climbed up onto the windowsill before jumping to the grass below. It wasn't a big jump; the house was only one level besides the basement and the attic. I climbed through, jumping to the grass below before reaching up and shutting the window behind me gently.

Running up the side of the house towards the side gate, I glanced to make sure none of the Pack members were in the front yard. It was exceedingly early still. The sun had only just started coming up, light starting to break through trees that surrounded the house. I grabbed Lily's hand and started jogging towards the bus stop at the end of the dirt road, which was also the driveway. As we neared the end, I could hear the bus coming past. We ran faster to the bus stop, getting there just in time. I threw my arm out, waving the bus down. The bus driver smiled when he saw us.

"Hey, Bill," I said, getting on the bus and passing him our bus fare.

"No smile today, Lily?" he asked, smiling down at her. Her lips tugged at the sides before she gave him a big toothy grin.

"That's my girl," he said. We moved to the back of the bus. The drive into town was only ten minutes long, and Lily stretched out on the seat next to me, placing her head in my lap.

"Ari, I'm hungry," she said, gazing up at me.

"I know, I will make you some lunch and breakfast when we get into town," I told her as I leant down to kiss her head.

I gazed out the window watching the trees and morning birds. I was over having to live this life. My stepfather was a cruel man, and he was the Alpha of one of the most notorious Packs in the city. I would have left when our mother died, but he wouldn't let me take Lily. I don't know why, it's not like he was ever a father to her. He hated her from the moment she was born, blamed her for our mother's death. I still remember when he brought her home and told me my mother died during childbirth. He shoved little Lily in my arms and said, "Look after it." I remember being confused. I was only thirteen at the time. I knew nothing about babies. I had to drop out of school, give up my entire life. I raised her, loved her, and she became my whole world. I didn't under-stand how he could reject his own pup, his own flesh and blood.

Lily was an adorable baby; Mum would have loved her. I named her Lily since David didn't even bother to do the paperwork. Lily was Mum's middle name. She was so excited when she found out she was expecting, and so was David, but when my mother died that excitement turned to hate. The Pack suffered for 6 years since. Petrified of him, they would never go against him. He was Alpha for a reason. So here I was, a high school dropout raising my baby sister. Luckily, Mum had everything ready for her arrival before she passed because the Alpha didn't help me with anything. I had to get formula off Pack members. Luckily, even after Mum's death, they didn't hate her or me. They felt sorry for Lily so they would sneak me tins of formula and nappies.

When Lily turned five and was old enough for school, I enrolled her and started looking for a job so I could try and provide for her. It wasn't much, but it was better than having to ask or beg Pack members for anything she needed. I still remember the beating I got when I asked David for some money to buy her school uniform. He split my lip open before dragging me to the basement, where he beat me until I passed out. I shook my head at the memory before looking down at Lily, who was playing with my father's necklace that hung from my neck.

The necklace had a wolf on one side and a man with fangs on the other side. My father died when I was two, I don't remember him. My mother used to tell me how loving he was, but after the Alpha took us in when I was seven, she didn't really speak about him. Alpha David didn't want to hear about her past life. She was his mate, he always thought it was a betrayal that she had a child with someone who wasn't her mate sent by the Moon Goddess.

What made it worse is my father wasn't a wolf. He was a Vampire and my mother was a wolf, therefore making me a Hybrid, which isn't all it's cracked up to be. I'm an abomination. I can't completely shift like other wolves. I can grow claws when needed, which is quite painful, and I can also mind link. From my vamp side, I get their speed and sense of smell. I also can't heal like a wolf or a Vampire unless I drink human blood. Being raised in a wolf Pack means I don't get blood, which is okay. I can live without it simply fine, but it means I'm always weaker and I can't heal. Alpha David forbids me from drinking blood, and besides him, the only other people who know what I am are my mother and Lily. I hoped one day, Lily and I would be free of this hellhole so I no longer must hide what I am, but that will never happen.

The bus pulled up out the front of the diner I worked at. I quickly pushed Lily towards the exit, stepping onto the footpath.

"Come on, Lily. If we hurry, I will get Marcus to make you some pancakes before school."

Lily took off into the diner to her usual spot, which was close to the kitchen. I watched as she slid along the booth seat, placing her bag down on the red leather seat beside her. Lily loved the diner; she came with me every morning before school and after school, because my shift didn't finish until 6. I would use my lunch break to pick her up from school, but the biggest bonus of working here was Zoe.

The owner was a human woman who owned "Joe's Diner". Her husband was Joe. He died years ago, and she took over her husband's business. Zoe was in her late sixties. She has long white hair that's always pulled into a bun with green eyes and rosy cheeks. She is a bigger woman but one of my most favourite people I know. She always smiled and loved Lily, and since she didn't have children of her own, she kind of took me and Lily in. Zoe always made sure Lily had lunch for school and breakfast and dinner. After Lily got seated in the booth, I greeted Zoe with a hug before walking out to the kitchen. Marcus was standing at the stove with his hippy tie-dyed shirt and jeans, already making Lily pancakes.

Marcus was probably my only real friend; he was a good-looking bloke with his blonde hair and blue eyes, but unfortunately for me, he was also gay. I waved to him as I walked past to find my apron. Lily has pancakes every morning before school. I grabbed my apron and wrapped it around my waist before walking back out to grab the coffee. I started refilling a few customers' cups.

Joe's Diner was always busy no matter the time of the day. When I finished refilling cups, I walked back into the kitchen to grab Lily her pancakes.

By the time Lily finished her breakfast, it was 8 AM. I cleaned up the booth Lily was at and ducked back into the kitchen to grab Lily's school bag, which I kept in the duffle bag. As I was walking back through the kitchen, Zoe was already waiting with a paper bag.

"I made her ham and salad sandwiches, and Marcus threw in some quiches from yesterday for her,," she said, smiling, placing the bag in my hand. Lily came running into the kitchen, wrapping her arms around Zoe, her little arms barely making it halfway around Zoe's hips. Zoe smiled down at her before placing a kiss on top of her head.

"Have fun at school and learn new things," Zoe told her. I thanked Zoe before chucking the bag over my shoulder and grabbing Lily's hand to walk her to school. The school was only one block away, so Lily and I walked hand in hand the whole way. The streets were busy with everyone getting ready for work, and I quickly pulled to the side as a rush of people came out of the subway, just in time for us not to be trampled. We quickly made it to the school, stopping just out the front of the gates, and I gave her a quick kiss. "I'll see you at 3 o'clock, okay? Have fun," I said before giving her a quick hug.

I watched her run off towards her friends before turning and walking back to the diner. Once I got back to the diner, I quickly went to retrieve mine and Lily's clothes from the duffle bag, but when I opened the bag, it was empty. Before I even got a chance to close it, Marcus walked in.

"Zoe already put them in the wash for you," he said before walking back to the kitchen. I quickly retrieved my apron and went to start taking orders and refilling everyone's mugs. The day went by quickly, and before I knew it, Zoe came out of the kitchen, signalling for me to come over.

"It's quarter to 3, you have to get Lily, dear. Here, eat this on the way. I noticed you haven't eaten since yesterday morning," she said, placing a roast lamb sandwich in my hand with a napkin.

"No, I'm fine, really Zoe, you do enough for us already." She refused to take it back.

"You girls are like children to me, don't be ridiculous," she replied before quickly turning around and walking into the kitchen.

I ate the sandwich while walking to the school. As I did, I looked up at all the high-rise buildings. I loved the city; everything was so fast-paced and alive, constantly on the go. I loved watching people rushing around going about their lives. When I made it to the school, I waited out the front for the school bell to ring. I wasn't waiting long before Lily came bursting through the doors with a huge grin on her face. She ran straight towards me wrapping her little arms around me in a hug. I bent down, picking her up and placing her on my hip as we walked back to the diner. She told me all about her day and what she did in class. Once back at the diner, Lily grabbed her books out of her bag and went to sit with Zoe, who was already sitting in a booth waiting for Lily's arrival. Every afternoon after school, Zoe would help Lily with her homework and listen about her day. I waited tables getting ready for the afternoon rush when I suddenly felt eyes on me. I looked up from refilling Lily's cup with water, but no one was there. Shaking off the feeling, I walked back into the kitchen to get the next order ready.

Chapter 2

Reid's POV

HAVING JUST FINISHED ONE meeting, my Beta Zane texted to tell me the next meeting I had has been moved to Joe's diner. Apparently, it was on neutral territory; the Black Moon Alpha didn't want to meet on my territory. *Pussy*, I thought, shoving my phone back in my pocket before adjusting my tie while walking to the elevator. I stepped in the elevator, hitting the button to the bottom floor when the elevator doors closed. I watched the buttons, watching the floors go down. When it got halfway down, it stopped, the doors opening. I growled, annoyed. Two women, one with red hair and the other a blonde both were quite attractive. One of them I recognised, the redhead. Michelle was a Pack member. The other was a human I didn't know, and a short stumpy man from the tech floor walked in after them. They quickly stepped back, realising who I was. They dropped their heads looking at the floor. "Sorry Boss," said the man. I'm fairly sure his name was Peter. I remember him coming up to my office to update the computers. I pushed the button for the doors to close. Listening, I heard them let out a breath just before the doors shut completely. I stared down at my Rolex watch, 2:30 PM. Shit! I was going to be late.

Once down at the foyer, my Beta was waiting with my keys in his hand. He tossed them to me. Catching them, I quickly threw them back at him. "You drive, I don't know where this place is." I walked out to my black Bentley getting into the passenger side and opening the window. We were driving to the south of my Pack's territory, and just as we left the border, I felt my wolf stir, trying to come forward.

"What's gotten into you, Ryder?" I asked. He didn't reply. I could feel that he was anxious. *Maybe this meeting wasn't a good idea,* I thought to myself. Feeling him pressing beneath my skin, I knew my eyes must have changed when I let out a growl, warning him to stop.

My Beta pulled the car over to the curb. "You alright boss?" he asked. Hair was spreading across my arms, my wolf fighting for control.

That's when it hit me, the most intoxicating scent. I looked around; we were pulled up out the front of a primary school. I couldn't see anyone, so I stepped out of the car. My wolf instantly calmed down, happy that we stopped. I looked towards the primary school across the road then looked up the street. I couldn't see anything except trees along the footpaths and a group of mothers waiting along the school gate, none of them standing out to my wolf and they were definitely human. As I was getting back in, the breeze shifted, and the intoxicating scent got stronger. It smelt like strawberries and citrus; it was making my mouth water.

My Beta got out staring at me questionably, and that's when I noticed her. She was standing behind a tree next to the gate of the school. She had long dark hair that was pulled into a ponytail. I wanted to run my fingers through it. She also had an hourglass figure. I stared at her back, hoping she would turn around, she was dressed in jeans and a plain white blouse with long legs. "MATE. MINE." I growled. Ryder echoed the same thing in my mind.

Zane smiled, a knowing look on his face. I went to walk across the road when the bell rang, and the little girl jumped up into her arms. I stopped before crossing and growled. Turning my back on her, I quickly got back in the car.

"What are you doing?" asked Zane, staring at me in disbelief. "Go get her,"

"What do you expect me to do? She has a kid," I said, pointing at her.

"First of all, you don't know if she has a kid. Secondly, I don't think she would be old enough to have a kid that is already in school," he stated.

"Fine, cancel my appointments and follow her," I snapped back. I watched Zane as he instantly sent a few messages before pulling out from the curb to follow her. My wolf wanted her. She was extremely attractive, but I am not one to separate a family. I watched her hips and arse move when she walked into the diner, feeling my pants becoming a little too tight. I adjusted them, stupid bloody wolf giving me dirty thoughts of what he wanted to do to her.

My eyes followed her through the window of the diner that I was supposed to be having a meeting at. The little girl ran to a woman that was seated in the booth. Zane and I watched her as she walked out the back before returning with an apron on and a glass jug with water and filled a glass up before handing it to the little girl. She must have felt me staring at her because she suddenly stood up, looking around cautiously.

"So, what do you want to do?"

"Drop me back to my office and come back to watch her for now. Try and find out which Pack she belongs to," I ordered him. Zane nodded his head before driving me back to my office.

The entire drive back, my wolf wouldn't settle down, trying to come forward, wanting me to go back and claim the girl. Stepping into the elevator, I hit the 20th floor where my office is. My wolf lurching forward, making me hit the elevator walls, trying to fight me for control.

"Settle down, Ryder, or I will reject her," I growled. The thought of rejecting her caused a stabbing pain in my chest and my lungs to restrict. How could she have such an effect on me already when I haven't even spoken to her yet? Stepping into the corridor, my secretary came running over to me. She was a nice girl, not much to look at, very plain Jane, in my opinion. She was like a stick figure, no arse and no boobs, but she was good at her job.

"Sir, I couldn't stop him. He said it was urgent, he is in your office,," she said, fear evident on her face.

"Who is?" I asked, annoyed.

"He said his name is David, sir." I nodded before throwing open my office door and glaring at Alpha David. I cancelled my meeting with the Black Moon Alpha earlier; I didn't think he would have the balls to show up to my office.

When I walked in, he was sitting behind my desk in my seat, his muscles bulging from his shirt. It looked ridiculous, as if it belonged to his little sister. He stared up at me with a smirk on his face before cracking his knuckles.

"Alpha, you're back," he stated. I growled warningly at him.

"Yes, I am. Now get the fuck out of my seat," I spat the words at him. He put his hands up in surrender before getting out of my seat and leaning against the window, looking down towards the street. Taking my seat, I sat back before asking Melody, my secretary, to make coffee and bring it in.

"What can I do for you, David? Why the sudden interest in meeting me?" I asked.

"That's Alpha to you," he snarled.

"Don't push me, David. You're in my territory now. You may have one of the strongest Packs in the city, but you know as well as I do that you don't stand a chance against me or my Pack. Now what the fuck do you want?" I said using my Alpha voice, forcing him to submit.

"I'm sure you're aware of the rogue attacks at my borders. I need help. I'm losing too many of my warriors. My guys keep pushing them back, but they keep coming."

"So, you dare come to my territory, try and challenge me in my office and then ask for my help?" I laughed, shaking my head. "You got balls, I will give you that. Now, what do I get out of this?"

"What do you want?" he asked.

"Nothing you can give me clearly. I don't need anything, and I don't want to get mixed up in your gang rivalries and drug business. I will do this as a favour for now, but just know when I do need something, you will do it. Understood?"

Alpha David nodded his head before giving me his hand to shake. "Deal," he said.

"Fine, I will organise my Beta to send some of my men over to watch the border. Tell your guys to expect them. If any of your Pack attacks one of my men, I will declare war."

Aria's POV

The last week and a half, I have been getting this strange feeling that I am being watched. Would Alpha David be sending someone to watch me? I wonder what he is planning. I know the Rogue attacks were getting out of hand and that he had to ask the Blood Moon Pack's Alpha for help. They have been along the borders. I have run into a few of them in the last week. Their auras are very dominating. I thought our Pack was sinister, but theirs is on an entirely different level. They even make me want to retreat, and that's saying something because not even Alpha David can make me submit with me being a Hybrid. The only reason I do is because I know I can't beat him. Sometimes it makes me wonder if I had human blood how much stronger I would be than my Pack. I know that's the only reason Hybrids are hunted down because we would be the dominant species, but there are so few of us that we don't stand a chance against a werewolf Pack. Therefore, I will always have to remain hidden and do as David says, because if he leaks what I am out, I will be hunted down like the rest of the Hybrids that have stepped foot into the city. I also know if I drink blood, they will realise straight away that I'm not just a wolf, and I really don't feel like being attacked by my own Pack. Lost in my thoughts, I didn't realise someone had come into the diner until they grabbed my elbow as I was walking past to clean some tables.

Placing my hand over my heart and jumping back, I looked at the customer.

"Sorry, I didn't see you. You nearly gave me a heart attack," I said nervously. The diner was extremely quiet today. The man just stared at me; he was quite handsome. He had shoulder-length hair that was pulled into a ponytail at the back of his neck. He was very lean and muscular, and he had green eyes and tanned skin.

He was wearing a grey suit, so he looked like he just stepped out of an important meeting.

"That's fine Hun, I was wondering if I could get some menus."

"Sure," I replied, going back to the counter and retrieving one. I passed it to him and waited for him to order. I could tell he was a werewolf by the way he carried himself, plus his scent was a dead giveaway. I wonder what Pack he is from.

"For now, I will just get two coffees black, no sugar please," he said politely.

I quickly ducked to the kitchen, putting the coffee on. I glanced over to him, which was a mistake as he was staring directly at me, watching what I was doing. Marcus came over standing behind me, "Order?" he asked.

I shook my head, turning to him.

"He hasn't ordered yet; I think he is waiting for someone," I said, grabbing two mugs and the jug, walking back over to the booth he is sitting at. I placed the mugs down before pouring the steaming hot coffee in the mugs. As I was about to leave, he stopped me, grabbing my elbow again. I looked down at him.

"What's your name?" he asked.

"A... Aria," I stuttered. He was starting to make me uncomfortable. I looked back towards the kitchen where Marcus was watching in case this bloke turned all creep on me.

"Nice to meet you, Aria. My name is Zane," he said, smiling at me. He had perfectly straight pearly white teeth. Looking down at his hand that still had hold of my elbow, I could feel my face getting hot. I quickly moved out of his reach, stepping back only to turn and walk straight into what felt like a brick wall. But it wasn't, it was another man. He was about 6.5 feet tall, had short dark hair, and I could feel his abs through his shirt when I walked into him. I looked up to apologise when his scent hit me. He smelt amazing, he had an earthy aroma like rosewood and sandalwood. I leaned in and inhaled without realising, when I heard someone clear their throat awkwardly. My eyes snapped open, and I stepped back quickly, apologising before taking off back towards the kitchen.

Once in the kitchen, I tried to calm my racing heart by taking deep breaths. "What's wrong with me?" I asked myself, not realising I said it out loud.

"Nothing is wrong with you. If I had to go serve those two hotties, I would be hyperventilating too. Damn girl, they are fine," said Marcus, coming up behind me.

Straightening out my apron, I followed him back towards the kitchen, stealing glances towards where they sat at the back of the café. I was secretly hoping Zoe would be back from her doctor appointment before I had to serve them.

A few minutes passed before they waved me over. I cautiously walked over making sure to stay a few feet away so I wouldn't get distracted by his intoxicating scent.

"What can I get you?" I asked, not looking at either one of them.

"What Pack do you belong to? I can tell you're a wolf, but you smell different from any normal wolf," asked the new mystery person.

Instead of answering, I just repeated the same question. "What can I get you?" My tone sounded bored.

The man smirked before reaching forward and grabbing my hand. As soon as he touched me, sparks flew through my hand and arm, leaving a tingling sensation. I quickly pulled my hand back as if I had just been burned. Taking a step back, I looked at him. His eyes turned pitch black, even the sclerae. It only lasted a few seconds before going back to their normal silver-grey colour.

He smiled at me; I couldn't bring myself to look away, completely mesmerised by his gaze.

"I'm Reid, Alpha of The Blood Moon Pack. What Pack do you belong to?" he asked, using his Alpha voice.

My heart rate sped up fear consuming me. His Pack was the Pack helping ours, and he had an even scarier reputation then Alpha David. He was known for being cruel and merciless to those that have stood against him. Alpha Reid was also said to have wiped out complete Packs when they wouldn't agree over territory disputes, but he was also an Alpha no other Alpha could go against. He had the largest Pack with over 500 Pack members, 95 percent of them being Pack warriors. Their Pack has been undefeated, and even if other Packs tried to stand against theirs, it would be a bloodbath. He is also the one responsible for killing off all the Hybrids. He made me want to run away or submit, which no Alphas have that effect on me.

"Ari, you got to go get Lily," Marcus sang out from behind the counter, distracting me and also saving me from submitting and answering him. I looked in his direction relieved, thanking the Moon Goddess for my escape. I quickly ripped off my apron, chucking it at Marcus, not daring to look behind me as I ran out the door to get Lily from school.

Chapter 3

Reid's POV

I WATCHED HER ESCAPE THE diner. I heard her heart rate spike when I told her my name. She has every right to fear me, but I don't want to scare her. My wolf wanted her. All of her, and so did I. Never in my life have I wanted something as much as I wanted her to be mine, but what was the most interesting thing about her was the fact that she could fight my Alpha's voice.

I could tell by the look on her face she wanted to submit, but she was also determined not to reveal anything about herself. Her scent radiated fear. It took all my strength not to chase after her and mark her. The bloke behind the counter came over and introduced himself as Marcus, pulling me out of my thoughts. He smelt human. We gave him our orders before deciding to move over to the table and chairs, where I know the girl Lily always sits after school. Zane raised an eyebrow at me when I moved but followed anyway.

"So, what's the plan then?" he asked.

"Well, if she won't talk, maybe her daughter will," I stated.

Marcus brought our food out, placing it in front of me. I looked down at my food and started eating. It was good. After about half an hour, the door opened to the diner. As predicted, the little girl ran straight for her usual spot directly across from us and started getting her homework out. We finished eating while they were gone, but I flagged Marcus down and ordered more coffee and a hot chocolate and cookies. When he placed the coffee on the table, he went to place the hot chocolate and cookies down. I shook my head and pointed to the girl. He quickly placed them down in front of her and thanked me before placing a kiss on the girl's forehead and walking away.

I could feel eyes on me. I knew my mate must be watching me carefully to see if I was going to hurt her pup. The girl looked up and smiled before thanking me. She set out to do her work, and after a few minutes, my mate brought her over a sandwich, placing it on the table in front of the girl as she looked at the girl's work.

"Where is Zoe?" asked the girl.

"She is still at the doctor. That one is incorrect, try again,," she said, pointing at the page at some math work before walking away to serve some new people who just walked into the diner.

I turned back to Zane. "You should head back to the office; I'm going to stay here for a bit." Zane nodded before standing up and leaving. I watched Lily struggle with her homework before getting up and sliding into the booth sitting across from her. She looked up at me with her blue eyes and chubby cheeks. She was adorable, her blonde curls hanging down around her face.

She looked up at me. "Hi, thanks for the hot chocolate,," she said. I just nodded and looked down at her work; she was doing three times tables. Really, they make kinders do times tables now?

I then proceeded to grab the little bags of sugar from the jar on the table and set up three lots of three and told her to count them, she looked down and using her fingers, she counted all nine.

"Nine," she said happily.

"Then that's your answer," I said to her, pointing at her page. She started using the sugar to help work out her math problems while I watched. After a while, I asked her some questions.

"So, what's your mother's name?" I asked, pointing at my mate who was standing behind the counter, her eyes glued on me.

"Aria, but she isn't my mum, she is my sister,," she said while still looking down at her page.

"So where is your mummy?" I asked, taking a sip of my coffee.

"She died when I was born. Ari looks after me. Has since I was born," she stated matter of factly.

"What about your dad then?"

Lily got all nervous. Her shoulders slumped, and her heart rate picked up. She was scared. I could smell it on her coming off in waves, so I quickly changed the question.

"How old are you and what grade are you in?"

She immediately relaxed. "I'm six, and I'm in grade one."

"And your sister?"

"Ari is nineteen." *So, she has been looking after her sister since she was thirteen? What about school,* I thought to myself.

"How old are you?" she asked.

"How old do you think I am?" I asked in return. She smiled.

"Old," she replied. I laughed at her answer. Kids always say the first thing that pops into their minds.

"I'm 28," I told her.

"So, you are old." She giggled.

"You won't think it's old when you are my age. So, it's just you and Aria?" Lily looked up. I could tell she was mind linking. Her eyes glazed over before she nodded. I knew her sister would have been listening in our my conversation.

"Aria said I shouldn't talk to strangers." I looked over to her, she was talking to the owner who just stepped in. Lily noticed my stare, looked up, and saw Zoe. She squealed before running over and wrapping her arms around the woman's waist.

I observed my mate. I could tell she was very protective of the pup, but there was something else I just couldn't put my finger on it. I knew she was a wolf, but she didn't seem quite as affected by the mate bond. I knew she felt it when I touched her, and she leaned in, inhaling my scent, but most wolves can't help but be all over each other like an elastic band that keeps pulling them back together. But for the most part, she seems unaffected unless she is close to me.

"She hasn't got a wolf," Ryder spoke up in my head.

"What do you mean she hasn't got a wolf. She is a werewolf?" I asked him.

"Yeah, she is, but she has no wolf. I have tried talking to her wolf, but it's like there is a blockage, or maybe her wolf died somehow." I could feel his sadness spilling into me at the thought of her not having a wolf, so I pushed him to the back of my mind.

Aria came over to clean the table. It was now dark outside. She placed Lily's stuff in her bag before wiping the table over.

"Aria," I asked.

Aria's POV

"Aria," he asked while I tried to clean the table as fast as possible.

"That's your name, isn't it?" he said, reaching out and grabbing my hand before standing up and pulling me into him. He lent forward and ran his nose along my chin to the crook of my neck.

The sensation made me shiver. He smelt so good it made my mouth water, made me want to lean in and touch him. I reached up and put my hand on his chest, inhaling his mouth-watering scent. I heard him chuckle softly before he kissed my cheek softly, which sent sparks all through me.

"Why do you smell different than a normal wolf?" he asked, which then snapped me out of my trance. I quickly stepped back. He looked upset for some reason and took a step toward me, I quickly grabbed Lily's bag and walked fast back behind the counter. He did not leave though. He sat at the front of the diner watching me, and no matter how much I tried to ignore his presence, my eyes would always go back to him. Deciding I should go out the back and check on Lily, I saw Lily was eating her ravioli Zoe had made. I thanked Zoe before walking back out to finish my shift. Only an hour to go.

When I came back out, I made myself a coffee before walking back out to the counter only to find the Alpha now sitting at the counter. I sipped my coffee, looking towards the two truckers that came in earlier, but they were still eating happily. Deciding to get the jug, I refilled the Alpha's mug. He smiled at me and kept watching me. *What the hell is his problem*, I thought to myself.

Marcus came out to speak to me, placing his hand on my lower back. I turned to look at him. Over my shoulder, I could hear a low growl coming from Alpha Reid, so low I looked at him wondering if I heard it. He was glaring at Marcus's hand. Not wanting him to kill my friend, I quickly stepped to the side, which made Marcus drop his hand.

"Lily is falling asleep. She has finished her dinner. Zoe said to knock off early, she can handle it from here. It looks like it's going to be a quiet night tonight." I nodded before walking out the back, and sure enough, Lily was fast asleep next to her empty bowl. I quickly grabbed her bag, taking off my apron. I chucked it in the washing machine before putting the washing in from today, along with all the tea towels and napkins then I turned it on. Grabbing my jacket, I put it on.

I picked up Lily and walked out towards the entrance where it was pouring down with rain. Placing Lily's bowl in the sink, I passed Lily to Marcus before taking my jacket off and draping it over Lily so she wouldn't get wet. She nestled into me. Marcus followed me, grabbing his keys. Zoe walked out just behind him putting an apron on.

"I'm not letting you walk home when it's raining." I nodded, thanking him before saying goodnight to Zoe.

Alpha Reid stood up. "I can take them home."

I politely declined his offer. He looked disappointed for some reason which made me feel bad. The drive to the Pack house was a lot faster by car. As he went to pull onto the dirt driveway, I stopped him. "It is okay we can walk from here," I said, opening the door before Marcus could protest. I could feel the Pack members' eyes on us through the trees, where they were watching. I grabbed Lily from the backseat, unclipping her seat belt before thanking Marcus for the lift home. It was still pouring down with rain by the time we got to the front of the Pack house, and we were both drenched and freezing. As I was about to walk up the porch steps, the Alpha came bursting through the front door growling. He stalked towards me. Quickly placing Lily on the ground, she stood behind me. I motioned her to run inside. I could tell it was me he was after. His eyes hadn't left mine since he nearly broke the door when he burst through it.

I took a few steps back and to the side of the house. Lily ran behind and up the porch steps and into the house just as he got to my position. He punched me straight in the face, forcing me to stumble. I stood back up when he raised his fist again; it connected with my jaw. I could taste the metallic taste of my blood. The third time he tried to hit me, I blocked him and stepped out of his reach.

"How dare you bring some random person to our lands."

"It was just Marcus, and I didn't. He dropped us off down the end of the driveway. I would never bring anyone to the Pack house," I screamed at him.

He didn't listen; he smelt strongly of whiskey. Pack members had started to crowd around to see what the commotion was. Alpha David lunged at me, but I jumped back at the last second, which was a huge mistake. It pissed him off when he missed, and instead, he decided to shift. This time it was his beast that took over. His wolf was a menacing dark brown with patches of black. He was growling, advancing on my position. He swiped at me with his giant claws, cutting deeply down my rib cage. I clutched at my side, which was bleeding profusely, stumbling back and onto one knee. When he went to lunge at me again, another wolf jumped in blocking him. I recognised the grey wolf instantly. It was his Beta Michael. He mind linked with me

"Get inside, Ari." Getting to my feet, I ran up the stairs and into the Pack house. I could hear growling outside. I knew Michael was the only reason I was not dead right now.

Running into my room, I slammed the door shut, leaning up against it for support. Lily was hiding underneath the blanket on the bed. "It's okay, Lily, it's just me."

She popped her little head out from underneath the blanket before running at me. Lily grabbed me around the waist sobbing. I flinched on impact, and she stepped back, noticing the blood. Sliding down the door into a sitting position, I closed my eyes. The adrenaline was wearing off, and the pain was trickling in. I could feel my fangs coming out. Looking over at Lily, she took a terrified step back, my eyes snapped to hers. I could hear her heart pounding, hear the blood pulsating in her veins. I could smell it.

Knowing it would not be long before my hunger kicked in, I raced into the kitchen to where the basement door is. Throwing it open, I raced down the stairs so fast, I tripped halfway down and rolled down the rest of the way, making me groan in pain. Once at the bottom, I crawled to the back of the basement where different herbs and plants were dried out and stored. Just as I went to reach up and grab the wolfsbane, a gloved hand grabbed it for me. I watched as Beta Michael placed the herbs in a bottle of water before passing it to me. I stared at him, confused and frightened. How did he know what I was?

I grabbed the bottle and chugged it down. It felt like acid burning down my throat, but I knew if I didn't, Michael would start looking like dinner. Wolfsbane instantly muted my blood-lust. Laying back on the cement floor, I could feel the wolfbane burning every cell in my body.

My stomach turned violently, and I reached for the closest thing to me, a box, and threw up the entire contents of my stomach, which was not much. Sitting up, I leaned back on some shelving before bringing the bottle back to my lips and forcing myself to drink more down. My throat was killing me. I could feel the burn all the way to my stomach, making me want to double over and scream.

"How?" I ask, my voice sounded strangled and breathless.

"We have always known, at least all of the original Pack members. When you joined this Pack, I saw your mother feed you a few times. The Alpha had sworn us to secrecy," he stated.

I looked at him. His eyebrow had a cut on it, but it was almost completely healed beside his clothes being a bit of a mess. You wouldn't think he just got into a fight with a werewolf, let alone an Alpha.

"I don't care that you're a Hybrid, you're still one of us. Everyone else thinks the same, but Ari, you need to get out of here," he stated.

"Tell me something I don't already know, but I can't. He won't let me take Lily, and he would find her straight away, being that the dick is technically her father!" I replied dryly.

His eyes darted up to the door nervously before falling back on me. "Get her to reject the Pack when she steps over the border. You do the same, then leave the city. Ari, we can't go against him, but we are all sick of his shit and watching him abuse you," he whispered. I could see the sadness in his eyes; he truly did care for Lily and me.

I nodded, not really knowing what to say.

"But her wolf isn't awake yet. How can she reject the Pack when she hasn't awoken yet?" I asked.

"You don't need a wolf to reject the Pack, Ari. You should know this seeing as you haven't got one either. You can also reject the Pack at any time. It's wolf genes, not the wolf itself!"

Nodding my head, I lifted up my shirt. There are 5 deep gashes across my ribs. The blood running down my stomach and thighs was pooling on the floor. Beta Michael grabbed a cloth and put pressure on it until it stopped bleeding before placing a waterproof dressing over it. It was going to take a good few days before it healed. I can't heal like a wolf but still faster than a human even without blood.

"Thanks," I croaked out.

"I would give you my blood, but the Alpha will notice straight away when your scent changes, and then we will both be dead and no one to look after Lily."

"You don't have to explain, I understand." Gripping the shelf, I pulled myself up before leaning back, regaining feeling in my legs. Michael passed me a jar. It had syringes filled with a gold liquid and two water bottles of wolfsbane.

"Just in case you need more, show Lily the syringes in case she ever needs to use them on you. They are concentrated levels of wolfsbane. I know wolfsbane can't kill you, but they," he said, pointing at the syringes of gold liquid "will even put you on your arse for a while, okay? And tell Lily not to drink from the bottles," he said.

I looked at him questionably. "It's fine. I noticed every time you got injured, my wolfsbane supply went down or completely went missing. I figured out it was you. Also, I could smell it on you."

He pushed me towards the stairs, and I climbed up them. Every step hurts. Even breathing hurts. I could feel my wound stretching with every movement I made. Once to the top step, Michael's mate Elizabeth was standing in the kitchen. She hugged me carefully before speaking.

"There is hot stew in your room. The Alpha is passed out drunk, so eat then have a shower,," she said before placing a box of pain-killers in my hand. She walked me to my room and watched me and Lily eat the stew. It was delicious. I didn't realise how hungry I was until I walked in and smelt it, my stomach instantly started growling. I polished off the whole bowl and even soaked up all the juices with a piece of bread. Elizabeth handed me a glass of water and pushed the pills into my hand again. I quickly swallowed two of the little pills before getting up and placing the jar and bottles of water in the duffle bag after explaining to Lily what they were.

"Remember Lily, you can't drink these. They will kill you and only use these on me if you have to," I said, making sure I spoke clearly so she understood what I was telling her.

Elizabeth took the bowls and bread plates out before bringing in towels. Getting up, I pulled Lily up with me, and we walked down the hall towards the bathroom, which was in the middle of the house. Stepping in, I flicked the light on. The bathroom was huge, bigger than our bedroom and had a large clawfoot bathtub and a huge shower with multiple showerheads. The room had grey tiles on the walls and black tiles on the floor. The fixtures were a gold colour, it was beautiful.

I turned the shower on letting it heat up the room before I slipped my clothes off. Lily pulled hers off as well and stepped under the water. My dressing was already drenched in blood from the wound reopening with movement. Climbing in behind her, I adjusted my shower head temperature, making it hotter. My muscles started to relax, not realising how tense I was. Looking down, I watched as blood and dirt went down the drain. We showered quickly, washing Lily's hair before getting out.

The pain killers were starting to kick in, and everything felt like it was going dull. I felt no pain, but my body felt heavy. I turned the water off and wrapped a towel around Lily. Grabbing our toothbrushes, we quickly brushed our teeth. I looked at my reflection in the mirror. I had a huge black bruise on my jaw, and on the other side, a black eye. Great, now I need to borrow makeup from someone before work tomorrow.

Once back in our room, Lily put on her pyjamas, and I slipped on a shirt and panties before climbing into bed. It did not take long before the pills knocked me out, and I fell into a dreamless sleep.

Chapter 4

Reid's POV

LEAVING HOME EARLY, I decided to head straight to Joe's Diner, not bothering to send Zane today. Besides, I also had a meeting at 9:00 with Alpha David. Seeing as we have cleared his rogues, he wants my men off his territory now.

I was extremely tired. My wolf kept me up most of the night. Even now Ryder was starting to become agitated and restless, and I had been struggling to keep him contained. All night he kept telling me something was wrong but did not know what. Getting in my car, I drove quickly, ignoring the speed limit, not taking me long to arrive at the small diner. Parking the car on the curb out the front, I got out and went in. I was greeted by the owner, Zoe. She was a nice lady. I sat at the counter, looking around, trying to see if she was in. Zoe came over, placing a mug of coffee in front of me. Reaching for it, I took a sip. After about an hour, she still wasn't in.

I looked at the time and saw it was 8 o'clock already. Zoe looked worried too. She kept glancing at the clock a few times, and she even stuck her head out the door looking towards the bus stop, but no Aria or Lily.

"I knew something was wrong. It's been nagging me all night," Ryder growled angrily in my mind.

"Shut up, you can't know that," I replied, annoyed, shoving him into the back of my mind. Feeling him still growling at me I got up and walked to the window looking out but no sign of her, so I walked back to the counter to speak to Zoe.

"Is Aria not working today?" I asked nervously.

"She was supposed to start at 6 this morning. I'm not sure what's going on," she replied. I could tell she was concerned, she kept glancing at the door and the clock.

"Is Aria usually late? Does she have a phone?" Zoe looked back at me before refilling my mug.

"No, never she is never usually late or misses her shift unless…" she hesitated then regained her composure. "No, she hasn't got a phone."

"Unless what?" I ask. I could tell she was going to say something before she stopped herself.

"No, it's nothing you should concern yourself with."

When Zoe went to walk away, I stopped her. I could tell something had her on edge, but before I could say anything, she stared me down.

"Look, I know she is your mate. It's quite obvious to me, but really I can't tell you anymore. She has enough on her plate without you causing trouble for her; you need to leave her alone," she snapped before glancing at the door again.

"What? How do you know?" I shook my head. trying to wrap my mind around what just came out of this human woman's mouth.

"My husband was a hunter. I know what goes on in this city; I may be old but not blind."

"Was a hunter?" I asked, shocked by her admission.

"Yes. Joe, my husband, was a hunter until he realised his best friend was a Vampire. That's when we realised Vampires and your kind aren't much different from humans. Most just want to live in peace, so he quit, and that's what got him killed. He died protecting his best mate when the Hunters came for him. My husband got in the way trying to protect him, they both died." She told me this completely unaffected, not like she did not care, but like she had come to terms with it and accepted it.

I just stared, completely shocked. Most Hunters wouldn't go and tell someone like me they were Hunters unless they were cocky or downright suicidal, but Zoe spoke as if it were a lifetime ago. I could tell there was no hate in her for my kind at all, just acceptance. I watched her go out the back, and I just sat thinking of what Zoe had just told me.

While I was lost in my thoughts, I felt a hand touch my shoulder. Looking up it was Alpha David and another man. Alpha David introduced him as his Beta Michael, we quickly shook hands before taking a booth in the far corner. Zoe came over and asked if we wanted to order anything, and we all just ordered coffee. I wanted this meeting over with as soon as possible so I could find Aria and Lily.

Looking at the Alpha, I could tell he was tired, and his breath smelt strongly of whiskey. *Was he still drunk?* I thought to myself. His clothes looked like he slept in them. He was wearing a flannelette shirt and jeans. His beta was dressed in a suit, he looked like he was angry with the Alpha over something. Whenever the Alpha would ask him something, it was short answers, and he practically spat the words at him. The Alpha was definitely drunk or extremely hung over because he wasn't even paying attention to how his Beta was speaking to him.

Zoe brought our coffees over, and the Alpha started gulping his down before he spoke.

"Well, Alpha Reid, I just wanted to let you know your warriors did an excellent job and we haven't had an attack the last 3 nights now, so if you wanted to pull your men back, you can. I really appreciate your help," he stated.

"If you don't need them any longer, I am happy to have them come back home. I know my men are missing their families. Even though they talk every day, it's still not the same for them when they are used to being with their mates and children daily. You would understand; you have kids yourself, don't you, David?"

His Beta stiffened, looking towards the Alpha. I observed as Alpha David clenched his fists tightly on the table then unclenched them, not bothering to answer me. Suddenly my wolf started to get all anxious. I was about to mind link Zane to send some of our warriors out to look for Aria and Lily when her scent hit my nose so quickly I thought for sure I imagined it, until she bolted past the front of the diner quickly, apologising to Zoe for being late before she took off to the back where I couldn't see her.

Looking towards Zoe, I saw concern on her face before she followed Aria to the back somewhere. *What the hell was going on?* Straightening out my suit, I turned back to Alpha David and his Beta. At least she was safe.

"Glad you think so. Are you really that blind, Reid? I could see from the back of your mind. She is hurting, you bloody arse-hole. Plus, I could smell it on her. I knew something was wrong," growled Ryder. He pushed at me, trying to take over. To run to her, to chase her and make sure she was okay. But I would not give him the control he wanted. I could not let him rip apart the diner and scare everyone here or have Alpha David think I was challenging him.

"You okay, Alpha Reid?" asked Michael

"Yes, sorry, I'm fine. I just zoned out for a second, sorry about that." We made small talk while we finished our coffees. Well, mostly Michael and I talked while David just looked hungover and didn't know what day it was. After about 20 minutes, Aria came out. I kept glancing over to her, watching her. When she got closer, I got a strong whiff of her scent. I instantly got goosebumps all over me. Ryder was trying to push forward because she smelt terrible. I could smell blood on her. Aria's scent was extremely weak, and I could smell something else.

"WOLFSBANE," growled Ryder. He was pissed that someone had hurt our mate using wolfsbane. Just before she reached my table, she froze for a second. Both the Alpha and the Beta looked up to see who I was staring at. Aria quickly dropped her head but not fast enough, I could see she had a black eye and bruises along her jaw. She quickly filled our cups, and before taking off behind the counter, which made me feel relieved, the look that Alpha David gave her made me want to rip him apart. He looked at her with disgust. I didn't catch the Beta reaction to her, he was looking everywhere but at me. I thought I saw his eyes glaze over though like he was mind linking someone.

"Well, since everything has been sorted, we might as well keep this meeting short. I will have my men off your territory straight away, and if I ever need anything, Alpha, I will be sure to contact you to collect that favour," I said.

The Alpha nodded before getting out of his seat and walking out. His Beta Michael got up shaking my hand before saying, "Sorry about him, he had a rough night last night and a few too many drinks."

"I figured as much. He smells like a bar."

Michael chuckled before taking his leave. Walking up to the counter, I went to take a seat when I saw her just out of the corner of my eye, standing next to the sink in the kitchen. I watched as she took some pills when I felt Ryder push me over. Before I knew it, I was standing behind her.

She turned around and walked into me "You can't be back here, sir," she said nervously.

I looked down at her, then grabbed her and crushed her against my chest. Reaching into her back pocket, I pulled the sheet of painkillers out and read it. "Codeine. What are you taking these for?" I asked her. Werewolves heal fast, no need to take pain killers unless severely injured. She quickly stepped out of my grasp and snatched them out of my hand.

"That's none of your business. Now please, you can't be back here." I could tell she wanted to get away from me, so I turned and walked back out and sat at one of the booths. Someone had hurt her. The evidence was all over her face, and I could smell blood on her like she was still bleeding, and she strongly smelt of wolfsbane. It must be on her clothes, or maybe she spent the night around it, because from how strong it smells, she should be dead.

Chapter 5

Aria's POV

THE NEXT MORNING, I woke up, and Lily was already dressed for school, quietly waiting, leaning against my side. Sitting up slowly, my body ached. I reached for my watch glancing down at the small screen that said 9:30 AM. "Shit, we are already late," I told Lily.

"I tried to wake you; we missed our bus," she replied, putting her shoes on and trying to tie the laces herself.

"Come here," I said. She walked over, and I quickly tied her laces. "Pass me my uniform please, Lil." She quickly did as I asked, passing me my clothes. Putting my bra and panties on, I reached for my blouse Lily was holding. As I moved, I could feel my wound reopening. I slowly placed my hand over it, trying to hold it together. Lily helped me put my black slacks on and my shoes.

I quickly tied the laces, before putting my blouse on. I peeled one side of my dressing back, it was starting to heal very slowly.

Pulling the dressing off completely, I quickly reached into my duffle bag, pulling out a new waterproof dressing and covering it again. I then put my blouse on, grabbed our bags, and walked down the hall to the kitchen with Lily following closely behind me. Elizabeth was standing in the kitchen at the sink, washing the dishes from breakfast when we walked in.

"The Alpha isn't here if that's what you are wondering."

"No, I need a lift to Lily's school. Is Michael still here?"

"No, he is with the Alpha, but I will go grab my keys and run you myself. Meet me in the car,," she said, walking out of the kitchen towards her room. Lily and I grabbed our bags and walked out to the garage where a heap of cars were lined up. Finding Elizabeth's green hatchback, we waited beside it until she came out and unlocked the doors. I pulled the front seat forward so Lily could climb into the backseat before getting in the passenger seat.

"Here, take these pain killers when you need to. They won't make you drowsy but will relieve the pain, and this is my make-up bag. Your bruises are already fading but are still quite visible," she told me, dumping the makeup bag on my lap. I put the pills in my pants pocket before using the visor mirror to try and conceal my black eye and a bruised jaw. It helped a little, but anyone looking too closely would easily see them. Elizabeth also handed an apple to Lily in the back seat and told her to eat it for breakfast and a lunch box.

"Here Lil, some sandwiches and chips for lunch." Lily thanked her before eating her apple.

The drive to the school was fast. Elizabeth wasn't the best driver; she is very heavy-footed; I'm not even sure she knows what a brake is. It was usually a ten or fifteen-minute trip, and she got us to

Lily's school in half the time, which I was glad for. Her driving was starting to make me nauseous. Once we pulled up out front of the school, Lily and I quickly walked to the main office where I signed her in as late before I walked her to her classroom. After saying my goodbyes, I started to walk to work which was surprisingly more exhausting than I thought it would be. My ribs were throbbing, and I knew the dressing was saturated with blood already. Putting pressure on it with my hand while I was walking stopped it from tearing open completely.

As I got closer, I was walking past a group of teenagers when I felt my gums start to tingle. I moved to the side of the footpath, pressing up against the brick building as they walked past. Just as they did, my fangs came out, overwhelming my senses completely. I listened to the sounds of their beating hearts until they were out of view, too afraid to move from my position. All I wanted to do was chase them down and rip into their carotid arteries and feed until I drained them.

Once they were out of view, I took off running to work. When I opened the diner door, I held my breath and ran straight past everyone and to the back, dropping my bag on the ground. I grabbed the wolfsbane bottle and took two huge gulps of it before placing the lid back on the bottle. Zoe was bound to come out soon to check what was wrong with me. Since I didn't have time to change my dressing again before she came into the back, I placed another straight over the top of it before fixing my blouse, just as she walked back a worried expression on her face.

"You okay, dear?" she asked, rushing over to me.

"Yes, sorry, I'm late. We missed the only bus, and I had to wait for a lift into town," I told her before picking up my bag to put away.

"Are you sure you're okay? You're sweating, and you look a bit pale,," she said, staring at me. I knew she must be able to see my bruises because she was directly looking at them, making me nervous. Plastering a fake smile on my face, I nodded quickly before answering.

"Yes, I'm fine. It's because I ran here from the school," I told her before walking out and putting my apron on. Grabbing the coffee jug, I walked around to all the tables and quietly refilled everyone's cups. When I reached the last booth, I noticed Alpha Reid sitting dressed in a black suit with a silver tie that matched his eye colour. He was talking to someone who had their back to me. Hearing me approach from behind, the man turned around and glared at me, it was Alpha David and Beta Michael. I dropped my head and filled their mugs quickly. My hands were shaking, making me nearly spill the coffee on the table. Beta Michael looked at me before looking away.

"I can smell wolfsbane all over you and blood," he told me through the mind link.

"I know I'm sorry, Beta."

"Just stay away. Alpha Reid won't hesitate to kill you if he notices you are a Hybrid," he stated.

"Why the meeting?" I ask.

"We no longer need his help. This is just a casual meeting, thanking the Alpha for his help, that is all. So don't worry but don't come back over, we will be leaving soon anyway," he replied.

Moving out the back to the kitchen, I asked Marcus if he needed any help and started cutting up fruit and vegetables for him.

After about twenty minutes, Zoe came out to the kitchen and asked me to clean up some tables on my way out. I grabbed a glass and filled it with water before reaching into my pocket. I popped two of the painkillers in my mouth before quickly swallowing them down with a mouthful of water. When I turned around, I walked straight into Alpha Reid.

"You can't be back here, sir," I stuttered nervously. He stared down at me, making me feel tiny next to his tall, muscular frame, before pulling me to his chest. He wrapped his arm around my waist, causing me to wince in pain from the pressure on my ribs. Using his other hand, he reached into my back pocket and pulled out the small sheet of pain pills which only had two left in them. He then let me go before reading the little Packet.

"Codeine. What are you taking these for?" he asks, raising an eyebrow.

Snatching them out of his hand, I quickly placed them back in my pocket before talking.

"That's none of your business. Now please, you can't be back here," I said now annoyed. He turned and walked back out and sat back in one of the booths. Watching him walk away, my pounding heart started to slow down. Zoe walked out with a glass of water in her hand, and she placed it in front of me on the counter.

"Here, drink this. Are you sure you're okay? If you need the day off, it's ok, Ari. I can manage on my own with Marcus,," she said, placing her hand on my neck. She rubbed her thumb over the bruise on my jaw worriedly, and I saw she had tears in her eyes.

"Really I'm fine, Zoe. I'm just tired," I told her. I drank the glass of water down, soothing my dry throat before walking out with a tray to clear the tables.

Alpha Reid stayed all day watching me. Doesn't he have work to do? Why is he hanging around the diner? Does he know what I am? Is he waiting for me to leave so he can slaughter me? My brain was working overtime, trying to figure out what his sudden interest in me was. When it came time to get Lily, I quickly took off my apron before walking out the door, towards the school.

When I was out of sight of the diner, a pair of hands clamped down on my arms. I knew instantly it was Alpha Reid by the sparks that ran all over my body. He pushed me against the brick wall of the building, pressing his chest against mine. He leaned in, breathing in my scent. My heart was pounding so hard I could hear it. I froze, waiting for him to kill me. Only he did not; instead, his hand moved underneath my blouse where my dressing was. He ran his nose along the top of my shoulder before lifting my blouse, revealing the bloodied dressing. He ran his fingers over it, letting out a menacing growl that paralysed me on the spot. "Who did this?" His voice was deep and menacing.

"No one," I stuttered, my voice so low it was nearly a whisper. I tried to move to escape, but he growled warning me not to, so I stood there not daring to move an inch. Running his nose to the crook of my neck, he inhaled deeply. I could feel his canines protruding, pressing against my skin. They were sharp. I inhaled deeply, not realising I had been holding my breath.

"Why do you smell of wolfsbane? Is that why you're not healing?" His voice was dangerously low. Frightened, I tried to push him back, but he did not budge.

"Please, I have to get Lily," I cry out. Stepping back, he let me pass. I quickly took off in the direction of the school.

After I picked up Lily, we went back to the diner where Reid was waiting next to the door. Reid stepped right into my path, blocking us from moving further into the diner.

"Hello Lily," he says, passing her a giant choc chip cookie. Lily took the cookie, smiling up at the Alpha.

"You can help with my homework if you want, Mr. Reid," Lily told him excitedly, but before he could answer, Zoe saved me from telling her no and stepped forward, wrapping Lily in a hug and forcing the Alpha to move out of the way. Lily walked off to her usual booth, and I pushed past the Alpha before going into the kitchen to put my apron on. Reid never left. When my shift was about to end, I walked out the back to retrieve my bag and grab Lily, who was sleeping in the back part of the store where Zoe's little studio was.

When I was bending down, grabbing our clothes out of the dryer and placing them in the duffle bag, I felt familiar hands brush my sides. I knew it was Reid, his tantalizing scent hit my nose just as he touched me. Sparks stretching throughout my body. *Why does he have this effect on me?* Thinking to myself, I spun around only for him to push me back so my ass was pressed against the washer and dryer. I watched him lean in, breathing in my scent. His other hand reached up into my hair pulling my head back, forcing me to look up and meet his gaze. Just as I was about to tell him he couldn't be back in this part of the diner.

He smashed his lips hungrily into mine, catching me completely off guard, but the most surprising part was my own body's reaction to him. An involuntary moan escaped my lips, and I felt my core tighten. His tongue traced my bottom lip, wanting access which I granted before he deepened the kiss, pressing his body into mine. Just as fast as he kissed me, he pulled away, I heard him chuckle to himself, "Now that's the reaction I have been wanting."

Confused, I was about to ask him what he meant when Zoe walked in. I felt my face flush with embarrassment as I stepped out of the laundry. Grabbing Lily, I quickly collected our things and ran out the door, not even bothering to say goodbye. I walked home as quickly as possible, and after an hour of walking, I finally reached the driveway.

Reid's POV

As soon as I saw her walk to the back, knowing her shift was about to end, I couldn't help myself, I followed her. I stood in the doorway, watching as she bent down to remove the clothes from the dryer, completely unaware I was watching. She bent over to grab the last of the clothes, and my dick instantly went hard as I stared at the shape of her plump ass in the air. I reached over, placing my hands on her hips, and she instantly froze. I watched as she sniffed the air slightly, spinning herself around so she faced me. I pushed my body against hers. I could feel her skin heating up under my touch. This is the reaction she should have had the moment we met, but she is only affected when I'm close or touching her.

Curious to see her reaction, I ran my hands up the side of her body and into her hair before grabbing a handful. I pulled it back so her face was looking directly at me. I could see lust and fear in her eyes; she wanted me to kiss her, but she still feared me. My lips crashed into her soft pink lips, making me growl. My wolf was howling in my head, pleased to finally taste her. I sucked her bottom lip before running my tongue along it, wanting entry to taste her more. I felt her lips part, and I plunged my tongue into her mouth, tasting every bit of it. Her scent was sending my wolf crazy. He wanted to claim her right now, but I knew it would scare her, so I pulled back.

"Now that's the reaction I have been wanting."

She stared at me, confused. She was about to say something when we were interrupted. Zoe walked in, and my mate's face flushed adorably with embarrassment. Zoe glared at me, then my mate took off. I turned to Zoe, crossing my arms across my chest.

"I told you to stay away from her," Zoe's voice was calm but demanding, which irritated my wolf.

"She is my mate; you know this already."

The old woman stepped forward. "That girl has enough going on. You think you can just come in here and confuse her? She doesn't even know you're her mate and she won't until you mark her. She won't throw Lily away to be with you. Ari has raised her since she was born. Loves her like a daughter, not a sister. Just because you are her mate, don't think she will choose you over her."

My wolf growled. Zoe raised a brow at my reaction to her words but did not look bothered. My body trembled as I tried to fight my raging wolf from trying to take over.

"I never said I would make her choose between us. I know wherever Aria goes, Lily will be with her. I'm not trying to separate them. I fucking love her and Lily. I don't fucking care what you say she is mine," I snap at her. Zoe's composure faltered, not expecting my anger before her eyes softened and she let out a breath of relief.

"I thought you wanted to take her away from Lily, but it still doesn't change anything. She doesn't know you're her mate, and Lily's father isn't going to just let Lily leave with Aria."

"What do you mean, how do you know so much about her? They are siblings, and who is Lily's father?" I was becoming more annoyed and confused by the minute, and my wolf had gone awfully quiet. I could tell he knew something I didn't, but he just retreated to the back of my mind where I could not reach him.

Zoe's face went pale, and she started to sweat. I could smell her fear coming from the pores on her skin. Now I was starting to get pissed off. First my wolf runs off and now Zoe has all of a sudden gone quiet too.

"What the fuck is going on? What aren't you telling me?" I growled at her. Zoe looked around nervously.

"I knew her mother and father, that's all I can tell you."

"What? Whose mother and father?"

"Aria's. Lily and Ari have the same mother but different fathers."

Now her words made sense. He would not let Ari take Lily when Aria wasn't even his daughter. So, if Lily's father is alive, why is Aria raising his daughter? I had so many questions that needed to be answered, but I could tell Zoe would not be the one to give them to me.

Storming out of the laundry and back into the diner, I looked everywhere for her. I wanted answers, and she was going to give them to me even if I had to force them out of her. But she was not here. Where did she go? I don't even know what Pack she is in, so I can't just turn up and demand that her Alpha hand her over. Stepping outside, I tried to pick up her scent, but she was long gone.

Chapter 6

Aria's POV

WALKING UP THE LONG driveway, Lily moved in my arms, waking up. I placed her on her feet. The night was cold, and the walk home took longer than usual since I was still in pain from the gash on my ribs. It was starting to get cold, and the breeze made it a little chillier than normal. I could smell an earthy aroma telling me it was going to rain later. When we were nearly all the way to the Pack house, Lily looked up at me tugging on my hand, I looked down at her.

"Can I run ahead please? I really need to pee." I chuckled at her; she was wriggling around while she walked.

"Go on then."

She looked relieved and took off running towards the Pack house, which was only about ten metres away now. I watched her run up the steps and into the Pack house. As I got closer to the Pack house, I pulled the duffle bag off my shoulder, about to climb the stairs, when a new sensation took over me, making me drop the bag on the ground. A horrid feeling churning in my stomach, overwhelming all my senses.

Fear. Pure fear. The sort of fear that makes your skin itch. When you can feel every hair on your body rise, when you feel like your skin is crawling. Fear that makes your body freeze paralysing you on the spot. That's the sort of fear I felt when I heard her blood-curdling scream.

The only thing was, I was her big sister. I couldn't run away. I had no choice but to move, go to her. I forced my legs up the front porch of the Pack house, running in the direction I could hear her screaming my name. My feet pounding on the floorboards in panic. I was moving so fast, I felt myself slipping on the hallway rug, making me skid along the floor and into the wall. My head and shoulder twisting at an awkward angle into the kitchen door frame with enough force that black dots danced in front of my vision. My collarbone and shoulder sending shooting pain through my body, as I feel my shoulder dislocate on impact.

"Aria! Aria!" Her petrified scream echoed through the house. Jumping to my feet, my head spun. I turned the corner into the kitchen to see the Alpha dragging my sister by her hair into the basement with a whip in his other hand. I start running to her, grabbing the basement door frame just in time for him to slam the door shut on my fingers. My own scream escaped my lips in agony. Reaching for the door handle, only to find it's been locked. I start trying to yank my hand free. I could hear her crying and screaming for me on the other side of the door.

"LEAVE HER ALONE!" I screamed at him, banging on the door with my fist. Slamming my body into the door, trying to free my fingers and get in. Not being able to get a run-up, I threw my body with all my might towards the side where my fingers were stuck. The door moved just enough for me to free my injured bloody mangled hand. My fingers were definitely broken as they twisted and jutted out at unnatural angles

Backing up into the kitchen, I ran full force into the door and bounced off, knocking the air out of my lungs. I stood up, backing up again and ran harder. I dropped my shoulder hitting the door with so much force it burst open. My feet hitting air as my body was thrown down the stairs landing at a weird angle and my head smashing into the basement's concrete floor.

"Aria!"

"Aria!"

Her cries made me pull myself to my hands and knees. The Alpha was standing above Lily, who was cowering on the ground at his feet, tears staining her rosy cheeks. As he went to raise the whip, I threw my body over hers just as it came down, tearing the back of my blouse open. I could feel my flesh being torn. I screamed, shoving Lily out from under me and to the side. I turned over and kicked my leg up straight between his legs. The Alpha grunted in pain before kicking me in the stomach. I tried to get to my feet, but he grabbed me by my hair, forcing me to look at his rage-filled face.

This man is a monster. I tried to mind link Michael but was punched in the face, his fist connecting with my nose making blood spill everywhere on the floor. I could hear Lily's frightened screams making my blood boil.

"I saw you today cosying up to Alpha Reid. You think you can betray me, girl?" His voice was menacing; I could smell his putrid whiskey breath on my face which just fuelled my anger. I felt my claws extend, and I didn't think twice as I plunged them into his thigh, making him let me go.

"You're fucking dead now, bitch," he screamed. My eyes widened when I heard his bones snapping. He changed so quickly, jumping into his wolf form in a split second. He lunged at me, my body slamming violently into the shelving along the walls. Feeling his teeth sink into my side, I let out a strangled scream. My breathing was laboured, and I was fighting to stay conscious when I felt his teeth sink into my thigh, feeling my flesh being ripped away.

Black dots tried to take over my vision. I could hear Lily screaming and frantic footsteps above us.

I tried to look for Lily, but all I could see was fur, the Alpha violently throwing me around like a rag doll. I hit more shelves. Just as the Alpha went to lunge for my throat, he let out a scream. I looked up trying to figure out what happened when my eyes fell on Lily. She was holding a bucket. Her fingers were bleeding, and she looked on the verge of collapse. That's when I put the pieces together. Wolfsbane. She had grabbed the bucket of wolfsbane off the shelf, tipping some on herself before she threw it at the Alpha.

Adrenaline kicked in, and I ran to her just before she collapsed. The Alpha was on the ground naked, screaming, turning back to his human form. I didn't wait to see what would happen next. Scooping up Lily, I started running up the stairs. Halfway up, Michael and one of the Pack warriors raced down the stairs. I saw him look over my shoulder at the Alpha on the floor. A loud growl echoing through the basement.

When we made it out of the basement, I went to place Lily down, but Michael stopped me. He jammed a chair from the dining table under the door handle so the Alpha could not get out.

"Run. We won't be able to hold him for long, especially if he commands us to grab you." He sounded panicked, so did the person with him, who must be new as I did not recognise him. He kept glancing between the basement door and me.

"Go Aria, get out of here while you still can." Michael's voice dragged my eyes away from the newcomer.

I took off out of the Pack house, adrenaline the only thing that kept me moving. I should be dead, and once I stopped moving, that might actually become a possibility. I could feel blood running down my legs and face. Stepping onto the porch, the breeze was cold, making me shiver. I could feel Lily starting to come to, which meant the Alpha wouldn't be far behind us.

Running down the stairs, I grabbed the duffle bag when I ran past and started running through the forest that surrounded the Pack house. Michael mind linked me as we got close to the border. My legs felt like giving up, and I spent most of the run holding my breath so I did not attack Lily. Slowing down, I listened to the Beta.

"He is awake, don't forget, Ari, you need to wake her and make her reject the Pack." Stopping just on the border, I shook Lily a bit, and she stirred in my arms.

"Come on Lily baby, I need you to wake up." I kept repeating what I said until her eyes fluttered open. Tears sprang in my eyes seeing her look up at me.

"Ari,," she said, her voice sounding so weak.

"Come on, Lil, I need you to wake up and repeat after me." She was too weak to stand, her eyes fluttering closed again.

"Come on, Lil, stay awake for a few more minutes." Her eyes opened, and she groggily repeated after me.

"I, Lily Violet Blackwood, reject the Black Moon Pack and understand by doing so I will become a rogue." I felt her link snap just as she drifted off to sleep in my arms. Getting up, I did the same.

"I, Aria Rose Peyton, reject the Black Moon Pack and understand by doing so I will become a rogue." I felt my teether to the

Pack snap just as I heard vicious howls. He has told them to find us. Running as fast as I could with Lily in my arms, I listened to my surroundings. I could hear a car. If I could just get to the road before they found us, we might be able to escape.

Running was difficult because I felt like passing out. Seeing the brake lights up ahead through the trees, I ran faster. Branches and sticks were scratching up my legs. I could still see the brake lights when I realised the car must be stopped at the train crossing. I listened as much as I could, straining to hear over the thunder from the storm that was coming. I could just make out the sound of a train passing when I felt what felt like razors cutting through my skin.

Looking around, lantana bushes were everywhere, blocking our escape. I forced my way through the branches trying to shield Lily as much as possible. When I came out the other side, I was on the road. My clothes were in tatters. My legs were almost bare from the lantana stripping and scratching away my pants, leaving cuts everywhere they touched my skin. My blouse was only held on due to me holding Lily, and I could feel one of my bra straps hanging on my back.

I quickly looked over, and the train had passed. The ute was just waiting for the gate to lift before it could cross. Not wasting another second, I put Lily in the tray before climbing in behind her. There was an old tarp in the tray underneath a box. I quickly pulled it over us just as it started to belt down with rain. Only when I felt the ute move and start to accelerate did I let out the breath I was holding and closed my eyes.

Chapter 7

Aria's POV

WAKING UP WHEN THE ute came to a stop, I laid under the tarp, frozen. Listening carefully, I could hear music blaring loudly and lots of voices. I was not sure how long we had been in the tray because not long after our escape, I had given in to exhaustion. When I was sure the coast was clear, I stuck my head out from under the tarp, trying to find anything that might tell me where we were. We were in a parking lot. Looking out, I could tell we were at a bar, one that I had never heard of, so we were not on Black Moon territory, but where were we exactly? Feeling Lily move beside me, I clamped my hand down on her mouth. She looked up groggily at me as I motioned with my finger to my lips telling her to keep quiet. When I heard voices, I quickly stuck my head down and back under the tarp lying motionless.

The voices stopped right next to the tray. The voices sounded like they were right next to us two male voices. Focusing on what they were saying, I heard a man with a deep voice speaking to whoever was with him.

"You smell that, Mark?" I listened as they sniffed the air.

"Rogues," the other man growled. My body tensed at his aggressive growl. Shit, we escaped only to end up on another Pack's territory.

"They couldn't have got far; the scent is too strong, and they are injured too, so I doubt they will put up much of a fight." The first man laughed.

"Alert the Alpha; it's time to go hunting." Mark sounded like he was excited to hunt us down. Lily's breathing started to get louder. I could tell she heard what they were saying. Lily gripped my hand tightly, and we waited until they moved away. As soon as they did, I pushed the tarp off us. I slowly climbed out, ducking behind the tray, I quietly gripped Lily from under her legs and arms, lifting her out of the tray.

Grabbing the bag, I flung it over my shoulder. I did not know where we were, but one thing I did know was we had to get off their territory before they found us. Carrying Lily, I ran down the street and behind a hardware store. Sitting behind the dumpster out of view of the street, I placed Lily on the ground, forcing her to stand.

"Lily, I need you to run. I won't be able to carry you. Don't stop until I tell you, and whatever you do, don't let go of my hand." She nodded, clutching my hand tightly. Looking above the dumpster, I tried to find a street sign to tell me where we were, but there weren't any. The streets were pretty much deserted besides the bar around the corner, so it must be late.

Grabbing Lily's hand, we stayed low and walked as quietly as possible to an alleyway that was behind the hardware store. I couldn't recognise any of the streets because it was dark and my vision was already blurry. Sticking to the back streets and alleyways, we made our way to a residential area. All the house lights were off; only the dim street lights illuminated the roads. Quickly as possible, we climbed a small hill in the residential area once at the top. I looked around trying to find anything that would let me know which side of the city we were on.

My heart stopped when I saw a huge skyscraper building in the distance. The giant lit-up sign on top that said Pharma enterprises. My blood ran cold, we were on Blood Moon territory. Pharma enterprises was a Blood Moon owned business. Grabbing Lily's hand tightly, we started to run down the hill when we came to some bushland. It wasn't very thick, so didn't offer much coverage. Lily started to slow down to the point I was half dragging her. Stopping behind a tree, I let her catch her breath.

"Okay, Lil, catch your breath. We can't stop again; we need to get to the other side of the city."

"I'm thirsty, Ari." She had tears in her eyes, her hair was all matted, and she was sweating.

"I know, baby. When we get to the other side, I will find you something to drink, okay? But we aren't safe here. I need to get you out of here first," I said, rubbing her face gently. Lily looked down and nodded before I felt her freeze. She tugged on my hand, pulling my eyes down to what she was staring at on the ground. Blood and lots of it. In my panic, I forgot I was bleeding; it was leaving a trail straight to us.

Lifting up my shirt, the place where the Alpha bit me was just a piece of flapping skin barely hanging on except for the fact the remaining parts of my blouse were sticking to it, holding it together. My thigh wasn't much better. A huge chunk was missing, and my blood was turning a blackish colour. Just Lily pointing it out made me very aware of the fact that I had somehow ignored the hunger I felt. Pulling off the blouse that was only held on by the arms as the back was completely ripped open, I made a makeshift bandage by wrapping it around my stomach and side holding the flap of skin in place. I can't do much about the leg unless I walk around naked, which is not going to happen.

Throwing the bag over my shoulder, I gripped Lily's hand tightly and started running, pulling Lily with me. Now that Lily pointed it out, every step I took was leaving an obvious trail behind us. When we reached the end of the small bushland, we heard howls. We were in another residential area and only a few blocks away from the city centre. Running down towards the city centre, I knew if we could make it to the subway, we would be able to catch a train out of the city. Just as we stepped on to the main drag, I heard a vicious growl catching us from behind, and a huge brown wolf stepped out from behind a building. I turned to face it, pushing Lily behind me protectively, forcing my claws to extend; they painfully ripped my fingernails off. Then more growls came from the side. We were outnumbered, six wolves were surrounding us. The only way out was the direction we were running in, but they would easily outrun us. I could feel Lily shaking behind me, pressed tightly against my back.

"Lily, I need you to run and don't stop, no matter what, okay?" I felt Lily shaking her head against my back.

"Please, no, Ari," she whispered.

"Do as I say, Lily. Run and don't stop," I growled at her. The brown wolf was slowly prowling, sizing me up as the others moved in.

"Run Lily," I growled just as the big brown wolf launched himself at us. I smashed into it, grabbing it before it could grab Lily. Lily screamed then took off running. I watched as another wolf pounced, its claws digging into my back painfully. I was thrown to the ground violently. Just as another smaller grey wolf went to jump on me going for my face, I lifted my hands, my claws digging into its chest. Using my legs, I pushed it off and away from me.

The only thing on my side was there were too many of them to attack at once without injuring each other, but at the same time, I couldn't catch my breath. My lungs felt heavy, and I understood this was going to be how it ends for me. So long as I could be a distraction and Lily could get enough distance, she might stand a chance of making it off this territory. I just needed to buy her some time. A grey and black wolf I noticed out of the corner of my eye went to chase after Lily. I jumped, sinking my claws into its back and hanging on before I was thrown off and into a brick wall. Jumping to my feet, I lunged at it, only to be hit from the side, slamming me to the ground again.

Black dots started to take over my vision. The last thing I remember seeing was the black and grey wolf snarling and snapping its teeth at me, running at me. The next thing I see is oblivion. Complete darkness. No pain, just a feeling like weightlessness, like floating. Is this what death is like? Darkness? Nothing? They were my last thoughts before everything went black.

Chapter 8

Reid's POV

ECIDING TO LEAVE THE diner, I mind linked Zane. "I want everyone on the lookout for Aria and Lily."

"Everything okay, Boss?"

"Yes, I just need answers. I had an interesting conversation with Zoe, the owner. She told me a few things that aren't making any sense, but she won't say anything else. I will explain when I see you. Just find them and bring them back to the Pack house. Is there any news on which Pack they belong to or last names?"

"No, Boss, whoever Aria is, someone has gone to great lengths to keep her hidden. Same goes for Lily. There are no birth records for Aria, not even banking information. Zoe must pay her in cash, and Lily's records are sealed seeing as she is a minor. Public records wouldn't hand out her information when we visited. It was weird, though. When we went to the school, they said they could not find her files."

"Hmm that is interesting, keep looking."

"Yes, Boss. Want me to come grab you?"

"No, I'm almost back at the office, anyway."

Cutting the mind link and walking to the elevator, I hit the button to my office floor. When the doors opened, I went straight to my office. My secretary was still sitting at her desk when I walked in.

"Why are you still here, Ellie? Go home."

"Just had some filing to do. I'm about to leave, Boss."

Nodding my head at her, I walked into my office. Ryder was lingering just below my skin, agitated. His feelings were starting to mix with my own, making me angrier. "What are you hiding, Ryder? What do you know that you're not telling me?"

He didn't answer. Having a wolf doesn't mean we share everything, but we do feel everything together, and I could tell he was hiding something. Something he was worried about me knowing. Something to do with Aria. A few hours later, I was still in my office looking over some documents. My bad mood only got worse when one of my Pack warriors alerted me to two rogues running through my territory.

"They are running north of the office. They are running through the bush heading straight towards your location, Alpha."

"Fine, keep following them. I will meet up with you."

"What about the child, Boss?"

"There is a kid?"

"Yes, Boss, woman and child,"

"Don't kill them, catch them."

"Yes, Boss." The mind link is cut off. Putting on my suit jacket, I decided to take the stairs, running down them 2 at a time, pumping my adrenaline in case they decide to put up a fight. Maybe this will settle Ryder down; he always loved a good chase. I felt him jumping forward, he was excited just as much as I was.

Once on the bottom floor, I sniffed the air. Nothing but the smell of rain. The sound of howls could be heard in the distance. Jogging slowly and turning at the corner of the street, I started to run up towards the outer parts of the city towards the housing estates. Just as I was running through a small industrial area, I cut through an alleyway. I could hear growling then footsteps running on the pavement towards me. Picking up my pace and turning another corner, I stopped dead in my tracks.

Lily was sobbing, running directly at me. Her clothes were covered in blood, and she was running like her life depended on it. Noticing me coming towards her, she stopped, her eyes going wide, fearing I was someone chasing after her before recognition hit her.

"Reid?" Her voice cracked, and she ran at me, grabbing me around the legs.

"Lily, what are you doing here? Where is Ari?" Placing my hand on top of her head, I looked around frantically. Aria would never leave Lily on her own, especially in this state and this late at night. Lily was sobbing uncontrollably and shaking.

"They're going to kill her! Help her please," she begged, clutching my pants leg.

More growls could be heard. Running in the direction of them getting closer, I got a whiff of her scent. She was up an alleyway up ahead. I could hear Lily puffing and panting trying to keep up behind me. Turning into the dark alley, I could see Pack members circling around the intruder, and I caught sight of Aria being slammed onto the concrete. Just as one of the Pack members went to lunge for her throat, I was standing over her in a split second, moving with inhuman speed. My hand grasped around the grey wolf's throat. Merle, his name was. Squeezing until I heard a sickening crack, his body going limp in my hand. "MINE," I snarled.

Dropping his lifeless body at my feet. I stepped over him towards my men, growling. They all moved back, and they lowered their heads whimpering.

"We didn't know, Boss," one of them whimpered out through the mind link. Turning around, I gazed down at Aria's limp body. She was saturated in blood, her clothes were torn, and her top half was completely bare except for her black torn bra. Bending down, I scooped her up, clutching her to my chest. I nuzzled her neck, breathing in her scent. Her body felt cold against my hot skin, my wolf instantly calming. She was alive, her breathing shallow but alive.

"Let me fucking kill them," Ryder growled.

"No, we will deal with them later. We need to take her home."

"Zane, get here now." I mind linked.

"Yes, Boss." Not even two minutes later, Zane turned up in his wolf form. Shifting into his human form, he quickly pulled on his jeans that were tied to his leg before walking over.

"Grab Lily," I said, nodding towards her. She was standing shocked, staring at Aria's limp body in my arms. Zane walked over, picking Lily up from under her arms before picking up the duffle bag that was at her feet. Lily clutched it tightly as he rested it on his shoulder.

"Where to, Boss?"

"Home. The Pack doctor is meeting us there. I already called for her."

"What about Mark and the others?"

I growled warningly at them, and they backed up, lowering their heads.

"Not now," I snapped, looking down at my mate. I could feel her blood running down my arm, where I was holding her legs. One of the Pack members pulled up at the end of the alleyway, opening the door of my black SUV. Throwing the door open, I climbed in, pulling Aria on my lap. Zane placed Lily beside me, putting her seat belt on. She was sobbing uncontrollably, still clutching the bag that was over Zane's shoulder. When she wouldn't let go, he slid it onto her lap before closing the door and hopping into the passenger seat.

Looking down, I pulled the shirt that was tied around her stomach slightly. Blood started gushing out except it was not red; it was black and thicker than normal blood. I quickly placed my hand over it, putting pressure on it.

"Why isn't she healing?" I asked out loud. Zane peered over the front seat looking at her before my glare made him turn around, quickly realising she was barely clothed. Pulling her closer, I looked over at Lily, who was rubbing Aria's leg with the hand that was not clutching the bag.

Trying to take her mind off Aria, I asked her, "What's in the bag that's so important, Lil?" She clutched the bag tighter and looked at me but did not speak.

We got to the Pack house quickly. As soon as the door opened, I ran out and up the stairs clutching Aria to my chest. I kicked the door open and ran to the infirmary where the Pack doctor Mavis was standing next to the hospital bed, in her white coat. Her red hair was a mess, telling me I had woken her. I could see she was still in her pyjamas under her coat, and she only had socks on and no shoes. Placing Aria on the gurney, Doc quickly started to work. Zane walked in a few minutes later with Lily still clutching the bag tightly.

I bent down to look at Lily. "You okay?" She shook her head and sniffled. Her blonde curls were tinged red covered in blood, and some was dried on her face. "Are you hurt?" She shook her head again.

"The blood is Ari's. She was carrying me," she stuttered, trying to hold her sobs in. I could tell it was Aria's; I would know her scent anywhere.

Looking down at her drenched clothing, I noticed what looked like blisters along her hands. Pushing the sleeves of her shirt up her arms, I found more blisters and burns. I could smell wolfsbane on her clothes, which would be causing her pain. Immediately, I signalled for the nurse that was with doc to come over.

She took one look at her before confirming, "Wolfsbane,"

"Is that why my mate isn't healing?" She looked uncertain.

"Maybe. Come on, let's get you cleaned up,," she said, holding her hand out to Lily to take. Lily looked uncertain but took her hand anyway.

"Why are you so quiet, Ryder?" I asked.

"You will find out soon," was all he replied. I knew he was scared for our mate. She looked so small and fragile, laying on the hospital bed. The Doc was stapling her leg while another nurse was stitching her side. She was completely unconscious. If I couldn't see her chest rise with each breath she took and hear the slow beating of her heart, I would have thought she was dead. A tall man in a white coat walked in before placing an IV in her arm and attaching a bag of fluids. I watched as he took some blood samples before walking out of the room again. Both doctors kept giving me nervous glances.

"Maybe you should go wait in your study, Alpha," said Mavis. I have known her for years, and I could tell something was making her nervous. That I was making her nervous.

"No, I'm fine here."

"Sir, I don't think you should be here when she wakes up."

"She is my mate, I'm staying." Mavis looked shocked for a second, glancing at Tom, the male doctor who had stepped into the room again before looking down at my mate with a look of fear on her face.

"Sir, I'm afraid I need to insist you leave. Mavis or I will come see you soon. It's for your mate's safety," said Tom.

"Safety? I am not going to hurt her. She is mine." Tom wouldn't budge, instead gestured towards the door.

"Please, we will be able to work more efficiently with you not here."

Storming out of the room and slamming the door behind me, I made my way down the hallway to my study. The study was dark. Turning on the light, I looked around the room trying to find something to distract myself, looking over at the shelves of books. I didn't feel like reading or working, instead deciding to just sit behind my desk. Running my fingers through my hair, I leaned back in my chair, closing my eyes.

I must have dozed off because Zane walked in with a plate in one hand and a mug of coffee in the other. He placed them down in front of me.

"Eat," he ordered, pushing the plate in front of me.

"Any news?"

"Yes, but you're not going to like it. I had my suspicions earlier but didn't want to say anything,"

"What?"

"Please just eat and wait for Doc." Just as he mentioned her, she walked in with some papers in her hand. She looked over to Zane nervously before he nodded, and she walked further into the room.

"Well, take a seat, Doc." She shook her head before looking down. Mavis was making me uneasy; it cannot be that bad, surely, she was breathing and alive. "What, did she die?" I asked, my voice breaking at the thought.

Doc shook her head. "No, of course not but there is something you should know."

"Like?" I threw my hands up impatiently. Doc glanced at Zane again before looking down at the papers in her hand.

"You said she was your mate?" I nodded, confirming her words. "Well, she had lethal doses of wolfsbane in her system. Enough to kill 10 or more wolves to be precise." she said, placing a piece of paper down in front of me.

"But she is alive. She will be fine, though, right?" I asked, glancing down at the paper.

"Yes, Sir, she will live, but she needs blood to heal. We don't have any here. I am organising some to be sent over."

"Ok, so what blood type is she? I can organise some Pack members to donate blood if needed?" Now she is really worried. She looked around anxiously, her hands began to shake, and she moved closer to Zane. "Am I missing something? What's going on? Docs she have a rare blood type?"

"No sir, you're not understanding, she…. your mate needs blood to heal. She is a hy… Hybrid," she stuttered over the last word.

I burst out laughing. "Nice try Doc," she looked towards Zane. Before he stepped forward, his hand gripped my shoulder squeezing lightly. He looked at me and nodded his head, confirming what the doctor said.

My blood started to simmer. She can't be a Hybrid, but at the same time, so many things made sense now, her unique scent. The fact that she could not heal. Why she wouldn't know of the mate bond? Why she had no wolf. Why she was not dead when

I smelt wolfsbane on her. My head was spinning. "This is what you wouldn't tell me, huh Ryder?"

My anger reached breaking point, boiling over. Gripping the desk, I flung it against the wall, narrowly missing Mavis. My mate was a fucking Hybrid! Mavis darted out of the room. I wanted to break something. I wanted to kill something. No, I wanted to kill her. Is this my fucking punishment, Moon Goddess? Did you do this to fucking torture me? I will not have a Hybrid as a fucking mate. Trashing the room, there were no shelves left standing. The windows smashed from flying furniture. Zane did not move, just stood in the doorway, waiting for me to finish. When I went to walk out, Zane stepped in my way.

"Move," I growled, grabbing his shirt and slamming him into the door frame.

"Why? So you can kill her? You kill your mate, the Moon Goddess will not grant you another. Reid, think about this. Do not let your hate control you. Don't let it destroy her."

"I won't have a Hybrid as a fucking mate," I spat at him.

"Killing her will only weaken you. Be reasonable."

"I made a fucking promise to wipe them from existence. She doesn't change that," I screamed, shoving him out of the way.

"And I won't let you hurt our mate," Ryder, finally speaking up, growled at me. Fighting me for control.

Chapter 9

Aria's POV

THE CEILING, I REMEMBER the ceiling. All I can see is the fluorescent light above my head, shining brightly down on me, making a bead of sweat run down my neck. My head is pounding against my skull, heart throbbing in my ears. I could not remember if I were asleep or awake. I only remember the ceiling. Were my eyes already open or did I open them? Turning my head to the side, my head felt heavy, and my limbs felt like they were held down by weights. The whole room appears to be white. Too bright for my eyes, so I close them. My eyelids felt heavy, and I was trying to concentrate on breathing, sucking a big breath in to fill my lungs before I let it out again.

Hearing a single click, I try to turn to look in the direction it came from, but I felt too heavy. My throat felt raw and dry like a desert. Inhaling the air slightly, I force myself to roll onto my side, when I hear a noise like a hummingbird's wings flapping hard against the wind. I focus on the noise, opening my eyes slightly, and I see a figure standing next to a black door. I can see their bare feet on the tiled floor. Forcing my eyes up to see who it is, stopping briefly halfway, I notice they are wearing butterfly pyjamas. Why did they look familiar to me? My eyes search them trying to find the noise that is consuming the room and overwhelming my senses completely. I need to know what the sound is, such a sweet melodious noise. My eyes stop at their neck when I notice the steady movement of a vein twitching, pulsating.

I watch captivated as the vein pulses to the rhythm of the fluttering, completely mesmerised by the sweet sound vowing to satisfy my thirst. I inhale the smell of the sweet-smelling liquid emanating through their veins calling to me. Promising me everything I have ever craved. Promising to extinguish the burn in my throat.

Standing up, I move on instinct following the alluring scent. When I am in front of them, I can hear inaudible noises like talking, but I could not comprehend what they were saying. All I could focus on was the hypnotic sound of their blood that flows through their veins. Lifting my hand, I caressed the white flesh of their neck lightly with my fingers. They shuddered under my touch, fear only making their delectable scent sweeter. Gripping their shoulders, I tugged them to me, leaning down and brushing my lips against their soft, warm skin. Just as I was about to sink my fangs into their neck and drink their sweet nectar of life, the door was thrown open, making me pull back. Uncontrollable hunger seized me. All I saw was red. The intruder grabbed me roughly around the shoulders, and my mouth was jammed against warm flesh, sinking my fangs into it. My senses became overloaded when the warm sweet taste of blood flooded into my mouth, soothing my painful dry throat. A soft satisfied moan almost like a purr rumbled through my chest as I gulped down the most delightful soothing liquid ravenously.

Ryder - Reid's Wolf POV

Listening to my human speak venomously about our mate was scraping my insides. Hmm… he thinks he can go against the Moon Goddess. He is just my vessel, two minds for one body. I do not like being in control of our human side. To me, it is just a pound of flesh, but I will not stand idly by and watch him obliterate our only chance at happiness. Foolish humans and their off-centre emotions. I observe from behind the veil of his mind, watching him lose control, waiting for my chance to overthrow him, to take full control. I have only had real control in my wolf form, not in this weak sleeve. Yes, he lets me come forward but never gives in completely. He knows my taste for blood. Knows I will kill without hesitation, so I do not blame him. The human world and its politics I know nothing much about, so it is best he has control, but not now. Not when he is the one about to give in to his hatred.

Aria is ours; Aria is mine. I watch as he destroys the office. I don't fight, but when I hear him tell Zane he wants to kill our mate, I know with every fibre in my body that he means it. I understand his hate. I have always been with him, so I know his secrets, I know his anger, but she doesn't deserve that hate. She doesn't deserve his wrath. I'm glad for Zane's distraction as Reid doesn't feel me getting closer. His fury and hatred shadow me until the last second. "I won't let you kill our mate." I pounce, gripping the teether we share and ripping him into the depths of our mind. He puts up a fight, but even he recognises he won't win, not when he is fighting out of anguish. He isn't thinking straight. Lunging forward, I shove him to the pits of darkness, where he likes to shove me when I get under his skin. Lurching forward completely, I take control.

"Ryder, thank the Moon Goddess," Zane exclaims. "I was wondering when you would appear. I knew I couldn't hold him forever." I watch as Zane's grip on me relaxes before sagging against the door in relief.

"Where is my mate?" Zane, standing up straight, straightens his shirt, wiping off some invisible dust.

"She is in the infirmary."

"And Lily?"

"She should still be with the nurses."

"Lead the way then." Zane turns and starts walking down the hall, and I follow closely behind. When we reach a black door, a nurse comes forward. Looking up, she goes to say something before looking directly at me. She does a double take before she takes a step back. Understanding Reid is no longer in control before bowing her head slightly, revealing her neck in a sign of submission. "Alpha, I didn't realise we would be seeing you." Looking down at her hands, she continues, "Doc has just stepped out to gather some blood for your mate."

I nod in understanding "The girl?"

"She is with her sister." Using my wolf senses, I listen. I can hear Lily talking.

"Aria, it's me." I hear her sob in distress. Kicking the door open, I ran into the room. Aria is leaning in, and from the angle it looks like she is about to cuddle the girl, except her eyes are no longer the vibrant green. They are the eyes of a predator about to kill its prey; they are now an orange burning like embers of flame.

Without hesitation, I tackle her around the shoulders, plummeting to the ground against the wall, her back pressed against my chest. I feel her fangs sink into my forearm. Her bite is not painful like I thought it would be, it must be a mate thing. Aria lets out a moan that vibrates through her chest, biting down hungrily. I can feel her sucking, hear her swallowing. She is completely overwhelmed with bloodlust. When Doc walks in, taking in the scene before her, she holds up a bag of blood. I motion for her to throw it to me. Doc obeys, tossing it. I catch it with my free hand, pulling her head as gently as possible from my arm to get her attention.

I pierce the bag slightly with my nail. Smelling the bag of blood she rips it from my hand, biting straight into the side. Blood spurts out like a burst water balloon all over her face and mine. Knowing it will not last long enough, I motion for the doc who throws a second bag, ready for when she finishes the first. Aria is sitting on my lap. Pulling her closer and brushing her hair to the side and out of her face with my fingers, I gaze down at her. She truly is an extraordinary creature. When she grabs savagely for the second bag, I know I will never get a second chance. I sink my teeth into her neck to mark her. The metallic aftertaste of her blood on my tongue brings me satisfaction, and I growl softly before running my tongue along the mark to seal it. Aria collapses into my chest, the blood bag falling from her fingertips. I wait a few minutes before I lift her up bridal style and place her back on the bed. Raising her hospital gown slightly, I watch as her lacerations close and all the bruising vanishes.

"She will be out for a while. A normal wolf's marking will take a toll on the body, but an Alpha's mark?" She looks down at my sleeping mate. "I think she will be out for the rest of the night." Nodding I tuck the blanket around her, kissing the top of her head before walking out to where Lily is in the hall.

"Reid?"

"No, I'm Ryder. Come on, how about we get you to bed."

Lily hesitated. "When is Reid coming back?" she asked. I must be scaring her.

"I'm sure he will be back by morning; he doesn't like to be kept in the dark for long." I chuckled to myself. Reid cannot kill her now, not without killing us in the process. Feeling proud, smiling to myself, I know now she will be safe from us.

Chapter 10

Aria's POV

THE NEXT MORNING, I awoke early to someone opening the curtains and letting the light into the room. Sitting up, I stared at the person who appeared to be a nurse. She was wearing blue scrubs and white sneakers, her blonde hair pulled tightly in a bun. Noticing my movement, she turned around to face me. Surprise was evident in her blue eyes.

"You are up."

I just nodded my head in reply. Feeling confused, I tried to remember how I got in this room, but the only thing I can remember is telling Lily to run and then a wolf snapping its jaws, lunging at me before being plunged into darkness. The memory sent a shiver down my spine.

"Where am I?"

"You are on Blood Moon territory." Petrified, I tried to get up, but the nurse ran over, pushing me down by my shoulder.

"Luna, you're safe here." Dismissing what she said as a mistake, I shook my head. Looking at her name tag that was pinned to the bottom of her shirt, I discovered her name was Wendy.

"There was a girl with me. What happened to her? She is 6 years old with blonde curly hair, dark blue eyes." As I was describing Lily to the nurse, I could feel tears start to brim. My throat felt thick with worry. The nurse, noticing my distressed state, came and sat on the bed next to me.

"Luna, calm down. Lily is fine. She is in the rec room playing with the other Pack members." My shoulders sag, feeling relieved that she is ok and safe. But that still didn't answer how we got here.

"How did we get here? How long have we been here?" Confused, I just keep shooting questions at her, but she does not seem to mind.

"Alpha Reid found you and Lily and brought you back here. You're currently in the Pack house infirmary, and you have also been asleep for two days since your mate marked you."

"Mate? I don't have a mate." Reaching up I slid my fingers over my neck and shoulder, flinching when I hit the tender skin of a mate's mark. It stings a little, but mostly when I touch it, it just tingles. Shocked, I instantly start to panic. Getting up, I glance down at my clothes. I am in a green hospital gown. Looking around, I do not see my duffle bag or my shoes. The nurse watches worriedly but does not stop me. Now I just need to find Lily, and we will be on the next bus out of the city. Walking over to the black door, I tried to open it, but it had been locked. Spinning around, I turned to look at the nurse who placed her hands up in surrender.

"It's for everyone's safety and yours, Luna. I understand you're confused, but everything will work out soon."

"Everyone's safety? Why do you keep calling me Luna? I'm not your Luna," I yell, starting to feel trapped and angry.

"You are our Luna or will be once everything settles down and yes our safety. You really don't remember anything when you woke up after you arrived here?"

"No, I don't. I'm not going to hurt anyone. I just want to get my sister and we will be out of everyone's way. Now open the door," I demanded.

"Why don't you have a shower? I will get you some clothes and bring you some breakfast."

"I want to see my sister," I say, sitting back down on the bed. Placing my head in my hands, I try to think of an escape plan. I know it is not going to be realistic while locked in this room.

"I will bring Lily in after you have a shower and breakfast, deal?" She tries to bargain with me.

"Fine," I say storming off into the bathroom. Stripping off the gown, I realised I was completely bare under it, but that wasn't the most startling piece of information. I was completely healed, not even a scar. I know I was in bad shape after our escape from Alpha David, and knowing I can't heal properly, it's either they have some crazy voodoo doctor or they gave me blood. In fact, I feel the best I have in years, not a single ache, no pain at all.

Preferring the crazy voodoo doctor, I walk over to the small mirror above the basin. Peering into the mirror, I jumped back, not expecting the reflection that was staring back at me. No scratches, no marks covered my skin, but my eyes were no longer their normal green. Instead, they were bright amber orange glowing dangerously back at me.

They gave me blood; they know what I am. Why haven't they killed me? Nothing is making any sense. Why would they help two lowly Rogues?

Chapter 11

Reid's POV

I CAN'T BELIEVE MY WOLF would go against me. How dare he betray my trust. We are supposed to be a team, supposed to be one whole. He knows the promise I made and yet he still went against me for her. Marked her against my will, all because she has spelled his wolf with her phony humanity. Hybrids are an abomination; they are barbaric savages. They exist to kill, and it's incredible she has managed to conceal her true self this long. To hide the monster she truly is. It is only a matter of time until she slips up and kills someone.

"Do you hear yourself? Really Reid, you sound like a whiny bitch. I did you a favour, you'll see."

"I am not whining, you betrayed me. If you were doing me a favour, you would have slaughtered her," I tell him before shoving him back to where he belongs.

I haven't slept in two days since he marked her. Concerned he will force his way back in control when I'm vulnerable, I won't allow him to cause more irreversible damage. Leaning back on my office chair, I try to rest my eyes. When that doesn't work, deciding I need more caffeine, I walk down the hall towards the kitchen. On the way, I find Lily stopped outside the infirmary door with Wendy, the nurse. Lily, noticing me, starts walking towards me, before stopping in front of me. She is wearing her butterfly pyjamas again, carrying her duffle bag, which she hasn't let go of since she arrived. "Are you visiting Ari?" she asks.

Her innocent little face peers up at me. It's not her fault her sister is a monster. "No, I'm getting coffee. Why are you still in the same pyjamas? Don't you have more clothes in the bag?" I ask, reaching for her bag, but she tugs it closely to her chest, shaking her head.

"No, just my school clothes. We didn't have time to grab anything else."

"What do you mean? Who are you running from, Lil? It's okay, you can tell me."

Lily doesn't say anything, just steps back, walking back to the door where the nurse is waiting.

"You're not letting her in there, are you?" The nurse seemed confused, and Lily looked up questionably.

"I promised she could see her sister, Sir."

Grabbing the nurse's arm tightly, I pull her to me. "You are aware she is a Hybrid, aren't you?"

"Yes sir, but she isn't dangerous. She is in control."

"For now, she is. Don't let her fool you."

"Sir, I understand your dislike for Hybrids, but Ryder marked her. She is our Luna and your mate. How long are you going to deny her?" Wendy's reply touched a nerve.

How can the whole Pack be so accepting of her already? She hasn't been here five minutes and she already has my Pack wrapped around her fingers. I am fucking Alpha, for god's sake. I don't care if she is supposed to be my Luna, I will never stand beside her. She will never be my equal. Wendy pulled her arm from my tight grip before opening the door, stepping out of view of the door. I watched as they walked in before going to the kitchen.

Aria's POV

Getting in the shower, I washed quickly, eager to see Lily. Not having her close to me and not knowing where she is was making me anxious. When I got out of the shower, I wrapped the towel around me before sticking my head out the bathroom door. Laying on the bed were some clothes. Walking over and picking them up, I realised they were exactly my size.

Wendy left a pair of light blue jeans and a white tank top, along with a black bra and panties set and a pair of socks. Quickly putting them on, I was drying my hair with the towel when Wendy walked in carrying a tray. She placed it down next to me on the bed. Pancakes. My stomach growled hungrily at the sight of them. Embarrassed, I quickly thanked her for the clothes and breakfast before she walked out.

After breakfast, Wendy did as she promised and brought Lily to visit. The relief I felt upon seeing her is unexplainable. Never since Lily has been born have I spent a night away from her. Not seeing her was making me extremely anxious. Lily walked in, wearing her familiar butterfly pyjamas before she dropped the duffle bag and ran to hug me, just as excited as I was to see her.

"Ari!" Lily squealed excitedly. Brushing her curls out of her face, I bent down and picked her up, placing her on the bed.

"You okay now, Ari? Wendy said we can stay here now." Lily spoke excitedly.

I motioned for Wendy to leave. Instead of leaving, she shook her head and stood next to the door. Shaking my head, annoyed, I turned back to Lily.

"That's great, Lil, but remember we have to leave the city as soon as they let me out." Lily looked upset, tears shining in her eyes, but she didn't let them fall.

"Ok, but they said we would be safe here. Alpha Reid said we could stay; he even gave me my own room," Lily replied disappointedly.

"I know, but this isn't permanent. We have to leave, and when did you see Alpha Reid?'

"He was in the hall when I arrived, but I spoke to him last night. He said we won't be leaving because you are his mate and his wolf marked you."

Shaking my head, I sat back flabbergasted. That's why he hung around the diner, and that's why he took us in. I wasn't even aware I could be someone's mate. I tried to remember him marking me, but I have no memory of even seeing him since I got here.

"Hello, Ari, are you okay?" Lily sang out, waving her hands in front of my face, pulling me from my thoughts.

"Sorry, Lil, I was thinking."

"About what?"

I shrugged my shoulders. "Nothing in particular, it doesn't matter, Lil."

Wendy walked over. "Only 20 minutes then we have to go, Lily." she said.

"Go where? She can stay with me," I replied, annoyed. It was like they were trying to keep us separated.

"Sorry Aria, but Alpha…" I didn't let her finish, instead jumping to my feet.

"I don't care what the Alpha said. Lily is my sister and my responsibility. He has no right keeping her from me when I am the one who raised her." I didn't realise I was yelling until I had to take a breath. Wendy's shocked expression showed she wasn't expecting my outburst. But I didn't care, who does he think he is? Marking me, then ordering me around. I never asked for this, I just wanted to get as far away from the city as possible with Lily.

Wendy motioned for Lily to take her hand. Lily hesitated, confused on what to do, before walking to me taking my hand. But Wendy clearly refused to go against her god damn Alpha and went to grab Lily's hand, only fuelling my anger. Without even thinking, I growled at her and took a step forward, putting myself between them. Wendy took a startled step back. I could hear her heart rate spike, then that was all I could focus on. My hands became clammy, and I could feel my hunger for her blood starting to overtake my senses.

I could smell her fear oozing off her skin, and I started to advance on her. When Lily grabbed my hand, I ripped my hand from her and spun around my glare now on her. When she took a frightened step back, something clicked in me. They are trying to help. Holding my breath, I pushed Lily towards Wendy, who grabbed Lily and ran out the door.

Sitting on the floor, I placed my head between my knees, trying to regain control, but just thinking of Wendy and our argument would make it flare up like an erupting volcano. Sitting up, I rested my head on the wall, my eyes falling on the duffle bag by the bed. Quickly getting up, I raced over to the bag, ripping it open, relieved to find two bottles of wolfsbane and the jar of syringes. Nobody has looked in the bag because if they did, they definitely wouldn't have left them with a six-year-old.

Undoing the lid of one of the bottles, I swallowed down two painful mouthfuls, gagging and choking instantly. I always forget how much this crap burns, but knowing it is the only way to control my bloodlust means I'm just going to have to deal with this torture.

After about five minutes, the door opened again. I was still sitting on the floor trying to stop myself from dry heaving. Looking towards the door, I see a pair of black sneakers and looking up. I instinctively know who it is by the feeling in the pit of my stomach. There is no doubt now that he is my mate. My breathing instantly increased, my heart was racing. I always thought I didn't need anyone besides Lily, but I needed him. I never realised how incomplete I was until he walked into the room, making me realise he was the missing piece in my life. The other side to my soul, two souls fitting perfectly together becoming a whole. How had I not realised sooner?

Breathing in, I inhaled his intoxicating scent. My nerves felt like they were on fire, every fibre in my body trying to pull me to him. Standing up, I stared at the man who was everything I didn't realise I needed or wanted. Through his shirt, I could see the outlines of his abs, see the lines of his muscular chest. He looked like he had been carved out of marble. He was dressed very casually compared to when I would see him at the diner. His hair was a bit of a mess like he had been running his fingers through it. His gaze was intense, not his usual soft gaze.

I watched as he clenched and unclenched his jaw. His hands were fisted tightly, and he looked tense like he didn't want to be here. Moving closer, I went to place my hands on his chest and ask him if he was okay. But he moved so quickly, my heart skipped when he grabbed hold of my wrists tightly, too tightly. Any tighter I was sure they would break. The usual sparks from his touch did nothing to help the ache of my bones being crushed in his strong grip. He then shoved me back, making me stumble.

Looking up at him, I could see his breathing changing. It was getting faster, I could tell by the rise and fall of his chest moving rapidly. He was angry, he didn't want me. Rejection was like a slap in the face, only coming from him, it hurt more than any of the times I had been punched by David. Feeling tears brim in my eyes, I turned my head and wiped them, not wanting him to witness me breaking.

Why does this hurt so much? Once I was sure my face wouldn't betray me, I looked back at him. He went to say something but then stopped, his eyes flicking between him and his beast before going back to their silver-grey, showing that Reid was undeniably in control. I wanted to comfort him, ask why he was upset, but the look on his face was full of disgust like he couldn't look at me, like I was beneath him. Like some trash he had just come across. He turned and walked out of the room without saying another word, locking the door behind him, leaving me more confused.

How could he mark me then reject me like that? Was it a mistake? Did he mark me by accident? Or is it because of what I am? An abomination, an atrocity. As soon as I find a way out of here, Lily and I are leaving. We don't need anyone, never did, so this won't be any different.

Chapter 12

Reid's POV

WALKING IN, SEEING HER on the ground, I couldn't help the pull I felt towards her, even after knowing what she is. The mysterious mate bond had other plans. I am supposed to hate her, but being in front of her, the bond won't allow that. Only the need for her. Her feelings of disbelief, surprise, understanding, then lust all flowing into me through the bond. I could feel every emotion rolling off her and into me. Her desires becoming mine. When she moved towards me, I could feel her intention. She just needed to be close, to touch me. I could feel Ryder pushing me to give in to her, which aggravated me, distracting me enough to think clearly to realise my reason for being here wasn't to snuggle up with some bloody Hybrid. I grabbed her wrists before she made contact.

I felt Ryder jump at me trying to fight me for control, but I held strong, too strong. I didn't realise I was squeezing her wrists so tightly until I felt her bone-crushing pain sink into me through the bond. Letting go abruptly, she stumbled to the floor, landing on her ass. I could feel her embarrassment, then sadness leaking through the bond, I could smell the saltiness of the tears she tried to hide. Ryder kept pushing for control. He was screaming in my head, angry. I only came in here to find out who she was running from. Instead, this shit happens, making everything more awkward than it needed to be. Seeing her hurt gaze staring back at me, I couldn't handle it any longer. Turning my back on her, I walked out the door, locking it behind me. Going back to my office, Zane was standing against the office door.

"We have a problem, Alpha."

"What is it?" I snap, pushing past him into the office.

"The Black Moon Pack have been at the border. They want permission to look for some Pack members that escaped,"

"Let me guess, a woman and child?"

"Yes, Boss."

Aria's POV

After Alpha Reid left, I was locked in for most of the day. Wendy came in a few times to check on me, but other than her, I spent the rest of the day alone plotting our escape. In the afternoon, I got that chance. Wendy came in and said the rest of the Pack had to go out on Pack business and that I could explore the Packhouse. When she left the door wide open, I thought it was a trick. Fifteen minutes had passed when I realised the door wasn't going to be slammed in my face, and I couldn't hear anyone loitering behind the door or in the hall.

Stepping into the hall, I felt soft carpet under my feet instead of the cold tile floor in the hospital room. The hallway walls are a soft light grey colour with white trims and black dome lights hanging from the ceiling. I walked down the hall until I came to what I thought was the end but was actually just an open ceiling and balcony overlooking the floor below. Peering over, I could see the foyer below and hear children playing. Walking down the huge white staircase to the floor below, I followed the noises into some sort of media and games room. I watched for a little while before walking in and interrupting the children's fun. Lily was playing Mario Kart with another little girl. Seeing me walk in and standing behind the huge lounge, she jumped up, bringing her new friend with her. "Amber, this is Ari, my sister."

Amber had dark straight hair that was cut just above her shoulders and pale skin with rosy red cheeks. She looked like a porcelain doll.

"Hi, I'm Ari," I told her, waving to her. She shyly waved back before taking off back to her spot on the giant navy-blue horseshoe-shaped lounge. Sitting down, she grabbed her controller and resumed playing. Just as Lily was about to go back and play, I pulled her aside.

"This may be our only chance to leave, we have to take it."

Lily shook her head. "I don't want to leave Ari, I like it here!" she yelled, crossing her arms over her chest and pouting.

"We can't stay here, Lily, we have to leave," I said, grabbing her arm, pulling her gently towards the stairs to retrieve the bag so we could leave.

"No, I'm not going!" Lily yelled and took off up the stairs. Just as Lily took off, Wendy walked in. Just my luck, now I must find Lily and not tip Wendy off to our departure. Turning to Wendy, I plastered the fakest smile I could muster.

"Everything okay, Aria? I thought I heard yelling."

"Yes, everything is fine, we are just playing hide and seek," I lied.

Wendy smiled politely, believing my lame-ass excuse. She then turned around and walked off through a door on the other side of the media room. As soon as she was out of view, I darted up the stairs. Going back to the infirmary, I quickly grabbed our duffle bag, chucking it over my shoulder before turning and walking out of the room, shutting the door behind me. Making my way down the hallway towards the foyer, I opened every door, but each room was either an office or storage rooms.

How big was this house? I felt like I had been walking around opening random doors for hours, even though it had only been 10 minutes tops. That's when I decided to go back the way I came. Starting back at the infirmary, I turned in the other direction which led to another hallway turning the corner into the new hallway. I came across another office, this one was richly decorated. Mahogany bookshelves lined the walls loaded with books. I loved reading, I used to borrow books off the pack members back home. Some of the teenagers still in school used to borrow them for me since I didn't have a TV in my room to watch. But as Lily got older and I started working, I didn't have much time to read, and when I did, I was too tired.

In the centre of the room was a mahogany desk which looked brand new, as it still had plastic over the top of it. The carpet was thick and black, warm under my feet. Walking back out of the room, I went to the next door and the next until I came to another hallway of doors. Opening the first one I realised was a bedroom. Knowing Lily must be hiding somewhere here, I started opening every single door. I came to the last one next to a set of stairs that led to yet another floor of this mansion of a house. Opening the door, I could tell straight away it was a child's room. It was pink, and there was a white 4 poster single bed with a frilly pink unicorn bedspread. It had fairy lights hanging from the posts and had lots of toys and a fluffy purple mat. Looking over, I saw a built-in cupboard, and opening it, I found Lily sitting in the bottom sobbing.

"Come Lil, we need to go before everyone gets back," I told her, trying to get her to understand. Lily wasn't one for tantrums, and this was the most difficult she has ever been, but slowly, she sniffled, wiping her nose on the sleeve of her shirt.

"Do we really have to go, Ari?"

"Yes, we need to leave. We have to leave the city before your father finds us or Alpha Reid hands us over to him." I left out the part of Reid hating Hybrids and was probably in his torture dungeon plotting my death somewhere. Lily slowly nodded and stood up. Pulling the pyjamas off her, I quickly rummaged through the bag, pulling out her winter school clothes and dressing her quickly. Once Lily was dressed, we snuck down the stairs, going to the front door. I tried to open it, but it was locked with a key.

Knowing that Wendy must have the key, I quickly walked through the media room to the door on the other side, pulling Lily behind me. Sticking my head through the doorway, I found that it was a kitchen. Everything was white tile, the benchtops white marble over grey cupboards. There was a gold chandelier hanging from the ceiling, and all the appliances were restaurant quality. Seeing that Wendy wasn't in the kitchen and stepping completely into the room, I noticed on my examination there was a set of double doors leading outside. Racing over I twisted the handle, they were unlocked.

Pushing Lily out the door, we walked out to what must be the rear of the property. We were on a huge patio area that overlooked a pool. Running down the stairs quickly, I saw that the entire property was surrounded by trees, making it very private. Moving quickly across the lawn, we made it to the tree line. Looking back, I could see that the place was indeed a mansion. It looked more like a white sandstone castle than a mansion actually. Not giving it another thought, Lily and I started running through the trees. After a while, we came to a dirt side road. We must be outside the city. Where? I had no idea, but luck must be on my side today because, after about two minutes of walking, a silver car with an old couple pulled up beside us and asked if we needed a lift into the city.

Knowing if they were psychos I could easily just turn around and eat them. We accepted and asked if they could give us a ride to the closest train station or bus depot. The old couple were quite talkative. On the drive, they told us they had been married for 40 years and had 7 children who were all grown up and 16 grandchildren. Their names were Norman and Enid. Pulling up to the front of the train station, I tried to offer them money for fuel, but they declined. The train station was small, covered in graffiti, and the signs were ripped down so I couldn't even tell which station we were at.

Walking up to the ticket booth, we met a girl. She had piercings all through her face, black and pink hair, and she looked very emo, chewing on bubble gum with a frown on her pale face. Raking through my bag, I told her I needed two tickets out of the city. When she asked where, I told her as far away from the city as possible, not really knowing where I was going. I would call Zoe and let her know we left when we found a phone at our new destination. Grabbing the tickets, I passed her the cash before she said the train was five minutes away.

Once on the platform, I found some vending machines. Putting some change in, I got Lily some chips and peanuts for the trip and a few cans of lemonade. I wasn't sure what we were going to do once we got there, but I would have to figure out something fast. I had some money we had saved up, mostly tips from the diner, but it wasn't going to last long, maybe a month max. I would have to find a job as soon as possible.

When the tin can also known as our freedom, pulled up at the station, we jumped straight on finding some seats, which was easy since the whole train was empty. It consisted of 3 carriages so we must be out of the city a fair way, because the city trains were huge and modern looking. On this train, we had to open the doors ourselves, and the leather seats were ripped. It had a weird odour to it. Sitting in the green leather seats, I rolled up my work uniform so Lily could use it as a pillow. I wanted to put my feet up, but after seeing how filthy my feet were decided against it, not that it would matter with the state of seats.

The first thing we needed to do was find a shop with shoes because I couldn't go around barefoot forever. Pulling the socks out of the bag that Wendy gave me, I quickly placed them on so my feet wouldn't catch a disease from the filthy carpet in the train carriage. After about 20 minutes of being on the train, it came to an abrupt stop, making us jerk forward in the seats. Lily, laying with her head in my lap on her makeshift pillow, nearly completely fell off her seat. Getting up, I peered out the window. We weren't at another station yet. All I could see was farmland. Walking over to the other side, I looked out.

My heart nearly stopped, there were about 7 black SUVs along the tracks. Like some scene from a movie, the doors opened, men stepping out. I knew it was Reid's Pack members. I recognised his beta, Zane. They got out in their suits. I could see the train driver out talking to someone. When they spun around, I could tell it was Reid. He looked furious. He was showing the driver a picture, which I was guessing was us, and all the Pack members started boarding the train. Grabbing Lily, I pulled her through to the next carriage, intending to run out the last door. Halfway through the carriage, the door opened. Zane and another Pack member walked towards us, smirks on their faces like they found this amusing. Spinning around, I went to run the other way, when an angry Alpha stormed through the door we just came through, blocking our escape, making me gulp and take a step back. Fuck this, I'm sick of playing nice.

$Chapter\ 13$

Aria's POV

URNING ON AN ANGLE so I had a clear view of both ends of the carriage and those blocking the exits, I shoved Lily into the seat, not taking my eyes off Zane or Alpha Reid. "Lily, close your eyes please, and hands over your ears," I said, not even looking in her direction. I couldn't afford to take my eyes off them. Knowing they were waiting for me to turn my back on them, Alpha Reid crossed his arms over his chest, making him look even bigger if that was possible. I may not win nor be trained like them, but I'll be damned if I go quietly to my death. Zane, noticing my intent, smiled. His bulky friend standing beside him chuckled like he thought I was joking about trying to fight my way out. Peeking over at Reid, he looked amused, taking a seat in the first chair at his end just as another Pack warrior walked in, standing in his place. Okay, not the best scenario. I may not be trained, but I am a Hybrid. Not having blood for 2 days now is a disadvantage, but I know I have had enough, that my speed and reflexes outmatch theirs.

"Let's see what you got then," said the cocky shit standing next to Zane. He was shorter, around my height, but Packed with muscle, too much muscle. I knew he would be slower than me. He was a fair bit shorter than Zane's 6-foot frame. The carriage wasn't big, but I knew that would work in my favour. I didn't need as much room to move. Zane shoved him forward, he stumbled about a metre away from me.

"You first then," he threw at him with a grin on his face. The warrior looked back at Zane, taking that as my opportunity.

I grabbed his outstretched arm he was going to use to stable himself, taking him by surprise. Using his momentum, he jerked forward, underestimating my strength, just as I lifted my knee, which connected with the side of his head. Shocked, he didn't have time to recover, his body being pushed back by the force of my knee, making him land on his arse. I quickly stomped on his manhood, making him squeal while he clutched at his groin. Zane immediately stepped forward over his friend's body and tried to grab me, but I jumped back just in time. Forgetting the person behind me, they grabbed me in a bear hug from behind. Thinking fast and using my legs, I pushed off the ground, shoving both feet into Zane's chest, making him trip over his recovering buddy, who was still laying on the ground cradling his balls.

Throwing my head back, I connected with my hugger's nose. Their hands let go instantly. Spinning around, I watched as they clutched their nose, which was bleeding, running like a tap. My own growl ripped through my chest and escaped my lips, not a normal growl, more primal, savage. It was disturbing, the growl of a predator. The smell of their blood reaching my nose filled me with hunger. Alpha Reid stood up. Shoving his Pack member out of the way, he landed on the seat, stomping towards me and grabbing my arm just as I went to lunge for the fallen man's throat.

Letting out another growl of annoyance, I slapped at his hand with my free one not realising my claws had extended, leaving a gash running down his chest and arm, making him growl back at me. Reid's grip tightened, ripping me forward. I landed into his chest. The force knocked me out of my blood-filled trance. Struggling against his grip, I dropped my weight, making my body go limp until I hit the floor landing on my back. Not expecting me to play dead, Reid fell on top of me. Using my legs, I pushed him off, making him somersault over me. Getting to my feet and spinning around, I saw Alpha Reid had a smile on his face, which confused me. Was he having fun? Not giving me a chance to lunge at him, he tackled me, knocking my feet straight out from underneath me.

Just when I thought for sure my head was going to crack open like a dropped egg on impact, he twisted so instead of landing on the filthy floor, I was once again on his chest. His arms wrapped around my own, and he squeezed, forcing the air out of my lungs. I would have been amazed at his strength if it weren't being used against me.

"Nice try," he whispered in my ear, confusing me, making me very aware of the closeness of his body pressed against my own. Trying to get out of his grip that has caged me in was useless. He outweighed me and easily overpowered me.

Rolling to his side with me still caged in his arms, he stood up, pulling me with him like I weighed nothing. *I guess he never misses leg day then,* I thought to myself, making me chuckle. Reid turned his head looking at me questionably, wondering what I thought was so funny. I could feel his breath fan my face making me instinctively lean into him wanting more.

Letting me go, he took a step back and to the side motioning for me to move past him to the exit.

"What? You expect me to go back willingly to my death?" I asked, raising my eyebrow. Reid pointed toward the exit again. Looking up at the exit, Zane was leaning against the frame of the door with Lily in his arms, who was talking happily to the person who's junk I crushed. My shoulders sagged instantly.

"You weren't the target. We only needed to distract you to get to Lily. I know you won't risk endangering her. If we wanted you dead you would be. I only told them to grab you or grab Lily. Nice try though, it was quite entertaining." Alpha Reid's tone was mocking, making me think he thought this whole situation was childish.

Stomping past him, I followed Zane. When I came up behind him, I went to reach out for Lily. Shaking his head, he continued walking before stepping off the train, while I followed. Walking up to the car Lily was being placed in, I went to get in, but the door was slammed shut in front of me. Spinning around to confront the person who slammed it, I came face to face with the bulky wolf from the train.

"Low blow, don't ya think? Nearly crushed my baby-makers," he said jokingly. "I'm Rick by the way. Nice to finally meet you, Luna."

"I'm not your Luna, and I'm umm sorry about your family jewels." Just as he was about to say something else, I felt a pinch in my neck. My hand reflexively going to my neck, I turned around to find Alpha Reid standing there with a syringe in his hand. "What?" My body instantly weakened. "Son of a Bitch." My words sounded slurred, my body went to jelly, and I slumped into Alpha Reid, who scooped me up. My head landed heavily against his shoulder just as my eyelids began to shut. I heard him laugh, the rumble echoing through his chest.

Reid's POV

We didn't even make it to the Pack border before Wendy mind-linked me to tell me Aria and Lily escaped. We'd been driving for 40 minutes only to turn around. I was furious. I finally found out what Pack they belonged to and who had been hurting my girls, and now they were going to do a runner from me. I may hate Hybrids and am having trouble figuring out if I want to give into the mate bond, but she is mine. Whether she likes it or not, she will be coming home. Aria believes she can leave my wolf and me. Not happening.

"Spin around head back towards the Pack house," I tell my driver. The car makes a sharp U-turn, spinning back around the way we just came. The rest of the vehicles behind us instantly spun around and followed.

"What's going on, Boss?" Zane's mind link came through.

"Aria thinks she can leave. She gave Wendy the slip."

"What about Alpha David?"

"Tell Dominic to deal with him for now. Tell him to tell the prick he isn't getting them back."

"You want to start a war?"

"Why are you scared?" I mocked.

"Pfft yeah, pissing in my boots," he sarcastically spat back.

Driving back to the Pack house, Wendy was waiting out front. Jumping out of the car while it was still moving, I walked over meeting her halfway.

"How did she get out of the room?" Wendy looked down, giving herself away instantly. "You let her out…. FUCK!"

"She had been in there all day, Alpha. I thought she might want to look around. I didn't think she would run. I thought I locked all the doors."

"Obviously, you thought wrong," Pinching the bridge of my nose, I let out a breath "It's fine Wendy, she couldn't have got far on foot unless she was picked up along the road. We didn't pass any cars so if she did get picked up, she must be in one of the outer towns. Closest is Larse, we will head there."

Everyone waiting next to the cars got back in. Four cars went one way at the T section, my car and 4 others went the other direction heading towards the small town out of the city. We drove for about 20 minutes before we came to a derelict train station. Sending Zane to the ticket booth to see if she had been seen, I waited by the car.

"They got on a train about ten minutes ago, Boss. Heading out of the city."

"Lead the way, we can cut the train off." Getting in, I told my driver to get out of the driver's seat, and he quickly slid into the passenger seat. Putting my foot down and leaving a cloud of dust behind us, we tore out of the train station to chase after the train. After about five minutes, we hit farmland. Driving up to the train tracks, we turned, driving alongside the tracks, when we saw the train up ahead. Putting my foot down, I overtook the train before driving up onto the tracks about a kilometre ahead of it to give it a chance to stop safely. The train driver instantly slowed before coming to a stop just before my car. An elderly gentleman with his grey beard and hair wearing overalls stepped off the train raising his hands in surrender. "I don't want any trouble."

"Settle down, we aren't here to cause problems. I'm looking for a woman and child; they got on at Larse station." I showed him a picture on my phone that I had Zane take when he was watching her at the diner.

He briefly looked at it before saying, "The middle carriage, son. You aren't going to hurt them, are you?" He genuinely looked concerned for them.

"Of course not, why would I hurt a defenceless woman and child? You have been watching too many action movies, old-timer," I replied. He looked relieved, nodding his head, he climbed back into the carriage.

Walking along the train, I made eye contact with Zane before pointing to the last carriage. He immediately obeyed. I knew she would run for the back one, so predictable. Pushing the sliding door open, I climbed into the train before opening the carriage door inside. Aria was protectively shielding Lily.

"Just grab her. If not, grab Lily. She will comply; she won't risk her safety."

"Yes, Boss." Everyone replied before I cut the link.

I observed. Aria wasn't really thinking she could get away, surely, she would know better.

"Lily close your eyes and put your hands over your ears," Aria called out. Glancing over at Lily, she did what she was told no questions asked. Lily really is a great kid; Aria has raised her well considering. Looking back up, Aria had turned, so she had a view of both ends of the carriage. HMMM, she is really going to try, interesting.

"Our girl is a fighter. Let's see what she can do," Ryder says excitedly. "Should have brought some popcorn." I muffle my laugh, but luckily no one was paying attention. Zane shoves Rick forward, but what happened next, I wasn't expecting. Aria seized the opportunity and cracked him a good one with her knee before stomping on his nuts. I internally cringe as I watch her foot come down.

Next up is Zane, who I could hear laughing at Rick's downfall. Aria was ready though, jumping out of reach. But she wasn't expecting Mitch behind her. After she kicks Zane in his chest with both her feet, he trips groaning.

"Fuck, I feel like I just been kicked by a horse. What have you been feeding her?"

"My blood," I laughed back at him. Hearing a terrifying growl, I look back up and notice a crazed gleam in her beautiful amber eyes. Hunger. Looking over at Mitch and seeing he is bleeding. Crap. Getting up, I shove him to the side, making him land on the seat. I grab her just as she lunges for him, but she is quick to swat my hand away, along with it my bloody skin. My own growl matches hers. Yanking her, she turns and lands against my chest but then goes limp catching me off guard and we start to fall to the ground. Only she is prepared and shoves me straight over the top of her. She isn't as weak as she looks. Amused, I feel a smile creep onto my face. Just as I lunge at her, tackling her, she starts to fall, but I twist at the last minute, pulling her onto my chest.

She squirms for a bit before realising it's useless. My arms wrapped around her warm body, and I could feel her breasts pushing against my chest, her scent driving me and my wolf crazy. I could feel my dick going hard at the thought of having her pushed up against me. Rolling to my side and using my legs, I pull us to a standing position. Not wanting her to know the reaction being close to her gives me. Letting her go, I instantly lose the warmth of her body.

"What, you expect me to go back willingly to my death?" she asks, raising her eyebrow at me. I indicate towards Zane, and her eyes follow before she recognises defeat.

"You weren't the target. We only needed to distract you to get to Lily, I know you won't risk endangering her, if we wanted you dead you would be, I only told them to grab you or grab Lily. Nice try though, it was quite entertaining." She stormed off the train.

"Isn't she marvellous? I'm so glad we decided to keep her," says Ryder, obviously impressed.

"Think you mean you decided to keep her. I wanted to kill her, but she is kind of growing on me."

"Hmm something is definitely growing, and it isn't her," he bites back sarcastically. Looking down, I discover a tepee rising in my fucking pants.

"Settle down, Ryder, you filthy dog." His anger at me calling him a dog made my erect dick instantly go down. Walking back to my car, I reach over and grab a bottle that has a sedative in it. Grabbing a syringe from the first aid kit, I stick the needle in the bottle, drawing some out. Walking back over to Aria, who was having a discussion with Rick over his hurt balls, I jab her in the neck while she is distracted.

A confused expression appears on her face when she notices the syringe. "What?" She falls into me before she mumbles something else that doesn't make sense. I think she called me a bitch. Picking her up, I inhale her scent. *Little wolf won't be escaping now,* I think to myself. I climb into the car with her sitting across my lap and wait for the driver. The train has pulled away now, and I watch her sleeping body in my arms. Brushing her hair out of her face, I ran my nose against her jaw to her ear then along my mark Ryder gave her. She moved a bit at my touch but didn't wake. I placed a kiss on her head just as the driver's door opened and Mitch climbed in the front.

Chapter 14

Aria's POV

WAKING UP, THE BED felt soft, comfortable, and warm. Not like the infirmary bed, which was a rubber mattress with flannelette sheets and thin cover. I was also aware I wasn't in bed alone. A heavily muscled arm draped lazily over my torso, his body heat seeping into mine from his chest pressed tightly against my back. Turning my head, I looked over at the sleeping Alpha. Must be deep in sleep because he snores like a bloody chainsaw. It was the middle of the night; I could see the moon sitting high in the sky through the windows that wrapped around half the room. Rolling onto my back, I freed one of my arms and lifted his arm that was now placed under my breasts, moving it off my body. I sat up and put my foot on the soft carpet, about to make a run for it.

Looking towards the door, I started to get up when I realised the snoring stopped. Glancing over at him, he was no longer sleeping; his eyes open staring at me. "I wouldn't. I mean, you can try if it makes you feel better. I will even give you a head start." He rolled on to his back, closing his eyes.

Getting up swiftly, I darted to the door. I could hear the Alpha laughing behind me. Throwing the door open, I ran out, a cold breeze sending goosebumps all over my body. Looking down, I realised I only had an oversized shirt on that was only just covering my bare arse. Where the fuck are my clothes? Running back into the room, I turned around and glared at the Alpha.

He was sitting up in the bed back propped up against the wooden headboard. Reaching over, he flipped on the lamp that was on the bedside table. "Well, that was quick. Forget something?" He smirked, raising an eyebrow before looking down at my bare legs. Suddenly feeling naked, I tried to pull the shirt down to try to cover my exposed flesh.

"Where are my clothes?" Alpha Reid put his hands up in surrender.

"I promise I didn't peek, and I thought you would be uncomfortable sleeping in jeans."

"So, you thought I would be uncomfortable in my underwear as well?" I asked, crossing my arms over my chest glaring down at him. His eyes dropped to my legs again. He smiled. Looking down, I realised by crossing my arms, I had hitched the shirt up even higher, nearly exposing myself completely. Quickly ripping the shirt back down, I felt my face heat up.

"I wonder how low your blush goes?" Looking back at the Alpha, his head cocked to the side with a smile on his face. I watched his eyes flicker oddly in the dim room to his wolf before settling back to his normal stormy grey. I stood awkwardly at the door, trying to cover myself and my embarrassment, which he seemed to be enjoying.

"You can have your clothes in the morning," he said, pulling the blanket back and patting the empty side of the bed.

"I'm not tired. Might have something to do with you knocking me out."

"Well, I am. Now get in the bed."

"No, I will go sleep with Lily. Where is she?"

"Why? So you can run the first chance you get? Not happening." He patted the bed expectantly. Knowing I wasn't getting anywhere, I walked over to the bed and climbed in. The Alpha tried to pull me closer, but I wriggled out of his grip. One minute he was glaring murderously at me, the next he was almost playful. Why am I in his bed? He wanted nothing to do with me the other day.

"My wolf will sleep better closer to you, and so will I, if you stop questioning everything." Confused, I looked over at him, his eyes were closed. "I can hear your thoughts when you're close, now can you please go to sleep?"

What? Can he hear my thoughts? My face heated up, instantly mortified, thinking of all the inappropriate thoughts I had of him in the diner. Why can't I hear his then?

Propping himself up on one elbow, he looked down at my reddening face.

"I can hear yours because I have marked you and you are close to me. You haven't marked me so, therefore, you can't hear mine. As for the dirty thoughts, I didn't know of them until you just remembered them, now please go to sleep."

Oh my god kill me now. I mentally face palmed myself. Rolling over to my side, I tried to go back to sleep, but it just wasn't happening. Trying to think of anything other than the Alpha's warm body next to mine, I started counting back from a 100. "Not helping, please stop talking."

"Stop listening then, I never asked to be in here. I can't sleep with you next to me."

"You were sleeping just fine before. I can help if you want."

I rolled my eyes and sighed dramatically. "How? Are you going to drug me again?" I laughed.

"I have other ways." Before I could ask what they were, he was on top of me, his legs pressed against my thighs, his head pressed to where my mark was. The next thing I remember is his canines brushing up against it before his teeth sunk into it, remarking me, then I was out like a light.

Waking up the next morning, I could hear water running. Groggily opening my eyes and peering around the room, I blinked, waiting for my eyes to adjust to the light shining in through the floor to ceiling windows. His room looked like something out of a catalogue. All the furniture was made from oak, and the carpet was black and thick, making the room quite cosy looking with the furniture. The king bed was also made from oak with a huge headboard that had two wolves facing each other carved into it. Getting up, I noticed straight away I still only had his shirt on. Walking over to the dresser, I opened the drawer which had briefs and socks in it, going to the next drawer I opened it. Inside were boxers and pyjamas. Grabbing a pair, I slipped them on before taking a pair of his socks and putting those on too. Wanting to leave before he got out of the shower, I quickly opened the door and started running down the stairs, which were located next to the bedroom door I found Lily hiding in.

Opening the door, I popped my head in, but the room was empty. Closing the door, I walked down the hallway, passing the infirmary after a few turns. I knew this side of the house, so finding the stairs leading down to the main floor was easier today than when I tried to escape. Walking down the stairs, I could smell freshly brewed coffee and bacon. My stomach growled hungrily. I followed the scent all the way to the kitchen, where I found Lily, Beta Zane, and a blonde woman with the little girl Lily introduced me to. Standing in the kitchen was Wendy and another man whom I'm assuming must be her mate, as he had his arms wrapped tightly around her waist. His head rested on her shoulder while she was standing at the bench drinking what I'm assuming is coffee or what I like to call liquid gold.

As soon as I swung the wooden door open, all eyes turned to me. Not one of them seemed shocked to see me. Wendy smiled and walked up to me with her arms open, embracing me in a warm hug.

"I'm so glad you are alright. You had me worried when you left."

I hugged her back before stepping back and looking at her. "I'm sorry I hope you didn't get in too much trouble."

"Don't worry about the Alpha, I can handle him." She winked before smiling back at me.

"Oh, this is Mitch, my mate. You already know Zane, and that is Christine, Zane's mate," Wendy said, pointing to each one. Mitch had short blonde hair and blue eyes and a round face. He was taller than Alpha Reid but leaner. Christine had blonde curly hair that sat on her shoulders, her facial features were softer, and she had green eyes and pale skin. Waving at them, I instantly recognised Mitch was the one I headbutted.

"Sorry about yesterday," I said, looking at him. Mitch just nodded his head. His nose was already healed, not even a scratch, but that didn't make me feel any better especially knowing he was Wendy's mate.

"What, I don't get an apology?" asked Zane.

"I barely touched you, and you fell over your own feet," I threw back at him with a grin on my face.

Zane shook his head, smiling before taking a sip of his coffee. Lily stopped eating her pancakes and came over to me, wrapping her tiny arms around me in a hug, before running back to the table to sit next to Amber. Walking over to the jug, I poured myself some coffee and lent on the counter with my arms next to Wendy and Mitch, who had gone back to the same position they were in when I walked in. Come to think of it, Christine also had some part of her touching Zane. When each would move, they would readjust some body part whether it was arms, legs, or hands to keep touching each other like magnets. Must be a mate thing and werewolf thing because I don't feel like touching Alpha Reid. I feel like running from him.

Speak of the devil, and he will show. Just as I was taking a sip from my coffee, in bursts Reid with his wet hair that was dripping on his clean blue shirt and a pair of jeans. The panicked look on his face made me jump back before his features softened and relaxed upon seeing me standing next to Wendy. Walking towards me, I took a step back, bumping into Wendy.

"He won't bite love; he is alright once you get to know him."

"That's because you haven't been bitten by him." I could hear everyone chuckle. My hand reflexively went to my mark where he decided to take a bite last night. Who is she kidding? I have every right to fear him. He hates me and my kind.

"I don't hate you, don't think that."

"Will you stop doing that? It's an invasion of privacy," I said, gritting my teeth. Grabbing my coffee, I went and sat next to Lily, drinking it slowly.

"So, how many Pack members live here?" I asked.

"Only us, the rest have their own places. It would cause too many fights having everyone under one roof, and Pack warriors love to fight," Christine said, speaking up for the first time since I walked in. Made sense, Pack warriors are hunters and loved fighting, so I would assume amongst themselves too.

Looking around the room, I noticed the Alpha leaning casually on the counter staring at me, his dark eyes burning into me with a look on his face I couldn't decipher. Looking back at Lily, she had finished eating.

"Can we stay here now, Ari?" she asked excitedly. Before I could answer, the Alpha was standing directly behind me.

"Your home is here now, you aren't going anywhere," he said, placing a hand on my shoulder. His touch sent sparks flying down my shoulder to my core, desire coursing through my body. I pressed my thighs together, trying to stop the ache between my legs. Looking up, the Alpha was looking down at me with a sly smirk on his face over the effect he was having just by touching me.

My face instantly heated up. He chuckled softly before removing his hand and walking back to the counter. When I looked around, I found everyone was staring at me smiling, like they were in on some joke I was unaware of. Wendy broke the awkward silence.

"Zane reckons Alpha has no effect on you. Alpha wanted to prove him wrong." If looks could kill, he would be dead ten times over with the daggers I was throwing his way.

When Lily walked out, I was quick to follow, pulling her to the side.

"Lily, where is our bag?"

She looked nervous, looking down before answering. "Alpha Reid took it; I think he took it in his room. He had it when he was carrying you," she said, still looking at her purple socks.

Looking over at her clothes, I noticed she was in brand new ones. She had on black tights and a pink unicorn shirt that matched her bedspread.

"Okay, I will try to find it. Stay with Amber."

Lily nodded before running over to play with Amber in the games room. Walking back up the stairs, I quickly ran back to the Alpha's bedroom, looking in all the drawers before going into his walk-in closet and rummaging around trying to find my duffle bag. I knew if I didn't find it soon, we would have problems. Ever since the night I came here and they fed me blood, I have started craving it more and more, not just when I'm injured or angry. The thirst is now always there waiting for a reason to take over.

Realising it's not in the bedroom, I make my way down to his office which I know is the one with the new desk simply because it's the biggest. It was nearly as big as his room, plus it was kind of in the middle of the house. Feeling relieved when I opened the door to see he wasn't in there, I made my way over to the bookshelves which had filing cupboards underneath and started opening them.

When I opened the third drawer, I found the bag. I opened it, noticing it felt lighter. My stomach dropped when I realised the bag only had my work uniform and my wallet. Standing up, my back was turned to the door, so I hadn't realised the Alpha had walked in and was now sitting behind his desk watching me. Shit, where did he put them? I couldn't find them anywhere.

"Looking for these?" His voice was low, making me jump. Turning around, he was sitting at his desk holding up a jar full of syringes. Relieved, I went to grab them, but he pulled them away at the last second.

"I need those, please," I begged.

"Why?" not willing to answer. I tried to snatch them from him, but he was quicker, moving them out of reach again.

When I went to grab them a third time, I noticed one of the bottles of wolfsbane at the end of his desk. Quickly snatching it off his table, I walked out and slammed the door.

Chapter 15

Reid's POV

WATCHING HER LEAVE AND slamming the door behind her, I wanted to chase her down and force her to tell me what she wanted the wolfsbane for. It was unusual for a wolf to want it. Was it for protection? Does she feel safer knowing she has it on her? Lily refused to tell me when I asked why Aria smelt of it at the diner and why Aria had so much in her system when we found them. The only thing Lily said was that they used it against the Alpha when they escaped. I'm assuming her old Alpha forced her to drink it as punishment, knowing it wouldn't kill her. I just didn't understand why they would have so much in the bag. Just as I was about to follow her, the door opened, making me come to a stop. It was Doc. She walked in holding a bunch of paperwork.

"You are going to want to take your seat, Alpha. I have some surprising news for you."

Walking back over to my desk, I sat down waiting for her to explain what the hell she was talking about. Mavis sat down before pushing the papers in front of me.

"What is it?" I asked, confused. The documents looked like blood work documents.

"When Aria came in here, we took some vials of her blood. Out of curiosity I had her DNA tested because even for a Hybrid she had ingested way too much wolfsbane. Enough to even kill a Hybrid."

"What are you getting at? I don't understand." Looking at the papers, they were just numbers on a page to me. I could never understand all this medical gibberish.

"We got the test results back. Aria isn't a typical Hybrid. She is 83% Lycan or in simpler terms a pure wolf, but her Vampire side is also pure. Aria isn't just a werewolf/Vampire Hybrid. Her DNA is older, her bloodline is ancient, and she is more wolf than any of us. Whoever her parents are, they are old, incredibly old. Aria's bloodline is so pure that she is, in every sense of the word, a mythical being."

"That's impossible. Lycans died out centuries ago. There are none in existence. Run the tests again."

"We have multiple times. I thought it must have been a mistake as well, but I assure you Alpha, it's not."

Lycans were the first of our kind. They don't have a wolf because they are the wolf. Meaning if what Mavis says is true, her bloodline isn't much younger then the Moon Goddess herself. The Moon Goddess was Lycan. It's said that one of her grandchildren fell in love with a human, therefore creating a mutated version called werewolves. When the Moon Goddess found out that her grandchild mated with a human, she had a witch help her, and in turn, the Moon Goddess created the mate bond to try and keep the bloodlines pure. What she didn't realise was that humans and Vampires could also be mates for Lycans and Werewolves, so after time, the Lycan blood was eradicated. Werewolves like myself are a mutation over Lycans mating with humans. No wolf today has Lycan blood, we are half-human, but that means Aria is from an original generation of Lycans. It also means that if she wanted, she has more power over any Pack and is rightfully a queen of Alphas. It also means the Moon Goddess is either her grandmother or her aunt because the last Lycans alive with as much purity as Aria were the Moon Goddess's siblings or her children.

"What about her Vampire side?"

"It's the same. I have no idea who her parents were, but you said Lily and Aria share the same mother. Lily's test showed she has normal wolf genes, and she comes from an Alpha bloodline. So that means it was Aria's father who was an original Hybrid. Aria's Lycan side is more dominant than the Vamp side for now. From what I gathered from her blood test, she hasn't drunk blood in years. Her Vamp side was almost dormant until you gave her blood. I'm actually surprised at how well she is adjusting, her thirst must be excruciatingly painful for her. Giving her blood would have awoken her Vampire side, she would probably be ravenous."

"What do you mean she would be ravenous? Has she come to you to get blood?"

"No, I figured you must have been feeding her, but if you haven't been feeding her, that means she hasn't had blood since you fed her the first night here. She would be a ticking time bomb if she doesn't feed." Doc's worried expression has me concerned. If she is a ticking time bomb, then how safe is my Pack with an original Hybrid in the house?

"And you're sure no one has given her a blood bag?"

"Yes, Alpha. It's not something we keep here. Not much use in a Pack house full of werewolves with super healing abilities." She chuckled lightly.

"Well, you are going to have to order some."

"Yes, Boss." She walked out of the room, leaving me to my own thoughts.

So, if Lily has Alpha blood, does that mean Alpha David is Lily's father? No Pack has two male Alphas. And who was Aria's father? Does Aria know what she is?

"And you called her an abomination, she is more werewolf than us," Ryder spoke up.

"Shut up, Ryder. We have more pressing issues like where our mate is and what she is hiding. We also have to sort out the Black Moon Pack and that Alpha of theirs."

Leaving my office, I followed Aria's scent to look for her.

Aria's POV

Running from the Alpha's office, I quickly made my way to the Alpha's bedroom. I didn't want Lily to worry, and I was also worried she might tell the Alpha I was craving blood. I didn't need to give him any more reasons to kill me. I knew he wouldn't follow me because as soon as I left, Mavis, the Pack doctor, walked in straight after me. Going to the bathroom, I quickly chugged down half the bottle before crumbling to the floor. My thirst was beginning to become a problem. I haven't wanted or needed blood so badly before, but it was like every fibre of my body was craving it. The wolfsbane burnt every cell, making me cry out in pain, clutching my stomach.

Come on, Aria, you can do this just a bit more. It will make the hunger stop. I tried to drink more down, but as soon as it hit my tongue again, I doubled over, throwing up into the toilet. I could feel my tongue sizzling from the poison. Blood started running down from my eyes and mouth. I thought drinking more would hold me off longer, but all it did was make me thirstier. My hunger became the only thing I could think about, taking over my thoughts completely. Laying on the cold tiled floor, I suddenly felt like my body was overheating, like I was boiling from the inside. I don't know how long I laid there. When I suddenly heard the bedroom door open, I could smell his alluring scent instantly. Closing my eyes, I tried to concentrate on anything but his scent, his blood calling to me. Sitting up, I quickly locked the door, but as soon as I did, he knocked on it.

"Open the door Aria," his voice sounded strained. I didn't answer because I knew if I did, it would come out pained or I would growl at him. Not trusting my hunger, I tried to drink another mouthful but only ended up choking gasping for air, when the door was suddenly kicked in. Alpha Reid walked in a pained look on his face; his breathing was ragged, and he was clutching the door frame tightly with his hand.

"Stop whatever you are doing," he gasped. I tried to get up but only stumbled back onto my hands and knees. So instead, I leant on the wall. He walked back out to the bed sitting on the edge, "The stronger the mate bond gets, the more I feel what you are feeling, including your pain."

Looking over at him, I suddenly took in his appearance. He had sweat running down the sides of his face, and his shirt was drenched in sweat as well. He sat there until he regained his strength before pulling his shirt over his head, dumping it on the floor next to him. Placing his elbows on his knees, he brushed his fingers through his hair before looking over at me sitting on the floor.

"Is that why you drink it? To stop the bloodlust?" Nodding my head, I faced the wall. I had been holding my breath for a few minutes now. Knowing as soon as I took a breath, I would be consumed with hunger again.

Getting up he walked back over to the bathroom door, leaning on the door frame. I watched as a drop of sweat ran from his neck down his muscular shoulder over his pecs and down his 6 Pack to his V-line before stopping at his jeans. He really was built like a god.

"If you're done eye-fucking me, get up off the floor and breathe. I know you're uncomfortable,"

"I can't," I said, gritting my teeth.

"Why? Because you're hungry…because you need to feed?"

Looking up at him, his eyes were soft. He didn't look angry, he just looked worried. Does he really care, or is this some trick to see if I can control my hunger? Well, if that's the case, I won't give him the pleasure of seeing me break.

Reid, figuring out I wasn't going to listen, showed me his palm. His claws extended, and he ran his index finger down his palm, slicing deeply. Blood started running down his hand onto the floor. He was baiting me. I could hear his blood dripping onto the floor. My face distorted just at the sight of it; my lips parted, my fangs breaking through my gums painfully. I growled at him in warning, trying to tell him to back off, but he didn't even flinch. I took a breath through my mouth, my growls getting angrier like a predator about to attack its prey.

"It's okay, Aria. It's not a trick I promise." Looking away, I closed my eyes, but my eyes snapped back to his when I heard his skin be resliced, only deeper. He was healing but reopening the wound. Teasing me. Obliterating what little self-control I had left. Why is he doing this to me? I felt tears brimming in my eyes, threatening to spill over. *You are stronger than this Aria, you can do this, he is just trying to bait you.*

Chapter 16

Aria's POV

GETTING UP OFF THE ground, I shoved past him. I didn't get far before his hand reached out to grab my shoulder. Spinning around, I grabbed him and pushed him. He flew backwards and landed on his back on the bed. Climbing on top of him, my legs straddling either side of his hips, anger and fear began taking over.

"Is this what you want? To see me break, to lose control? So, you can prove I'm the monster you think I am, to give you a reason to kill me?" I screamed. Lifting his shoulders, I slammed him back onto the bed.

He had a look on his face I was having trouble deciphering. He didn't look happy, just concerned, sad. Reaching his hand up, he placed it on my cheek, his thumb tracing the veins that were exposed under my eyes. His touch sent shivers down my spine. My body wanted to lean into his touch, but I refused, pulling back. I watched him; his hand dropped to my hip, squeezing it lightly.

"I don't want to break you. Just let go and give me control, Aria. I... It's hard, but I can't reject you. You're not like them, I know this now." His voice was soft.

"Not like all the Hybrid's you killed. What did they do that has you hating us so much that you would be sick enough to exterminate us completely? You want control? You're an idiot if you think I will give you control. People only want control because it's power over the other person, something to use against them," I spoke through gritted teeth.

"I wouldn't do that; the mate bond wouldn't let me. Why can't you see that? I was wrong, what I did was wrong. I know that now."

Pfft, I refuse to bow down to anyone anymore. I'm sick of being a pawn in everyone else's game, sick of hiding, sick of fighting what I am. As I was about to climb off him, he sat up, holding me in place. I went to shove him back with my hands, but he gripped both my wrists, holding them firmly to my sides. He lent in and placed a kiss on my jaw.

My eyes widened before they closed, a moan escaping my lips. His head dipped lower, kissing my neck. Reaching up, he grabbed my hair, wrapping his fingers in it softly pulling, giving him better access to my neck. I could feel his erection pressing against his jeans. I inhaled his scent, arousal flooding me mixed with hunger. Pulling back, he looked up at me. I hadn't realised I was growling at him. Not in anger but hunger and desire, both fighting against each other not sure which was going to win.

Reid pulled my face down so we were looking at each other, his eyes holding mine. Desire coursed through me as he leaned in, kissing my lips softly. His lips moving against mine filled with desire. I answered his kiss. Kissing back fiercely, both of us fought for dominance. My hands moved to his chest, and I ran them along his shoulders. His arms wrapped securely around my waist, pulling me closer. Kissing him behind the ear, I heard him moan against my shoulder.

Moving closer to his neck, hunger took over, devouring my senses. My fangs pressed against his flesh. I tried to pull back, to run, to stop from hurting him. His grip only tightened, one of his hands reached into my hair, holding my face to his neck.

"Shhh…. it's okay Ari, let go. I won't let you kill me," he whispered, pressing his lips on my cheekbone. Hearing him use my nickname and the tenderness in his voice, I let go. My walls came crumbling down, no longer scared, no longer hiding what I am. Trust, something I never thought I was capable of, trusting someone completely and of all people, I truly did, at this moment, trust him. Sinking my fangs into his neck, his blood rushed into my mouth. I gulped it down greedily, yet he didn't scream like I thought he would. Instead he moaned, pressing me tighter against his chest.

I could feel his emotions flooding into me: love, acceptance, desire. His intoxicating scent was nothing compared to how he tasted. I could taste every emotion he felt, making me want more. I was sure I could get drunk on his taste. Pulling back before he had a chance to, I ran my tongue along my bite. I watched as it sealed but remained the same as the mark he gave me, marking him. I didn't realise I had tears running down my cheeks until he wiped them away before kissing me.

Rolling me on to my back, he kissed me harder, his legs pushing between my thighs. I could feel the bulge in his pants pushing against my core, moaning loudly at the friction. His hands running beneath my shirt until they reached my breasts, my nipples hardening under his touch. Pulling my shirt off, he sat up, looking down at me. There was so much in the way he was looking at me. I could feel how much he wanted to touch me. How much he loved me, how much he wanted me. He didn't hate me. Just how had I been so blind to see it. His love for me outweighed the anger he had for my kind.

I pulled him down, pulling his hips into mine. I arched my back, wanting more when I felt his teeth graze my nipple as he took it in his mouth. I wanted him, all of him. I don't know why I felt so bold. Reaching for his belt buckle, I started undoing it, my hands shaking. Seeing me struggle, he gripped my hands, holding them in one hand above my head. He hungrily kissed my neck before I felt his hand push inside my pants, slipping his fingers between my wet lips, leaving me moaning against his touch. He rubbed his fingers in a circular motion around my clit, my core throbbing in anticipation as he slipped a finger into my flooding hole.

"You like that?" His husky voice sent thrills all through my body. I didn't respond, my moans were my answer. Opening my eyes, he was watching me, seeing my reaction.

A seductive smile appeared on his lips. He slipped another finger in, curling his fingers, hitting my g-spot, my hips moving against his fingers as he slipped them in out. My skin started to burn up. My legs began to shake as I could feel my release coming, just sitting on the edge building up until I felt my walls clamp down on his fingers. He slowed his movements, letting me ride out my orgasm. Slipping his hands out of my pants, my face flushed when I watched him suck his fingers clean, tasting me on his fingers. Kissing my neck, he sat up. I just laid there never feeling so relaxed as I did now.

"You might want to get up, we have company." His voice ran clear in my mind. Shocked, I looked over at him. He had a cheeky smile on his face.

"Did you just mind-link me?" I asked. Instead of answering out loud, he mind-linked instead.

"Yes, I did. You're part of this Pack now that you have marked me. You are my Luna."

I blushed all the blood rushing to my face thinking back to me marking him. Now everyone will know what we just did. How embarrassing.

"Don't be embarrassed." I couldn't help it though; I was never one for public displays of affection. Looking at the mark on his neck, it was red, angry. It was no longer bleeding but clearly on display, much to my horror. Seeing how uncomfortable I was becoming, he put out his hand. I gladly accepted it, letting him pull me to my feet.

"Why are you so uncomfortable? If you're this embarrassed now, I would hate to see how uncomfortable you will get after the mating ceremony." The mating ceremony oh my god, how awkward. Now I'm glad we didn't have sex. The whole Pack would know, be able to smell his scent on me, claiming me as his.

"Are you a virgin?" he asked. I stared back mortified, and he chuckled softly.

"Well sorry, but I have been a bit busy raising my sister. I didn't have time to being throwing myself at randoms," I said sarcastically, trying to hide my embarrassment. His eyes glazed over, his wolf taking charge. Gripping me, he pulled me to him, crushing me against his chest. I relaxed in his hold before someone awkwardly cleared their throat. If I had been paying attention, I would have heard them come in. Stepping back, Reid's eyes were back to normal, his wolf no longer holding control. Looking over at the door, I saw it was Zane.

"Lily wants to know if she can go see Zoe?" he asked, raising his eyebrow a small smirk playing on his lips as he took in my dishevelled appearance. I nodded, embarrassed, walking past him to go search for Lily.

Chapter 17

Aria's POV

WALKING DOWNSTAIRS, I FIND Lily playing with Amber. They were both sitting peacefully playing with a dollhouse and some barbies. Sitting next to them on the floor, I watched.

"Can we visit Zoe? I miss her," Lily asked with a frown on her face.

"I can send Zane with you; I have a few things to look into," Reid said, walking over to us. Lily beamed at him. Excitedly, she stood up, running off before coming back with some pictures she drew.

"Can I also go back to school?" Lily asked. I went to tell her not yet, but Reid decided to answer for me.

"Would you like to go to school with Amber at the Pack's school?" asked Reid. Seems like he has everything figured out, so I didn't object.

"Yes," she squealed excitedly, throwing herself in my arms. Looking up at me, she sniffed me before sitting back. "You smell different, Ari."

"That's another thing we have to talk about Lily, we are going to join the Blood Moon Pack, that's why I smell different." I thought Lily may be a bit disappointed joining another Pack that wasn't connected to our family, but she looked just as excited.

"Really, we don't have to hide anymore?" I shook my head, tears springing in my eyes at her excitement.

"Come on, we will go see Zoe and talk about it more when we get home," I told her. Zane walked out standing beside me. Reid was on the phone now but pulled the phone from his ear as we were about to leave. "We are going to have a bit of a ceremony to introduce you to the Pack as the Luna. We can also do Lily's initiation ceremony as well," he said, handing me his credit card. "Here, find something nice to wear. Zane will escort you just in case you run into anyone from your old Pack," he said before kissing me on the cheek.

When we arrived at Joe's Diner, Lily took off and ran straight through the doors. Walking into the diner myself, I was greeted with a hug from Zoe. She hugged me so tight I didn't think she would let go. Marcus also came out, picking Lily up and throwing her up in the air.

"Let's go make pancakes, Lil," he said excitedly. Lily followed him to the kitchen.

Turning back to Zoe, she had tears in her eyes. "I thought that Alpha killed you, but when he came in looking for you and Lily, I knew you must have escaped."

Being shocked at her words was an understatement, I was completely gobsmacked. Zane gave me a nod before sitting in one of the booths. Zoe ushered me out of the diner and into her studio, walking behind the tv that sat in the corner off the wall. She pushed on the wall, which opened up, showing some stairs. I followed her down the stairs. As we walked down, lights started flicking on. They must have been motion sensor lights, little LED lights were running on each step. When we reached the bottom, the lights turned on and revealed a bunker.

Along the walls were tv screens. I could see different angles of the diner and the street outside as well as the back entrances. Looking at Zoe, she gestured for me to sit down at a long stainless-steel table that looked more like a medical table than one you would eat at.

"What's going on, Zoe? What is all this?" Looking at Zoe, I came to realise I didn't know Zoe as much as I thought I did. She never really spoke much of her life with her husband. Mainly she asked about us or told us what she had planned or what she might have done that day, but nothing personal. I just assumed the memories of her life with Joe were too painful, and so I never pushed her for answers.

"I'm shocked Reid didn't say anything."

Looking back over to her, I said, "What? He knew all along?"

"No, only recently when I figured out he was your mate. I kind of told him to back off and leave you alone," she mumbled.

"So, what is all this?"

"My husband used to be a Hunter. This was our weapons bunker." Zoe got up and pressed a switch on the wall. The wall opened a hidden compartment, and the whole wall on the inside uncovered an arsenal of weapons. Standing up, I walked over, examining them carefully. There were weapons for every sort of supernatural creature plus some I had never seen before.

"What's this," I asked, pointing to a ground ball with a pin in it. It appeared to be a grenade but was clear with a gold liquid in it.

"It's a wolfsbane grenade." A shiver ran down my spine. Turning back to Zoe, I watched her carefully. She didn't seem fazed about being in my presence. No matter who Zoe is or what her past contained, I knew I could still trust her.

"I know you have questions. If you take a seat, I want to show you something." Sitting back at the table, Zoe walked back up the stairs and came back with a photo album. Opening it up, I saw a picture of Zoe with her husband. "I married Joe when I was 18. Joe was 19 at the time. I came from a Catholic family, so when I found out he was a Hunter, I instantly thought I married a nutter." She giggled at the memory. "But after a little time, I came to see for myself. I never agreed with any of this, I couldn't bring myself to stand on the sidelines either, so I was also a Hunter for a while. I helped track them down but didn't get involved in the war, Joe preferred it that way anyway. He was a bit old fashioned, said it was too dangerous for a woman. Joe came from a family of Hunters, and when his parents died, he took over. He was raised to believe all supernatural creatures were dangerous and merciless killers and that he needed to rid the world of their evil. When he was in his early twenties, he met a man. They became best friends, but he soon discovered his friend wasn't human."

Zoe turned the page revealing a picture of Joe and another man. The man had black hair and a strong jawline; he was tall and strongly built, he also had orange blazing eyes. But that's not what I found the most astonishing thing to this story; the necklace around his neck- it was my necklace. Picking up my necklace between my fingers, I looked at the wolf's head before turning it over to see the back, which I realised had the same face as the man in the picture. It captured his features perfectly, even the eyes which were the same orange as mine now.

"That's my father, isn't it?" Zoe nodded sadly.

"Yes, your father was my husband's best friend. When he found out, he was shocked but then realised his view on them was ruled by fear. They weren't much different than us. Yeah, you have your bad eggs, but they usually keep to themselves. So, after he found out about your father, he quit. Your father was a good man, and after a while, he became family. A few years later, as you know, me and Joe couldn't have kids, so we went and visited an orphanage, and we adopted a little girl. She was 3 at the time. She was abandoned on the side of the road when the authorities found her, and we raised her like our own." I looked at the little girl in the picture. She reminded me of Lily.

"When she grew up and was about 10, she shifted into a wolf for the first time. Gave us quite the shock, but your father knew all along. He helped teach her to hunt, how to bond with her wolf. Your father also helped us keep her hidden. When she was 21, our daughter and your father established a relationship. They fell madly in love." Turning the page tears sprung in my eyes. It was my mother standing with my father and a huge baby bump. "Not long after you were born, the Hunters my husband worked with found out about your father. My husband tried to get them to understand that he wasn't like the rest of the Vampires they had come across, but they refused to listen. One day they trapped your father and Joe. They were ambushed when they were out hunting, killing them both. My husband tried to save your father, but in the end, it got him killed. Your mother was devastated, and for a while, she left. She came back a few times when you were younger but never stayed long."

"So, you're my grandmother? Lily's grandmother?"

Zoe smiled sadly. "I'm sorry I didn't tell you, but Alpha David refused to let me be a part of your lives. So when you stopped in that day looking for a job, I knew it was my chance to be a part of your lives. Your mother used to send me photos of you growing up before she died. Alpha David was very controlling when he met your mother, and when he realised she was his mate, he kidnapped her. I thought I lost her. He forbade her from having contact with me, but after a while, the bond was too strong, and she stopped fighting to leave. A few years later she had Lily. We kept in touch secretly, but once David came into the picture when you were 7, I never saw you in person, only by photos. David forced your mother to have you hypnotised to forget about me. That's why you have no memories of me." Come to think about it, I haven't got many memories from my childhood, only dribs and drabs.

I had tears running down my face. Standing up, I hugged her tightly. I still have a family; Lily and I aren't alone anymore. I have someone to connect me to my family.

"Aria, there something else, your father wasn't a Vampire, he was Hybrid. A powerful one at that. He wasn't a werewolf. He was a Lycan. When we met your father, he was 440 years old. My husband discovered after a lot of research that your father was the first Hybrid in existence. Your blood holds so much power. I didn't want to tell you earlier because if David found out that you could take him and his Pack, he would have killed you, and I knew you wouldn't want Lily left behind to be raised by that monster." I just nodded my head. There is no way I would want him anywhere near her, especially after finding all this out.

"The more you feed, the stronger you will become, but you also need to be careful about the Hunters. You may not hear of them, but they are still around. They find out about you, they will come for you. Your bloodline is old, rightfully you would be considered an original Hybrid. You can't shift because you don't have a wolf. Your Lycan blood means you aren't a mutation, you're something special. Your blood holds the past of when Lycans ruled when Lycans were considered Gods of Alphas."

"We shouldn't tell Lily, not yet I don't want to confuse her or scare her," I said, which Zoe agreed.

"So how is everything with Reid?" Changing the topic to a lighter, almost casual topic. Honestly, I was glad for the change in subject. I was having trouble wrapping my head around this whole Lycan stuff and the fact that I have a living relative not only connected to my mother but my father also.

"It's okay. I thought he hated me when he found out I was a Hybrid, but he has come around. Now we are having a little ceremony tonight to introduce us to his Pack."

"Go easy on him dear, he has his reasons for hating Hybrids. He has a pretty tragic background himself, but the mate bond will correct all faults. Trust in the Moon Goddess."

"How do you know so much about him?"

"I have my ways; granny still has connections, and I have cameras all over the city. I have seen a lot over the years."

"So does Marcus know about all this?"

Zoe nodded. "Marcus is also a Hybrid but just a normal Wolf and Vampire Hybrid."

"How does he hide it?"

"Well for starters he drinks blood, so for the most part to the werewolves he smells human. After a while your eye colour will dim a bit, but he wears contacts mostly. His bloodline isn't like yours, your eyes will probably stay like your fathers growing brighter with hunger and strong emotion, but you can try contacts if you're that worried. Your father wore contacts before we discovered what he was." Just as I was about to say something else, we heard a commotion upstairs racing up the steps.

I ran towards the entrance of the diner, where I could hear growling and things being smashed around. Stopping when I got to the counter, I saw Marcus had Lily pushed behind him. Zane was fighting with Alpha David and his Beta. Quickly racing forward, I grabbed Michael and threw him into a table. Alpha David turned. Knocking Zane out of the way, he stalked towards me. Lily screamed loudly, distracting me just as David punched me, knocking me to the ground. Zane and Marcus were quick to jump at him though, forcing him back before he could lunge at me. Getting to my feet, I grabbed Lily and pushed her towards the back of the diner. As I went to go help Zane and Marcus, I heard Zoe walk out from behind the counter, a shotgun in her hand pointed straight at the Alpha. She cocked the gun. David froze, a snarl on his face. His claws extended and his canines elongated.

"I won't miss, mutt. Now get out of my diner." David growled at her, and Michael got to his feet and moved to David's side.

He went to take a step closer to Zoe, who had Lily behind her. She lifted the barrel, so it was directly pointed at his head. "You think you can take my daughter away, my heir. I'm her father?"

"Your daughter? How dare you? She isn't your daughter. Being her father implies you cared for her and raised her. The only thing you ever did was push your responsibilities on to me. You are nothing but a coward. Lily is mine, I won't let you take her," I screamed, outraged that he thinks he can even give himself the title of being her father.

Michael gripped David's arm, trying to pull him towards the door and out of sight of the gun that Zoe held. They reluctantly leave.

"This isn't over you will pay for this; I will get her back." David sneered from the door.

"Pfft, you can try, but you don't scare me. You are delusional if you think I will just hand her over to the likes of you. Mum would be disgusted in you. You're no Alpha, you're weak and pathetic."

David growled at me, trying to push past Michael. I must have hit a nerve. Fuck him, who does he think he his suddenly wanting to claim parental rights. The Alpha and Beta Michael left in a fit of rage; David smashed the glass doors, sending glass everywhere on his way out.

Zane came over, placing a hand on my shoulder. "We should get back before he sends for back up. Reid wants to come get you."

"Tell him no. We are leaving anyway, we can meet him at home."

"Yes, Luna."

Picking up Lily, I turned back towards Zoe, who placed a kiss on Lily's head. "You should come with us; it won't be safe here." Zoe shook her head.

"I have Marcus here, and I'm not some defenceless little old lady. I can hold my own, Ari. I refuse to be scared out of my home."

Marcus got a broom and started cleaning up the broken glass with a broom. Embracing him in a hug, I said my goodbyes. As I was walking through the busted door, I heard a low growl from behind me. Reid was standing there, glaring at Marcus. Marcus growled back, shocking me. I always thought of him as human, so it was quite shocking to him growl at someone, especially an Alpha. He must feel comfortable being himself around me now that I knew. I sort of understand why he remained hidden. This city isn't the safest for Hybrids. I'm his best friend, he shouldn't have felt the need to hide it from me, but now I am seeing him in a totally new light.

Reid took a step forward, reached out his arm and grabbed Marcus. I stepped between the two of them and glared at Alpha Reid.

"Move Aria."

"You are not going to touch him; he has done nothing wrong."

"He is a Hybrid, fucking move." He growled, shoving me to the side. Spinning around, I passed Lily to Zane before jerking Reid back by his jacket, who had tackled Marcus to the ground.

"I said no. If you want to kill him, you can go through me first. Marcus is my best friend. I won't allow you to hurt him."

Marcus got up and went back to sweeping, seemingly unfazed by Reid's show of dominance. Marcus could probably hold his own, but he isn't very confrontational and would rather diffuse a situation. The only time I had seen him get angry or hit anyone was when I had customers being inappropriate or vile towards Zoe or me, but Reid needs to get over his aversion to Hybrids seeing as I am one.

Storming off, Reid got in the car that was parked on the curb, slamming the door behind him. Zane took Lily in his car, while I got in Alpha Reid's.

"Why are you here? I told Zane to tell you to wait at home."

"You're my mate. As if I am going to sit at home like some house husband while my mate is in trouble, and then I show up and you're cuddling up to some Hybrid."

"Really, you're jealous? That's what this is about? Well, I'm afraid to burst your bubble, but you and Zane are more his type. Marcus is gay, and he is my best friend, so grow up. I don't know why you hate Hybrids so much, but if I catch you trying to hurt Marcus, Lily and I will leave, and then you will have no mate."

Chapter 18

Aria's POV

*D*RIVING BACK TO THE Pack house, Reid didn't say much. He seemed to be thinking about what I said. After about ten minutes, he finally spoke. "Do you know why I hate Hybrids?"

Shaking my head, I looked over at him. Reid was staring out the window. "No, I don't know," I said. Reid thought for a few moments before speaking again.

"I wasn't an only child. I had an older brother: his name was Alexander. He was 4 years older than me, and he was meant to take over the Pack when my father died. He never got the chance, though. When I was fourteen, my father took me away on Pack business with him. My mother and older brother stayed behind. Alexander was meant to go, but I begged my father to take me instead. We were gone for three days when my father got called through the Pack link saying the Pack house was under attack. We shifted and ran all the way home. My father screamed in agony every time he felt a Pack members link break, but he didn't stop running because he knew his Pack needed him. When we arrived at the Pack house…" Reid went quiet, trying to find the words to express what haunts him.

"When we reached the Pack house, Pack members bodies were strewn across the place. Men, women, even the children that didn't have a chance to get to the bunkers. All ripped to pieces, their blood staining the soil where they lay. My brother was fighting for his life and the Packs, but we were outnumbered. My father screamed, clutching his chest. It was the most agonised scream I had ever heard. I felt like my chest was being crushed. I will never forget the feeling of my mother's link breaking. My brother dropped to the ground feeling it too, feeling my father's heartbreak through the Pack link. I ran towards my brother to help when a man put his hand through his chest, ripping his heart out right in front of me. I killed the man, ripping him limb from limb. The last image of my brother has haunted my dreams ever since..." Reid's hand clenched into tight fists white-knuckled he continued.

"When my father managed to get to his feet, he became crazed at the loss of his mate, my mother. The loss of my brother was the last straw. He slaughtered every single one of them. We lost half the pack that day. My father wiped out the entire other Pack, every single person. He didn't care if they were involved or not, he went after them anyway. They were a rival Pack, my father had a dispute with them a few weeks before. They waited for my father to leave so they could attack, and they enlisted the help of the Hybrids. I hate them for what they did, not just the fact that they killed my family but for what they did to my mother. The Hybrids ripped her to pieces. It took us hours to find her entire body.

"My father went on a rampage and killed every Hybrid in the

city with my help. I promised him I would kill every Hybrid I came across, promised to keep the Pack safe. A few years after, when I was sixteen, my father took his own life. My father couldn't handle the pain of losing his mate. I found him hanging from the ceiling in my office. Losing a mate will send a wolf crazy or make them bitter and angry. My father went crazy and killed himself, leaving the Pack to me. That's why I hate Hybrids. It doesn't matter if they weren't involved. I have seen what they can do, I know the destruction they are capable of."

I sat silently listening to everything he said, letting it sink in. He didn't look at me or add anything else. Reid just sat there gazing out the window trapped in his memories. Reaching over, I grabbed his hand. Reid ripped his hand out of my grip, and a growl escaped his lips, making me flinch and pull my hand back. We had pulled up outside the Pack house. Opening the door, Reid walked inside, slamming the car door behind him, leaving me sitting in the car. I felt terrible not because he rejected me but because he had his own secrets, his own pain. A pain I couldn't take from him. Feeling through the bond, I could feel how hard he struggles with himself being around me, but at the same time, I could feel how much he rejects those feelings, pushing them aside for me. I felt guilty. I know I didn't kill his family, but that didn't make me feel any less guilty knowing that my kind were the ones to cause his heartbreak and knowing I was also making him break the promise he made to his father.

After a few minutes lost in my own thoughts, Zane came over, opening the door. He waited for me to get out. "Let him calm down. He doesn't mean to push you away."

"I know," I said, hopping out of the car. Zane looked at me, worriedly. "I'm fine, Zane. Reid is the one that needs you, not me." Zane nodded his head, following his Alpha.

Walking into the Pack house, I find Lily, who is in the kitchen talking to Wendy excitedly about the upcoming celebrations. Looking at Lily, it made me think of what Reid said about losing a mate. How it sends a wolf crazy. Alpha David lost his mate, my mother. I could, for the first time, understand what he went through. I know if something were to happen to Reid, it would kill me. The mate bond was that strong, it would be like losing a piece of your soul. How was David able to live with it? I couldn't forgive all the horrid things he had done, how he rejected Lily, but for the first time, I did understand it. He blamed her even though she didn't deserve that blame.

For the first time since my mother died, I felt sorry for him, but sorry doesn't erase what he has done. Sorry doesn't make me think any better of him. I just hope one day Lily could have a father figure in her life that adores her. But if not, she always has me. I will always make sure she knows that above everything. That her happiness will always be more important than everything else that life throws at us. But to keep her safe I will have to try to speak to her father. They may never build a relationship like I used to hope they would when she was baby, but I also didn't want to risk Reid's Pack, our Pack, if we were to go to war.

I know Reid would go to war if we needed to keep her safe. I just hope it doesn't come to that, and if there is any way to stop it, I promise Lily I will try. After all, as much as I can't stand David, it doesn't change the fact that he is her father. Lily may want nothing to do with him now, but that could change when she is older, and if there is a chance they could build a relationship, I will have to make sure she gets that chance. So, for now, I need to find a way to defuse the situation before it becomes out of hand.

Walking over to Lily and Wendy, they walked out the back onto the patio area that overlooked the pool and backyard. Following behind them, the first thing I noticed was heaps of Pack members. There were about a hundred people in the yard setting up long tables and placing out chairs. There were men setting up what looked like a DJ station and dance floor. Women were happily chatting amongst themselves, setting the tables. A large group of teenagers were hanging lights from the trees and on the huge gazebos. How did they set up all this in the time while we were gone? Everyone seemed buzzed and excited about the ceremony. I wondered if they would feel so excited when they discovered they have a Hybrid for a Luna. I suddenly felt inadequate. I was a noone, now I'm expected to help lead the Pack.

Wendy, noticing me, walks over, wrapping an arm around my shoulders. "This is all for you, Luna, you and Lily. The Pack members are excited to meet their Luna finally. We never thought Reid was going to find his mate. He has always been so closed off to everyone until you came into the picture, so everyone is naturally curious."

Her words only made me more anxious. Stepping away from her, I made my way back inside. Deciding to go upstairs, I walked into Reid's room, not really knowing where else I could hide from everyone. I looked for a linen cupboard, wanting to take a shower, but couldn't find one after a few minutes. I walked back downstairs to the hallway. Walking past the bedrooms before coming to Alpha Reid's office, next to it was a cupboard and opening it, I grabbed a towel out. As I was about to turn to walk back upstairs, I heard talking. "Calm down Alpha, if you go back and kill him, Aria will never forgive you."

"I don't fucking care. I hate them, hate them all." I quickly dropped my head going to walk off back to the stairs when the floor creaked. Looking through the gap of the door. I made eye contact with Reid, who was glaring directly at me. His canines protruding, his face was distorted with anger. I couldn't seem to pull my gaze away from him. His anger was strong, thick, reaching to me through the bond. I suddenly felt like my blood was boiling, making me feel hot. His anger was burning hot and unrelenting. Zane stepped into my line of vision, breaking my eye contact. He looked at me, smiling sadly before closing the door.

Running to the room, I locked the door before walking into the bathroom. His anger scared me. I felt frightened of what he might do if I pissed him off. I knew he can't kill me without destroying himself, but that didn't make me fear him any less in this moment. Jumping in the shower, I turned the taps on, washing my body with the shower gel and a loofa. I washed myself slowly, not wanting to get out of the shower. My muscles were tense, and I was on edge. After about five minutes, I heard the door handle to the bedroom break. It dropped to the floor with a soft thud. My heart skipped a beat, and my stomach dropped when I heard the door handle to the bathroom twist before opening.

Dread consuming me, I froze. Reid's imposing frame walked in. Watching him, I had the sudden urge to not turn my back on him. He was still angry. Reid stripped his clothes off before stepping into the shower and turning on the other showerhead at the other end on the wall. Putting his head under the hot stream of water, I watched his shoulders relax, and he let out a breath. I quickly washed my hair before turning my own shower off. Grabbing my towel that was sitting on the sink basin, I quickly wrapped it tightly around my body. When I looked up, Reid was staring at me, his jaw clenched and eyes blazing. Rushing out of the bathroom, I quickly closed the door behind me.

Sitting on the bed was a dark aqua coloured dress. The dress was beautiful, it was a mid-thigh off-shoulder silhouette with a plunging neckline which would show a lot of cleavage. Picking up the dress, I stared at it. I couldn't remember the last time I wore a dress, maybe when I was a little girl. I wouldn't usually wear something so revealing. Next to the dress was a blue suit, which must be what Reid will be wearing. Wrapping the towel tighter, I went to the draw and pulled out some underwear. The dress wouldn't allow for a bra, so I slipped my panties on, just as the door opened. Wendy and Christine excitedly stepped in. "You like the dress?" asked Christine excitedly.

"It's gorgeous but don't you think it's a bit revealing?"

"Nonsense, it will look great. Come on, let's get you changed," said Christine grabbing my hand, pulling me from the room and down the stairs to her room. Christine was wearing a lilac floor-length dress. Wendy was wearing a strapless blue mid-length dress that flared out at the bottom. Both of them looked stunning.

$$Chapter\ 19$$

Aria's POV

WENDY AND CHRISTINE DIDN'T waste any time; they excitedly did my hair and make-up. I just let them do what they wanted. There wasn't any point in trying to argue with them, I had more pressing issues consuming me. How were Reid and I going to get along when he had so much anger and hatred towards things that were out of my control? I can't change what I am, but I won't stand for him, making me fear him. I have always been submissive to how mine and Lily's life turned out, taking it as it comes. I'm not willing to sit and take it anymore. I know who I am now. More importantly, I know who I want to become, and that's not a person who gets pushed aside and walked all over. Only I can control who I am supposed to be, and standing there and taking blow after blow didn't work in the past. So, learning from those mistakes, I refuse to devalue myself for the sake of pleasing others or fearing the reactions of those who won't agree. Lily needs to know it's not normal hiding from everyone, not normal to fear everyone, and the only way I can get her to see her own strength is to display it myself.

I was brought out of all-consuming thoughts after about an hour of Wendy fiddling with my hair and makeup when they asked me to get changed into the dress. The dress fit like a glove, though I must admit I wasn't comfortable with the length, but they insisted it wasn't too short. Slipping the black heels on, I stood in front of the mirror. Wendy had curled my long hair and put it half up half down, the curls raining down to the middle of my back. I had to admit they did a really good job. I looked nice. I looked how a Luna should look. Standing there, staring at myself in the mirror, I had a newfound confidence. I was starting to become excited about the celebrations. Today may not have been the greatest in terms of Reid and I getting along, but I pushed those thoughts aside. Even if he chooses to ignore me or not even show up, I will manage on my own. I won't let the Pack see what a nervous wreck I am on the inside. Just smile, fake it until you make it, I guess.

Walking out into the foyer, Lily comes bounding up to me. She had a pink frilly dress on that went to her feet. Her blonde curls shaping her angelic little face to the middle of her back and white sandals on. She looked like a little princess.

"You look pretty Ari," she said excitedly, pulling on my curls gently. I smiled down at her.

"So, do you, Lily, just like a princess." Lily laughed excitedly, spinning in a circle to show me her dress, the bottom flaring out as she spun around. Holding my hand out, Lily took it, and we walked towards the back yard. Beta Zane walked out with Christine and Wendy. The girls, noticing some Pack members, ran to go chat and mingle, leaving me there holding Lily's hand. Zane stepped over in his black suit putting his arm out for me to take.

"Luna." He nodded. "You look great, Ari."

"Thanks, you scrub up nice yourself," I replied, smiling. Lily, Zane, and I walked over to the end of the patio. The entire yard had been transformed. Fairy lights shone brightly from the trees, making the whole yard glow. There were small fire pits scattered around, the tables were all set up and decorated. Music was playing loudly. There were tables of food. Lily looked excitedly at a group of kids around her age that were dancing on the dance floor that had been set up in the middle of the yard. Noticing her excitement, I nudged her. "Go play, Lily, it's alright."

"But what about you?"

"I'll be fine. I have Zane, and I'm sure Alpha Reid will be down soon," I answered, not so sure on the last part. I watched Lily run off towards the crowds of people. Every Pack member was here. Everyone standing around talking, dancing, drinking, and eating. The atmosphere was very relaxed and happy, carefree. Everyone was enjoying themselves.

"Ready?" asked Zane.

"Yep, as ready as I'll ever be."

Zane led me down the stairs. He introduced me to a lot of people. I could tell some thought it was weird that Zane was showing me around and introducing me to everyone instead of Alpha Reid. But no one said anything. They all seemed excited to meet me, and I was just as excited to meet the other Pack members. After a few hours, I did start to worry that Reid wasn't going to make an appearance. Pack members whispered amongst themselves. I even heard someone call me an unwanted mate. I didn't let it bother me, choosing to ignore the whispers. Their opinion of me didn't matter, and I didn't care to hear it either.

Letting go of Zane's arm, I walked over to the bar area and grabbed another drink. The gentlemen behind the bar passed me a flute of champagne. He had red hair that jutted out everywhere, making him appear younger than he was. He had a strong build but wasn't as tall as most male werewolves. He wore black slacks and a t-shirt that had a picture of a tie on it.

"So, you're the Luna. It's a pleasure to finally meet you. My name is Damien." He bowed his head slightly.

"Nice to meet you, Damien. I'm Aria."

"Where is that Alpha of mine? Haven't seen him all night."

"He is somewhere, I'm not quite sure either." He nodded in understanding. I could tell by the look on his face that he had heard the whispers. Does everyone think I'm the unwanted mate? As the night went on, I started noticing the women kept glancing or smiling sadly at me. Like they felt sorry for me. I didn't want their sadness or pity. I wanted to feel like one of them. Everyone was polite but didn't go out of their way to talk to me. Wendy and Christine came over, finally finding me sitting on a stool at the bar. This time I was drinking red wine. Wendy took the glass from me, taking a sip before she passed it back to me.

"I'll have that one please, Damien," she told him. He quickly handed her a glass as well, and she motioned for me to follow her. We sat at one of the tables. Watching everyone, I saw Lily dancing with a group of kids on the dancefloor. Laughing amongst themselves. Zane came over with a huge tray of food. There were various types of meats and cheeses, and we tucked in eating, watching everyone. After we were done, Zane put his hand out for Christine. She happily took it, and they made their way to the dance floor. Wendy's mate also came and grabbed her. I watched them excitedly. But after a while, I found I was the only one still sitting at the table. I didn't mind, I was happy just watching. I knew it wasn't normal for the Alpha not to be at a ceremony he had organised. I tried to reach him through the bond, but he pushed me out.

When Wendy and Christine came back over, they both put their hands out. Gripping their hands, they pulled me up before dragging me to the dancefloor with them. Feeling a bit giddy from the wine, I joined them, dancing with them and laughing at Zane, who was trying to impersonate Mick Jagger's strut. The whole night seemed to be passing by, but I didn't care. I was having fun dancing with everyone, dancing with Lily whose face was red with exertion.

After a few hours of dancing, everyone was clearly intoxicated and there was still no sign of Reid. There was a commotion at the end of the dance floor. Zane walked off to go deal with it. When the voices got louder, though, I decided to walk over to see what was going on. Three Pack members were arguing, throwing punches. Zane was trying to separate them. They were too intoxicated and weren't listening to his commands, caught up in fighting each other. A crowd had started to grow around the idiots that were fighting. I saw Zane mind-link the Alpha presumably, but just as his eyes regained focus, he was punched making him stumble. There was a collective gasp from the crowd. Walking over, I put my hand out to help him up.

"You okay?"

"Yes, Luna, I'm fine. I will deal with this go back to enjoying your night." I went to walk away when one of the men threw a punch, forcing the other man to stumble into me, knocking me to the ground.

"You fucking twit, show some respect to your Luna. Apologise now," Zane ordered. Getting to my feet, I dusted some leaves and dirt off my dress.

"Luna? Reid doesn't want a Hybrid for a mate. He isn't even here; she is no Luna."

"Watch your mouth, Tom. She is your Luna. Now apologise." The man scoffed at me, rolling his eyes childishly. Lily came over wondering what was going on.

"That's enough, there are children present," I spoke up, looking towards Zane and the other man.

"See, that isn't a Luna. She is weak."

This bloke was really starting to piss me off. One of the other men threw another punch, and it started all over again. Zane was trying to separate them.

Reaching through the mind link, "Reid can you come down here, please. If not for me, do it for Zane. Things are getting out of control."

Reid never replied. I know he heard me; I felt the connection go through. I could even feel him listening. Zane managed to get them separated. People were talking in small groups, agreeing with the man about my authority or lack thereof.

The man from earlier, the one who knocked Zane down, stopped fighting. Walking towards me, he stopped directly in front of me. I could smell the bourbon on his breath. His white shirt had been torn from the fighting, he had a cut on his lip, and his blue jeans had blood on them from the other man. He had leaves in his blonde hair, which was all matted. Christine was right about one thing; having so many Pack warriors under one roof would be a disaster waiting to happen. The amount of testosterone in the air was ridiculous.

The man smiled cruelly. I could tell he was up to no good. I also knew if I backed down, he would see me as weak and no one in the Pack would respect me. The man started jabbing me in the chest with his index finger. Zane went to walk over, but I put my hand up waving him off.

"You're not fit to be Luna. Even the Alpha agrees because he isn't even here."

Some of the Pack members were nodding their heads, agreeing with him. Looking over at Lily, she was scared, worried I was going to get hurt. When the man jabbed me in the chest with his finger again, I grabbed his hand. His eyes widened, and he growled at me. Angry, I started twisting his hand. I bent it back, he tried to manoeuvre out of my grip, but I was stronger. Twisting his wrist until I heard a sickening crack. Snapping his wrist, it hung at a weird angle. Everyone took a step back. I was pissed off. He may be drunk, but that's no reason to be disrespectful. I could feel my anger boiling bubbling in my veins. I knew my eyes were blazing, my fangs elongated. The man let out a shriek as his wrist broke, clutching it to his chest. He snapped it back into place, then glared at me.

"You bitch." He sneered, lunging at me. I stepped out of his way. He landed face-first in the dirt. That didn't stop him lunging again. I don't know if it was his embarrassment or his ego, but he kept lunging trying to gain an advantage. Trying to land a blow. I was too quick, my reflexes were faster than his. It didn't help that he was completely shitfaced either. After the third punch he tried to land, I had enough. Gripping him by the collar of his shirt, I shoved him away, making him stumble into someone. Getting to his feet, I yelled at him.

"Enough!! Sit down and shut up." My voice echoed through the trees surrounding the yard. The man instantly dropped to his knees and went silent. I didn't realise how much authority I put behind what I said. I used an Alpha voice, one I didn't know I contained. Only realising the extent of my command when I looked up. The entire Pack was on the knees with their heads tilted to the side, baring their necks in submission. The whole yard had gone silent. Even Beta Zane was on his knees, though he had a silly smirk on his face.

Looking around, I noticed Reid's imposing frame walking towards me. He looked over at the crowd of people on their knees at my feet. The man my command was aimed at started shaking and whimpering when Reid approached. Reid looked handsome in his navy-blue suit. Placing his hand around my waist, he pulled me into him. He gently placed a kiss on my cheek, his earlier anger completely gone. Now he just looked shocked but proud. Using his Alpha voice, he commanded the whimpering man that was at my feet. "Apologise to your Luna now." The man quickly apologised, stumbling over the words. Everyone let out a breath.

"You may rise," he said to the crowd. Everyone started to get up from their positions on the ground. Seizing my hand, Reid pulled me towards the small podium at the front. Up on the podium, Reid pulled me to his side, his fingertips rubbing circles on the small of my back.

"Well everyone, by now you have all met your Luna. You would also have distinguished by now that she is Hybrid. Despite what I have said in the past about their kind, I expect you all to show her the respect she deserves as the Alpha Female. I'm sure she will put you in your place like earlier if you do cross her." Raising his glass which I didn't even see him grab on the way to the podium, "To the Luna," he said.

In unison, everyone replied before cheering. Having Alpha Reid beside me, no one dared to speak out against me, but after the little show earlier, I think they realised my ability, and I had asserted my authority. The crowd sipped their drinks. Alpha Reid waited for the cheers to stop before speaking again. Waving his hand in the air, everyone fell quiet.

"Now Lily, I would like you to please step forward and come to me." I watched Lily excitedly skip up to the stage. Her pink dress was now covered in dirt and grass stains from playing, but she still looked adorable. The crowd watched as Alpha Reid took a knee, coming down to her height. She smiled happily gazing back at him.

"Place out your hand for me, Lily." Lily raised her palm up in front of Alpha Reid. He clasped it gently between his own. "Now Lily I would like you to repeat after me." Lily nodded looking out at the crowd shyly.

Lily repeated after Alpha Reid, her voice was calm, and she didn't stumble over the words. "I, Lily Violet Blackwood, accept the Blood Moon Pack and accept you, Reid, as my Alpha." The Alpha took a small knife and sliced Lily's finger before slicing his own hand down the palm. It was quite unusual to have a child be brought into another Pack. Usually, this was for adult newcomers or rogues that weren't killed, but a child was pretty much unheard of. If Lily were my child, there would be no need for him to slice her finger because she would have been a Pack member the moment Reid marked me. Children were usually born into a Pack. Since we left ours, this was the only way for her to become part of the Blood Moon Pack. I was grateful that Reid didn't slash her palm like he did his, though. Lily's finger would heal quickly with her wolf gene. By morning, it would probably be gone. Lily didn't flinch when he pressed his palm to her fingertips, but she did gasp when she felt the Pack link merge, linking her to everyone.

The audience all cheered excitedly, and for the first time, I felt emotional not because I was sad but proud of how far Lily had come. She was no longer the scared little girl, like in our old Pack. Here she was vibrant, happy, and everyone loved her. Lily started jumping up and down, not being able to contain her excitement. "We are home now, Ari; we have a home." Picking her up, I cuddled into her, hiding my tears in her shoulder.

Chapter 20

Aria's POV

AFTER LILY'S PACK INITIATION, the party went on for a few more hours. Reid went off to talk to other Pack members. Looking for Lily, I found her asleep next to one of the fire pits. Lily was laying on a chair cosied up next to the fire. Taking a seat next to her, I took off my heels because my feet were absolutely killing me. I felt relieved taking them off, rubbing my heel. A few minutes passed, I decided to pick Lily up and put her to bed. Getting up with Lily in my arms, I looked around for Reid, but he was still busy talking to Zane and Damien at the bar. Walking up the stairs, I made my way inside and to Lily's room, placing her on the bed before removing her sandals. Tucking her in, I sat on the end of her bed. Tonight had been a long night. I still wasn't sure where I stood with Reid, because as soon as Lily's little ceremony was over, he disappeared into the crowd.

Feeling tired myself, I climbed in beside Lily, pulling the covers up. I snuggled into her tiny frame. It didn't take long before I fell asleep.

I felt like I had only just fallen into a deep sleep when I was jostled awake by movement. I felt familiar tingles running up my back and legs. Reid's familiar scent hitting me, I nestled into his chest. Reid had found me and had taken it upon himself to put me in bed. Leaning into his warmth, I fell back asleep. I vaguely remember him unzipping my dress, but I was too tired to care. The next morning, I woke to find Reid leaning over me, intently staring. Opening my eyes to see his face so close made me jump in fright.

"Good morning," he said, before pushing his face into the crook of my neck, inhaling my scent.

"You seem in a better mood."

"Hmm," was the only reply I got. His hands running along my body before slowing just under my bare breasts. Reid's palm ran up and over my nipple, causing me to shiver and nipple to harden.

"So receptive," his deep voice whispered just below my ear. I could feel his breath on my neck. Reid sucked on my mark, sending pleasure all through my body straight to my core, making me lean into him. I could feel him chuckle against my skin, his lips curving up into a smile against my skin at my reaction.

Turning to face him, I placed my hand on his hips and pulled him towards me. Reid's hand running along my side then my arse before pulling my leg up, so it was draped over his hip. Just as his lips smashed into mine, the door burst open, and Lily bounced into the room. Reid groaned in annoyance, disappointed. I could only laugh at his reaction at being cock blocked. Lily, unaware of what she nearly ran in on, jumped on the end of the bed, jumping up down like it was a trampoline. "Wake up, wake up," she squealed. Reid rolled on to his back.

"And why must we get up?"

"I want to play outside. Zane's setting up a jumping castle in the backyard for me and Amber."

Reid shook his head. "So why must we get up?" he groaned.

"So you can play too." I heard him mumble something annoyed.

"We will meet you down there, Lil," he told her. Lily bounced off the bed, jumping to the floor with a thud and went to run out the door when Reid called to her. "Shut the door." Lily obeyed before darting back down the stairs. Turning back to me, he nuzzled my neck. "Now where were we?" I laughed, pushing him away.

"I'm having a shower."

"No… why? Stay here." He pouted.

"No, I'm going to play with the kids, go on the jumping castle," I told him, walking into the bathroom.

"I have something you can jump on," Reid sang out from his position on the bed.

"Tempting, but I'm already up," I sang back, turning the shower on. Grabbing my toothbrush, I quickly brushed my teeth, trying to rid the dry taste in my mouth from the wine last night. Washing my hair, I felt Reid's hands slide up my hips before he stepped in behind me, hogging all the water. "There is another shower head over there. Move over," I said, trying to get the soap out, that was now burning my eyes.

"I'm good here," I heard him laugh before he pulled me into his chest under the stream of water. Quickly turning around and washing the soap off and rinsing my eyes, I looked up at him. The obsidian eyes of his wolf looked back at me; he had a sly smile on his lips. "What are you doing, Ryder?"

"Reid said you want to play." His voice was deeper, rougher than Reid's. His eyes flickered before going back to their normal silver colour.

"Your wolf is a horn dog." Reid laughed before pulling me back into him. I could feel his rock-hard erection pushing into my stomach. "Stop Reid, we have to go meet Lily."

He ignored me, nipping at my neck before his hands found my ass, running his fingers to just under my thighs before he lifted me. Forcing my legs to wrap around his waist, he pushed me into the shower wall holding me in place. I could feel his erection pressing against my core. Excitement pooled in my stomach.

"You sure about that?" he asked, not giving me a chance to answer as his lips found mine. His tongue brushed my bottom lip. I parted my lips, and he plunged his tongue into my mouth, exploring every inch of it. His hot tongue playing with mine made me moan out, wrapping my arms around his neck. I kissed him back. He pushed his hips up, his cock pressing between my wet folds, making him groan into my mouth.

Pulling him into me with my legs that were wrapped around his hips, the tip of his rock-hard cock pressed inside, stretching my tight walls. He inched himself in, giving me time to adjust and stretch around his large size. Pushing the length of his thick cock in slowly until he was completely in. His lips found my neck as he pulled out before thrusting back in, making me gasp. "So tight," he whispered, as he pulled back out before thrusting back in even harder. Holding onto his shoulders, I could feel my pussy clench around him, my juices coating his thick cock. Pleasure rippled throughout my body as he plunged his cock repeatedly into my tight pussy, making me scream out in pleasure. His fingers digging into my thighs only made me wetter. His flesh pounding against mine. I could feel my orgasm building as my walls tightened around him. Digging my nails into his shoulders, I bit into the soft flesh of his neck, making him groan against my shoulder as his cock plunged into my wet pussy repeatedly.

Pulling back his lips smashing against my own, his breathing became rapid as I found my release. Reid slowed his movements while I rode out my orgasm, making me see stars as my pussy clenched around his cock. Finding his release, he groaned leaning into me, pushing his cock deeper into me. I felt his hot cum shoot into me before he came to a stop, resting his forehead against my shoulder. Letting go of my legs, I slid down the shower wall, standing on my feet. Reid pulled me towards him, wrapping his arms around my shoulders.

"Come on, let's get cleaned up and go downstairs," he said before kissing the top of my head.

Chapter 21

Aria's POV

RUNNING DOWN THE STAIRS and racing out the back, I saw Zane had set up a huge jumping castle. It was a princess one with a huge slide and on the side a climbing wall and a jumping pit. Christine was on it, bouncing around with Lily and Amber. Seeing me walking towards them, she waved me over, telling me to get in. I hadn't been on a jumping castle since I was a kid. The jumping castle looked intimidating, an injury waiting to happen. As I went to climb up, my legs were suddenly ripped from underneath me, making my stomach drop and the air to leave my lungs before I was tackled, my body bouncing in the air on the jumping castle. My legs stretched out in a not so lady-like manner.

Looking over, I see it was Wendy. She was laughing hysterically at her actions, which nearly caused me to have a heart attack. The worst part though was looking back out through the netting and seeing Zane, Reid, and Mitch were laughing, sitting on the bench seat watching. Getting to my feet, I tackled Wendy onto the slide, and we both ended up rolling down before I ended up landing on top of her on the grass. Jumping to my feet, I took off running. Wendy started chasing me along with Lily and Amber, who jumped off the castle to help her. When they failed to catch me, I heard Wendy's cracking bones as she dived into her wolf form. Her wolf was a light grey with a bluish tint to it. She had a white streak that went from her head to her tail, and she was big even in wolf form. Growling playfully, she ran at me, before lunging. I dropped to my knees, landing on my back, sliding along the grass. Wendy went straight over the top of me landing on her paws, spinning around. I stuck my tongue out at her before taking off heading straight towards where Reid, Zane, and Mitch were sitting. Darting behind her mate, I shoved him at her just as her wolf went to tackle me.

Mitch landed on the grass with a loud thump. Lily and Amber both jumped on him, holding him down. Knowing Wendy couldn't climb on to the castle in her wolf form without popping it, I tried to sneak back to the jumping castle to catch my breath. Wendy, noticing my hesitation looking between the trees and the castle, chased me down, her fast on my heels running around the back of the jumping castle. I took off towards the trees when I heard a loud growl.

Looking back towards everyone, Reid was taking off his shoes. Wendy's wolf collided with me, knocking me to the ground before she started playfully sniffing my face, telling me she won. Looking back over, I watched as Reid took his shirt off. Damn, that man is fine.

Reid had a silly smirk on his face that turned into a devilish grin. Christine mind linked me, her voice ringing loudly through

the link. "I would run if I were you. The big bad Alpha is coming."
I watched as everyone turned to look at the Alpha. He shook his
head at Christine for dobbing him in. I watched as he started
running towards me. I heard the sickening crack of his bones
snapping mid-jump as he took his wolf form. Landing on the
grass about 40 metres away, I stared at him. His wolf was more
like the size of a bear, completely black, his shiny fur had not a
patch of colour anywhere. Even in his wolf form, Ryder seemed
to be smiling, baring his teeth. Jumping to my feet, I ran straight
towards the trees.

I could hear Ryder gaining on me, hear the twigs breaking under
his giant paws. Running through the forest, everything became a
blur. I felt free as the trees whipped past me, the branches hitting
my skin. My adrenaline pumped with excitement as I weaved in
and out when suddenly I hit a clearing. Nowhere to hide, I turned
to the left, running along the tree line. Ryder still hadn't caught
up. Using that to my advantage, I climbed a huge tree standing
on the branch, I waited.

A few seconds after knowing the branch would easily hold
my weight, I got comfy on my branch, draping my legs over
either side. Ryder came into my line of sight he was sniffing the
ground. I placed my hand over my mouth to muffle my giggling.
I watched as he kept running past then stopping after losing my
scent. Turning around, he was at the bottom of the tree I was
hiding in.

I watched as he sniffed the tree before looking up, his gaze
landing on me straddling the branch. He tilted his head to the
side. "Ryder can't climb, but I can." Reid's voice coming through
the mind link, my smile dropped. I looked down before climbing
another branch. Going back to his human form. I heard him
laugh, making my eyes dart back to him. Reid was standing there

in all his naked glory, smiling back at me. He started climbing the tree alarmingly fast. I took off running along the branch before jumping to a nearby tree, gripping the tree with my claws before I steadied myself. Looking at the ground, I gasped. That's a long way down in my adrenaline rush I hadn't realised how high I had actually climbed. Frozen on the tree, Reid jumped over landing on the branch above me. "You can run, but you can't hide."

"Ha, that's what you think," I threw back at him before clenching my teeth. I jumped off the branch the ground rushing towards me, making me let out a high pitch squeal, my feet landing on the ground below. I was now looking up at Reid who looked like he was about to have a heart attack at my little stunt. I saw him mutter something under his breath but couldn't make out what he was saying. I knew he would have to climb down. His human form isn't sturdy enough to jump the thirty or forty metres to the ground.

"You could have hurt yourself doing that."

"Don't you mean, you would hurt yourself if you tried that?" He shook his head at me. Climbing down the tree while I watched his nice firm ass. I giggled to myself watching him swinging from branch to branch, like Tarzan.

"What are you laughing at?"

"The view," I called back. He smiled at me. Before hanging from a lower branch by his arms, he let go landing on his feet in front of me. I stared at his gorgeous body covered in sweat, his tanned skin shining in the sunlight. My eyes running down his body to his V-line.

"Hey, my eyes are up here."

Rolling my eyes at him. I shoved him to the ground, making him land in the dirt, and took off running towards the Pack house. I could hear him shifting back into wolf form just as I broke through the tree line. Seeing his clothes laying on the ground, I reached down and grabbed them, only leaving his shoes. Zane and Mitch watched as I darted inside, locking the door behind me. Everyone was standing inside the kitchen, watching amused. I knew Reid wouldn't fit inside the door in wolf form, his shoulders were too wide. I watched as he breathed on the glass, I waved his clothes at him.

"He is going to kill you when he gets inside," said Christine.

"Has to find me first," I said, running through the kitchen door and towards the foyer. I could hear everyone laughing behind me.

"Bring my clothes back, Aria." I ignored him walking up the stairs. I listened as he Pack linked everyone asking for some clothes so he could shift back.

Everyone ignored him except Zane. "Can't get involved, boss man" I laughed to myself, before hiding in his office. After a few minutes of him not being able to get in. I heard him use his Alpha voice through the link demanding clothes. He sounded annoyed.

Being cheeky, I knew mine would overrule his commands. "No one help him, I'm trying to find somewhere to hide," I called back. I heard him growl annoyed.

"You're gonna regret that, Ari, when I get inside. I am going to punish you." I laughed back at him. Deciding he would find me in his office, I ran back downstairs and into the kitchen. Reid was no longer at the door.

"Where did he go?"

"I have no idea, but you better hope he doesn't find you," Mitch chuckled. I heard banging. Looking through the window I see Ryder/Reid had jumped on to the lower part of the roof. Whoops didn't think about the windows. I knew as soon as he was out of sight of the kids he would shift back and climb through a window. I looked at Zane for help, but he put his hands up.

"Don't look at me. I'm staying out of it."

Christine nodded towards the walk-in pantry. Just as she closed the door, I heard Reid landing on the floor in one of the upstairs rooms.

Everyone darted out of the kitchen, leaving me in the pantry. It didn't take long before the pantry doors were thrown open and a not happy Alpha was staring down at me with his arms folded across his chest.

"I see you found some clothes," I nervously giggled.

"I'm glad you're enjoying yourself at my expense." Reaching forward he gripped my wrist, making me smack into his rock-hard chest before he threw me over his shoulder.

"How very caveman of you." He stormed out of the kitchen and past everyone, who were now sitting on the lounge in the games room. I could hear Reid muttering to himself while I flailed around trying to make him put me down.

He didn't let me go, and much to my embarrassment as we were walking past everyone, his hand slapped my arse. I flinched at the impact of his huge hand coming down on my arse, making me hiss at the sting. Did he just spank me? Zane smirked, shaking his head and waved at me. I, in turn, flipped him the finger. Reid started climbing the stairs with me still half upside down over his shoulder. On the plus side, I got a nice view of his ass. Returning the favour, I slapped it. He grunted before slapping my arse even harder. "Do that again, and you won't be able to sit for a week."

"You're a brute, you know that?" I could feel the vibration of him laughing. My belly was starting to hurt as his shoulder pressed into it. Just as I was about to demand he put me down, he kicked the bedroom door open and dumped me on the mattress, making me shriek. Reid stood looking down at me.

"You think what you did was funny?" he asked, tilting his head to the side. His lips turned up and into a menacing smile. Excitement ran through me. I couldn't help the smile that crept onto my face as I nodded my head. His smile didn't waver, and it sent a chill down my spine. I laughed at his expression. I couldn't tell if he wanted to kiss me or kill me. He raised an eyebrow at me and clicked his tongue. Gripping my ankle, he yanked me towards the end of the bed.

Chapter 22

Aria's POV

REID GRABBED MY OTHER ankle and flipped me over so I was belly down on the bed. I squirmed, trying to break his hold on my ankles. Reid growled at me warningly before gripping my hips and pulling them towards him. My feet were forced to the ground while the rest of my body was draped over the bed. Lifting myself up onto my elbows, he forced me back down. Pushing his hand between my shoulder blades to hold me in place.

Reid then pushed his groin into me. I could feel the bulge of his erection pressing against my ass. Stepping back a bit, he ran his other hand up my thigh. Stopping at my shorts, his fingertips moving along my panty line between my legs teasingly, sending delightful shivers to my core. Removing his hand from beneath my shorts, he started rubbing my arse, making me quiver everywhere he touched. I could feel my underwear becoming moist. I pushed into his hand, shaking my ass at him.

His palm came down, connecting with my ass cheek. I could feel his handprint burning into my flesh. It stung, but it also turned me on even more. Reid rubbed his hand over where he slapped. His hand then finding its way back into my shorts, using his fingers, he pushed my panties to the side before sliding his fingers between my wet lips. Reid bent over me; I could feel his breath on my neck below my ear.

"You liked that?" he growled, before shoving his finger inside me, making me moan out loud. Pulling his finger out slowly, he pushed another finger inside me. My body quivered at his touch, becoming more aroused. I want more.

Then his fingers were gone, his touch was gone. Rolling over, I looked up at him. Reid's eyes were glazed over, telling me he was mind-linking someone. The look on his face was pure rage. His eyebrows furrowed together. His canines protruded. Hair was spreading across his arms. I watched as his nails turned into claws. His breathing got deeper and faster. He was fighting himself for control. A terrifying growl ripped through him, vibrating through his chest. I flinched and pulled away. His eyes darting to me. The glazed look left instantly. His eyes softened. Reid walked towards the door. Getting to my feet, I went to follow him.

Just as I was about to ask what was going on, he spun around. His eyes pinning me to the spot.

"You stay here, and don't leave this room."

"What's going on Reid?"

"Nothing you need to know about. Just for once do as your bloody told." He walked out the door, pulling it closed behind him. I heard the latch click over. He locked the door. Rolling my eyes at his abrupt change of mood. I don't know why he expects the door to keep me in. Maybe a deterrent, but it isn't Hybrid proof. Deciding to give him a head start at whatever was bothering him, I opened my mind feeling for Wendy through the link. I could feel her wolf. It was restless.

"Wendy, why has Reid locked me in the room? What is going on?"

Wendy didn't answer straight away. I could tell she was trying to fight my Alpha command.

"Wendy, do not make me ask again." I could feel every fibre of her being trying to shake off the command, but she wouldn't be able to hold for much longer. Her wolf was whining, wanting her to give into me, and she did.

"Why are you making me go against him? I can't tell you; he doesn't want you involved."

"Wendy, what is going on?" I emphasised every word. Saying them slowly, forcing my Alpha command on her. I heard her wolf whimper through the link, making me feel bad. I know it is painful for her trying to fight against my will.

"Alpha David and his Pack are at the border." The words spilled out like word vomit. I could hear cars leaving. Moving fast.

"What's happening then?"

"Alpha is going to warn him or…"

"Or what? Wendy-"

"Wipe them out. He sent all our warriors to the border."

I gasped shocked. The Blood Moon Pack would annihilate the Black Moon Pack. They weren't big enough or trained enough to go against the Blood Moon Pack. Why would David do this? It was suicide. I couldn't let Reid's Pack slaughter everyone. I may not be a part of that Pack anymore, but I still considered them to be family. As weird as it sounds, it is the only family we have known. And a lot of the Pack members are good people. I also couldn't let Reid kill Alpha David; he is Lily's father. But what can I do? I know Reid will lose it if I command everyone to stand down. He would never forgive me for taking his authority from him. I may be Luna, but this is rightfully his Pack.

Trying to think, I heard the door click unlocking. Lily walked in, tears running down her face. Wendy walked in behind her; her head was down. "Lily, what's wrong?"

"Reid is going to hurt Uncle Michael," she sobbed. Damn it I was going to kill Reid. That's if my idea doesn't get me killed first.

"No, Lily. I am going to fix this." Lily looked up at me hopeful. Quickly hugging her, I walked towards the door. Wendy gripped my arm, stopping me as I walked out. "It's fine, Wendy. Don't warn the Alpha," I said, forcing my Alpha command on her.

Wendy's shoulders slumped in defeat. "I'm sorry, but I can't have you warn them, you know he will come after me." Wendy nodded her head. I felt terrible, Wendy was my best friend here. I hate causing her pain. I hate putting her in this position where she has been forced to choose between her Alpha and her Luna.

Running down the stairs and out the front door, I ran towards the tree line. The border was half an hour away by car. I could run there in a quarter of the time. Then I just have to convince them to go back to the Pack house and try not to kill or be killed by one of Alpha David's Pack warriors, and hope they are still in human form so I can speak with them.

Sprinting through the forest, I came to a hill. I could see the convoy of SUV's driving along the dirt road below. Cutting straight across through the trees, I raced across the paddocks, overtaking them. I remained hidden in the tree line. I ran towards the city. Reid must have felt my heart rate picking up, sensing I was up to something because I could feel Wendy whimpering not giving in to his commands and threats. I felt him trying to force a link between us, but I just pushed back harder. Running faster, I came to the edge of the city, heading east towards the border. The sun was starting to go down. I knew by the time I reached the border, it would be dark. Running through the streets, I slowed down a bit. I knew the border couldn't be too far from here. The streets were starting to look seedier. The north side was what I used to call the posh area. The street I was currently running down definitely wasn't part of the north side. Some of the houses were burnt out, and there was rubbish strewn across the streets. Lawns overgrown, gardens completely overgrown with weeds. There was even a burnt-out van on the corner of the street. Running to the end of the street, I looked for a street sign.

Melrose street. I was already over the border. I hadn't realised I had crossed over it. Which meant they would know I have crossed the border already. Slowing to a stop, I waited. I listened to the noises trying to pick up any movement. It didn't take long before I heard the ferocious growls of my former Pack members. The street was completely dark now. The broken streetlights didn't offer any light. No light from any of the abandoned houses. The only light came from the moon. It was a full moon tonight, making it seem eerier than normal, or maybe it was the fact I am standing in an abandoned street.

When the first wolf stepped out in front of me, I could tell it was a Pack warrior by its size. They send warriors when they sense a threat. The only problem was, I am no threat to them. I just want to talk, and hurting one of them was only going to cause a war.

When another 2 wolves stepped out, I placed my hands in the air, surrendering. Falling to my knees, I watched them circle around me. The biggest one, a grey one, came up to me, baring its teeth. Growling in my face, I stared it down, making sure not to move to suddenly. He pushed me with his nose, trying to get a reaction out of me.

"I'm not here to fight. I just need to speak to Alpha David."

The wolves all growled, stepping closer. Closing in on me, they must think I'm threatening the Alpha. This wasn't working, I couldn't talk to them. I wasn't a Pack member. I didn't understand what they were saying. "I'm not here to start anything. I just need to talk to my stepfather." The last word rolled off my tongue, leaving a sour taste in my mouth. But it seemed to get the attention. The grey wolf stopped in front of me. My heart rate slowed down, and I listened as theirs did too. I could hear their breathing. Hear their blood moving throughout their bodies. I calmed my mind, trying to come up with a way to get them to understand.

"What do you think? Should we take her to the Alpha?"

"Call for Michael, he will know what to do with her." Glancing behind me, I looked to see who was talking. But it was only the three wolves in the street. No one in human form except myself.

"Call Michael. He can verify who I am. My name is Aria," I pleaded.

"How did she know what we were mind-linking?" asked the red wolf, who was standing behind me.

I looked at the grey one, he stepped forward right into my face. "Can you hear us?"

I nodded my head. I could hear them but couldn't push the link back. I don't know how, but right now I didn't care. I just needed to get to Alpha David. I waited as they linked Michael.

"Follow us," the grey wolf demanded.

I followed them all the way to the Pack house. I knew Alpha Reid wouldn't be far off the border. I just needed to find out what Alpha David wanted and try to create an arrangement with him. To try and stop this war that will come if he tries to challenge Reid.

Walking up the Pack house driveway, I was hit with a sense of déjà vu. The last time I was here, I was running from the place not trying to break into it. The Pack house looked the same, still an oversized farmhouse. Standing up on top of the porch was Michael. He had a distressed look on his face. He was standing next to Alpha David. Alpha David had his arms folded across his bare chest, the only clothing he had on was a pair of jeans. He looked intimidating.

I wanted to run, but I wasn't that scared, weak girl anymore. I refuse to run from him. If anything he should be begging at my feet. I know what I'm capable of now and I know who I am. I'm not going to let him walk all over me anymore. I'm doing this for Lily, for his Pack. I know he is a crazy bastard, but I also know he doesn't want his Pack killed.

Alpha David wore a smirk on his face, dropping his arms to his side. He started walking down the steps. He never took his eyes off me. I could hear a low warning growl coming from him as he walked towards me. I stood straighter, not breaking my gaze, refusing to look away. When I didn't submit, the rest of the Pack started circling around us, growling at me threateningly. Michael didn't move off the porch, he just stared at me, trying to warn me with his eyes. He looked petrified not of me but for me. What the hell have I just walked into?

$Chapter\ 23$

Aria's POV

WATCHING DAVID, I NOTICED he didn't look shocked to see me. I then realised this was his plan all along. I realised I was his bargaining tool, his way to get Reid to comply. I was Reid's weakness. If something happens to me, it weakens him, and he can get Lily back.

Too busy watching David trying to think of a way to convince him to sort this out amicably, I didn't hear the person sneaking up behind me until I felt the sting of the needle as it pierced my neck. The burning sensation bled into my skin, burning my insides like fire consuming my body. I gripped my neck, trying to get the pain to lessen, trying to stop it from spreading. Turning around, I see no one behind me but my former Pack members and a syringe at my feet containing gold liquid concentrated wolfsbane.

I felt my surroundings start to spin as fire consumed my veins, overtaking all my senses. I could feel myself burning up.

I screamed in agony, trying to stop the burn. My legs collapsed under me. My body felt heavy, I was losing to the pain. For the first time in my life, I welcomed the darkness, praying I would pass out so the pain would end.

I could feel my body falling, my head hitting the soil, but I didn't even feel it. All I could feel was wolfsbane burning through every cell in my body. I smiled when I felt everything getting darker, my surroundings starting to dim. Michael's words came back to me. "This stuff will even put you on your arse." He was right. If I weren't in so much pain, I would have laughed at the fact it did exactly what he said it would.... I thanked the Moon Goddess as I finally slipped away into the darkness of oblivion.

Reid's POV

Torn between going to fight beside my Pack and staying and protecting Aria and Lily, I reluctantly left. I had a Pack to protect. We raced through the winding back roads towards the city. The trees blurring into one at the speed we were moving. Alpha David crossed the line, and now there is no going back, I will finally rid the earth of that scum who dared torture my woman. Aria can't hate me for protecting my Pack... our Pack. I was doing this for her, for Lily, and for us. Driving towards the border, the city came into view. We were only a few kilometres out. The only thing surrounding us were trees and farmland. Just as we hit the outskirts of the city, I felt a cold wave of a feeling I couldn't recognise rush over my skin. Ryder instantly tensed and tried to lurch forward.

"What is it?" I ask him. He pushed underneath my skin forcefully. Hair spreading across my arms, my claws extending tearing the leather seat.

"Aria is getting away from us," I heard him snarl at me in reply. No, Aria was at home where I ordered her to stay. She wouldn't defy me; she wouldn't betray my trust like this. I locked her in, the door was sealed, and wolf proof. The glass on the windows is even impenetrable. Mind-linking Wendy, I felt her push back, trying to ignore the link. Furious that she tried to ignore my call, I shoved back forcing her to accept the link. I could hear her groan as I pushed through the tether. Mitch, who was in the front seat driving, whimpered at me, feeling his mate's pain come through the bond. Wendy let go and stopped trying to shove me out, knowing it's a battle she can't win.

"Where is Aria?" I demand. Wendy didn't answer. Mitch tried to get her to answer by asking the same question I just did. I could see his grip tightening on the steering wheel, his knuckles turning white. Wendy whimpered from the pressure of her mate.

"I ca…can't," she stuttered almost breathlessly. Aria has done this; she is the only one who is strong enough to bind someone against me. Her tricks don't work on me, but the rest of the Pack is defenceless against her commands. But I also know she wouldn't force that burden, that pain to go against an Alpha on Lily. Linking Lily, I could finally get answers.

"Lily, where is your sister?" Lily didn't resist, meaning Aria hadn't commanded her to keep quiet.

I heard Mitch let out a breath when I dropped the link to Wendy.

"She went to speak to the Alpha, um, my dad." Lily sounded unsure on the last word like she hadn't used the word before. I growled, pissed off that she disobeyed me. I felt Lily cower through the link, she doesn't understand I'm not angry at her. Cutting the link, Mitch looked at me through the rear-view mirror.

"Speed up, Aria is heading to the border." Mitch nodded before putting his foot down, overtaking everyone like they were standing still.

Jumping out of the car before the car even stopped as we reached the border, Dominic, one of my warriors, came up to me. "They all retreated about 5 minutes ago, Boss."

"Where is the Alpha?"

"Don't know. He never showed up here. Only their warriors showed up, but they left. What do you want to do, Alpha?"

"Stay alert, they have your Luna." Dominic growled in reply. I tried to reach out to Aria but got no reply. Trying to come up with a plan with Zane, we had no idea where the Pack house was having never been there. We knew it wouldn't be anywhere in a populated area. Most Pack houses were away from the human population and near bushland so we could let our wolves out. So, it's probably on the outskirts of the city. Dominic brought some maps of the city so we could search for secluded areas of the east side. Unfolding the maps, I sprawled them out on the car bonnet. The only place big enough and secluded enough was the bushland along the railway tracks. It was backed onto a wildlife reserve. I know that is where I would build a Pack house if it was me.

Suddenly feeling like I was being skinned alive, I fell to the ground panting. My body felt like it was being doused in acid. Ryder pushed forward, forcing me to shift. My clothes tearing as I took my wolf form.

"Aria," snarled Ryder. Jumping over the border, I could feel him trying to run towards her until I suddenly felt cold, my body going numb, my vision blurred. Pushing forward I regained control, forcing us to shift back. Zane was right behind me. Clutching his stomach he shakily handed me some shorts.

"We can feel her, Alpha, make it stop." he pleaded before collapsing next to me.

Sitting up, I look around to find all my men on the ground, shaking and writhing in agony. How is this possible? The bond only works on me. Ryder was pacing in the back of my mind, anxious. Reaching out to Aria, I feel nothing through the bond, no connection at all. Which could only mean two things: she has passed out or she is dead. I knew she wasn't dead; I would feel that. The thought alone was painful like my soul ripping out of me, so I knew she was still alive. But the question was how she affected my entire Pack.

"Lycan Blood. She is our rightful queen. They were all bonded the moment you marked her," growled Ryder. My body felt weak; I shakily stood and put the blue shorts on before collapsing to the ground again. We just had to ride it out. Once she was completely out, the pain would end, I hoped.

Aria's POV

"Now what do we do with her?"

"We use her to get my daughter back. Alpha Reid will come for her. If he wants her he will hand Lily over."

"He will kill the entire Pack. This is insane even for you. You're willing to risk everyone?"

I could hear whispers. Alpha David was talking with someone. Slowly opening my eyes, I stay as still as possible to not alert them that I'm awake. I was in Alpha David's office. I could see shelves of books and a desk that had papers and maps all over it. I was placed on the brown leather sofa in the centre of the room. I could see Michael with his back to me, talking to the Alpha who was seated at his desk.

My throat felt incredibly dry. I felt like I had a major hangover. My head was pounding against my skull. Testing out my limbs, I realised I could move my legs and arms. I was weak, but I had feeling back. That wasn't the only feeling I had though. Hunger. I was ravenous. I needed blood. I could hear four heartbeats in the room. My own standing out above everyone else's thumping loudly in my chest against my ribs. I knew two belonged to the Alpha and the Beta, but the fourth person must be behind me somewhere. I could feel my fangs breaking painfully through my gums, my mouth filling with the metallic taste of my own blood.

"You hear that? She is waking," said the mystery person behind me. Looking over in the Alpha direction, I hear him stand up. Michael made eye contact with me.

"That's impossible, she should have been out for hours," he stated.

"Dose her again before she regains her strength," ordered the Alpha through the mind link to the person behind me. Obviously, he forgot I can hear them, or maybe his Pack members forgot to mention that detail. I heard the person behind me start walking towards the back of the sofa. Just as his hand reached over to inject me, I gripped his wrist, pulling him over the sofa making him land on the floor.

Sitting up, I still had hold of his wrist that was gripping the syringe. I squeezed his wrist, making him cry out and drop it. I saw the Alpha and Michael about to lurch forward to stop me as I ripped the man towards me, sinking my teeth into his neck. I drank voraciously, draining him in a few seconds before rolling his body off me and onto the floor, his lifeless eyes peering up at us in shock.

I grabbed the syringe that had fallen at my feet, twirling it between my fingers, admiring the poison that just knocked me out cold. I heard shuffling as the Alpha went to try to stop me from attacking first, but I had no intentions to fight; it would end in their deaths. I sat back on the couch, getting comfortable.

"I understand it now, why you did it," I said clearly. The Alpha stopped. Looking up at him, he looked confused. Michael wore the same expression, trying to figure out what I was talking about. I observed the Alpha. He didn't look the same. I no longer feared him. He looked rather normal in his blue denim jeans and a black t-shirt. I could tell he lost weight, his eyes were dark with sleep deprivation, He looked like he aged ten years since I last saw him at the diner.

Now I just felt sorry for him. I knew I shouldn't, but I couldn't help it. He was a monster to us for years, but now I see a broken man, not someone to be feared.

"What are you talking about, Aria?" asked David, crossing his arms over his chest he leaned back sitting on the edge of the desk.

"I'm talking about why you hated Lily and me. Why you abandoned your own pup." The Alpha bared his teeth at me and growled. "I understand it now. I know a wolf goes crazy without their mate. I understand what it does to them. I don't agree with your actions, but I do understand," I told him.

"You know nothing, Aria. Don't pretend you know anything. I just want my daughter back."

"You mean the daughter you dumped in my lap to raise? The daughter you pretended you didn't have? That daughter?"

"Watch it, girl,"

"No, you're right. I don't know what it's like to lose a mate. But I understand why you are the way you are. Most wolves kill themselves after they lose their mate, or they go mad. You went mad with anger and blamed her. When you should have put all the anger you had into loving her."

"Aria, shut up," warned Michael. Looking back over at the Alpha, his face was red with anger, veins sticking out along his arms like he was a ticking time bomb. But that no longer scared me.

"Listen to Michael, Aria. You know nothing of what you're talking about. You can't sympathise with me."

"You think I don't know what it's like to lose her? You lost your mate. I LOST MY FUCKING MOTHER," I screamed. "I was thirteen, and you threw Lily in my lap. I couldn't even attend her funeral because you were too gutless to be around your own daughter. Mum's flesh and blood. You didn't just lose her. I lost her too. Then I lost my childhood. I threw everything away to raise her. ME, not you. I took care of her, and now you expect me to hand her over to you."

"She is my daughter, Aria."

"Yes, you're right, she is, but she doesn't know you. She knows only to fear you. You spent so much time hating her, but did you ever think of what Mum would have wanted? I know she wouldn't have wanted you to abandon her flesh and blood. She would have wanted you to be the father you promised her you would be. Now after six fucking years you want to claim her back."

Alpha David walked back to his desk and took a seat. He knew I was right. Lily doesn't know him the way she should, and he doesn't know her. "So, what do you suggest then, Aria? You think you're calling the shots? You think you have all the answers?" Michael relaxed a bit before sitting on the edge of the desk. I sat back understanding the Alpha was willing to compromise.

Looking at the clock, it was a little after 8pm. The Blood Moon Pack was already at the border, but why haven't they crossed over yet? Reid would know I'm here by now.

"I am only here because of Lily. Despite the hell you have put her through, she still feared Reid was going to kill you. She wanted me to stop this. You and I still have unfinished business, but for now, this is about Lily, so I suggest you prove you deserve to be a part of her life. Maybe visit, get to know her, but she remains a part of my Pack." The Alpha growled at me about to disagree and argue back. I held my finger up at him, motioning him to let me finish.

"When she turns 18, we let her decide if she wants to take over the Black Moon Pack. For now, until I can trust you, you can get to know her and then maybe down the track if Lily decides she wants you in her life we can sort out custody agreements."

"Shared custody, she is my daughter,"

"Listen to her, Alpha. She has a point. You can't just rip Aria away from Lily and expect Lily to be okay with that. Aria is all she has ever known."

The Alpha seemed to think about it. I heard Michael start to mind link him and blocked him out, giving them some privacy to speak. Pushing through the bond, I could tell Reid was close.

"Reid you there?"

"Where the fuck are you, Aria? Do you have any idea of the damage you have caused?"

"Calm down, I'm with Alpha David. I will be back at the border soon." I could tell he was using the bond to find my location.

"No, I'm coming to get you. Tell David to tell his warriors to let us through or it will be a bloodbath."

"Just wait there, I will be there soon," I argued back.

"No, you went against me. This could have been avoided, but you had to defy me. I'm coming to get you, and that's final." He cut off the mind link. I could feel his anger pouring through the link.

"Reid is on his way. Tell your warriors to stand down." They both stopped talking and looked at me. Alpha David raised an eyebrow at me. "I tried to stop him, but he is coming anyway. Tell them to stand down. I don't want our people hurt."

"Our people?"

"Yes, I might not be a part of this Pack anymore, but they are still family to me, despite what you may think. I don't wish any harm to anyone here. Please."

"Very well. I will tell them to let them through, and as for Lily, we have a deal for now."

I smiled, genuinely excited for Lily. She may just get the father she wanted, after all. I always had that hope for her that this monster would eventually come to his senses and see what a great little girl she was and how much like Mum she is.

It didn't take long before we heard cars pulling up in the driveway. Following David and Michael out we made our way through the Pack house.

It hadn't changed much. I had so many horrid memories here, but it was home for so long it just felt familiar, comfortable in a way. Which is absurd, but it was home. It's where I lived with my mother for 6 years, where some of my earliest memories were. This place will always feel familiar.

Once outside, five black SUVs were parked out the front. Men piled out of the cars, standing alongside the vehicles. Reid stepped out of the one that was parked in front of the stairs. He only had blue shorts on, and his chest was bare. He was covered in dirt and sweat. Meeting his eyes, I went to walk down to him when I noticed him glaring directly at me. I froze on the step. He was furious. My heart skipped a beat when I heard him speak.

"Aria, get in the fucking car." I was frozen. I didn't react which just pissed him off even more. Marching forward, he gripped my arm, ripping me towards him, making me stumble into him. I heard Michael growl at him behind me at his forceful grip.

Reid shoved me towards the open rear door. "Get in the car NOW!" he shouted at me, making me flinch. Alpha David came down the stairs and extended his hand to Reid in a polite gesture, trying to diffuse the situation, but Reid just spun on his heel and punched him breaking his nose making David stumble back falling onto the steps.

Chapter 24

Aria's POV

THE ONLY SOUND WAS a collective gasp from everyone who was present. I held my breath when I saw David scramble back to his feet. He dusted himself off before rubbing his already bruising jaw. Michael's eyes flicked to my horrified ones, begging me to do something before this got out of hand.

But I didn't have to, the most shocking thing happened when David clenched his jaw and walked back up the stairs and inside the house. Everyone kind of looked around confused by the Alpha just walking away from a fight. No one was more surprised than Alpha Reid.

"What? You are just going to walk away and be a coward?" Alpha David just kept walking ignoring Reid. Michael quickly followed behind. For the first time ever, I was actually proud of the way he handled himself. He didn't give in to his anger, he just simply got up and walked away not wanting to risk the agreement we have come up with. Maybe he really is going to try and right his wrongs.

Looking around, my former Pack members eyes quickly darted away from the scene and they went back to patrolling, leaving just the Blood Moon Pack standing around. I must have missed an order through their Pack link since there were no threatening growls or any attacks from anyone. Reid's Pack looked tense like they were expecting retaliation, but there wasn't any. They all simply walked off like we weren't intruding on their land.

Walking over I went to place my hand one Reid's arm. He spun around so quickly and gripped my wrist before I made contact. His eyes burned with anger. If looks could kill, I would be a pile of dust by now. I wasn't sure if he was more pissed that David turned his back on him or my escape. I think it was a mixture of both.

Difference is if I walk away, he will chase after me. So instead, I calmly relaxed in his death grip. When I didn't pull away, Reid started dragging me towards the open rear door. Once we were close enough, he shoved me inside. I landed on the seat, my legs still hanging out the door. I moved to the other side of the car just as Reid sat down. He didn't say anything, but when I went to turn and place my feet on the ground, he gripped my ankle and yanked me towards him until I was half on his lap with one leg draped over him the other awkwardly bent next to him. Reid didn't let go. I watched the fall and rise of his chest while he tried to calm himself and his wolf down.

After a few minutes I tried to remove my leg that he gripped and was forcibly pulled back to the same position. When I heard a growl emit from him, I froze my movements and watched him warily. I could feel his hot breath on my neck.

Being around him is like walking on eggshells. My leg was starting to cramp from the position I was sitting in. Deciding to move, I sat in the middle seat trying to find a more comfortable position, when Reid suddenly pulled me completely onto his lap, so I was straddling him.

He dropped his head into the crook of my neck and started inhaling my scent. His strong arms wrapped around my waist, he started to relax after a few minutes. I had to hold back a moan when he started sucking on my mark, my eyes rolled into the back of my head just from his touch. Pulling away slightly, I looked around embarrassed. Zane was driving back to the Pack house but was paying no attention to us in the back seat. I tried to hop off his lap when his fingers dug painfully into my waist.

"You will not leave again without my permission. Do you understand?" His deep gravelly voice spoke just below my ear near my neck. I tried to get off his lap by pushing off his chest with my hands, but his strength was unrelenting as he held me in place with one arm, his other hand snaked out and gripped my chin forcing me to look at him.

"Do you understand?" he asked. His intense gaze made me gulp nervously. His eyes hardened when I didn't answer his grip on my chin tightening. I quickly nodded my head, not trusting my voice not to break if I answered out loud. He let my chin go and his grip on my waist loosened. I climbed off of him and scooted as far as the seat would allow away from him.

Reid turned his body so he could watch me, draping one arm along the backrest of the car. I looked in the mirror to be met with Zane's sympathetic eyes staring back at me before he quickly glanced away.

"What happened with Alpha David?" asked Reid. I had this entire scenario played out differently in my head. I wasn't expecting it to be so tense nor was I expecting him to punch David without giving me a chance to explain.

"It was about Lily," I told him my voice firm, annoyed that he was treating me like I was some omega. Angry that he nearly ruined the deal I have with Alpha David.

"And?" Reid asked, annoyed at my answer. I had to fight the urge to roll my eyes at him, his way of talking down at me was starting to really get under my skin.

"And it doesn't concern you, David and I will organise things later around Lily's school schedule." Reid growled at my response and my tone of voice. I knew I sounded bitchy, but what did he expect after the way he just treated me.

"When it's about you and Lily, it does concern me Aria. You are mine, now lose the attitude and tell me what is going on,"

"Really, lose the attitude? I'm sorry if I won't bow down to you. Until you start treating me like your equal, the attitude stays." I retorted.

Reid reached over and gripped my arm. I see Zane glance nervously in the mirror before his eyes went back to the road. Through the bond, I could feel that he was a ticking time bomb, his rage just swirling inside him looking for an escape even Ryder was angry. Pissed off he didn't get the challenge from Alpha David like he hoped he would. Both of them were annoyed, feeling like I was challenging them.

I wasn't, but I also wasn't going to put up with their anger issues. Not wanting to be suffocated by his testosterone-fuelled rage at me, challenging him, I gripped the door handle and shoved the door open.

Ripping my arm out of Reid's grip, I jumped from the moving vehicle, Zane instantly hitting the brakes. My body collided with the rough gravel; I could feel my flesh being ripped away as I rolled along the road. The car behind us screeching to a stop about a metre off me. My clothes were torn, and I had cuts and scrapes covering every bit of exposed flesh, including my face. I was too angry to notice. I just wanted away from him, away from both of them.

Pushing up off the ground onto my hands and knees, I groaned. Maybe that wasn't the smartest idea I had thought of. Standing up, I dusted myself off pulling small rocks out that were embedded in my hands, I turned and started walking towards the forest that led to the Pack house. I could hear people's rushed voices calling after me before the car that nearly hit me left, driving towards the Pack house.

Reid screamed at me, demanding I come back to the car, but I was not in the mood to deal with him. I ignored him and kept walking. Next thing I know I am being knocked down onto the grass from behind as Reid barrelled into me. Hitting the grass with an oomph as the air was knocked out of me. Reid rolled me over onto my back; I just stared, dazed.

"Where do you think you're going little one?"

"Where do you think I'm going… Home. Now get off me."

Reid glared down at me, challenging me. I glared back at him, not submitting. When he realised I wasn't going to back down he growled warningly at me, but I just growled back. How dare he challenge me. We are meant to be mates, equals. I don't own him just as he doesn't own me. I won't submit to him or anybody. I'm not going to be his little bitch that he can treat like garbage then think I will forgive his brutish behaviour.

When I growled back, Ryder's eyes peered back at me. Ryder may love me, but Alpha's don't like to be challenged even by their Luna. Most Luna's are submissive to their mates. I'm not a normal wolf, I'm Lycan and not going to back down to him whether he is my mate or not. Ryder seemed to realise that I could tell Reid was fighting for control, his eyes flickering between him and his beast. I shoved him to the side and went to get up when hands gripped my shoulder's pulling me back down.

Ryder pulled me, so my back was pressed against his chest, his arms holding my arms at my side, I felt him move my hair over my shoulder, exposing my neck to him.

Suddenly feeling teeth bite down harshly on my neck, trying to get me to submit, I struggle against him when I feel his canines bite through my flesh harder pinning me in place. Ryder growled menacingly at me, but I refused to submit. When I felt him bite deeper, I could feel the blood start to run down my neck and arm, any harder he could rip my arm off.

His growling got louder, trying to force me to give in. Instead, I pivot, his teeth ripping harshly out of my shoulder and neck. Gripping him I bite him back, I sink my teeth into his neck, but the blood loss from his bite starts to make me woozy as I feel myself getting sleepy, I drop to my side my body feeling like it's being weighed down.

Why didn't I just let Ryder win? I knew better than to challenge a wolf. Reid is one thing, Ryder is completely different. The wolf side loves the chase and loves a challenge, but one thing they won't do is show weakness, especially in front of their mate. So, me challenging Reid brought Ryder forward.

I feel my body being lifted, and my head hits Reid's shoulder as I fight to stay conscious. I can feel movement before I am placed on his lap. Hearing the car door close I know I'm back in the car on Reid's lap. I could hear Zane speaking.

"Luna alright, Alpha?"

"Yeah, she just bit off more than she can chew with Ryder, she just needs blood,"

I feel the engine start and the car move. When I give into exhaustion.

I'm nice and warm. My skin feels like it's vibrating, tingles are spreading down my sides where Reid's hand is drawing patterns in my skin. I leave my eyes closed, enjoying the sensations and my heightened senses. I breathe in his intoxicating scent. His masculine smell making my mouth water. I can tell we are laying on our sides, my face resting on his arm, his breath fanning my face. Wriggling closer Reid tucks my head under his chin, pulling me tighter to his chest.

I growl low, almost a purr at our closeness, I have an overwhelming need to taste him, running my nose along his chest, I lift my head and start licking and sucking his neck softly. He moves onto his back, pulling me with him, so I'm lying on his chest. I breathe in his scent, which is teasing me, making me thirstier. My eyes still closed; I run my nose along his collarbone, breathing him in. Reid pulls me up higher, so we are face to face. I open my eyes to see Reid's soft gaze staring at me. I lean in and kiss his lips softly, his fingers softly drawing circles on my lower back.

Dropping my head back on his chest, I listen to his heartbeat thump in his chest, my own heart falling in sync with his.

Chapter 25

Aria's POV

"I SHOULDN'T HAVE LET RYDER have control." Reid's husky voice broke the silence. My hand instinctively went to my neck, remembering the feel of his anger as he bit into my soft skin. My neck was smooth, having already healed. Lifting my head up, I stared at Reid's face. He was fully in control now his gaze soft, but I could feel his worry seeping into me through the mate bond. I could feel his guilt thick and strong. Reid's silver eyes searching mine waiting for me to say something.

Leaning over, I kissed his lips softly before getting up. I climbed off the bed and walked into the bathroom, I wanted to shower so I could go see Lily and tell her about my meeting with her father. When I opened the bathroom door Reid sat up, he must have felt my intentions through the bond.

"Lily is asleep. I wouldn't wake her; she has her first day of school tomorrow."

"What do you mean? What time is it?" I asked, confused. I didn't feel like I was out that long. It was the middle of the night when we left David's, I feel like I only had a short nap.

"It's 2:00 AM Aria, you have been out for three days now." His voice got lower as he looked down at the bed. Three days I have been out, Ryder knocked me out for three days. No wonder he feels so bloody guilty.

Turning my back on him, I push the bathroom door open. Stripping my clothes off I turned the shower on, my body felt a little stiff but other than that I felt fine. I certainly didn't feel like I had been asleep for three days. I was fairly hungry though my bloodlust was strong, but it was strong before Ryder bit me. I will have to go see if I can find any blood in the infirmary. Dr. Mavis said she would stock it there in the fridges for me.

Halfway through washing myself, Reid walked in, I watched as he stripped his clothes off and turned the other showerhead on at the opposite end to me. I watched as the water ran down the muscles on his back. His arms braced on the wall in front of him, his head under the stream of water.

Reid must have felt my eyes on him as he turned around and stared back. His eyes running up my body stopping at my hips then my breasts, before looking me in the eyes. His gaze stirring my insides, as arousal started to flood me. I wasn't sure it was completely mine or just Reid's desires coming through the mate bond. Scanning my eyes over him, I watched his chest move with each breath, my eyes sliding down his abs then slowing at his V line when I noticed his erection standing proud. I turned away, definitely not just my own feelings I was picking up on. I didn't want to give him the satisfaction.

Abruptly ignoring my arousal, I turned the taps off and stepped out of the shower. He will have to tend to himself, I could feel the hint of a smile creeping onto my face at the thought. Grabbing a towel, I wrapped it around myself and walked out, closing the door behind me. I heard Reid groan with frustration.

Since it was night-time, I decided to put my pyjamas on. Leaving the room, I snuck down the stairs and opened up Lily's door, she was sleeping peacefully snuggled up to her purple unicorn plushie. Closing the door, I walked to the infirmary. My gum tingling in anticipation. Just as I'm about to reach out and open the infirmary door, Zane steps into the hallway.

"Luna, you are up," he said noticeably shocked at finding me walking the halls so late at night.

"Yes, Zane, good morning. Why are you up so early?" My voice was breathy, my fangs had already protruded from my gums, making it difficult to speak.

"Patrol duty, are you sure you're alright?" asked Zane, reaching out he gently touched my arm. I pulled back. I tried to calm myself, but in this empty narrow hall, it was hard to ignore the beating of his heart, the sweet smell of his blood racing through his veins. I was struggling. I was fine, but as soon as the infirmary came into view, my hunger took over knowing what waited on the other side of the door.

I watched the vein in his neck lost in a trance. I could hear his concerned voice talking to me, but his words didn't register. My mouth started to water; I could feel my eyes blazing in hunger. Just as I went to lean in to taste him, he pulled away startled. My eyes flicked to his concerned ones.

"Luna… Luna, Aria." I could hear him speaking, but they were just words. They held no meaning at this moment. Moving towards him, he put his hands up, trying to ward me off. My only response was a guttural growl. Just when I went to take another step towards him, I felt arms wrap around my own, distracting me.

Reid's arms, the familiar tingles spreading throughout my body at his touch, his intoxicating scent making me lean into him instinctually, calming myself down. Reid pulled me closer, tucking my head under his chin.

"Beta you are free to leave. Let me know if you have any problems while on patrol." Reid spoke with authority. Beta Zane sounded relieved to have Reid walk in. His heart rate instantly slowed down at the sight of his Alpha.

"I will see you later. Luna, feel better," he said as he walked off towards the foyer. I let out a shaky breath and tried to pull away.

"Where are you going?" Reid asked.

"I need blood," I stated, my voice still slightly distorted.

"I know, but why you are going into the infirmary?" I looked at him confused. I know blood isn't stored next to the milk in the fridge downstairs. Reid pulled me back towards our room. Wriggling out of his grip, I opened the door to the infirmary.

"I told Mavis not to store blood here for you after the last batch went off."

"Why would you do that?" I asked in disbelief. Was he going to force me to go without it like David?

Reid grabbed my hand and walked me back to our room, why would he tell Mavis to do that? Is it because I challenged him? Because I went behind his back? Was this his punishment?

Once back in the room, Reid pulled his shirt off and sat on the edge of the bed. "You don't need blood bags when you have me, I don't want you drinking random peoples blood Ari, only mine."

I watched him waiting for him to tell me it was a joke. I searched the bond and found no deceit, no indication that he was going to go back on what he was telling me. I could tell he felt strongly about me drinking only his blood, his possessiveness making him even want to control who I drink from. I didn't mind, he tasted just as good as he smelt.

Reid put his hand out and tilted his neck towards me, I watched the vein in his neck, throb to the beat of his heart. His scent perfuming the room, the sight of his neck was making my mouth water. I hesitantly stepped towards him and grabbed his hand. He pulled me on his lap, I was starving, but I was also worried about hurting him after what happened in the hallway with Zane.

"I won't let you kill me, Ari, stop worrying," When I didn't move, Reid reached up and slid his nail across his shoulder where it met at his neck. Drawing a thin line of blood. His blood spilling over and running down his shoulder onto his chest.

I couldn't fight the urge anymore, seeing his blood running down his skin, the temptation became too much. I licked up the trail of blood. Reid shuddered under my hot tongue, running over his flesh. When I reached his neck, I sank my teeth into his tender flesh. Reid moaned loudly at the sharpness of my teeth. Through the bond, I could feel that he actually enjoyed me feeding off him, like he found it erotic.

His blood dribbled down my chin as I drank from him, my hunger felt insatiable, when I went to pull away, Reid shook his head, he could feel my hunger radiating through our bond. I sank my teeth back into him, I knew my eyes and sclerae were burning red as the colour of his blood started to take over my vision. Making the room appear tinted red.

Adjusting my position, I could feel Reid's erection pressing between my legs through his jeans.

Chapter 26

Aria's POV

PULLING BACK, I WENT to get up when Reid tugged my hips back down, thrusting his hips into mine. I could feel his rock-hard cock pressing against my core. Reid held me in place with one arm tightly secured around my waist. His other hand reached up towards my face. He gripped my chin between his fingers, forcing me to meet his hungry lust-filled gaze. The intensity of his eyes made me squirm in anticipation.

Reid's thumb rubbed over my chin before brushing over my bottom lip. Parting my lips, my tongue brushed against his thumb softly. I could taste his blood on it. Swirling my tongue around the tip of his thumb, I sucked on it. His delicious taste enticed my arousal more.

Reid's hand dropped to my breast, he palmed it firmly, fondling it with his warm hands, as he hungrily smashed his lips into mine.

Rolling my hips over the bulge in his jeans. I felt moisture pool between thighs at the friction, making me moan against his lips, earning a growl from him.

"You still aren't forgiven," I told him. My voice sounds breathy and desperate.

"We'll see." His husky voice spoke just below my ear as he sucked the skin on my neck.

Reaching between us, I undid the button and zip on his jeans, reaching inside. I grabbed his large thick cock in my hand. Squeezing it, he thrust into my hand. I stroked him, slowly teasing him.

Reid grabbed my ass with both hands, squeezing so tightly, I knew his fingers were going to leave a bruise. My body betrayed me when he squeezed even harder, making me moan out.

Flipping me over, Reid sat on his knees between my legs. The silk slip dress riding up, revealing my wet panties. Gripping my panties, he ripped them off, my skin stinging as the fabric tore into my flesh, making me hiss.

Pulling me towards him and spreading my legs wide apart for him. I watched as he rubbed his fingers over my bare pussy, sliding his fingers between my swollen wet lips. He rubbed softly between my moist folds before pushing two fingers inside me, my pussy clenched around his fingers as he slowly pulled them out before adding another, his fingers moving in and out of my pussy torturously slow.

"So wet." Reid's husky voice made me quiver.

I pushed against his fingers, trying to get the release I was sitting on the edge of. Pulling his fingers out completely, I suddenly felt empty.

Watching as he placed his fingers in his mouth, sucking my juices from them.

"And so sweet." His gravelly voice making my stomach tighten.

Leaning over me, he smashed his lips into mine, his tongue playing with mine fighting for dominance. I could taste myself on his lips as he took over my mouth.

Standing up, he removed his jeans, his cock springing free from the confines of his pants. He stroked himself while watching my reaction. Sitting up on my elbows, I watched as his hand stroked and squeezed his cock.

My juices running down and onto my thighs, at the sight of him standing over me, I rubbed my legs together to try and soothe my throbbing desire.

Sitting up, I grabbed hold of his thick cock, I felt it jerk in my grip. Looking up and watching his reaction. I flicked my tongue out and licked his knob, before taking it completely in my mouth.

Sucking his cock, I felt his hands slide into my hair. Gripping a handful, he thrust into my mouth, making me gag. His cock twitched when my throat constricted around his hard length.

Sucking harder, he thrust into my mouth again. This time I was prepared for it and relaxed my throat.

Reid continued to fuck my mouth for a few minutes before reaching down. He grabbed my dress and pulled it over my head, before shoving me back, making me fall on my back on the bed.

Using his hands, he spread my legs apart, before laying between them. I moaned out when his hot breath came in contact with my skin as he sucked on the inside of my thigh. Moving closer to my core, his hot breath fanning my skin as he ran his tongue over my swollen lips.

His hands running up and over my belly to my breasts, everywhere he touched sparks ignited, making my sensitive skin tingle.

I writhed in pleasure as he sucked and licked the small bundle nerves, he then slid a finger inside of me, making me grip the sheets. His tongue giving me no rest as he tasted me. I tried to slam my legs shut, but he pulled them open holding them in place, my stomach tightened, and body tingled as my orgasm took over as my pussy clamped around his fingers, slowing his movements so I could ride out my orgasm.

I laid there trying to catch my breath when Reid suddenly flipped me over onto my stomach, grabbing my ankles. He ripped me towards the end of the bed. I yipped at the speed, thinking I was going to be thrown off the bed when suddenly my feet touched the soft carpet. My body still bent over the bed, trying to sit up, I felt his warm large hand shove me back down before the sound of his slap echoed through the room as his hand swatted my arse. I could feel his handprint burning into the tender flesh of my arse as he rubbed it soothingly.

Using his feet, he kicked my legs apart, his hand gripping my hips, pulling me closer to the edge of the bed, leaving me face down with my ass in the air. I felt as he shoved his erection between my wet folds teasingly. My stomach tightened in anticipation, reaching between us, Reid's hand ran over my ass gently before sliding his fingers between my wet folds and rubbing my core, my wetness coating his fingers.

The low hum like a purr rumbled through his chest deep and low making me insides clench, when suddenly his fingers were gone as he slammed his hard cock into me. I cried out at the shock and force of his cock slamming relentlessly into me, my cries turning to moans as I became putty beneath his hands.

The only sounds were moans and the sound of our flesh as his hips slammed into mine, it didn't take long before I felt my core tighten and my skin heat up as another orgasm washed over me. My pussy clenching around his cock as I rode out my orgasm, I could feel his movements become harder as he finally found his release. Spilling his seed into me, we both collapsed onto the bed.

Waking up a few hours later, the sun was now up, making my way into the bathroom. I quickly peed before jumping in the shower to wash away the remnants of last night's shenanigans. Getting out, I quickly chucked on jeans and a shirt, sliding on my slippers, I quickly made my way down to Lily's room.

Opening the door, Lily threw herself into my arms. The relief I felt being able to hold her in my arms was overwhelming; my eyes instantly pooling with tears. Lily let go excitedly, she was wearing a navy blue skort and light blue button-up blouse.

'"I get to go to school today," Lily said, jumping up and down excitedly. "I'm glad you're awake, you will love my school. Reid took me to the Pack school yesterday so I could meet my teacher. She was so nice, and she has Pink hair like a princess." Lily explained, her excitement never wavering.

"Pink hair? What's her name? Did you like her?" I asked just as enthusiastically as Lily.

"Yes, her name is Mrs. Tatt. She is nice, and she even wears princess dresses with frilly skirts." Lily replied, just as Reid walked in, he was wearing his usual black suit and white shirt looking very formal and work ready. In his hands, he was holding a pair of black Nike joggers and some socks. I watched as he got down on one knee in front of Lily. Lily instantly sitting next to him as he placed her socks and shoes on her feet before tying her laces.

I kind of felt a little left out. I was so used to doing this stuff for her, it was kind of weird seeing someone else dress her and get her ready for school. I felt unneeded. Reid sensing my emotions looked up at me and raised an eyebrow at me. His voice slipping into my mind.

"You're not jealous, are you?" I didn't reply. I know it was child-ish, but I actually was a little jealous.

"Don't be, someone had to look after her while you napped. Besides, it is good practise for when we have kids. I even did her hair." I was gobsmacked. I didn't really picture Reid as the type to want kids, let alone see myself wanting kids. I guess I never really thought of myself ever having a mate either. Never wanting children of my own, I always classed Lily as my own. Now the thought of having my own scared me. Looking at Lily, Reid had indeed done her hair, it was a little out of place but looked ok still, her blonde hair was parted down the middle and pulled into pigtails, I smiled at his attempt. Watching him with Lily, I could see another side of him, one I never knew existed.

I knew I wasn't ready for kids; I only just found my mate, and now he wants me spitting out a litter. Hell no. Reid stood up and hugged me, wrapping both arms around my waist and resting his head on my shoulder; his lips gently kissed my cheek.

"I didn't say right away stop stressing; I can feel your anxiety.... calm down. When you're ready, we will talk about it,"

I will never be ready. I thought to myself, it was never a desire I ever had.

"Yes, you will one day." Reid whispered in my ear.

"Stop reading my thoughts," I retorted.

"Then stop hiding your feelings, and I won't have too."

Lily was digging through her new unicorn backpack, completely oblivious of my inner turmoil or mine and Reid's conversation. Lily was excitedly getting ready for school, when the doorbell rang loudly, echoing throughout the house. Lily looked at me, nerv-ously. I was confused at her reaction, Reid stiffened beside me as his hands tightened around my waist. Kissing my neck, he let go.

"You should get that," he stated. I walked out of the room and walked towards the foyer. As I was coming down the stairs, Wendy opened the front door. His scent hit me instantly. I would never forget that scent having spent half my life around him. Confusion took up my mind. I could hear Lily and Reid coming up behind me just as Alpha David stepped in the foyer.

He was clean-shaven wearing jeans and a loose-fitting blue shirt. He also looked like he had a haircut. His hair was neatly done, and he was even wearing deodorant instead of his usual foul whiskey smell, which usually followed him like a dark cloud. He looked good clean, but most of all, like a normal father instead of a dirty rough biker.

I froze on the steps. I could feel Lily tug my hand gently when she grasped it. David looked panicked for a second upon seeing me frozen on the steps.

"Am I late?"

I stared, confused. Wendy piped up when I didn't say anything.

"No, just in time. We were all about to have some coffee while the kids ate breaky then we will head off."

David nodded. I made my way down the stairs slowly, never taking my eyes off him.

"Okay... I am missing something, what's going on?"

"You messaged saying it was Lily's first day of school and I could attend if I wanted, so here I am" David spoke in a nervous voice.

Reid walked up behind me. "I didn't text, I don't even have a phone" I replied confused. Reid reached into his pocket and pulled out an iPhone.

"Well, you do now, and I invited David on behalf of you. Now come on, let's go have some coffee" Reid said , placing the phone in my hand and walking towards the kitchen. Lily stared up at me nervously before chasing after Reid. I nodded for David to follow as we all made our way to the kitchen.

$$Chapter\ 27$$

Aria's POV

ONCE IN THE KITCHEN, I started making coffee with Wendy. The atmosphere was a little tense not knowing how to react to having someone that wasn't a Pack member in the Pack house. David looked extremely uncomfortable, and he and Reid sat across from each other at the table watching each other closely. Neither of them trusting the other. Walking over, I placed a coffee in front of both of them. I don't know who's as more shocked Lily or myself when David thanked me for his cup.

I stared speechlessly, so did Lily, the words sounded alien coming out of his mouth. Quickly masking my shock, I took a seat between both Alpha's, my own cup in hand and watched as Lily and Amber munched on their breakfast. Wendy offered everyone pancakes, but Alpha David declined, and I suddenly lost my appetite. How could I eat when everything felt uncomfortable? I didn't trust myself to not choke on my food.

When Lily finished eating, she grabbed her bag, chucking it over her shoulder. I stood up and reached for her hand. She grasped it tightly, I could sense she was nervous. I just didn't know if it was about starting a new school or the fact that David was following behind her. Reaching the foyer, Reid stopped in front of us.

"I have to go to the office. When you're done at the school head over if you like, Mitch will drive you wherever you want to go" He told me, placing a kiss on my lips before stepping back. Just as he was about to bend down to talk to Lily. David stepped forward.

"Actually, is it alright if after I have some time with Aria? I have a few things I would like to discuss with her?" I was once again left speechless. The man I had always feared asking permission like a child and using manners too. What happened while I was out, he was like a completely different person.

Reid glanced at me quickly, and I shrugged my shoulders before he looked back at David.

"Fine but Mitch stays with her, wherever you take her, he is to stay with her understood." David nodded and thanked him. Agreeing to the terms.

"Okay, let's get Lily to school" I announced, drawing everyone's attention to what we were meant to be doing. Reid bent down and placed a kiss on Lily's head.

"Everyone will love you and have fun kiddo," he told her before walking out the front door. David looked down at Lily and smiled. The smile seemed genuine and held no malice, it was weird seeing him smile. I hadn't seen the man smile since my mother was alive. Oh, how things were changing.

Walking out behind Reid, I watched as he jumped into his car with Zane following behind him, before jumping in the driver's side and leaving. We watched the car go down the driveway, Mitch pulled up out the front in a black SUV, I walked over and opened the back door for Lily. Lily climbed in, placing the seat belt on while I slid in next to her. David stood awkwardly. I could tell he was unsure whether or not he was supposed to come with us or follow.

"Just jump in the front, we can drop you back to your car when we are finished at the school." I yelled out to him. David made his way to the front passenger seat climbing in and buckling himself up. The drive to school was silent and luckily a quick drive, the school was only ten minutes from the Pack house.

Jumping out of the car, the school was only small, compared to the ones I went too. One huge building surrounded by high fences. Kids were talking and hanging around in groups, there were even older teenagers. I looked at Mitch, confused. Noticing my confusion, he stepped closer.

"The school is K to twelve. There are only around 200 students that attend the school, so instead of having two separate schools, we joined them into one. Makes it easier for the warriors to watch over everyone. The classes are smaller, so the students get a lot of one-on-one time with their teachers. First half of the day is spent doing your normal human sort of education, maths, English, science, etc. The other half of the day is spent learning about werewolf history and training," I nodded my head in understanding, it was a lot different than the schools I went to.

I went to a mixed school, with a mainly human population that was unaware of the werewolf population walking the halls of the school. This seemed more practical, the kids didn't need to hide what they were and were amongst those they have grown up with, they also got the best of educations into both worlds. By the time Mitch had finished showing David and I around, we had stopped in front of a colourfully decorated classroom. The windows were covered in different art pieces the kids had drawn one window was covered in painted handprints that I'm assuming were Lily's classmates.

Stopping, I noticed we had quite the following of kids, they were crowded around us, staring up at Alpha David and myself curiously. Lily was talking animatedly to Amber, and another little girl who's name I learned was Tara. She had red hair and freckles wearing her navy-blue school uniform proudly.

"Is your sister our Luna?" I heard Tara ask, staring up at me excitedly. I smiled back, Lily just nodded her head and introduced us.

"This is Ari, my sister and this…" She stopped unsure of what to say when it came time to introduce David. Luckily, David didn't freeze, in fact, he looked quite proud. He waved at the children that were huddled around. I see a few kids sniff the air realising he wasn't a Pack member before they stepped closer to Mitch and myself. David seemed unfazed and introduced himself.

"I'm David, Lily's father," he said before looking at my face to see if I would deny him. I just smiled, and Lily did too. She looked relieved but also unsure of his new attitude towards her. I couldn't blame her; I was actually proud of how she was carrying herself; she really had come a long way from being the frightened little girl she once was. Now she was more confident and sure of herself, she still had a long way to go, but I now knew she would get there.

David watched Lily talk amongst her newfound friends, Mitch stuck close, never leaving my side just like Reid had told him. When the bell finally rang signalling the start of class, kids ran in all different directions to their classrooms and lined up. Lily took her place next to Amber in line and waited patiently.

A woman walked over to us. She eyed David warily before relaxing when she spotted Mitch and myself standing with him.

"Hi, you must be Luna Aria," she stated, giving me her hand to shake. Her handshake was gentle. She had soft features and caramel coloured skin and bright brown eyes with curly black shoulder length hair.

"I don't think I have met you yet. I'm Mrs. Tatt, but you can call me Nadia." She spoke softly. I said a quick hello before her gaze looked over my shoulder to the Alpha standing behind me.

"Ah, I'm David, Lily's father," he said, offering his hand to her. She quickly nodded and shook his hand. I could tell she was slightly confused. David Alpha Aura was strong, not as strong as Reid's but definitely strong. I was shocked he didn't introduce himself as an Alpha, instead just giving his first name like he was any normal person. I could tell she thought it was weird that a non-Pack member and Alpha was on Pack territory and that his daughter wasn't a part of his own Pack. I didn't have time to explain the very strange situation right now. So, for now, Nadia will just have to wait until I explain the unusual family situation to her.

Lily raced into class and put her bag at her desk. I watched her run back and wrap her tiny arms around me and give me a hug. She pulled away, and Mitch ruffled her hair while she swatted his hand away. She looked up at her father, not knowing whether to just walk away or shake his hand. I saw her raise her hand like she was going to wave when Alpha David placed a hand on her shoulder and lightly squeezed. I could tell he was just as unsure as she was. "Have a good day, Lily," he told her with a gentle voice.

She smiled and nodded her head before walking off to go back to her desk.

Walking out, I heard Mrs. Tatt calling out "Luna, Luna." I stopped quickly remembering I was, in fact, the Luna. That was still going to take some getting used to.

Turning around, I faced her. "School finishes at three as I'm sure you are aware but if you don't mind would you be able to stop by the class at 2:30 the kids would love to meet and get to know you,"

"Of course, I will see you then." She smiled excitedly, and I could see many faces pressed against the glass peering out at us. I waved at them before following Mitch back to the car. Alpha David walking beside me.

"I would like to speak to the principal here one day if that's okay. I like the idea of this whole werewolf populated school. The kids look a lot more relaxed when they aren't surrounded by humans," I raised an eyebrow, that had to be the most Alpha thing I have heard come out of his mouth. He did seem quite interested when Mitch was explaining the way the school was set up. Mitch answered for me.

" You will have to discuss that with the Alpha assuming Luna Aria is okay with that, I don't think Alpha Reid will have a problem": It was weird hearing Mitch address me so formally. I knew he was only doing it out of respect, and because Alpha David was with us. I really hope it doesn't stick though; I like being myself around everyone back home. But I feel it might change if everyone keeps calling me Luna. I didn't mind the title, but I also liked just being Aria.

"That's fine with me, we can discuss it later, now where did you want to have this talk at?"

"We can head back to your Pack house if you would be more comfortable there" Mitches mind-link pushed through to me. "Luna I would prefer if it was done at home, it is a lot safer there with the warriors, and I don't think Reid would like it very much if we left the territory."

I nodded in Mitch's direction. "Yes, we can head back to the Pack house and discuss things." I told David. Getting back to the car we made the short trip back to the Pack house.

Chapter 28

Aria's POV

ONCE BACK AT THE house, we headed straight towards the kitchen. I brewed coffee while David went and took a seat at the table. Mitch just lingered in the kitchen watching, keeping a watchful eye. David's whole demeanour changed once I sat across from him. He suddenly became extremely nervous like he didn't know how to start. I sipped my coffee and watched as he did the same. He kept glancing towards Mitch like he didn't want to speak in front of him.

"Does your friend need to stay?" he asked. I looked towards Mitch who was sitting at the counter reading the newspaper, having heard David speak, he looked up.

"I'm not going anywhere, so pretend I'm not here," he confirmed what I already knew. Reid had given him strict orders that under no circumstances I was to be left alone with Alpha David.

David realising this turned back to me while Mitch turned back to his newspaper and coffee.

"So, what did you want to talk about?" I asked, breaking the silence that seemed to be drawing on. I just wanted to get this over with.

"Well first, I wanted to say thank you for allowing me to try and form a relationship with Lily, I know it must be hard considering the past," I scoffed at his use of words, he was really trying not to mention any details, but at least he was attempting to apologise. Seeing my reaction, he put his head down. "Look Aria, I wasn't all bad. Before your mother died, I was a good stepfather, a good husband. It was just difficult after your mother died. I couldn't cope with losing her. I loved your mother, Aria."

"I know that, David, I do. I understand to a certain point now. I spoke to Reid; his father never recovered from losing his mate either. Now having Reid, I can't imagine life without him. That's not my problem though. I know who you are capable of being. I also know what you're capable of doing. I won't allow Lily to be put through that again. I know she is your daughter, but I am the one who raised her."

David seemed to be thinking, I could tell he was uncomfortable with being called out for his shit, and I could also see he really was trying to apologise for his actions.

"I do have a question for you, though," I said. He lifted his head and looked at me, his face unreadable. "Why didn't you tell me about Zoe? Why did you stop her from being a part of our lives?"

David sat back in the chair like he was trying to find the words. "If you knew about Zoe, you could have left, and she was a part of your mother's old life, the life she had with your father. I guess I was jealous that your mother loved someone other than me. I made it no secret that I felt betrayed that she had a child with someone who wasn't her mate, so I made her cut ties with her family." I was appalled at his reasoning. He basically made my mother choose her family or her mate, which it's almost impossible to go against the mate bond.

David seemed to grow tense under my glare. I didn't even realise I was glaring at him until I saw him look to Mitch, who was already on his feet staring at me. I closed my eyes and took some deep breaths through my nose, I could feel my fangs protruding and taste my own blood in my mouth. Regaining control, I relaxed. That was the first time I had actually managed to gain full control of my emotions and instincts. David's answer was so selfish it made my blood boil.

Once I was settled down, I grabbed my coffee and let the burn from the scolding liquid distract me from ripping him apart. I had no doubt in my mind now that if it came to that, I could easily overpower and kill him. I couldn't do that though I had to think of Lily.

"So, after Mum died, what was your excuse for not letting her see us? And don't say it was me running off because you and I both know I would never leave Lily in your care." He went to protest but shut his mouth.

"Well after your mother died, I just didn't see the point in bringing it up. You lived without her, so what's the point? Then when you started working there, I was quite shocked she didn't tell."

"She didn't say anything because she knew I would never leave Lily behind, and also so you wouldn't stop us from seeing her. She didn't care what sort of contact she had with us, she just wanted to be a part of our lives." David nodded his head in understanding. Listening to my words before speaking again.

"Well… so how do we go about this whole custody agreement?"

"What agreement, David? I haven't agreed to anything. Lily will remain with me until you either prove yourself, or she is old enough to choose."

"But surely, we can organise some routine so I can spend some time with her, or maybe even a time when you and Lily come and stay at the Pack house, so she is still around her Pack members?"

Mitch seemed to stiffen at the last part. There would be little chance of Reid ever letting me go back to my old Pack. "You would have to speak to Reid about that, David."

"But he isn't Lily's father. I should have some say,"

"I'm his mate, I will not go against him. If he won't allow me to stay at our old Pack house, then I am sorry David, but I will not allow you to be alone with Lily without me there. I didn't do this, you did. You made your bed so, for now, you need to lay in it and do things on my terms. If you don't agree to it, that is fine, I understand. But you won't be seeing Lily until I say so or she is old enough to understand and decide for herself." I would never back down when it comes to Lily's safety, and I had to lay it all out there because if he thinks I am just going to be pushed to the side and let him take over, he is sadly mistaken. I won't allow him to damage my sister any more than he already has.

David stood up about to protest, I remained seated, keeping calm. Mitch stood up and started making his way towards the table when Alpha David looked in his direction, he sighed before reigning in his emotions.

"I see at the moment we aren't going to agree on anything, I really need to talk to you about something else but wish to do so in private" Mitches phone suddenly started ringing, cutting David off. David looked at Mitch, who answered it. It was clear he was on the phone to Reid. "Some other time then Aria, can I pick Lily up after school with you?"

I nodded in agreement and told him to meet me in front of the school at 2:20. I promised I would stop in early to meet her classmates and teacher. That would also give me enough time to let the warriors that patrol the border to allow David back into the territory.

I escorted David out and watched him leave. Walking back inside, I was suddenly stopped by Mitch. He was carrying my jacket and had keys in his hand. "Come on Ari, Alpha wants you to come to meet him at his office. You really need to reign in your emotions. He has been hounding me the entire time you were talking to David, and now he is that anxious, he has ordered I bring you to him." I rolled my eyes at him, I could just overthrow him, but I know that would not only piss Reid off but also Ryder. The last thing I need is an angry possessive werewolf on a rampage to hunt me down so I decided it is best to go willingly.

Driving through the city, it was just starting to rain clouds rolling in from the mountains. The sky was grey, and the weather was turning miserable. When we reached the skyrise that was owned by the Pack, I made my way inside. The foyer was large; the marble floors made my wet sneakers squeak when I walked. At the front was a woman who, when I approached, bowed her head before telling me to catch the lift to the top floor.

Everything was so clean and polished, I could see my reflection in the buttons on the elevator, they were that shiny. When I got to the top floor, the elevator dinged as the doors opened. This office space was incredibly fancy, just what you would expect to find in a CEO's floor, everything was state of the art. The secretary at the front was a middle-aged woman in a pinstripe suit, she had glasses perched on the end of her nose and was gazing at her computer screen. When I approached, she looked up with a huge smile on her face.

"Good morning, Luna." I waved her off.

"Call me Aria. I am still not used to that title yet," I told her. She looked at me, nodding understandably.

"Alpha said to just go into his office." She told me, pointing to the blacked-out glass windows behind her. I couldn't see in the windows were tinted darkly, upon opening the door though his office kind of resembled the one at home.

Everything was clean and tidy with the same oak furniture; the only difference was the size of the room. It was huge, and the view from the floor to ceiling windows overlooked the entire city. Walking over I looked out and the view was breathtaking.

I stayed there looking out the window. I could just make out all the different territories in the distance. I was so absorbed in what I could see that I didn't hear Reid sneak in behind me. His arms wrapped around my waist, pulling me flush against his chest. His face pressing to the side of my neck as he breathed in my scent. Tingles and sparks ran through my body straight to my clit. "Hmmm," his voice changed to one of desire. I could feel his hard rod pressing into my arse. Deciding to tease him a little, I pushed my arse into him, making him groan. Reid's hands snaked under my shirt, and under my bra, he pinched my left nipple between his fingers while his other hand travelled south into my pants. Reid's finger pressing softly against my clit, his fingers moving torturously slow, my head rolled back onto his shoulder, Reid started kissing and sucking on my neck. Turning my head slightly, Reid claimed my lips with his, his fingers moving faster rubbing building me up, I moaned into his mouth.

Reid pushed his erection into me, and I reached back and grasped him through his pants. Reid growled before pulling his hand from my pants which earned him an annoyed growl from me. He smiled before shoving me towards his desk.

"You have no idea how much I have wanted to bend you over my desk and fuck you." Before I could say anything, Reid spun me around. "Hands flat against the desk."

I obeyed, placing both hands on the desk while he pulled my pants down, forcing me to step out of them. "Open your legs," he ordered, kicking my feet apart further with his own. I moved my feet, excitement flashed through me at his demand. I could feel Reid's hand between my legs playing with my slit before he rammed two fingers inside me. I moaned at the sudden intrusion. Reid moved his fingers in out of me slowly, so slowly I actually started pushing into him trying to get more friction and make him move faster. Reid's other hand snaked around my body back under my shirt and he squeezed my nipple hard making me cry out. It hurt but also kind of felt good, he is walking a fine line between pleasure and pain.

Moving his finger's faster, he built up my orgasm, only to pull his fingers from me entirely, leaving me feeling empty and frustrated. He kept repeating this until I cried out in annoyance. Just when I thought he was about to do it again, I felt something larger and a lot harder press between my legs. Reid's hand on my shoulder shoved me, so I was completely bent over his desk, my breasts pressing into the cold surface of the desk.

Positioning himself at my entrance, Reid slammed into me hard, my body jerked forward, my hips hitting painfully on the desk, but I didn't care. Reid relentlessly pounding his cock into me had me writhing and moaning in pleasure, finally getting the release I needed. When my pussy started to clamp around his cock, he picked up his pace slamming into me harder and faster. My orgasm came on hard and fast, my body twitching as Reid held me in place. In this moment I couldn't care less if anyone walked in and caught us, my body ached, and I was exhausted, my whole body completely relaxed while I rode out my orgasm, all the while Reid pounded into me until I felt him slow his pace before I could feel his warm cum shooting into me, coating my insides.

Chapter 29

Aria's POV

THE KNOCK ON THE door alerted us that someone was outside his office door. I managed to throw my clothes on with speed that would have put The Flash to shame. I could hear Reid chuckle at my embarrassment. Any werewolf walking in could easily smell what we had been doing. My dishevelled appearance would only be verifying it. I tried to flatten down my hair and smooth out my clothes. Reid was slowly buttoning up his pants, not even fazed in the slightest. I groaned with annoyance at his leisurely pace.

Without warning, Zane waltzed on in, taking in the room, a sly smile spread across his face as he leaned on the doorframe. Reid chuckled at my mortified expression. Before slipping his belt on. Zane cleared his throat. "Sorry about that, but by the sounds of it, you two were done. I couldn't very well wait in the hall all day, some of us have work to do," he stated.

My face flushed red. I could feel the blood rushing to my cheeks. Zane laughed at me. Reid eyed me like he wasn't the least bit embarrassed, it actually made me wonder had Zane walked in on Reid with some random bent over his desk before. The thought churned in my stomach jealousy, consuming me at the thought.

"Calm down, Aria, Zane is just playing. And no, he hasn't walked in on me before," he said, answering the question that was lingering in my mind. I hated when he did that, I can't even keep my thoughts private. "No, you can't so I don't know why you bother trying." Reid answered. Invading my mind again. Zane just watched our lover's quarrels. I sat on the edge of the desk and folded my arms across my chest. I know it was childish, but it really irritated me that invading my thoughts was becoming easier and easier for him and yet I could feel what he was feeling but still not see into that head of his.

Reid, ignoring my ranting turned to Zane. "What do you need?"

Zane smirked at me before turning back to Reid. "Nothing Alpha, I just came to see you about a breach in security," Reid's head popped up at that, all joking pushed aside while he listened intently on what Zane had to say. I unfolded my arms and leant forward on his desk to listen too. "Hunters were spotted sneaking around the territory, and they managed to breach the computer database, they stole some footage."

"Footage? Of what? And are you sure they were Hunters; we haven't had Hunters around in years."

"Positive Alpha, they left something behind. When we scoured the footage, we saw they left a note in the foyer downstairs. I'm not sure what they were looking for, but they stole the footage from the night Lily and Ari came to our territory. They didn't take the footage of inside the building but of the cameras on the streets," Reid looked back at me, panic on his face and leaking through the bond. I could tell he was trying to mask it. Zane's eyes darted to me quickly before his eyes glazed over. I could tell he was mind linking Reid as Reid's eyes lost focus before going to me. He growled lowly from the back of his throat, it sent chills down my spine and paralysed me on the spot.

"What?" I asked, demanding to know what had Reid so riled up. Zane looked back at Reid, who put his hand up before pinching the bridge of his nose in frustration. I could tell he was trying to pull himself together, so I waited patiently for him to answer.

"The note said to hand over the Hybrid, and they will show the rest of us mercy," I gasped in shock. There is no doubt in my mind the Hybrid they are referring to is me. My throat suddenly felt dry. If they know I exist, they would definitely know about Lily. Lily and I are always together, especially the night they took the camera footage from.

"Why, though?" My voice shook in fear but not for myself, but for our Pack and for Lily. I never should have stayed in town; I should have left when we had the chance. Now I have put everyone at risk and why now after years have the Hunters come out of hiding and feel brazen enough to break into one of the most feared Packs' business buildings.

"I have no idea, Aria, but it won't be for anything good, you aren't to leave without an escort from now on, in fact, you won't be leaving my sight." I shook my head that wasn't even an option in my head for the sake of Lily and my Pack, I may just have to hand myself over. No one is dying for my sake; I could never live with myself.

Reid growled menacingly, obviously reading my thoughts yet again. I rolled my eyes, but Zane seemed to get the message that I apparently missed because he left the room in a hurry, the door slamming behind him.

Reid gripped my arm tightly, pulling me towards him and wrapping his other arm around my waist, so I was flush against him. I could feel his anger radiating off him, the heat of his skin suddenly feeling like it was burning into me. "You will not be leaving my sight, Ari. Do you understand?" I looked up at him, my own anger bubbling to the surface. How dare he tell me to sit on the sidelines while everyone risked their lives for me. Over my dead body would I allow that. Reid's nails dug into the skin on the inside of my arm. I hissed at the sting and looked up at him. His eyes were no longer his own, Ryder's eyes peering back at me were blazing in fury at my defiance.

"Stay out of my head, Reid, or is it just you now, Ryder?"

"No, Reid is here too, but he isn't willing to do what needs to be done if you refuse." Ryder's voice was low daring me to defy him. I could hear the challenge in his voice like he really wanted me to try. I knew better, the memory of his bite still fresh in my mind. I hated that, but that didn't mean I was going to drop to his feet and beg for forgiveness. He was the one not thinking rationally.

"Bring Reid back now, Ryder." Ryder growled his nails digging deeper as he pulled me even closer, which I didn't think was even possible. His lips at my ear. "You won't be leaving Ari, will you?" I felt the blood leave my body, and my heart felt like it had moved into my throat. His voice was so menacing, I tried to swallow the lump that was caught in my throat, but my mouth felt like I was trying to swallow sand, the saliva leaving my mouth making it as dry as a desert.

"Bring Reid back, Ryder." My voice trembled and didn't come out as strong as I was hoping.

"Wrong answer," Ryder spun me, with so much force my surroundings blurred for a second, my back now pressed tightly to his front. Ryder's arm wrapped tightly around my waist, holding me in place. When I felt his canines brush my neck, I screamed and placed my hand just in time, so he bit into the back of my hand instead of my neck. I shrieked at the sudden pain and pulled my hand away.

Dropping down I twisted, so I was facing him. Lifting my hands, I hit him straight up under his ribs forcing him away from me. Ryder growled annoyed before getting to his feet. I watched him crack his neck, accepting the challenge. I didn't want to hurt him, and I knew deep down he didn't really want to hurt me. This was just his caveman side, brute force, and not much rational thinking.

Holding my hands up in front of me. "Wait, wait." Ryder halted, thinking I was agreeing to his terms. I used that to my advantage. Using my Alpha voice. "I said bring Reid back NOW!" I screamed. Ryder fought off my command easily. "Shit," I really hoped it would work with him being distracted. It didn't, why for once, couldn't I get the upper hand over him just once. Ryder seemed to think it was funny that my Alpha voice didn't work on him, because he was my mate. The look on his face was disturbing, primal, in this moment he truly looked like a predator and unfortunately for me, I was his prey.

I only had two choices: take a very painful nap for god knows how many days or give in to his commands. I chose the latter. "Fine, I will stay. Okay just bring Reid back please Ryder, you're scaring me." He smiled triumphantly before stepping forward.

"Promise you won't put yourself in any unnecessary danger." I nodded my head. I could agree to that unless it involved Lily, I won't put myself in danger. I made sure to remember to hold my walls up, so Ryder didn't read into my thoughts.

Ryder reached for me, tugging me to his chest, I could feel his face in my hair breathing in my scent. His grip around my waist was strong like a cage. I couldn't escape without hurting him, not that I wanted to, the familiar tingles running over my skin as his warmth seeped into. His arms loosened slightly, and I knew Reid had taken back control. I felt his lips kiss me on the top of my head. Pulling away, I glared at him before shoving him away.

Turning on my heel, I walked out of his office.

"Where do you think you're going, Ari?" Reid asked, reaching for my arm. I pulled my arm away.

"To Zane's office, don't worry, Alpha, I am not leaving your glass prison without you. With Zane, I don't have to watch out for his psychotic alter ego wolf attacking me" I spat at him. Reid growled, but I ignored him slamming the door in his face. Before I even got two steps out of his office., Zane walked up to me. "I hear I have been summoned," he said jokingly. I pushed past him and walked into his office and sat on his grey suede couch and pulled my mobile out.

Zane followed me back in shutting the door behind him. I tried to navigate the new phone Reid had given me. "Don't be too upset Luna, Ryder can be a pain in the ass, but he means well" I ignored him and kept scrolling through the contacts until I found the name I was looking for.

Zoe.

Chapter 30

Aria's POV

ZOE ANSWERED AFTER THREE rings. Her voice questioning "Hello?" I felt relieved upon hearing her voice. I have no idea why I was worried. I had no doubt that she could handle herself, but that didn't make me worry any less. I relayed the conversation between Zane and Reid, letting her know about the Hunters.

"And they are sure they were definitely Hunters?" Zoe asked concern laced her words.

"Positive, they also left a message demanding the Hybrid," I told her. Zoe seemed to think for a minute.

"How do they even know you exist? Only a handful of us know, and I know Reid wouldn't give you up or your Pack. The most intriguing question though, besides the obvious, is why specifically say they want the Hybrid, I wonder what they need you for?"

"I have no idea but, Reid won't let me out of his sight, so I won't be able to visit you until he says, I just wanted to let you know what was going on" I sigh frustrated.

"I still have some old contacts. I will see what I turn up, can I call you back on this number?"

"Yes, this is my number, call anytime," I told her. We say our goodbyes and hang up the phone. I turn to see Zane is pretending to ignore me like I didn't know he was eavesdropping on the conversation.

When two o'clock came. I got up from the couch and went to walk out the door, heading towards Reid's office. As soon as the door opened though Reid was already standing on the other side of the door. His face was unreadable but I could tell he was waiting for me to say something.

"I promised Lily's teacher I would come back early and meet the class, I also told David I would meet him at the school" Reid clenched his jaw but moved to the side to let me pass. Zane must have been called through their link because he was straight behind me following along with Reid. This is ridiculous, I rolled my eyes and shook my head. Coming to the elevator, I stepped inside, Reid's hand reached down, grabbing my hand in his death grip, Zane hit the button to go back down to the foyer.

Nobody said a thing the entire way down, you could cut the tension with a knife. When the elevator dinged signally, we arrived on the ground floor, I went to step out when Reid pulled me back to his side, keeping a strong grip on my hand. Its fucking daylight for god's sake, what does he expect is going to happen during the day?

"Don't test me, Ari, it won't end well for you." I gave up and relaxed my hand, Reid's grip loosened as we walked to the car that waited out front. Zane jumped in the passenger side, while Reid tugged me into the back. Mitch sat in the driver seat.

"Alpha," He nodded to Reid in the mirror.

"The school, Mitch." His words sounded bored. I sat back in my seat. Choosing to ignore Reid the entire time, I chatted with Mitch. When I slid to the middle seat and lent forward, I felt Reid's hand pull me closer, so our sides were touching. His arm pulled me back against the seat so I couldn't lean forward. He draped his arm across my shoulders. Jealousy raging through the bond, at me deliberately ignoring him and talking animatedly with Zane and Mitch. I looked over at him, his eyes racked over my face his expression was annoyed, but I could feel desire and an overwhelming need to touch him and reassure him flood through the bond. Giving up, I decided to not poke the angry wolf and leant into him, placing my head on his shoulder.

Reid's shoulders relaxed, and his fingers brushed my hair out of my face before gripping my chin. He tilted my head up so I could meet his eyes. His eyes softened, and he pressed his forehead to mine. I could feel his fear of losing me wash over me. I swallowed feeling suddenly guilty about earlier, remembering him telling me about his father going mad after the loss of his mate. I could never do that to Reid, I won't make him suffer because of my stubbornness. So silently I agreed I wouldn't put myself in danger and I would remain within arm's reach of Reid. Reid sensing my change or maybe he was reading my mind, kissed my forehead before pulling me tighter against him, I draped one arm lazily over his chest. Reid's other hand reached up and entwined his fingers in my hair.

When the car halted, I looked up, we were at the school. Mitch and Zane got out of the car and waited beside both rear doors like they were keeping watch. I noticed David's car parked in the parking lot. I could see him leaning against the bonnet. Stepping out, Reid followed behind me. When David saw Reid step out behind me, he looked taken aback but didn't comment. I walked over to him. "Ari, Alpha Reid." David nodded his head, and Reid entwined his finger through mine holding my hand. "Alpha David." Reid acknowledged. We all walked into the school and towards Lily's classroom. I could feel eyes on us, peering out of the classrooms. Before I even had a chance to knock, the door swung open. Lily's teacher smiled warmly back at me. Mrs. Tatt didn't hide her surprise at seeing Reid standing behind me along with our small entourage. "Alpha what a surprise, is everything okay?"

"Yes, Nadia everything is fine.", but I could tell she felt uncertain, as her eyes darted around to all the faces of her students in the classroom with alarm. She stepped outside, closing the door behind her. "Is something wrong?" Reid stopped her from continuing.

"Don't panic, Nadia. Everything will be fine; we just had a breach of security. Nothing for you to worry about, your students are safe." Zane and Mitch both nodded trying to reassure her. For some reason, my eyes darted to David, who shifted uncomfortably. I thought it was odd, but it was quickly forgotten when Lily opened the door and poked her head out drawing our attention back to the class who now had their faces pressed against the glass watching all of us with excitement. Moving past Mrs. Tatt, Reid reached down and picked up Lily and walked into the classroom.

The children instantly swarmed Reid excitedly. I could hear the children excitedly squealing Alpha trying to get his attention. I watched him play with the children and joined in too. Mitch and Zane stood outside the classroom, keeping guard. David sat awkwardly, watching the kids excitedly play with myself and Reid. When the bell rang signalling the end of school, I stood up, and Lily walked over to David and peered up at him. She looked uncertain, but David actually looked genuinely excited to have her attention finally.

"How was school, kiddo?" he asked, "Fun" she nodded and asked if he wanted to see her work. He nodded, and I could feel Reid's unease come through the bond while he kept a close eye on David.

When it came time to leave, I held my hand out for Lily and she ran over her little hand, fitting perfectly in mine.

"David, we need to talk. We had some intrusion on our territory." David nodded and walked over to Reid, who was leaning on the teachers' desk. He told David what had happened. To Reid he seemed concerned, but I knew David better, I could tell by the way he shifted nervously, his whole demeanour shifted, Reid couldn't tell not being around him all that much. I knew David like the back of my hand, and I could tell something was off. David, sensing my stare, looked in my direction before his eyes darted to the ground. I watched the exchange between them. Something was eating at me though. I knew David knew more than he was saying and admitting to.

"I will have extra patrols out to keep an eye along the borders. If we notice anything, I will ring you straight away. If Lily or Aria need somewhere to hide out for a while they can stay on my territory," Reid shook his head.

"No, the girls are safer with me. Our Pack is stronger, no one will get to them with us." Reid spoke confidently, I could tell he was proud of his Pack. David I could tell didn't agree but didn't voice his opinion on the matter.

"Very well, keep me informed, and I will do the same." Something felt off, the whole exchange on David's end felt false.

Walking out, Reid came over to me. We walked back to the cars, and David helped Lily in the car. Reid held me back, sensing my unease. His voice flitted through my mind through the link.

"What is it? What is wrong?" he asked, concerned.

"Nothing, just something doesn't feel right," I answered honestly. "I'm just being paranoid" Reid looked at me doubtfully like he didn't think my feeling was just paranoia, I didn't either, but I made sure to keep my walls up so he couldn't read my thoughts and climbed in next to Lily. I watched as David walked back to his car. His eyes darted over his shoulder in the direction of the car when he noticed me watching him. He nodded his head at me before getting in his car. David left, and we made our way back to the Pack house. When we stopped, Lily ran inside with Amber. Zane grabbed the girl's bags from the boot and followed behind them. Reid followed directly behind me, jumping out of the car, and Mitch drove the car off to the garage.

"I know you're hiding something, what is going on Aria?" Reid asked.

Chapter 31

Aria's POV

"I KNOW YOU'RE HIDING SOMETHING, what is going on Aria?" Reid asked.

Choosing to ignore him, I walked into the house. I have my suspicions on who might be behind this, but until I have proof or confront him about it, I can't very well go causing a war on a feeling. I would hate for Reid to go kill him, then later find out he wasn't behind it. Reid followed me into the house. Walking into the kitchen, Wendy and Christine were making the kids afternoon tea. Reid not wanting to cause a scene in front of the kids, let me be. I knew this wouldn't be the end of this discussion. I quickly made coffee for everyone before sitting at the dining table. Lily excitedly showed me her paintings they had done in class today. I watched but had trouble showing the enthusiasm she had about them.

I couldn't stop thinking about what an impact this will have on Lily if it is Alpha David who leaked information. I know Reid/Ryder would go berserk if they knew what I was thinking, but it was slowly eating away at me. I could feel it in every atom of my body that I was right. But now what, killing him doesn't change the fact that they have come out of hiding after years of keeping a low profile. When Lily got up to go play in the rec room, I followed her out, leaving her to play with Amber. I walked upstairs. I could feel Reid's lingering gaze on my back, I needed answers, and I know what he is going to say already, but I have no choice. I need to know, and I need to try and fix it.

Walking into the closet, I grabbed a jacket. Reid is going to pitch a fit when he finds out I plan on leaving to go to the Black Moon Pack, but the way I see it, he either comes with me and waits outside, which I know he won't do, or shuts his mouth and lets me go alone. I kind of need him to let me go alone, though. David will not admit anything if Reid is there. Just as I finished zipping the jacket up, in walked Reid. As soon as he saw me dressed and ready to leave, he crossed his arms over his chest and blocked my exit.

"Where do you think you are going?"

"I need to go see David," I tried to step past him, but his grip on my upper arm stopped me. Pulling me, so I was facing him directly. I huffed annoyed.

"You just saw David, why would you need to see him? Just ring him,"

"I know, but I need to speak to him privately," I said, crossing my own arms across my chest to match his annoyed and angry stance.

"Nice try, you're not going anywhere, Ari," I rolled my eyes annoyed at his childish behaviour. He needs to realise I am not some pathetic little girl. I am quite capable of taking care of myself.

"I will take Zane if it makes you feel any better."

"So, you will take my Beta, but I can't come?" I could feel his jealousy leaking into me through the bond. I raised an eyebrow.

"Really, you're jealous of your own Beta? Come on, Reid. I won't be gone for long just a few hours at most."

"Few hours? What the fuck could you possibly need to be gone that long for? I said no, and that's final."

Knowing he wasn't going to change his mind, I waited for him to turn his back and leapt at him. He didn't see it coming. I latched my arms around his shoulders, he tried to throw me off, but I was stronger but not by much. Now he is going to find out what it's like to be put to sleep.

I struggled to get a good angle, as he kept trying to throw me off, falling backwards on the bed, he was suddenly on top of me, his back to my chest. Wrapping my legs around his waist, I tried to hold him in place. I could hear Zane running up the steps leading toward our room, I needed to be quick before Zane stopped me. Reid hearing Zane's footsteps on the stairs as well turned to look at the door, he turned just enough that I got a good view of his neck and I took my opportunity.

My fangs extended and I sank them straight into his neck, I drank greedily, my hunger kicking in at the first taste of his sweet blood flooding my mouth, he moaned involuntarily when my teeth bit down into his flesh. I could feel his blood running down my chin and neck as he struggled to throw me off. His movements became jerky, and I could hear his heart rate slow, feeling him go slack, I unlatched my fangs from his neck just as Zane threw the door open. Shoving him off me, I got up and wiped my mouth and neck on a towel, cleaning the blood off.

"What the fuck have you done?"

"Nothing, now calm down, he is still alive. His wolf genes will kick in after a while, he should be fine."

"Should?"

"I promise he is fine; I can still hear his heart beating." Zane listened, picking up Reid's faint heartbeat before nodding his head.

"Is there a reason you put the Alpha to sleep?" he asked, confused.

"Well first, he deserved a taste of his own medicine, and second, I need to go to the Black Moon Pack, and you're coming with me."

"Why not ring?" It was the exact question Reid asked. I need to see David; I knew I could catch him out on a lie if he was in front of me. Over the phone not so much.

"Stop your questions and help me tie him up," I said motioning to Reid.

"Come again?"

Seriously, do I have to explain everything? "If he wakes up, he is going to come looking for me, help me tie him up, where are some chains?"

"Nope I'm out, you are nuts. He will kill me slowly, you - he will just kill." I rolled my eyes, walking over to Zane, I gripped his face forcing him to look at me.

"Go get the chains now," I told him using my Alpha voice. He rushed to do as he was told, not being able to fight my command. Dragging Reid up the bed closer to the headboard, I placed his head on a pillow and tucked him in. I laughed at the thought of tucking in the big bad Alpha, not so big and scary now are ya. I thought to myself.

Zane came back with some chains and two padlocks, I quickly wrapped them around his wrist then the foot of the bed on each side. I know it won't hold if he shifts, but I am hoping we will be back before then if he does wake up with any luck, the chains slow him down a little.

"Now what?"

"You and I are leaving, tell Mitch to watch the girls." Zane nodded and walked out. I walked over to Reid and kissed his lips. "Sorry, but you kind of deserved it, so I'm not really sorry," I told him, chuckling on my way out and down the stairs.

Getting in the car, we drove quickly to the Black Moon Pack border, upon arrival, two wolves stepped out but motioned us to drive through. We drove right up to the Pack house porch parking next to the steps.

"Ari, what are you doing here? Where is Reid?"

"Sleeping, I need to speak to you" Alpha David looked uncertain when Zane stepped out of the car. "He is fine, he won't cause any trouble" Alpha David gave Zane one last glance before showing us inside. Not that I needed showing I lived here most of my life, I followed after him anyway.

"Zane, go talk with Michael, I will be back soon," I said, leaving Zane in the loungeroom with Michael and his wife. Zane I could tell wasn't happy but didn't argue. I followed David to his office. Once inside, David took his seat behind the desk. I decided not to waste any time and got straight to the point. Time wasn't on our side, Reid will wake and come looking for me. "I know it was you," I told him, taking a seat across from him.

Alpha David looked at me, confused. "I know it was you, who told the Hunters about me." I clarified.

He went to shake his head, but I stopped him. "Don't deny it, I can tell when you're lying" He appeared to think for a minute, his eyebrows furrowed, and he pinched the bridge of his nose before letting out a breath and looking at me.

"I'm sorry, I thought you were going to take Lily from me, so I thought if I got you out of the way, Lily would be forced home, then after you and I came up with an agreement, I tried to tell you earlier to warn you, but someone is always with you. I didn't want to jeopardise our arrangement," I sighed, relieved my instincts were correct. I also had something else that had been eating at me since I first suspected, he was the one who was giving out information. "How do you know how to contact them?"

Alpha David looked taken back by my question but answered anyway. "I grew up with one of them. They aren't all bad, but most are raised from childhood to be Hunters. It is taught and passed down the family, generation after generation, doesn't mean they all agree. A lot of them don't have a choice," I thought for a few minutes before asking my next question.

"It was you, wasn't it? You knew Mum was your mate, so you told the Hunters to kill my father," I didn't ask it as a question, I knew I was right. He was the reason my father was dead, and my grandfather. His selfishness killed them. "How long did you know Mum was your mate before you had him killed?"

Chapter 32

Aria's POV

ALPHA DAVID GOT UP from his seat and walked over to the cupboard that sat next to the window overlooking the vast forest. His back was to me, I couldn't see what he was doing but could hear the clink of glasses and him pouring liquid into them. When he turned around, he held out a glass of whisky to me. I accepted the glass believing this conversation definitely warranted hard liquor. I could tell David was starting to get nervous and a little uncomfortable with the conversation topic.

I took a sip of the brown liquid. It was smooth tasting and had an oak taste to it. David downed his in one go and poured himself another. Finally, he sat back down across from me looking a little more confident with his glass in his hand. I took another sip from my drink and watched him over the top of my glass. "I knew she was my mate for five years. Your mother knew about me too but didn't want to break up her family. Your family Aria, not mine."

"So, what happened?" David ran a hand through his hair nervously and sighed, becoming resigned with the fact everything was about to be out in the open.

"I was pissed off that she would turn me down, reject me even though she never officially did reject me. She tried once but couldn't say the words. Couldn't bring herself to reject me. I told my friend about there being a Hybrid living in the city. I wanted to get rid of your father and try and have a life with my destined mate. I could tell your mother would never leave him for me. So, I took matters into me owns hands,"

I thought his words over trying to remember anything, but I was only two years old, so I had no memory of my father.

"It took another five years afterwards for your mother to accept me as her mate. She refused to move on, and I kept what I had done a secret for years, but I think your mother knew all along it was me. She just didn't say anything."

"So basically, you killed not only my father but my grandfather? Why didn't you just wait for the mate bond to work. The pull is stronger than anything I could have imagined. She would have given in eventually," I asked.

"I didn't want to wait. I waited five years before I acted, and as for killing them, they never died by my hands. I thought your father was dead. I thought he died along with Joe. They never found his body, and by the time your father came back, your mother was already dead."

"Came back? My father is dead."

"No, Aria, your father isn't dead, I saw him at the diner the other day when I had the meeting with Alpha Reid," I shook my head trying to wrap my head around what he just told me. How could my father be alive and not contact me?

"Are you sure? Why wouldn't he make contact?"

Alpha David looked confused for a minute and didn't say anything. He looked as confused as I felt. My father was alive and not only is he in the city, but he has also been at my work. Why didn't Zoe say anything, why didn't she tell me he was there? I have longed for my father for years, wanting to know him so I could know more about my past. The one I didn't know I had, to know more about my lineage.

How could he sit back, knowing I exist and not say anything?

"So, what's next then?" asked David.

"I'm not sure. We need to fix this Hunter's mess then I need to try and find my father if he is alive" I suddenly felt very sceptical.

"The Hunters won't be so easy to fix. When I told them you existed, they seemed really keen to get their hands on you, I'm not sure why. I think we will have a war on our hands. I am sorry Aria, I didn't mean, well I did, but I wasn't expecting everything to turn out the way it did, I promise to help with the Hunters, even if it means fighting alongside your Pack and as for your father, I won't say I'm sorry seeing as he isn't dead, but I do know where you can find him."

My head perked up, suddenly excited. Some good news has come out of this conversation, after all. I wasn't expecting what came out his mouth next, and the next few words shocked me to my core, how I had not put two and two together.

"He works at the diner; he is the cook there. He has changed his name but is definitely him. Marcus? I think his name is,"

My lips parted astonished, my father has been there all along, I didn't know how I felt. Shocked, angry? How could he sit idly by and not say anything he knew who I was all along. Also, how did I not recognise him, he looks nothing like the photo's Zoe showed me or like my necklace. I just assumed he was human until Zoe told me, what hurt the most was knowing Zoe kept this secret from me. I thought I could trust her completely now I was starting to wonder what else she was hiding from me.

Getting up, I wanted to scream, my anger was overshadowing everything. I needed to get out here. I needed to get home figure out my next move, placing the glass on the table, I stood up. Everything was falling into place, starting to make sense. I spent years grieving for a father who was there all along. Silently watching but not interfering. How could he just watch and not step in? How could Zoe not tell me? Why would they feel the need to keep this from me? Walking out of the office, I started walking down the hall. I just wanted to go home, I just wanted Reid. Zane, seeing me walk past got up off the lounge and followed after me.

"Ari, what's wrong?" I didn't answer, just kept walking to the car.

"Luna?" asked Zane as I got in the passenger seat.

"I think she might be in shock" David spoke behind us.

"What did you do?" Zane asked, suddenly becoming defensive.

"Nothing, I told her the truth," he said nodding in my direction, I nodded back and sat in the car. Zane looked between the car and David, who had turned his back and was now walking up the stairs. Zane waited for him to leave before getting in the car himself.

"Where to now?"

"I just want to go home" My voice lacked any emotion. I felt numb to all the new information I had gathered. I didn't say anything for the entire trip home. Zane kept glancing over at me, but I just ignored him and watched the trees and farmland pass by out the window. When we were about five minutes out I heard Ryder's voice, break through the thoughts circling in my head.

"Where the fuck are you?"

I ignored him, which I could feel ticked him off even more. I couldn't care less right now. I would take whatever punishment he decided to hand out. I wasn't in the mood to argue anymore.

"Ryder just linked me." Zane voice echoing in the silence. I just nodded, my eyes not leaving the window. "I told him we would be home soon; he sounds pissed, and I am pretty sure he's gonna eat me alive when we get back."

I turned to look at Zane, I could tell he was genuinely worried about defying not only Reid, but Ryder. Maybe I will have to deal with him, at least for Zane's sake.

"I won't let him touch you," I simply said. Zane seemed to calm down, and his grip on the steering wheel lessoned. His shoulder seemed to relax, and I could tell he was glad, I said something. I wasn't about to let Zane get hurt because of me. And I wasn't about to let Reid hurt his Beta, I could feel Ryder's burning rage as the Pack house came into view. Reid was standing out front pacing back and forth. The car pulled up, and I could see the tremble in Zane's hands as he put the car into park. Before I could even open my door, Reid was ripping it open. His glare was not his own but Ryder's. I could see his eyes flicking dangerously as Reid fought for control, Ryder was having none of that. Refusing to give in, I prayed Reid would regain control.

Zane got out of the car. He tried to sneak inside like a naughty kid caught doing something wrong, but his movements didn't go unnoticed by Ryder.

"Don't fucking move, Zane." Zane froze instantly under Ryder's command. I heard the front door open and could see Christine's horrified expression looking at her mate.

"Please don't let him hurt my mate." His voice came through the link, pleading desperately.

Standing up, I knew I had to get attention away from Zane. When I stood up, I met Ryder's angered eyes. "Leave Zane alone. He didn't want any part of it but wouldn't let me go alone," I stated. Ryder's eyes burned with anger, but he seemed to believe what I said. He looked at his Beta, they must have been mind-linking because he took off.

Christine's voice passed through my mind fluidly. "Thank you, good luck." When I turned to look at the Pack house. Christine had already run after her mate, leaving me with mine and his burning rage. Ryder's eyes fell down to meet mine.

His anger was so bad he couldn't even feel my emotions that were running all over the place. I didn't want to argue, I didn't want him to be mad. I just wanted to go to bed. I felt burnt out and exhausted.

Chapter 33

Aria's POV

OVING PAST RYDER, I felt my arm brush against his, I went to walk inside, Ryder was directly behind me, his glare burning into my back. I walked inside and made my way to Lily's bedroom. Ryder smacking into my back at my sudden stopping. I gripped the handle and twisted, opening the door, I popped my head in and could see her laying in her bed fast asleep, her unicorn plushie tucked tightly under her arm as she cuddled into it. Closing the door gently, I headed up the stairs towards our bedroom. Behind me, I could feel Reid's entire body shaking violently. His anger so much he couldn't see that I was breaking, about to come apart at the seams. When the door opened, I felt his sudden shift. Shifting in such close quarters had me thrown through the door, making me land on the floor on my stomach.

I have never seen them angry enough to see them shift out of anger so quickly.

Ryder's front paws were suddenly on both sides of my head, I could feel his hot breath on my neck and in my hair. I watched goosebumps rise all over my exposed arms. Yet I couldn't bring myself to feel fear. I felt nothing, rolling onto my back, I came face to face with Ryder's true form, and when he was angry like this, he really was a thing of nightmares, his teeth gleamed in the light sharp and fierce. The sort of teeth that could snap bones like they were toothpicks, his claws dug painfully into my shoulder when he raised his paw, bringing it down on my shoulder. I squirmed under his grip, but his anger was unrelenting. Blood started to trickle down into the crook of my neck pooling slowly. Ryder brought his nose down before licking at the blood that had pooled. I just watched without saying anything. When I tried to get up, though, I was shoved back down.

"Please Ryder, I don't want to fight with you right now." My voice breaking. I was done, so god damn done. I give up, I know he can't kill me but, in this moment, when my world just took a massive blow and was spinning out of control, I didn't really care if he did kill me. I not only have put two Packs in danger because of my existence, I put Lily at risk. I also find out Zoe and Marcus, or should I call him Dad, have been lying to me for years. My life was just thrown a curveball, and I didn't know how to react, how to deal with everything. Everything was falling apart, Hunters were after me, Ryder was out for blood. And I was falling apart. I didn't have the energy or willpower to argue right now.

"I fucking warned you Aria, and you disobeyed me anyway." Ryder's anger bubbling into his words as they boomed in my head. I flinched at the venom in them. Rolling to my side, I went to get up but only managed to scoot closer to the bed, propping my back against the leg I was able to sit up. Ryder watched me, his eyes burning with anger threatening to set me on fire. Tears brimmed in my eyes; I could feel them burn, as I tried to focus my vision back on Ryder but could only see my tears bubbling up before spilling over onto my cheeks. I squeezed them shut tightly and breathed out my mouth, trying to stop the feeling I was starting to feel flood me and drown me entirely.

"Just do it." My voice came out firm but soft. I really could use the sleep right now, he just needed to get it over with. I would do anything right now to be taken out of my own mind, sleep suddenly looked promising. I could feel Ryder's breath on my neck, and I squeezed my eyes tighter waiting for the pain of his savage bite, only it didn't come. I waited for it, braced myself for it, but no pain came. Instead I felt hands rub along my shoulders and up my neck. Opening my eyes, Reid was staring back at me completely naked, kneeling next to me. I threw my arms around him, making him stumble backwards, his arms wrapped firmly around me, holding me tight while I just cried into his chest. I felt his hand move into my hair, and he kissed my forehead.

"What happened, my love? I've got you now." His voice was soothing, and I squeezed tighter.

Reid felt warm against my cold skin, making me shiver, I inhaled deeply, taking comfort in his familiar intoxicating scent. I always felt safe with him, Reid was my safe place, so is Ryder. I loved them both, but right now, all I wanted is Reid. Reid's hands moved up and down my arms slowly, I could tell he was waiting for me to tell him what's wrong. I just didn't want to think about it right now, let alone tell anyone. Sitting up, I got an overwhelming sense of vertigo, maybe it was from laying down so long and my sudden movement to get up, but the entire room felt like it shifted as I stood up and I found myself staggering to the bed. Reid watched my clumsy movement's as I tried to get into bed.

"Have you taken something or been drinking?" he asked. He must be able to feel what I felt when I stood up.

"No, David gave me a drink, but that was it" Reid's growl tore through the room, as his hands clenched at hearing me mention Alpha David's name. His whole body began to tremble, Reid pinched the bridge of his nose and closed his eyes, I could feel through the bond he was trying to calm himself and Ryder down. Moving to the edge of the bed, I tried to stand, but the same sensation rolled over me, I gripped onto the nightstand, next to the bed to balance myself. When suddenly, a new sensation took over a violent need to throw up. I took off for the bathroom, kicking the door shut behind me. I barely made it to the toilet before I threw up the entire contents of my stomach. Reid burst through the door, just as I flushed. I stood up feeling a little better. Walking over, I rinsed my mouth and grabbed my toothbrush. Reid turned the shower on and hopped in.

"You okay? Do you think David put something in your drink?"

"No, he was drinking from the same bottle. I think I have just had too many emotions for one night," I mind linked back, seeing as I couldn't speak clearly with a mouthful of toothpaste. Reid growled lowly. When I finished, I gargled mouthwash and went to walk out, when Reid's arm reached out of the shower and pulled me in.

"You have blood on you, strip." I took my now wet clothes off, Reid helping me take my shirt off that was acting like a second skin. Chucking them out of the shower and onto the floor. Reid pulled me under the water, I rested my head on his shoulder, the shower steaming up, all I could smell was my own blood as it washed down the drain. Ryder's claws must have dug into my shoulder deeper than I thought, not that I could tell now though seeing as it already healed. Reid moved the loofah and soap over my skin, softly washing all the blood off before continuing to wash me entirely, his fingers moving through my hair as he washed it, combing it out with his fingers.

When he was done, I stood back, rinsing it off. When I opened my eyes, Reid was watching me, a look in his eyes that I was now familiar with, Lust. Moving closer, I kissed him, running my tongue across his bottom lip. My hand reaching down, I grasped his cock and squeezed, his eye's fluttered shut, and he groaned. Then I let go and stepped out of the shower. Reid growled, annoyed at me teasing him. I grabbed a towel and wrapped it around myself and walked back into the room.

I just finished drying myself and was rummaging through Reid's shirt drawer trying to find a shirt to wear, when I felt his arms wrap around my waist picking me up, he then dumped me on the bed.

I chuckled at his behaviour, I could tell Ryder was just below the surface, his eye's flickering. Reid stood at the end of the bed looking down at me. I squirmed under his intense gaze. When I couldn't handle him staring at me anymore, I lifted my knees and opened my legs slightly, Reid smirked and his eyes darkened, gripping my ankles.

I was yanked to the bottom of the bed, getting on his knees at the end of the bed, he pushed my legs further apart, I felt him kiss the inside of my thigh just next to my glistening wet cunt, he sucked on the skin and bit down, the stinging from his bite lingered but was soon forgotten when his hot tongue moved to my clit. Reid pushed my legs harder down into the bed so I couldn't move as he devoured me. My moans filling the room, his tongue swirled around the sensitive bundle of nerves. My legs began to shake, and my back arched as he sucked and licked relentlessly, making my stomach tighten and my skin heat up. Reaching down, I ran my fingers through his hair.

"Don't stop." My voice was airy, Reid sped up his movements, sitting on the edge, I spilled over, seeing stars as I came hard, Reid licking up my juices as they spilled out of me, making me slump back down on the bed while I came down from high.

Pulling me down the bed, I was exhausted, Reid pushed my knees back apart and into my chest before ramming his cock between my lips, my eyes opening at the feeling of his hard cock thrusting in deeply and hard. Moving my hips as he pounded into me, his cock hitting my cervix as he pounded hard and fast, my body reacting to his harsh movements, screaming out as waves of pleasure rolled over me again and again. Letting go of my legs, they fall to the sides suddenly feeling like they were made of jelly, Reid's mouth moving to my nipple as he sucked and bit down before soothing his bite with his tongue. I could tell he was close, gripping his hair, I pulled his face to mine, kissing him. I could feel his tongue playing with mine, fighting for dominance. When I felt his hot seed spill into me, his movements became jerky as he came inside me.

Chapter 34

Aria's POV

THE NEXT MORNING, I woke refreshed. I had the best sleep I have ever had. Rolling over and stretching, I notice Reid's side of the bed is empty. Sitting up, I looked around and listened, but he wasn't in the room or bathroom. Getting out of bed, I grab a pair of tights and a singlet, before walking downstairs. I run into Wendy as I enter the rec room.

"Where is Reid?"

She looked around nervously.

"Where is Reid?" I repeated using my Alpha Voice. I could tell she has been told to hide whatever is going on from me. Wendy tried to fight my command off, I have to give it to her. She lasted longer than Zane. Sweat started to form on her face, her skin losing colour as she fought against it. The pain becoming too much she blurted it out like rapid fire. "They went to see David, to see what he put in your drink because you have slept for over twenty-four hours" I stepped back flabbergasted. Twenty-four hours, I have been asleep for thirty-six hours. Grabbing my phone, I dialled Reid's number, he answered after the second ring.

"You're awake?"

"Come home, David didn't put anything in my drink. I told you this."

"Then why were you asleep so long?"

"Well, I don't know; I have no idea, I was just tired." Reid seemed to think for a second before I could feel through the bond, he was getting closer to me.

"Where are you?"

"We didn't even make it down the street when you rang." I hung up knowing he would be here any second, I walked out the front just as his car pulled up. Zane was first out followed by Reid. He walked over to me and wrapped an arm around me, kissing my temple.

"Sleeping beauty awakes." He chuckled. "You had me starting to worry, and Mavis is stuck in surgery at the hospital so couldn't come until tonight," he told me I just nodded my head.

"Well, I am starving; I am going to look for something to eat," I told him, turning my back on him.

I walked into the kitchen where Wendy and Christine were with the girls. They were eating happily and drawing. I walked over and kissed Lily's head, before helping myself to the bacon that was on the bench piled up for everyone. Taking a bite of it, I swallowed quickly, not wanting Wendy to think I didn't like her cooking. The food tasted bland, like eating paper. I struggled to swallow it down. Reid, feeling my reaction through the bond, walked over and bit off what was left on my fork. I heard his voice through the link. "What? It tastes fine." Him being so close overwhelmed my senses. I could feel and hear his blood moving through his veins. I was starving; I thought I needed food. What I actually needed was blood, and I was absolutely ravenous.

I didn't realise how hungry I was until I could suddenly hear every single person's blood pumping around me, hear the soft thrum of their heartbeats calling out to me teasing me. I growled completely lost, I could only focus on the sounds of everyone's heartbeats calling me, enticing me to rip their throats out and feed. The chatter in the room stopped, creating a deafening silence as everyone's eyes went to me. I could taste my own blood running out of my mouth and down my chin, as my teeth protruded going through my bottom lip. I was crazed with bloodlust, I tried to shake it off, but everyone's startled emotions made their delightful scents stronger. Fear sweetened their blood as it ran through their veins. I turned towards them when suddenly strong arms wrapped around my own. I threw them off like they were nothing. Mitch and Zane jumped to their feet, taking a protective stance in front of their mates and the girls. Lily and Amber started crying, they cowered behind Christine, who shoved them behind her as soon my growl ripped through the room, hunger taking over completely.

Then I smelt it, fresh blood. I turned in the direction of it. Reid's hand bleeding dripping onto the tiles, I was in a trance as I watched it drip onto the ground, so bright so tasty, my mouth watered, I could hear shuffling behind me, but I didn't care, all I could focus on was the blood calling to me. Reid moved closer.

"Focus on me, Hun." I glanced up to him, my eyes catching his worried one's, he was scared of me. It shocked me, I turned when I heard the doors leading outside open, I saw Lily run outside with everyone else. That's when I realised I was about to attack them, hurt my family. Holding my breath, I ran from the room. I could feel Reid catching up behind me as I took off up the stairs. I nearly hurt them, even Reid was scared of me. Now that I was holding my breath, I could feel his fear coming through the bond. He was scared, I was going to hurt them, not himself but everyone else in the room. He was scared for them. Closing the door, Reid's hand reached out, stopping it from shutting.

I looked at him, then at his hand, which was still covered in dry blood. Noticing my eyes drop to his hand, he walked into the bathroom and washed his hands with soap and came back out.

"What's going on with you?" he asked sitting beside me on the bed, he didn't sound angry, more worried.

"I don't know. I need to speak to my father he might know," I told him.

"Your father? He is dead, Ari."

"No, he isn't, David said he is alive." Reid turned me, so I was looking at him. His face showed confusion, I hadn't told him yet that my father was still alive.

"Marcus, my friend from the diner, is actually my father. I found out the other day. Alpha David, he recognised him. I don't know how? They look nothing alike, but I am assuming there is a reasonable explanation as to why" Reid thought for a second before speaking.

"Glamour, he used his glamour so you couldn't recognise him maybe?"

"Glamour?" I asked, my eyebrows raising slightly, I have no idea what that is, but Reid seemed to.

"Glamour - when they use a sort of mind compulsion to get people to do what they want or see certain things." I nodded in understanding, I wondered if I could do that.

"You do it every time you use your Alpha voice, I have noticed it the last few times, the more blood you drink, the stronger it gets," he stated. I just thought my Alpha Voice was stronger because of the Lycan blood running through my veins, not some Vampire voodoo. Reid mentioning blood brought my hunger back, Why was I suddenly craving blood so much?

"We will figure that out, but for now you need to feed, so you don't kill everyone." I usually hated when he invaded my thoughts listening to what I was thinking but it didn't seem to bother me as much at this moment. I looked at Reid, suddenly feeling scared, I won't be able to control my hunger once I start feeding, but he didn't hold the same fear for himself. I could feel through the bond that he knew he could stop me. I don't know what he thought could stop me, seeing as I just threw him across the kitchen earlier. He chuckled eavesdropping in my mind again.

"I have my ways, now here," He turned slightly, giving me a good view of his neck. The sight was too enticing, and I lurched forward, my teeth sinking into his neck. The craze coming back, as I tasted his blood that was filling my mouth. Reid didn't even flinch when I bit down again. I could feel panic start creeping into me as I fed longer than usual. I couldn't pull away, my claws extended digging into his shoulder, Reid didn't react like I would have expected. A normal person would have tried to fight me off, hc didn't. He calmly just put his fingers through my hair.

"Focus Aria, you don't want to kill me." But I couldn't focus on anything but his blood, his hand moved between us grabbing onto my breast rubbing his thumb over my nipple through the thin singlet, I moaned, my attention being pulled to his thumb as my nipple hardened under his touch. "Focus Aria," I did, my focus going to his fingers as he rolled my nipple between them. My claws retracted, and my grip lessened. Pulling my face back, I watched as his wound on his neck closed. His other arm wrapped around my waist, pulling me onto his lap, so I was straddling him. Reid kissed me, and I could feel him smiling against my lips. "I told you I have my ways." He whispered against my lips. I kissed him back, shoving him backwards on the bed, so I hovered over the top of him. I ripped my singlet off and clawed at his shirt, lifting it off over his head. I started kissing his neck, and up to his chin, Reid grabbed my hips, rubbing his erection into me through his pants. I moaned at the friction. Moving off him, I started pulling on his belt, undoing his pants and getting rid of them quickly.

I wanted him, all of him. The sight of his cock as it sprang free from his pants made me gulp, moving between his legs, I grabbed it. Kissing the knob before my lips parted and I took him in my mouth, I swirled my tongue around his knob, Reid's hand going to my hair as he grabbed a handful, forcing more of him into my mouth until I felt him hit the back of my throat. I started bobbing my head running my tongue along the smooth skin of his cock as I sucked on it, Reid's grip on my hair becoming tighter as he started pounding into my mouth making my eyes water. I let him fuck my mouth until he stopped and went to sit up, I shoved him back down, climbing on top of him, I positioned his cock at my entrance and slowly sat down letting his cock fill me completely. Reid's fingers digging into my hips as I started moving, my nails digging into his chest as he started to meet my movements with hard thrusts, as he slammed me down onto his hard cock.

I moaned out, my head going back as I rode him, one of his hands reached up squeezing my boob harshly, it hurt but was enough to send me over the edge as I came, my walls tightening around him, I felt him cum with me as I collapsed onto his chest. We lay there for a few minutes catching our breath before I rolled over his flaccid cock, leaving my body, I rolled on to my back next to him.

$$Chapter\ 35$$

Aria's POV

ROLLING TO MY SIDE. "I need to find out if he really is my father," I said as I was getting up. Reid rolled to face me. "Fine but I am coming with you." I looked over my shoulder at him and nodded. He jumped out of bed and started chucking a pair of jeans on. I grabbed my jeans and a bra before finding a white singlet. When I couldn't find a jumper, I grabbed one of Reid's flannelette shirts and rolled the sleeves to my elbows, I could smell the lingering scent of his aftershave on it. Once I was done, I grabbed my runners and followed after Reid, who was waiting by the door for me in his usual jeans and black shirt combo.

Reid grabbed his keys off the hallway table and walked out to his car, I hopped in the passenger seat. I thought it was strange Zane wasn't coming. He usually follows Reid everywhere like a shadow.

"You scared them, Ari, I told him he could wait here." I looked out the window feeling guilty. I was turning into a monster, I just hoped Marcus had some idea why.

"We'll figure it out," Reid told me, grabbing my hand before starting the car. We drove to the diner, when the car slowed, I wasn't sure if I wanted to go in anymore. I suddenly felt different about wanting to meet my father if that is indeed who he is. Reid pulled over to the curb and got out. I followed suit and got out before walking past him and into the diner. When I entered the bell sounded signalling our entrance. Zoe walked out to see who had stepped in, her face breaking into a smile upon seeing me. She walked over to me and wrapped her arms around me.

After a few seconds, I wrapped mine around her, she pulled me at arms lengths and looked behind me to Reid than the door.

"Lily didn't come?" she asked. I could tell she really hoped I had Lily with me.

"No, we had an incident, Aria is best away from her now," Reid answered. Zoe looked at me, but I just shook my head.

"She is fine, Zoe; I need to speak to my father." Zoe glanced between Reid and I.

"Aria, your father is dead." she answered.

"No, Alpha David said he saw him, recognised him. Where is Marcus?" Zoe glanced to the back where the kitchens are. I walked past her, just as Marcus stepped out. Only it wasn't Marcus, it was my father. How I hadn't recognised him after Zoe showed me a photo of him had me baffled, but it was definitely him in the flesh. Recognition shone in his eyes; he knew I knew.

"I can explain Ari," he said, looking between Zoe and I. Zoe didn't look shocked to see him. Therefore, she knew all along who he was and helped keep it a secret. Zoe moved past him.

"Shall I put the kettle on?" It wasn't really a question, more a statement as she darted behind the counter. I moved off to a booth and sat down.

Reid sitting beside me, my father sat across from me. His hair was the same colour as mine, even the eye colour, I could make out through his contacts were flaming orange and yellow. His skin was tanned, he was wider than before he was bulkier and no longer looked like a gay hippy man, even his clothes were different, no tie-dyed shirt just a remarkably simple white shirt and black slacks.

"Does he look any different to you?" I asked Reid.

"No, is he supposed to?" he asked. My father glanced between the pair of us, before putting his hand out to Reid. "I'm Abel, nice to see you have calmed some, Reid" Reid shook his hand. Abel, that was my father's name? I thought it would sound older than it is. I stared at the man, not sure what I felt besides confusion. "It's called a glamour; you should be able to do it." He spoke to me. His voice was different deeper, and he had a weird accent I couldn't place. It sounded old and not of this world.

"I know what it is ,Reid explained it to me. What I don't understand is why?"

"Why I hid myself from you?" he asked.

"Yes, and Mum. For years she spent grieving your loss, and you were here all along. How could you do that to her? Do that to me?" my voice breaking on the last word, I reigned in my emotions. I needed to hear this, hear the excuse he comes up with, not that that will change my anger right now from being lied to.

"I didn't have a choice, Aria. When the Hunters found out about me, they hunted me for weeks, you and your mother hid away. I couldn't let them find out about you. Your grandfather and I set up a trap hoping to let them think I was dead, only it backfired, and it actually got your grandfather killed. I pretended to be dead, waited, and when the coast was clear, I left the City. It was safer that way, they would know about your existence if I stayed, they would have found out and killed your mother and done only goddess knows what with you,"

"That doesn't explain why you didn't tell me when you came back."

"I didn't want to interrupt your life. I saw you had a sister and were raising her like your own. If I told you, it would have put both of you in danger, so Zoe and I decided to keep it from you, you're the only one that couldn't see me for me. I only glamoured you, that's why I look the same to Reid." I nodded in understanding, but that didn't make me feel any better knowing he was here all along just watching in the shadows.

"After David saw me, I knew it was a matter of time before he blurted it out."

"Yes, I went to see him after Hunters were spotted in the city. He has connections with them. David told them what I am," Panic took over my father's face as he looked around quickly as if we were being followed, Reid started shaking with anger, fur sprouting across his arms and his canines protruded. I forgot I hadn't told him about David being the one to alert the Hunters to my existence.

I placed my hand over his that was digging into the table because his claws were extended.

My father sat back and relaxed when he saw no one watching. Reid slowly calmed down, my thumb rubbing circles on the back of his hand. Zoe came over and placed a coffee in front of us. The smell instantly hit my nose and made me gag, jumping up Reid slid out, letting me out. I ran into the bathroom and threw up. My throat was burning, and my eyes watered. I threw up blood everywhere. Zoe walked in to check on me.

"Are you alright, dear?" I stood up and flushed the toilet before walking out and rinsing my mouth at the sink. What the hell is wrong with me?

"Yep, I'm fine," I said, trying to catch my breath. "This is why I needed to speak to my father." Zoe nodded and handed me the tea towel from her apron to dry my face. Walking back out, I made my way to my seat, holding my breath, so the strong smell of coffee didn't make me want to be sick again.

Reid was talking to my father, but I didn't catch what they were talking about when I sat down.

"Your mother used to do that, she even craved blood. The hormones would make her crazed with bloodlust." I looked at my father confused. My mother was a werewolf, werewolves don't crave blood.

"Reid told me how you have been sick, starving hungry and sleeping, it is the only thing that makes sense" He tilted his head to the side listening for something. "Don't you hear it?" he asked.

"Hear what?" I asked, looking between him and Reid, who was also listening intently.

Reid's face lit up when he heard the mystery noise, while I just stared at them both, Reid's face broke into a grin, and his eyes sparkled brightly.

"You're pregnant." He whispered.

Chapter 36

Aria's POV

"ISN'T THIS GREAT? WE are gonna have a baby," said Reid, kissing the side of my face. I was in shock. This was not the sort of news I was going to be excited about. Zoe wiped tears from her eyes as she excitedly congratulated us. I just zoned out and put my walls up, blocking Reid from invading my mind and my tumultuous thoughts. I didn't want kids; I have been raising a kid since I was a kid myself. This was far from anything I wanted. I didn't want a baby, to bring a baby into this chaotic world, let alone right now when we were about to go to war. A war I also didn't want a part of. This was far from any future plan; I had come up with in my head. The worst part is the excitement on Reid's face, how do I break it to him, that there won't be any baby?

I watched as my newly found father and my mate spoke excitedly about kids and potential baby names. Zoe, noticing my silence, placed a hand on my shoulder and looked down at me, her eyes knowing. Zoe knew I didn't want kids, and after seeing everyone's excitement, how do I tell them I don't want to be a mother. Zoe nodded her head in the direction of the kitchen, getting up I followed after her.

"That's some big news," she stated. While making up orders, I leant on the bench next to her. Keeping my voice low so Reid and my father didn't overhear.

"I don't want this, Zoe. You know this already." She nodded in my direction, so I knew she heard what I said.

"I know the timing isn't great with everything going on, but you will come around eventually dear, Babies are a miracle."

I shook my head. This was no miracle; this was a disaster. How do I tell Reid? I looked up at the ceiling, things were going to get worse before they got better and chucking a baby in the mix is just ridiculous.

"I am not keeping it. I don't want this, Zoe. He can't make me." Zoe put the egg flip down and glanced around paranoid someone overheard my words.

"You know Reid, even Ryder won't allow that, Aria. You do anything to jeopardise this pregnancy and Reid is going to lose it. Even I know werewolf pregnancies are sacred, you will be shunned and forced to leave the Pack Aria, think of Lily."

"I am thinking of Lily. I have enough on my plate without adding more to it. I need to focus on her, focus on keeping her safe, I can't do that pregnant. Besides, it isn't a real werewolf child. It will be a Hybrid so they can think what they want, it's my body, my choice," my voice coming out louder than I would have liked. Zoe stuck her head out, looking back into the diner, I did the same. My father and Reid were both happily bonding over baby news. I felt guilty for not wanting to keep this baby, but at the end of the day, it is my choice. Reid isn't the one that has to birth it. I am.

Zoe pulled me back into the kitchen. "You know, you won't get a say in this. You're going against the Moon Goddess Aria, you do anything Reid will see it as a betrayal, shit he might even kill you himself. You don't get a say in this, you know this." I rolled my eyes; this was stupid.

"Here I was thinking since it's my body I would get some say, what about all pro-choice, women have rights these days."

"Yes, you're right but not werewolf women or Hybrids like you. You don't get that choice the Moon Goddess chooses for you."

"Well in my case she chose wrong, I want no part of this." I could hear Reid, walking over to see what I am doing. I quickly shut my mouth so he wouldn't hear what we were speaking about. Zoe seemed to get the message and remained quiet.

"You ready to leave?" I nodded my head. My father walking in behind him, stepped past Reid and embraced me in a hug. I wrapped my arms around him too, it felt good finally knowing the truth and having everything out in the open, but at the same time, I wasn't forgiving so easily that they lied to me.

"Congratulations sweetie this is awesome news, I can't believe my daughter is giving me a grandbaby," he said gripping my shoulders. It would look funny to outsiders seeing as my father looked not much older than me, I would have to remember to ask him at what age he stopped aging, and also more about my family history. My father turned to Reid, "Make sure she has plenty of blood on hand, even though her mother was a werewolf, she craved blood like crazy, sometimes even became crazed."

He nodded, taking in the information. "This is such great news," my father stated.

"If you think so," I muttered, not feeling excited in the slightest. Zoe nudged me with her elbow warningly, and Reid raised an eyebrow at my comment but didn't say anything. Instead, he grabbed my hand and led me back to the car. *Can this day get any worse?* I thought, as I sat in the passenger seat. Reid started the car and started driving back to the Pack house. I could see Reid's reflection and seen him glance at me a few times, while I just stared vacantly out the window.

"I will get Mavis to come over so she can determine how far along you are," he told me. I didn't reply. The only thing I wanted to know is how to get rid of it. I didn't say that out loud, though. Reid noticing my silence, tried to push through the link to me. I shoved him out.

"What has gotten into you, Aria?" I ignored him. "Is this about the baby? Don't worry Hun, I won't let anything happen to either of you. The Pack will keep you safe, I promise." Great, the last thing I wanted to hear. I have no intention of keeping it, and I can see this is going to cause a huge argument. I just hoped he would hear me out. Surely though he wouldn't force this on me. I wonder if Mavis would speak to me alone. I know I am meant to get patient privacy, but I also know she fears Reid and I don't know if she would go against him even for her Luna.

When we got to the Pack house, everyone was waiting out the front.

"Can we not tell anyone yet? Please," I pleaded. Reid looked at me funny, I could tell he was a little taken aback by my request.

"Fine we can wait until after Mavis has checked you over." I nodded letting out a breath. It would be harder if he told the entire Pack I was expecting.

"I am going to lay down for a bit," I told him, wanting to be left alone. I climbed out of the car. Lily came over to me, and I scooped her up. "Sorry I scared you this morning" I whispered, kissing her chubby cheeks and rubbing my nose on hers. She wrapped her arms around my neck. "Want to watch a movie in my room?" Lily nodded excitedly.

"Can we watch the one with the snowman?" she asked.

"Yes, go grab it and meet me upstairs," I placed her on the ground, and she took off inside. I made my way upstairs and turned the TV on that hung on the wall across from the bed. Lily and Amber came running in and jumped on the bed, making themselves comfortable. I placed the DVD in and pressed play before laying down with them. I got lost in the movie being the first time I had actually watched it. When the movie was nearly over, Reid stuck his head in the door waving at me. Amber had fallen asleep, and Lily looked like she wasn't far off. I climbed off the bed and made my way over to him.

"Mavis is here," he said, pulling me from the room. I followed him down to the infirmary. Mavis was waiting there in her white hospital scrubs fiddling with a machine next to the bed.

"Luna." she said excitedly coming over and kissing me on the cheek. "I will get you to lay down and lift up your shirt." Great, Reid had already told her. I walked over to the bed and laid down. She squirted a cold jelly-like substance on my stomach, and using the device in her hand moved it around, she pointed to the screen. I didn't look. But I could hear Reid trying to get me to look at the screen.

"Do you want to hear the heartbeat?" Mavis asked.

"No," I said harsher than I meant for it to come out. Reid ignored me. I could feel his eyes boring into me.

"Yes, I want to hear the heartbeat," he told Mavis. Mavis turned a dial on the ultrasound machine. I could hear the steady hum of a heartbeat. I tried to block it out, but it was now forever burned in my memory.

"You are four weeks and 3 days along. Baby should be due around another twenty weeks seeing as Hybrid pregnancies don't last as long as human ones or werewolf ones," she stated. I sat up wiping the jelly off with some paper towel. I can't believe I have been here only one month; it feels so long ago that Reid found us, and it also means I got pregnant the first time we had sex.

"Any questions?" she asked.

"Can I speak with you alone?" I asked, looking at Mavis. She looked to Alpha Reid to see if it was alright.

"You can ask any question you like, Aria. Don't be embarrassed because I am present," he stated, denying my right to privacy. Mavis turned back to me. I suddenly felt like throwing up, nerves taking over. I knew Reid was going to flip his lid when I asked my question.

"So, what did you want to know?" I started sweating, both their eyes staring at me, I felt a bead of sweat run down my neck, and my throat went dry.

"How do I?" I tried to force the words out and glanced at Reid, who was watching expectantly, waiting to hear what I wanted to know. "How do I get rid of it?" My words came out so rushed, I didn't think she heard me. My heart rate spiked. I could hear it pounding in my ears. Mavis looked nervously back at Reid who looked like he was about to explode in rage.

Mavis stood up when his claws extended, Reid trying to remain in control.

"Mavis, leave," Reid commanded, his eyes blazing. I didn't want her to go, she looked unsure as well.

"Mavis, get out now." His voice booming echoing off the walls so loud the glass windows shook.

$\mathcal{C}hapter\ 37$

Aria's POV

I WAS EXPECTING THIS. THIS was the exact reason I didn't want to say anything in front of Reid. The fire in his eyes showed his fury. Although I knew he wouldn't hurt me, I still feared what he would do next. He was pacing back and forth, I could tell he was trying not to let Ryder out, who I could tell was just below the surface waiting to pounce on me.

When he stopped, I froze holding my breath, waiting for him to speak. Only he didn't. He walked over and grabbed my hand, ripping me to my feet with so much force, I was thrown into him. I smacked into his chest. He stormed out of the room, pulling me with him. I tried to pull my hand from his iron grip, he stopped in the hallway out front of the infirmary.

"Don't," he warned as I tried yet again to free my hand. One word but the malice in it made me freeze. Pulling me towards the stairs, Wendy and Zane stepped out of the rec room to see what the commotion was that had Reid so angry.

"Everything okay, Boss?" Zane asked, glancing at me before stepping out of the way, as Reid pushed past him. I watched as he pressed on the wall next to the stairs. The wall opened up to a concrete stairwell leading underneath the house. I pulled my arm back, trying to yank it free. Wendy and Zane glanced between each other, trying to figure out what was going on. I looked around panicking trying to find an escape, but there weren't any. Reid stopped trying to pull me down the stairs, realising I wouldn't go willingly. Instead threw me over his shoulder while I struggled to get free.

"Reid, stop. Let's talk about this." He ignored my pleas. I could hear his footsteps echoing on the concrete floor as he marched down them.

Zane and Wendy looked on horrified, as I was thrown into a cell and dumped on the bed.

"Boss, what's going on?" Wendy asked, running to my side and wrapping her arm around my shoulders.

"Any of you let her out, and you will have me to deal with." They looked at me wondering what it was I had done that would earn such treatment. "Now get out." Both of them bolted from the room. I heard Wendy's voice creep into my mind.

"What did you do, Aria?" Her panicked voice quickly leaving as Reid gripped my shoulders, shaking me out of the mind-link.

"You ask them to let you out, and I will kill them. Do you understand, Aria? Their deaths will be on your hands."

"You're being irrational. You can't keep me here, what is that going to do?" Reid paced around trying to think.

"I will not have you murder my child."

"So, what your going to keep me here until I spit out this baby?"

"Yes, if I have too. After that I will let you out. You don't get to choose this; this decision isn't yours."

I cut him off. "The Moon Goddess has no right choosing my life, Reid. This is my choice. It's my body." He lost it; I was shoved into the wall, his hands on either side of my arms while his face was barely an inch off mine. Ryder's eyes coming to the surface, burning rage simmering in the eyes of his beast. His voice distorted as his growl shocked me to the core, making my hair stand on end.

"Anything happens to that baby you are carrying, I will not only end you but everyone you love." His voice was cold and emotionless. It chilled me to the bone. I knew he wasn't bluffing. Ryder wasn't like Reid, he wasn't rational. Ryder acted out of instinct and anger, any emotion setting him off. I hated to admit that I did fear him when he was like this. I knew his threats weren't empty, they were a promise. One I knew he would keep if I pushed him. My mind went to Lily. Would Ryder really kill her? Would Reid let him?

The knowing glint in his eyes showed he knew where my mind went first. Where it always goes first, Lily. Everything I have done is for her. I would never willingly put her in danger. I would give my last breath for her; she is and always will be put above my own life. Ryder, realising I understood, retreated. Reid's silver eyes came back, showing Ryder had given him control back.

Reid kissed my forehead and then stood up, walking out, closing the concrete door behind him. I ran towards it, but it clicked into place, effectively locking it before I even had a chance to try and escape. I sat back on the bed, looking around at my new living arrangements. It consisted of a bed with a rubber mattress and a steel toilet with a sink attached up the top. This was a prison cell, usually prison cells were for rogues. It was cold and damp. There weren't any windows, so I couldn't see outside and the only lighting I had was from the fluorescent light beaming brightly above me.

Deciding to lay down, I pulled the thin sheet over me. Trying to get some sort of warmth. After a while, I felt myself doze off. I wasn't sure how long I was asleep for when I was awoken by the sounds of footsteps on the stairs outside the door. I felt like it had only been a few minutes but could have been hours.

Reid opened the door, stepping in, only to close it behind him. I sat up. Reid had a pillow and some blankets in his arms, as well as some food. I watched as he placed it on the end of the bed and walked out again, not saying a single word to me. I grabbed the blanket, wrapping it around me. The food didn't tempt me in the slightest, all it did was make me crinkle my nose from the strong smell of the cheese. I usually liked grilled cheese, but now, I couldn't stand the smell of it or food in general. Laying back down, I soon forgot about the smell as I went back to sleep.

I dreamt of Lily when she was a baby, only this wasn't a good dream. A dream of David taking her away, of never seeing her again as she was ripped from my arms, screaming, crying out for me. I screamed and smacked into him trying to get him to give her back, only for him to turn around, and no baby was in his arms, fear running through me at his empty arms. I awoke covered in sweat, my heart pounding in my chest as I tried to adjust to the bright light. Only I wasn't alone, Reid was watching me. An indecipherable look on his face.

"You have been asleep for three days. I asked your father and Mavis. They said it is normal. That its because the baby is growing more rapidly, faster everyday." I mulled over his words.

I noticed my clothes were different. I was in flannelette pyjamas and had white socks on. Did I really sleep that heavily? How did I not wake up?

"I will let you upstairs to shower. You try anything, anything at all, Aria…"

"I won't." I whispered, cutting him off and looking at the open door. My throat felt dry and itchy having not used it for days apparently. Reid nodded and stood up, walking to the door. He waited for me to follow. I sat up stretching, stretching felt different. I felt different, looking down to notice the small bump at the bottom of my abdomen. That's impossible, it's been three days and I could already see a slight bump proving my pregnancy was progressing. My hand went to it, to see if it was real and it was. The bump was really there. Reid watched me carefully like he thought I was going to hurt myself. Pulling my top down, I heard him let out a breath.

"Where is everyone?"

"They are upstairs, you won't be speaking to anyone Aria."

"Can I at least see Lily?" Reid turned back to the door, holding his head high ignoring my question.

"I don't have all day, hurry up," Reid said. He held so much hatred behind his words. It saddened me that one question could turn him against me. Why did I ask Mavis in front of him? I felt stupid.

I walked over to the door, and Reid gripped my arm and pulled me to the stairs leading into the house. Once we were standing in the foyer, I mind-linked Lily.

"Where are you, Lil?"

"Ari? I'm in the yard playing, where have you been? Reid said you are having a baby," she squealed in my head excitedly. I held my head as her squeal vibrated through me like a freight train.

"Shh, Reid has let me out to shower. Come to the bedroom."

"I can't Ari. Reid said I can't see you until he says." I looked at Reid who was watching me. He could tell I was mind-linking, probably even listening into my thoughts. I tried to shove him out, but he shoved harder, forcing himself back in.

"Aria, I will only warn you once, or I will take you back to your cell." I looked back at the stairs leading back below the house. I didn't want to go back down there, it was cold and too quiet. I started walking up the stairs towards our bedroom. Walking past the infirmary and past all the bedrooms before climbing the stairs that lead to the bedroom.

Opening the door, I could barely smell Reid's scent in the room. It was only faint like he hadn't spent much time in here. He answered my thoughts.

"I have trouble sleeping knowing you are locked down there." He did sound tired. But I refused to feel sorry for him. I didn't want to be locked down there, that's on him, not me. Walking into the bathroom, I found fresh clothes sitting on the edge of the sink basin, I really needed to pee. I went to close the door, Reid forcing it open as he stepped into the bathroom. "Door stays open."

"I need to pee," I told him. He turned to glare at me.

"Door stays open," he said emphasising the word open. He turned his back on me waiting for me to go. I refused; I was not comfortable going to the toilet with him standing there. Reid, seeing me refuse, walked over to the sink basin and turned it on.

"There, better?" He said, crossing his arms over his chest. I glared at him and walked over to the toilet and quickly peed. Getting up, I stripped my clothes off, Reid watched me from the door. I could feel his eyes follow me everywhere I moved, watching me like a hawk. Turning the shower on, I stepped in. The water warming my cold skin, I braced my hands on the wall and dipped my head under the steady stream, feeling my insides warm up. I sighed and relaxed under the feel of it running down my back. Reid was still leaning against the door, just staring at me, like I was about to run off.

"If you're gonna stare, can you at least get in? I feel weird with you standing there like some creeper."

Reid cocked his head to the side, considering my words before I saw him take off his shirt. I moved over when I saw he was going to hop in. Reid took off his pants and stepped in behind me. I started washing my hair when I felt his fingers take over massaging my scalp. I leant back into him, loving the feel of his hands touching me. He pulled me under the stream of the water, rinsing it out. I turned around only to open my eyes and see he was watching me again, his face emotionless. I reached up and put my hand on his chest, running my fingers through the small amount of hair.

"Please don't make me go back down there," I begged, leaning my head on his chest. Reid placed his hand on my cheek, rubbing his thumb down my cheekbone.

"I don't trust you anymore." His words hurt, stung as if he slapped me. I looked up at him, I could feel my eyes burn as tears threatened to break me. Through the bond, I could feel that he thought I was trying to trick him, get him to drop his guard. I stood back, moving away from him, and I turned my back on him and got out, grabbing the towel that was on the basin and wrapping it around my body.

Grabbing a pair of his thick track pants, I put them on and one of his hoodies. If he was forcing me back down there, I wasn't going to freeze. Reid got dressed quickly, afraid I was going to run. I had just finished putting on some socks when he stood in front of me.

"You need to eat." I ignored him and stood up and walked towards the door. Reid wouldn't let me pass, so I waited. "You need to eat, if not for you, do it for the baby." I glared at him.

"I'm not hungry, just take me back," I said. If he didn't trust me, I didn't want to be around him.

He moved out of my way, and I opened the door and started walking down the stairs. I could hear voices coming from Lily's bedroom. Stopping, I opened her door. Lily and Amber were playing with their dolls, sitting cross-legged on the floor. "Ari!" Lily screamed, throwing herself into my arms.

I hugged her tight and inhaled her scent. She always smelt of lavender. I felt Reid's shadow fall on me as he stepped in the room. Lily froze in my arms and looked up at him. "She came in Alpha; I didn't go to her." She didn't sound scared when she explained herself, but I didn't like the fact she had to at all.

"It's okay Lily, you're not in trouble. You don't need to worry." Reid told her making her relax.

"Reid said you're going to having a baby, that I will be an aunty." She looked so excited I couldn't help but feel excited for her, finding her excitement contagious.

"I have a bump want to feel," I asked. She nodded excitedly pulling at my shirt. Her little hands touching softly on my small bump.

"Can you feel it move? Do you know if it is a boy or a girl? Where have you been?" she asked excitedly, her blue eyes shining with happy tears.

"No, I can't feel it yet. At least I don't think I can, and no I don't know what it is, and I -" I didn't know how to answer her, I can't tell her Reid has had me locked in a cell downstairs. I didn't want her to be scared. "Maybe Reid will ask Mavis if she can do a scan and we might be able to find out," I told her, looking up at Reid who was watching me. His eyes were softer. I could tell he was probing into my mind seeing my reaction to Lily's excitement.

"I can see if she can stop by tomorrow. Do you want to know?" he asked me. I thought for a second. Did I? I just can't seem to picture myself as a mother. I felt excited for Lily, but could I feel excited for myself? Was a baby such a bad thing? Reid seemed to want this, maybe I would too.

"I don't know," I answered honestly.

He nodded his head. "You can think about it while you eat" I knew that was his way of saying It was time for me to leave.

"Can we watch a movie later? You have been gone for days, where did you go?" Lily asked.

I looked at Reid. "That is enough questions, for now, I will decide later if you can watch a movie if you behave," he said. The girls looked excited and went back to playing quietly on the floor. I knew he wasn't referring to them though. He didn't mean if they behaved. He meant if I did.

Chapter 38

Aria's POV

TAKING A SEAT IN the kitchen, Reid rummaged through the pantry, making something that I knew was going to turn my stomach upside down. The smell alone of him just getting the ingredients out was enough to make me dry heave. I felt light-headed and rested my head on the cool tabletop. Reid came over.

"What's wrong?"

I didn't say anything, refusing to give him any reason to send me back to the cell. Loneliness and the quiet down there was enough to send a person crazy. I was also scared that if I did go back down there, I would sleep. What if I slept the entire time away, slept until this pregnancy was over or worse never woke up. That thought scared me, the thought of leaving Lily alone in this world without me to protect her. I didn't want to go back to the cell. My own thoughts would send me insane, and I couldn't bear being away from Lily. I needed her like I needed air. She was the piece of my life I was proud of, the only thing I would fight to the death for besides Reid, who I wasn't so sure would do the same for me, at least not anymore. Making sure to keep my walls up so he couldn't invade my thoughts and think I was just trying to defy him. I could feel him probing trying to find a way in.

"Stop blocking me out, Aria," he growled annoyed. "I have warned you and yet you still go against the warning. Are you trying to piss me off?"

"They are my thoughts; you have no right to know them. If I wanted you to know what I was thinking, I would tell you." I told him, taking deep breaths through my mouth, so I couldn't smell the revolting stench of the bacon he placed on the counter. Reid gripped my shoulders, hauling me to my feet. The room spun before tilting. I bent over throwing up bile and narrowly missing Reid's foot. Walking over holding my breath, I washed my face under the sink and rinsed my mouth, trying to bring my temperature down. My body felt like it was on fire burning up and to think he wants me to keep going through this for another twenty weeks. Grabbing a tea towel and wetting it, I walked back over to where I threw up, intending to clean it. Reid snatched the tea towel from me.

"Sit, I will clean it." He sounded furious like he thought I did it deliberately. I suddenly wished to be back in the cell, anything to stop this heat that was overtaking my senses boiling me from the inside. I sat in the chair and watched as he cleaned the floor before walking out and chucking the tea towel in the laundry. A few seconds later, Wendy walked in with a mop.

"Here Wendy, I will do it," I said, trying to take the mop from her hand.

"Sit back down, Aria, I didn't say you could move." I glared at him.

"I'm pregnant, not fucking disabled." I spat back at him, snatching the mop from Wendy's hand. I was not going to make her clean up after me. Especially something so embarrassing like vomit. When I was done, Wendy took the mop and bucket and left. She didn't say one word to me the entire time. I wonder what Reid has said to them, usually even Wendy would have pushed the limits with Reid and tried to reach out to me. Only she didn't this time. Was she mad at me too for wanting to abort this pregnancy? Was I the only one who thought this was a disaster? Maybe I had gone too far, gone against the Moon Goddess.

I sat back down, my stomach starting to settle now that it was empty. Surely, I can't be sick again after throwing up already. That thought was soon proven wrong when Reid walked over, placing the plate in front of me. He had cooked bacon and eggs, toast, and fried tomatoes. I stared at it, not wanting to be anywhere near it. I knew the consequences of eating, I could feel it already in the back of my throat, threatening to come up at any moment. I could already taste the bile coming back up. Reid grew annoyed, his fist coming down on the table next to me, making me jump. The wood creaking and cracking up the centre from the force. I was quite surprised it actually didn't break and split down the middle. Looking up, Reid was glaring at me. If looks could kill I would have been turned to ash with the way he is glaring at me, the venom in his words made my heart sink to someplace deep and dark.

"Fucking eat, or I will force-feed it to you." I didn't want to know what that entailed, so I picked up a piece of toast and tore off a bit. Chewing slowly before trying to swallow, as soon as it touched my tongue, I heaved and ran for the sink. Only just making it in time and throwing up yet again in the kitchen sink. Reid was at my side in an instant gripping my arm making sure I didn't run off.

"Is this your plan to starve the baby to death?" How could he think that? I felt like slapping him. I have no intentions of harming it. I didn't ask for this. If I could eat I would.

"No, it's the food," I choked out.

"There nothing wrong with it, you will eat whether you want to or not, one way or another Aria, so fucking choose." I shook my head, rinsing my mouth again. I could feel my anger start to bubble. How could he think I would deliberately starve myself? I know I need to eat, but food right now is something I won't be able to keep down. Then it clicked. This baby doesn't want food, it's a Hybrid and Hybrids need blood. Just thinking of the rich, soothing taste of blood made my mouth water and brought my need to feed to the forefront of my mind wrapping around my senses.

I could hear the soft beating of Reid's heart and a fast fluttering of another heartbeat. I looked around my fangs protruding painfully. Where was it coming from? No one was in the kitchen with us. I realised, it was the only thing that made sense. I knew it wasn't my own. Mine was in sync with it, feeling it pushing the blood throughout my body. This one was faster and softer, the beating not nearly as loud. I looked down at the bump. The soft thrumming was coming from inside me, the life living within me.

I looked at Reid, shocked at what I could hear. How had I not noticed it before?

"I hear it." My words coming out distorted while my bloodlust takes over, my fangs getting in the way of my tongue.

"Hear what?" I looked down and placed my hands on my stomach. Reid's eyes followed my hands, watching.

"I can hear it." I whispered. Reid figuring out what I was talking about. Placed his hand over mine. Like he could suddenly feel it, although we both knew that was a couple of weeks off yet. Zane stepped into the kitchen, before realising, he walked in on something. He froze and went to turn around, but it was too late. My senses were already overloaded, his heartbeat just adding to the pressure snapping the control I had left. I lunged at him, the sound of his heart beating becoming too much.

Grabbing him by the shoulders, I bit into the tender flesh of his neck. Zane's blood filled my mouth. I could feel my eyes change as my vision turned red as I drank greedily. Starving and rabid, I had no control, but in this moment, I didn't want control. I just wanted blood and was willing to do anything for it. Zane tried to fight me off, but I was stronger, his hands pushing and yanking more of an annoyance, a distraction but not strong enough to fight me off. Shoving him into the wall and biting down harder this time into his shoulder, I had him where I wanted him pinned to the wall with no escape. It all happened so quickly not even Reid had time to react. I could feel Reid's hand wrap around my shoulders and yank me back, forcing me to let go of Zane. My teeth ripping away taking his flesh with me. I spun around quickly to fend off Reid. Only for his intoxicating scent to hit me, his scent filling my nose, as I breathed deeply my eyes fluttering closed, a growl tearing out of me vibrating through every cell in my body.

Zane's blood was nothing compared to Reid's. I craved Reid's blood. Zane's was sweet but bitter compared to the taste of Reids. Opening my eyes, I advance on Reid. I jump at him wrapping my legs around his waist, my arms wrapping around his shoulders, as I sink my teeth into him, drinking so fast I couldn't swallow fast enough, his blood running down my chin and neck. I could feel Reid trying to pull away, fighting me off. It was only when I heard her agonised scream ring in my ears that I stopped. The sheer pain in that one scream tearing through my heart and shattering my soul. All her fear and pain flooding me through the Pack link as she screamed out for her mate. Forcing myself trying to override the need to feed, I turned to find Zane slumped on the floor next to the kitchen door. Christine clutched onto his shirt, tears staining her face as sobs wracked her entire body.

Her wailing as she clutched his shirt, trying to wake him. Wendy and Mitch ran in. Wendy's hands going to her mouth trying to hide her shock as Mitch ran to Christine pulling her out of the way before leaning down and placing his hand on his neck which wasn't healing just spilling out his life's blood onto the tile. Zane's face drained of life as his skin started to lose its colour. Reid shoved me out of the way trying to get to his best friend and Beta. Then I see Amber and Lily step into the kitchen, Ambers screams shatter me as she runs trying to get to her father, only for Christine to grab her shielding her eyes away from her father's limp body bleeding out on the floor. What have I done?

Chapter 39

Aria's POV

I WATCH IN PANIC AS they try to stem the bleeding. When Reid walks over, ripping me up by one arm and dragging me to Zane's limp body, laying on the floor drenched in blood. Christine starts screaming at me. "Get her away, she has done enough damage!"

"She can help," Reid says, throwing his Alpha voice behind his words. Christine looks at me doubtfully but can't go against her Alpha. I hold the same doubt. I caused this, how was I supposed to help? Lily looks pale, standing in the door, looking at the monster I have become. Reid, not wasting any time bites into my hand, making me flinch. I try to pull my hand back, but he just yanks me forward. What the fuck is he doing? He presses my hand to Zane's mouth, my blood running into his mouth before my hand starts healing. Reid reaches up and grabs a knife from the bench and cuts down my hand where he just bit me, I squirm as he twists the knife and my blood pours down Zane's throat. Reid lets go of my hand, and I fall backwards, trying to figure out what he was just doing.

After a few minutes, Zane starts coughing and spluttering spitting, out the blood. I watch amazed as his neck starts to heal up. Christine gasps and throws her arms around him in a stranglehold. She starts peppering his face in kisses, and I suddenly feel relief flood through me that he is alright. I stare at my hand, confused. My blood saved him. How?

Reid, noticing me staring at my hand, shook his head at me. He was livid that I had hurt one of his Pack members. I stood up and bolted from the kitchen, intending to try and escape. I couldn't remain here not if it means risking their lives or Lily's life. I yank on the front door handle, only it's locked. I go to kick it open, knowing I could shatter its wood easily when Reid's arms wrap around my waist and rip me backwards. We stumble, and I land on top of him, my back pressed to his chest, his grip unwavering. I struggle and fight to get up.

"Stop it Aria," he says as he rolls to his side and stands up, pulling me with him to my feet.

I throw my head back, and it connects with his nose, I hear it crack, knowing I just broke it and quickly hold my breath as I feel his blood dripping on my back. Reid lets go with one arm while squeezing tighter on my shoulders, so I don't escape. I hear him break his nose back into place. Why the fuck is he so much stronger than me, I just fed for fuck's sake?

"Perks of being mated to a Hybrid, our bond doesn't just link us Aria, it makes me stronger, a better Alpha." Answering the question that ran through my thoughts. Reid pulls me back towards the cells I kick out, trying to get him to drop me, but he doesn't let go. Lily runs out and sees Reid trying to drag me to the stairwell.

"What are you doing, Reid, let her go," she screams, running over smacking his leg with her tiny fists.

Reid looks down at her, his gaze softening. I hear his voice in my head. "Stop fighting, you're scaring your sister, Aria. Look at her."

"You fucking are. Now let me go." I mind linked back. Reid looked down at Lily, and I felt like punching him when he used his Alpha voice on her.

"Lily, go wait with Amber and stay away from this door." Lily tries to fight his Alpha voice, but I can tell it causes her pain within a second. She gives up and walks out. Lily has Alpha blood, but her wolf hasn't awoken yet to even put up a fight.

"You fucking arsehole, you could have hurt her," I said whipping around and smacking Reid in the side of the head. Reid grunted at the impact but just managed to get a better grip on me and throw me over his shoulder marching down the stairs before depositing me on the bed. I went to get up and run for the door when Reid spun around.

"Don't forget what Ryder told you Aria, and just for your information, I won't fucking stop him especially after what you did to Zane!" He screamed, making me freeze on the spot. Tears sprang to my eyes. Reid just glared and walked out before slamming the door shut and locking it.

I sit back on the bed, trying to figure out what my next move is, how to get myself out of this situation and fix what I have broken. I nearly killed Zane, Reid's Beta. The look on Christine's and Amber's faces I was sure would haunt me. I nearly devastated their lives and possibly destroyed Christine in the process. I knew there was no way Reid would let me out of this cell now. Looking around, I started banging on the walls, but the concrete was too thick. Moving to the door, I tried pushing on it, then tried prying it open with my fingers, but the steel was too thick, and I couldn't get a grip on the frame itself, it was pointless.

Sitting back down, I lay on the bed, looking up at the ceiling. Trying to figure out a possible way to get out of this cell when I notice a vent just above the light. I pull on the bed, hoping to loosen it from the floor, I continue to pull and push on it. It gives a little, and I know I can with some effort get the bolts to loosen completely with the repetitive motion. I continue pulling and pushing until I hear the bolts snap, I do the same with the bottom end, eventually pulling it completely from the floor.

Dragging the bed, I moved it under the light. Standing on it, I reach up and punch the vent with as much force as possible. It dents but doesn't budge. I punch it again, the little louvres separating slightly. The third time I hit, it busts open. Gripping it with my fingertips, I pull it down, letting it fall to the ground. Jumping up, I grab the sides and pull my head through the ceiling looking inside. I let myself fall back down onto the bed. The vent narrows out, and a small child would struggle to get through the gap, let alone an adult. I huff annoyed I just wasted all that time and energy for it to fail.

Pushing the bed back into the corner against the wall, I stare at the mark dragging it left on the floor and the broken vent. Reid is going to blow his lid when he comes in. I pick up the vent to try and hide under the mattress before laying down.

With nothing else to do, I decide to sleep, but before I even start to nod off, I hear footsteps on the stairs, echoing loudly through the concrete walls. My heart rate picks up as I hear him stand on the other side of the door, but not opening it.

"Zane is completely fine," he says, I hear shuffling before he sits, leaning against the steel door. I get up and move to the door and sit with my back against it. I try to pry into his mind anything to know what he is thinking before his voice interrupts me.

"I wouldn't, Aria, you might not like what you find." I stopped because of the harshness of his words. I lean my head back against the door, waiting for him to speak.

"Hunters have been caught and stopped on the borders twice since you have been locked up." I could hear the regret in his voice but decided I must have imagined it. "We aren't sure why they want you, all three killed themselves before we could interrogate them," he stated.

"So, what's that mean then?" I whispered back, knowing he could hear me.

"Means they are willing to go to extremes to hide whatever it is they need you for, David asked if he could take Lily for a few days until things settle down," I froze my blood running cold.

"You're not letting him, though right?" I desperately ask the thought of her being away from me and in his clutches horrified me.

"He has changed Aria, you have to give him a chance. I know he won't harm her; I have spoken to him a fair bit, he has been over here every day to see her. Lily wants to go," he says, shocking me even further.

"No, she stays here Reid, you can't let her go with him."

"It's no longer up to you Aria, he picks her up in two days, this is only a trial Aria. He won't be keeping her." I get up enraged. I kick the door and feel him jump before getting to his feet.

"Anything happens to her I will fucking kill you, Reid. Mate or not, I will fucking end you," I scream while punching the door wanting to get to him. "He can't fucking have her!" I scream, my heart plunging into my stomach. "I have spent years protecting her from him. Now you're going to hand her over to him."

"She wants to go Aria; he is her father, and I have his word he won't harm her."

"His fucking word, that's what you're gauging his intentions off of?"

"No, Aria like I said he has been here every day while you have been in this cell. I think we can trust him, Aria."

"Clearly, you're fucking forgetting we are in this mess with the Hunters because of him," I spat punching the door, my fist leaving a dent.

"I haven't forgotten, but this isn't your choice anymore, Aria. When you realise my word is law maybe I will let you out," he said before I hear him stomp up the stairs. Two days, I have two days to try and get out of this godforsaken cell to stop him from handing her over. What the fuck is he thinking, to let her go with him, I don't care if she wants to, she is a child. She doesn't understand she is putting her life at risk. I can't picture David changing enough in such a short time span where I would feel comfortable leaving her with him for any amount of time.

Chapter 40

Aria's POV

I PACE AROUND IN THE basement, my mind reeling, anger consuming every cell in my body. My skin warming, getting hotter and hotter as my rage reaches boiling point. My claws extend, ripping my nails from my fingers painfully. My fangs push through my gums slowly tearing until they a through. I can taste the metallic of my own blood filling my mouth. I was losing control, a control I never really realised I never had control of in the first place. My entire body felt heightened, my senses overloaded. The light hanging from the ceiling becoming unbearable as it burned my eyes. I jump up trying to grab the bulb. Only instead of grabbing the bulb, I rip the entire light fixture from the roof.

The metal hitting the concrete floor clanging loudly. The cell was plunged into darkness, only it wasn't dark, my eyes adjusting to the change of light instantly, and I could see everything clearly as if it were still filled with light. Well, this was certainly new. I could always see in the dark, but this was completely different. Looking around, I suddenly become aware of every noise. I am also able to hear above me for the first time since coming down here. I can hear Wendy talking in the rec room, telling the girls to get ready for their baths.

Hear Christine and Zane, who were obviously busy making up for his near-death experience in a very sexual way. I wonder if they can hear Reid and me. I shake the thought away, not needing anymore desires other than getting out of this room right now. I listen and can hear Lily and Amber running up the stairs, and I hear Reid's office door click shut. I can hear every person in this huge house, my hearing zooming in and out listening intently.

Walking over to the door, I examine the hinges. They are pretty embedded only just sticking out slightly past the frame. The door handle, I know has five deadbolts that shoot into the wall bracing it, so I know there is no way to bust the door open from that side. But on the other side, I might be able to break it and open it just enough to squeeze through. Looking at the hinges, I kick one. The concrete cracks and I realise not only my senses are better, but I am a lot stronger. I wonder if that is why Reid is so much stronger now, he said it himself that being mated to me has its Hybrid perks, but this seems different. I also noticed Reid's Alpha voice is stronger now. The angrier he gets, the stronger he gets. Looking at the area where the hinges are. I kick it again; a chunk of concrete cracks, and I know it won't take me long to break them.

I continue to kick it until I hear both hinges break off the concrete and fall on the ground on the other side of the door. I freeze and listen. I hear Reid's office door open, and I hold my breath. Feeling through the bond, I can tell he heard something but is unsure of what it was. I feel him try and push into my mind, and I let him. Not wanting him to become suspicious of what I am doing. His voice popping into my mind.

"What are you doing, Aria?"

"Still rotting in the cell, like you want," I answer back sarcastically.

"You know I don't want that. You brought this on yourself, Aria."

"Last I checked you locked me in here, so that's on you, not me. You could always let me out." I move and shove the door slightly. The deadbolts on the other end bending but not breaking. I squeeze through the gap, the concrete scratching my flesh.

"I never wanted this, Aria. What did you expect me to do when you wanted to abort our child?"

"Respect my decision, Reid, instead you took my choice from me, and now it's too late," I reply while creeping up the steps toward the door leading into the house.

"You will come to see this is the right choice. I don't understand how you would want to destroy a piece of us."

"I don't want to argue, Reid. What's done is done," I state listening to hear if anyone is on the other side of the door. Which I find hard with Reid in my head because I am trying to answer him and not alert him to my escape as well as not think of what it is, I am doing. When I know the coast is clear, I open it slightly and pop my head out. I can hear the girls playing in Amber's room.

"Well make me understand then. I want to know why you don't want to be a mother when you're a great one to Lily."

"That's exactly the reason, Reid. I was forced to raise a child when I was a child. I have never once in my life done anything for myself other than raise a kid that wasn't even mine. I was completely alone, raising a baby. I put my life aside for her. I lost every part of myself I liked, as I was suddenly plunged into exhaustion, diaper changes and bottle feeds. While most thirteen-year-old were out hanging with friends and doing normal things, I was stuck raising a baby. It may seem selfish to you, but I don't want to raise another baby, have all that responsibility thrust onto me again. It's a baby, Reid. Something I will have to raise and keep alive and throw my life away for yet again." I hadn't realised I had stopped on the stairs until I stopped answering. Shit, I lost focus. I quickly moved up the steps and into the closet on the first level.

Just in time as I hear Christine and Zane walk past. Zane sounds like his normal self; you wouldn't even think he was knocking on death's door a few hours ago. I hear him stop and sniff the air.

"You smell that?" he asks Christine. "I swear I just caught Aria's scent."

"She is in the cells, you must have imagined it," Christine says. I hear them keep walking. Letting out a breath. Reid's voice popping in my head again.

"You won't be alone this time, Aria. You have a family now, you have me." I tried to focus on my task, but his words were bothering me. I could also feel his sadness through the bond seeping into me. I wiped a tear from my cheek and opened the door. I made my way to Amber's door; I could hear Lily playing behind the door.

"Aria what are you doing?" Crap, I must have let my guard down. I could feel him probing then realisation hit him, and I heard the office door swing open down the corridor. I looked in the direction that he would come down, Lily threw the door open and looked at me.

"Aria?" She looked shocked to see me. I went to grab her and run when I suddenly heard Zane behind me.

"Ari, you don't want to hurt her." I looked at him confused. I would never hurt Lily intentionally. Lily squealed loudly, and I looked at her. My claws were digging into her flesh. I quickly released her shocked, my hands going to my mouth, only to cut my own face. What the fuck was happening? Reid approached me like he was trying to cage a wild animal.

"Aria, focus on me." I thought it was strange he would say that. I took a step towards him. Panic taking over, my breathing became rapid. I could hear someone growling. I turn sharply to see who it is. Then I realise the growling is coming from me. Reid steps closer and my eyes flick to his. I see the concern in them and anger. I know something has gone wrong, everyone's body language proving my assumptions. The hallway tense and no one's eyes leaving me, no one moving. Goosebumps raise on my arms. I know if I move wrong, Zane and Reid are going to jump me.

My instincts for some reason were all over the place and completely out of control.

"It's the hormones Aria, you need to fight it." I try to force my claws to retract, but they don't. My body feels foreign to me like I am just an observer of its actions. Reid moves closer, and I step towards him, he holds his hands out, and I run at him. I know if I snap, he will be the only one to be able to hold me. I grab him around the sides he grunts when my body comes in contact with his. Then my hands feel warm and wet. I look down, and my claws are embedded in his sides. I hold my breath knowing if I catch a whiff of his scent, I will be gone, all control lost and start hunting them.

I go to step back away from him, but he holds me tight against him. "I'm fine, it's already healing." I feel tears burn my eyes. Reid's hands rubbing my back soothingly.

"They need to leave," I say through clenched teeth. The memory of Reid's blood, consuming my senses. I hear everyone quickly go after Reid nods to them to get out of here.

"Zane is going to take Lily to the Black Moon Pack." I nod, now realising she might actually be safer there then with me right now. We stayed frozen in the hall, my head on his chest, his hands rubbing my back softly but his grip tight. Reid moves his hand under my shirt, his hand coming in contact with my skin. Sparks ignite on my skin. I focus on the feel of them and feel him through the bond.

I can feel his worry, but I also feel that he doesn't fear me even when I'm like this. Even uncontrollable, he still loves me. Reid feels me digging through his mind but doesn't stop me. I feel how much he wants me and this baby, how much he loves his Pack and Lily. I look up at him, his gaze steady watching me.

"You're not alone anymore, you never will be with me by your side," he whispers before kissing my head. My body relaxing in his hold, and I feel his arms loosen.

"Come on, let's go upstairs. I am assuming you broke the cell door." I nod, but don't move. Reid tugs on my waist. "Come on."

"What about the others?" I ask, panicked. Maybe I really should have remained in the cell.

"They won't be coming back tonight. You don't have to worry. Mitch and Wendy have a holiday house a little away from here. Everyone will stay there."

"Lily?" I hate the thought of her being away from everyone, especially me.

"She will be fine; David won't let anything happen to her."

We had walked up the stairs, and I opened the door, how I missed our bed. I walked over to it and laid down rubbing my hands on the soft duvet.

Chapter 41

Aria's POV

*R*EID WALKS OVER TO me, leaning down he presses his entire body onto mine before kissing me gently. I answer his kiss, kissing him hungrily as the need to takes over. Reid, feeling my arousal through the bond, presses himself into me. I can feel the bulge in his pants. I rub myself against him, wanting the friction. I feel Reid chuckle against my lips, his hands going to mine, lifting them above my head. He holds them down with one of his, his other hand going to my leg as he wraps it around his waist.

I moan into his mouth, his tongue playing with mine, fighting for dominance and I don't fight back, loving the feel of him touching me. I grind my hips upwards. Reid groans, his lips going to my neck and his canines brushing my skin, before moving lower. He lets go of my hands and lifts my shirt off over my head before trapping them again above my head with his hand. I feel his teeth graze my nipple as he sucks it into his mouth, tugging on it with his teeth. My senses are fighting for control. Reid senses that and grips my hands tighter. "Fight it, give me control." I fight the urges and remain still.

Reid continues his assault on my nipples, sucking and biting. My body becoming impatient with need. I grind myself against him, needing the friction, needing him to touch me. Reid's hands go to my thighs as he lets go of my hands, my fingers going instantly to his hair, as I rub my fingers through it. I feel him shiver, his lips moving lower, stopping at my hip. He grips the waistband of my pants and yanks them off before reaching for my panties which are now soaked in my juices. I feel him kiss my knee as he slides them down. Reid suddenly moves his face between my legs, and without warning, I feel his hot tongue on me, parting my lips before plunging inside me, hungrily. I moan at the sudden contact, my back arching off the bed. My hands gripping his hair, wanting to tug him away, but Reid just pulls my thighs further apart, his tongue swirling around my clit before sucking it into his mouth.

I moan, my juices spilling onto my thighs and Reid's mouth as he devours me. My body reaching its peak, on the verge of exploding when I feel my stomach clench. Reid sucks my little button in his mouth hard and I am shoved completely over the edge. My legs shaking, trying to close around his head, but he holds them wide forcing them to rest on the mattress. His tongue not stopping as he licks up my juices.

I moan as I come down from my orgasm, Reid moves up my body, and I clutch at his pants. Needing him inside me, I undo his belt buckle and Reid using one hand, he slides them down his cock springing free, I feel it against my thigh. Using his legs, he kicks his pants off and onto the floor. I reach for his cock grasping it with my hand, I feel it twitch at the contact. Reid's lips finding mine. His tongue playing with mine as I move my hand up and down his shaft. Reid groans before thrusting into my hand, his lips not leaving mine. I move my hand lower, cupping his balls, I tug on them squeezing softly. Reid's lips go to my mark sucking on it, my legs wrap around his waist, pulling him to me. My hands go to his face as I kiss him hungrily. Reid positioned himself at my entrance and rams in making me cry out at the sudden intrusion. Reid finds his rhythm as he slams into me, His hands gripping mine above my head pushing them into the mattress, as he thrusts into me harder, making me moan out as his cock fills me to the brim. I meet his thrusts, moving my hips in time with them. My orgasm building up the faster he moves, slamming his cock into me relentlessly as he chases his own release. His thrusts becoming erratic, and I know he is close. I reach between us and grab his balls, squeezing them. I hear him groan, and I am sent over the edge, my pussy clenching tightly around his cock and Reid finds his own release, his warm seed spilling into me as I milk his cock coming down from my own orgasm.

Reid collapses beside me, his now flaccid cock leaving my body. We both lay there breathless, coming down from the high. I roll to my side, facing him when he pulls me on top of him. I rest my head on his chest, loving the warmth of his skin. Reid's fingertips running down my back to my waist and up again. I prop my head on my hands that are lying flat on his chest and watch him. His eyes not leaving mine as his fingers keep tickling my back. Reid lifts his head and kisses my nose, before rolling so he is now between my legs, holding himself up with his arms on either side of my face.

I watch him, he moves my hair from my face where it was sticking due to perspiration. I lean up to kiss him, and he moves his head back, a smile on his lips teasing. Reid presses his lips softly to mine.

"I love you," he says softly. I wrap my arms around his waist.

"I love you too." Reid's face moving closer to mine as he kisses me gently. I wrap my legs around his waist, and he chuckles.

"Come on, let's have a shower then you need to feed," he says, kissing my head. He goes to get up, and I wrap my legs tighter around his waist. He laughs but then sits up, bringing me with him, so I am now straddling him. Realising I am not letting go he stands up, his hand slapping my arse before he squeezes it, I can feel his growing erection pressing against the inside of my leg. I rub myself on it. Reid squeezes my arse but keeps walking into the bathroom, he turns the shower on.

My lips going to his neck where my mark is. He groans and grips my hips, rubbing his cock on my clit. I feel the water hit my back before I feel the cold tiles on my back, making me squeal and jump at the coldness. Reid chuckles. I feel it rumble in his chest. Before his hands push me lower, and he thrusts inside me again. My head going back to rest on the tile, Reid's mouth moving to my neck and collarbone nipping, and sucking on my skin. I grip his shoulders, moving my hips against his. I pull his hair, pulling his head back, his face getting wet under the water before I smash my lips into his, desire coursing through every cell of my body, my fluids coating his cock as he thrusts harder and faster, his grip on my hips getting tighter as he moves them in rhythm with him going deeper.

My walls gripping him, as my orgasm floods through me, my legs tightening around his waist as I moan out. Reid's hands moving to my face as he kisses my chin before biting my bottom lip. He finds his own release again, as he presses me harder into the wall before stopping. My legs aching from the strain. Reid steps back, and I unwrap myself from him. He steps under the water, pulling me with him. Grabbing the soap, I start washing his chest, my fingers brushing through the small amount of chest hair. He closes his eyes and lets me wash him before doing the same to me, my muscles relaxing under his touch. When we are done, he grabs my towel and passes it to me before wrapping his own around his hips.

I follow him back into the room, he chucks me one of his shirts before putting a pair of black shorts on himself. He sits on the edge of the bed and motions me to go to him. I hesitate. I have never feared feeding as much as I have for the last week. My hunger is insatiable, in fact, I am finding everything to become insatiable my hunger, my sex drive. I always feared feeding, all my life feared it because it is the one time you completely let go of control. I also know I have hurt people which now makes that fear stronger, I don't want to hurt Reid. I know he won't let me kill him, but I still fear going too far and him hating me for it.

Seeing my hesitation, he leans forward and grabs my hand tugging me, so I am standing between his legs. "Maybe we should use blood bags," I tell him. Reid pulls a face, I can tell through the bond he doesn't want me feeding on anyone else, the thought of having some other person's blood in my system repulses him.

"I let it pass that you fed on my Beta, you aren't feeding off anyone other than me."

"We can get female blood," I tell him. He shakes his head.

"You are mine, no one else's male or female. I don't want to smell anyone else on you."

He pulls me, so I am sitting on his lap, his hand going under the hem of the shirt resting on my thigh, his thumb rubbing against my hip. He kisses my lips softly. "You won't hurt me, I promise, your bark is worse than your bite."

"Really, is that so?" I raise an eyebrow at him. He kisses my neck before offering his own to me. The sight of his neck makes my mouth water, and I don't try and fight it, I let go. Trusting

Reid to take control and bring me back to reality. As soon as his blood floods my mouth, I swallow greedily, his blood soothing the burn and dryness of my throat. Replenishing every cell in my body, awakening my senses and overloading everything. Like fireworks exploding on my tongue. I could get drunk on his taste, I hear him moan, which only fuels my yearning, never enough. I knew I should pull away, but I couldn't, and Reid wasn't trying to stop me as I bit down again. Instead, offering more of his neck to me. I drink hungrily, wanting to drain him. I feel tears well in my eyes, my mind screaming at me to stop, and my body doing the exact opposite. It was a war one I had no choice but to wait for Reid to pull away as I couldn't physically do it myself.

"Babe, stop," he says, rubbing my back. Panic taking over and I will my body to stop, only it refuses to listen, my claws extending and digging into his shoulder. I hear him hiss at the sudden pain before he realises, I can't stop. Reid grips my shoulders and shoves me back hard, making me fall backwards onto the floor. My adrenaline kicking in and my hunger the only thing I can think of even though I know I need to fight it but I can't, all rational thoughts being shoved aside as my animalistic side overrides me. I lunge at Reid, but he manoeuvres, so I am forced to turn, and I land on the floor between his legs, his arms criss-crossed against my chest, holding me down between his legs.

"Sorry babe, I have no choice." I know what he is going to do, and I don't blame him, I actually welcome it. I feel his canine bite into my flesh, I scream. His bite is painful and savage as his teeth tear through my flesh. I feel myself start slipping, the room getting darker. I blink my eyelids grow heavier and heavier. I blink once more, and I can't open them, and I give in to the darkness letting it take hold, wrapping me soothingly as I drop into oblivion.

Chapter 42

Reid's POV

I WATCHED AS SHE SLEPT, I picked up her limp body. Guilt eating away at me, I could feel Ryder pressing against my skin. Itching to be released. I placed her on our bed, leaning down, I nuzzled into her neck. God, I loved this woman, but damn she infuriated me. I sometimes have to remember she didn't have the childhood she deserved, didn't have the support she craved. I inhaled her scent, Ryder instantly settling down. I placed my hand on her stomach, the slightest bump on her lower abdomen. I could hear the steady heartbeat of the life she was carrying. I knew Aria would be a great mother, I can't grasp why she would doubt her ability. Aria always puts her life second to Lily, no matter the consequences. I know she will be protective of our pup. I would lay my life down for all three of them. Lily was as much hers as she was David's, their bond was unbreakable. I know Aria feared that I made the wrong choice, but I know she will come around.

I can sense the change in David, the bitterness of the loss of his mate now leaving, and his love slowly being given to Lily where it should have gone in the first place. I was envious of the bond they had formed in the last couple of weeks.

How he was able to pull himself from whatever dark place he was in. My father was not so lucky, he couldn't live without my mother, not even for me. I brushed her hair out of her face and tucked the blanket around her. I heard the front door; I knew instantly it was Zane. What I didn't understand was why he was here. Something must have happened, for him to barge in when he was under strict orders to steer clear. I raced downstairs, Zane's appearance was dishevelled his clothes torn and barely staying on him. "What's happened?"

Zane tried to catch his breath, his hands on his knees while he was bent over. I mind linked him, knowing he was too out of breath to talk.

"Zane?"

"They attacked, there were too many of them. They took them, oh god Reid, they took her."

Panic coursed through my veins, my body tensing. I glanced up the stairs, knowing Aria was up there sleeping, unaware of the shit storm that just blew in. The timing couldn't be worse.

"Took who? Who took them?"

"My mate, oh god they took Christine. They had tranquilisers, we couldn't do anything. They took Christine and Wendy."

"What about Amber?"

"She is fine. Mitch ran with her taking her to the Black Moon Pack, she is with Lily" I felt instant relief knowing, the kids were at least safe.

"What happened?" I was already moving, my fingers moving a hundred miles an hour, texting the entire Pack to meet.

"The Hunters. They want Aria, Reid. They said they will kill them if we don't hand her over. They were watching the house as soon as we got inside the entire property was surrounded, they kicked the doors in and let off Wolfsbane grenades. Mitch grabbed Amber when I told them to run, but I couldn't stop them, I tried. I fucking Tried. But I WASN'T STRONG ENOUGH!" his voice screaming in my head. His anger boiling over, before crushing him. He was dying inside with guilt, dying with the thought of what they could possibly be doing with his mate.

"This isn't your fault we will get them back, Zane. I won't let them hurt your mate or Wendy."

Zane nodded, putting his complete faith in me. Ryder was hackled up in my head growling. "I am going to fucking slaughter the lot them" His growl ripping out of me before I felt the shift take over. I didn't fight it, I let him out. His instincts were to kill and take back what belonged to us. They were part of my Pack, and nobody fucking takes from me. Not unless they have a death wish. I looked up the stairs. I have to protect them, I will not let anyone touch what's mine.

"Go to the Black Moon Pack, take Aria with you. Warn them. Tell them to get ready, we are about to go to war." I took off knowing Zane would get Aria out of here and to safety. I have complete trust in him. He feels like he failed them, but I know he would have fought until his last breath if given the chance. I know if he did, they would have killed him.

Aria's POV

I woke to Lily and Amber crying, my instincts going on high alert. I grabbed them, hugging them to me before glancing around, looking for the threat they fear. I didn't recognise my surroundings, why were they here? Reid said they were staying away for the night. I push trying to feel for Reid, but I get nothing, he is blocking me out. The girls are hysterical. I try soothing them enough to get them to speak. I look around. I am in some sort of bunker, getting up. I peer around and huddled on the ground are hundreds of women and children. Fear consumes, what is going on?

I walk over to a woman, trying to figure out what the hell is going on. The lights flicker before I hear an explosion above us. Bits of concrete cracking off and falling to the ground. The room reeks of tears and fear, it was burning my nose, the stench nearly making me gag. The woman stands up when I approach, she is wary of me. But she can feel that I'm an Alpha female. The woman has sandy blonde hair and big brown doe eyes. She is lean and muscular, she is a trained fighter, and blood smears her clothes. A child is clinging to her leg, whom I assume is her pup; she looks around the same age as Lily.

I can almost hear the vibration of everyone shaking in fear. The room seems to buzz with tension. "What's happened? How long have I been out?" I ask.

"Two days, Luna. We are at war." she whispers as the girl clinging to her leg whimpers. War?

"With whom?"

"Hunters they attacked and took some Pack members two days ago, your Beta came and warned us Alpha locked us in the bunker, they attacked not long after. We fought, but there were too many, the Alpha said it was best we stayed here."

"Which Alpha? Reid?"

"No, Luna, you're in Black Moon Territory." I know something has gone terribly wrong if I am here and so is half my Pack.

"Who is in charge here?" I ask expecting to see Michael's wife pop up from the shadows, the place was crammed with bodies.

The room was huge like a football field, but not big enough for everyone to move or stretch their legs much. Another explosion was heard up above. I was worried the roof was going to cave in.

"You're in charge, Luna. Alpha David couldn't leave any warriors with us, there's too many of them."

Shit, I know what they wanted. Looking around the room, I tried to find Elizabeth, Michael's mate. I called out to her, but no answer.

"Does anyone know where Elizabeth is, your Beta female?" I knew she would have answers. Lily walked over, wrapping her arms around my waist, she was shaking.

"They killed her Ari, and they took Wendy and Christine." My blood ran cold. Ice in my veins, a growl tore from my throat so loud, it was actually painful. Vibrating out of my chest, everyone froze. I couldn't even hear the sounds of their breathing; you would be able to hear a pin drop, the silence deafening. They have them, they have my family.

An explosion by the door leading outside made everyone turn and shuffle towards me, trying to get away from the door. I shoved through the sea of people until I was standing between them and the door.

"Get the children to the back of the bunker now," I screamed, throwing my Alpha voice at them, forcing them to move and get organised. I heard banging on the door, someone was trying to break in. If it were Alpha David, I knew he would have just unlocked the doors, this was no friend this was foe. I let my claws extend so angry, I couldn't even feel them tearing my nails off. The women in the bunker shuffling around, shoving the children to the back, taking protective stances.

"Get ready!" I yelled, and everyone turned to the doors waiting. My fangs tear through my gums, my eyes blazing, I could feel every vein moving in my body as adrenaline pumped through me feeding my anger. I wanted blood, and I wanted to find my mate, but right now, I needed to protect my Packs. The door burst open concrete debris flying everywhere, filling the room with dust. The lights shattering above our heads, raining glass down on us. I didn't feel the sting as it cut into my skin. I could hear the woman and children's cries and screams behind me.

I had no idea what I expected when the doors burst, what I wasn't expecting though, was wolfsbane grenades. As soon as I heard the metallic clink and the roll across the floor and smelt the deathly sick smell, I screamed. "Cover the kids!" Just as they exploded. Everyone started coughing and dropping like flies. It burnt my skin, my growl ripping out of me as I am thrown backwards smacking into the people behind me. I jump to my feet. When I see the first sign of movement, I lunge straight for their throat.

Chapter 43

Aria's POV

I MOVE WITH PRECISION AND speed, my hands reaching straight for them, knocking the gun from their hands, as I bite into the flesh of their neck, blood spurting all over me, as I rip his throat from his body. Red dots filled the room, and I kept moving, reaching and grabbing for any part of them, as I ripped them towards me, tearing them apart. I could feel their blood dripping off me, could hear my Pack fighting behind me. Hear the screams of the kids, which only fuels my anger more. Another explosion goes off, as a second grenade is let off. I choke on the fumes, my lungs feeling like they are on fire, my eyes burning, my skin burning as if it had been doused in acid. I could hear the agonised screams of everyone behind me. I force myself to my feet staggering. I grab the first man I see in the cloud of dust and smoke. He has some sort of black armour on. The only skin showing is their faces and neck as I bite his face tearing the flesh of his cheek off. I spit it out, my teeth going for his jugular. His blood flooding my mouth as I drain him before dropping him at my feet, I step over his body, moving toward my next target. Only they kept coming, and the room was already Packed with dead bodies and people fighting.

I feel the sting of being shot in the leg. I look down and see a green dart in my thigh, I pull the dart out and lunge at the woman holding the gun that was pointed in my direction. Her scream dying in her throat as I tore it from her body. Everyone is running around in a panic, trying to escape the cloud and rain of Wolfs-bane falling onto everyone, suffocating us all. I watch as few escape when I am completely surrounded. Red dots appearing through the smoke all aimed directly on me at different locations on my body. I feel their sting as each one fires, the darts penetrating my flesh, making me woozy. I lunge grabbing the closest person, using him as a shield while I rip his spine from his body. Sinking my teeth into him, needing blood to regain some strength. I shouldn't be standing, I can feel whatever they shot me with moving through my bloodstream, hear the heartbeat of the life inside me thumping loudly. Anger courses through me. I keep fighting, but they keep shooting, dart after dart into me, making me weaker. I fall to my knees before I fall to my side, my eyes growing heavy, I fight the fog consuming me. Forcing my eyes open when a man walks in. The room has gone silent. Deathly silent.

The man walks over to me and crouches beside me. He has a white lab coat on and round glasses, his gaunt face looking down on me.

"Keep fighting, and we will kill everyone in this room." I growl because that's all I can do; my body is completely numb and limp. I couldn't fight even if I wanted to.

I hear Lily and Amber's screams resonate through the room. My head slowly rolling to my side, my eyes searching, until they find them through the thick smoke and people crowding around me. Their flesh is red, raw, and bleeding. They can't even stand only scream. I growl louder and try to lift my arm, but it doesn't move. Tears escaping my eyes running down my cheeks.

"Aria, please get up." Her voice breaks as she screams for me. My heart splintering off sharp edges, piercing my soul, knowing I can't get to her.

"Like I said Aria, don't fight and I will let those who remain alive go, which isn't many I must admit," My claws extend, I try and throw it at his face, but miss and my hand falls to the ground.

"Ah, Ah, Ah, Aria don't be foolish, we have your sister and her little friend. One wrong move and I will force you to watch as they die painfully" My eyes get heavy, and I try to fight the cold feeling consuming me as darkness takes over. I mindlink trying to seek help.

"Reid, Please Reid, you have to save them." I am out before he answers that's if he even heard me.

The dripping of water pulls me from my blacked-out state. I try to move my arms, but they don't budge. My head hanging forward heavily, my neck stiff, having not moved it for however long. I lift it, and I see I am braced to a wall. Metal holding me to the walls around my wrists, elbows, and shins, another around my chest. I look around my eyes lazily falling on Lily and Amber, who are cuffed to a metal table in front of me. Both laying with their heads on the steel surface.

"Psst Lily." She doesn't answer. "Lily." She moves her fingers, and I know she is alive, I can hear the slow beating of her heart. The room reeks of wolfsbane. Lily's flesh burned and peeling off. She was too weak to move, and Amber was in a worse condition. Slumped forward, nearly falling off the chair she has been placed on, her mouth open and a steady stream of blood pouring onto the floor from her mouth.

I hear coughing and turn to look beside me. I gasp when I see Alpha David braced to the wall beside me, I look on the other side and see Christine and Wendy braced as well. They are covered in bruises, and Wendy has a gash that isn't healing on her head. "You're awake?" Alpha David's voice sounds strangled and pained. I turn my head to him, making eye contact.

"Where are we?"

"Some sort of lab." He throws his head towards the front. I look up, and I can see clear glass. We are in some sort of glassed room resembling a huge fish tank. I can see scientists in lab coats walking around on the other side of the glass with computers and notebooks, all working, not paying attention to us trapped in the room in front of them. I look over to Christine and Wendy.

"Girls?" I call out to them, but they don't answer.

"They haven't woken since they got here, the doctor injected them with something. They keep coming back, testing their blood and injecting them."

"What do they want?" I asked.

"I have no idea, but we need to find a way out of here."

I nod, I try to mindlink but can feel some sort of barrier blocking me. I hear the lock to the glass door open and the man from the bunker steps in, a smug smile on his face.

"Nice to have you back with us, Aria."

I growl at him. "Let them go. You have me, leave them be."

He walks over to me; he has some stick in his hand. It is long and has two prongs on the end. He places it on my shoulder. Pressing the prongs into my flesh. I hiss at the sudden pain and struggle against my restraints. "I don't think so, see you aren't in any position to do anything; therefore, I can do as I please." He turns and presses the stick onto Lily's back. He presses a button near the handhold, and she starts screaming and convulsing, the buzz of electricity in the air. It's a cow prodder. I scream and pull on my restraints, and so does David.

"Leave her, fucking leave her, you fucking coward," David screams. The man turns toward David and jams him in the ribs with the prodder, turning it on. David tenses, his muscles bulging and rippling under the current. The man stops and turns toward me.

"That all you got, you fucking maggot," David screams at him before spitting on him. The man wipes his face and hits him again with the stick. I can smell his flesh burning, but he doesn't scream. In fact, he just glares pulling on his restraints. "I'm going to fucking rip you to shreds," he spits out venomously through gritted teeth. Lily stirs behind him, and her eyes go wide, realising her father is being electrocuted. Her eyes meet mine, and I mouth to her to stay quiet. I watch tears run down her cheeks before she freezes, holding back her sobs.

The man stops, and David fights against the restraints trying to break free. It is no use, though. The man walks around and sits across from Lily.

"Well, hello young lady." Lily moves back in her chair trying to get away from him.

"Well, now that I have your undivided attention, listen up. I am not sure if your father told you about the experiments we wanted him for." I stare shocked that he knows my father is still alive. "Oh yes, Aria, I have known for years. A body just doesn't disappear. Anyway, back to what I was saying. I need your blood, and I need a lot quite frankly. The blood we took from your father years ago has run out, and I need more and you, my dear will be, let's see, what's the word," he says, tapping his chin.

"Oh yes, my personal blood bag." His dark hair falls in his eyes, and he throws his head back, pushing it out of the way.

"And why is it that you need my blood specifically?"

"You're incredibly unique, and your blood holds the key to immortality, why else? Nothing more, nothing less. Although over the years, we have had some developments. Your friends there are living proof our science does work," he says, pointing to Wendy and Christine. I look over to them, still slumped forward, their faces hidden behind their hair that is acting as a veil. They do smell different.

Chapter 44

Reid's POV

W E HAD JUST FINISHED the meeting; every back member was called. We had to meet at the Pack stadium just to cram everyone in. We tripled the border patrols, made sure that we had a plan. A plan that I believed was solid and would work, that they wouldn't catch us off guard. The patrols were running smoothly for the first nine hours. My men were exhausted but alert. Geared up on needing to protect their families and our way of life. The Hunters haven't been seen or heard from in nearly two decades.

We soon learned they had been biding their time, accumulating more members, they outnumbered us. There were over five hundred Pack members in my Pack. This should have been an easy victory, especially with the help of the Black Moon Pack by our side. We sent word to the neighbouring Packs outside the city, everyone that we had alliances with. But even they couldn't get here in time. I had just received word that Alpha David had sent all the women and children to the bunker, we sent ours to be safe, or so we thought. I still don't know how many made it. One thing I learnt was that our bunkers were old and outdated, not for the size our Pack has grown. I hope they made it, but I know it's foolish to think they all did.

If we find a way out of this, if any part of the Pack survives, we will have hundreds of people to account for, hundreds to bury. Zane took Aria to the Black Moon Pack, to the safety of their bunker. Despite his past grievances and lack of training for his Pack, Alpha David was prepared for war. I was surprised when Alpha David told me to start sending my Pack members over there for protection. But it was a smart move less ground to cover if everyone was in one place.

What we weren't prepared for was the fact that the Hunters didn't need to cross the borders, they were already lying in wait for us, their numbers tripling both our Packs. They were well trained and had an advantage, they had something that weakened us. After I received the call that the Black Moon was under attack. I knew instantly that we failed.

We failed because to get to the Black Moon border, they had to get through ours. That's where we went wrong, we were so busy protecting the biggest border of the city, not realising they were already well and truly past our city border. Smack in the middle by the hundreds. They snuck up behind us, and when the first explosions went off, everything turned chaotic. They attacked both Packs at once leaving a clear divide between both. The woman and children fleeing caught in the crossfire between borders.

Every street, every building lit up like Christmas trees, as they were blown to smithereens effectively trapping us. Both Packs tried to get to the bunkers to protect them. But with the amount of firepower the Hunters had and the amount of Hunters we didn't stand a chance, they wiped out over half our people.

I had to block the mind link; nobody was able to fight properly, becoming distracted by the fear and screaming of their loved ones being ripped into the afterlife. I knew instantly when the bunker had been breached. I could feel Aria had woken, then I could feel her pain. Her pain as the explosions went off, I could feel the wolfsbane burning her skin, but she held on, and I knew exactly why. Aria wasn't one to go down without a fight, especially when her loved ones were at stake, when our Packs were fighting for their lives, I knew she would fight for them. I was well aware of everything she was thinking, everything she was feeling, but I couldn't focus on her alone when I could feel the teethers of my Pack, being cut and ripped away from me. I lost count after the first seventy.

The pain of their deaths only fuelled me to keep fighting. I knew if I stopped, I would break, it's unnatural to feel one death, let alone hundreds of links torn. Hundreds of people now memories. Then the feeling of everyone's heartache at having lost their mates, their parents, their children. It was too much to bear; I bore all that suffocatingly. I don't know how my father survived living through it for years after the attack that killed my brother and mother. I felt like my soul was being split away piece by fucking piece, the sharp edges cutting deeply, bleeding my soul right out me and creating a void, that was now being filled with guilt. Guilt that I couldn't save them. Guilt that I failed my job as Alpha.

When Aria finally succumbed, I felt that too, not only did I feel it, but the entire Pack was also linked to that teether we shared. We started dropping like flies. The Hunters did their research because they backed off as soon as she went down, going back to the shadows they came from. I tried to fight it, but her pull, the Lycan pull, was greater. Had I known being mated to her would cause not only me to fall but my entire Pack, I may have second-guessed marking her, although I knew that was a foolish thought to have, the mate pull is stronger than us, it would have been inevitable. The Hunters must have known, I don't know how they knew but without a Queen to command or fight for, the soldier's fall.

We all dropped, plunged into darkness as whatever they did to her knocked her down, effectively putting her out. I knew she wasn't dead, but I also knew that if they did kill her there would be no waking up, her link to this Pack was far too strong, stronger than we could have imagined as we were pulled into oblivion. I opened the link just in time to hear her.

"Reid, please Reid, you have to save them."

Then nothing but darkness. This was their plan all along. Take out the Luna and we all go down, so they can escape taking the only light in my life with them.

Aria's POV

This maniac of a man has been rambling nonsense for what felt like hours. I have never held so much anger towards one person before. I didn't just want to kill him; I wanted his death to be slow and painful, I wanted revenge. I wanted revenge so bad I could taste the bitter taste of it in my mouth. Christine and Wendy still hadn't awoken. Periodically men in white lab coats would come in and inject them with something. I demanded so many times to know what it was he was giving them, but he said we would find out soon enough.

We learned a few things about him like his name, which is Kade. I was going to kill Kade, no matter what, I knew when I went down, I was taking him with me. I watched as he finally walked out. Lily visibly relaxing as soon as the door clicked shut.

I looked to David, who was still clinging to consciousness after being electrocuted at random by the sick bastard.

"David?" He looked in my direction but couldn't even lift his head to look at me. At least I knew he was listening.

"Do you think you could shift out of your restraints?" His breathing was ragged, sweat dripping off his head and onto the floor. I could smell the burnt smell of his body hair, wherever the cow prodder touched, leaving behind round inflamed red blotches on his skin and bleeding holes. His blood was enticing my senses, trying to consume me.

"I am too weak, and I can't feel my wolf anymore, I haven't since we got here. I think they did something when I was knocked out." Even his speech was slurred and raspy. Lily looked at me, frightened. This was the man I feared for years and was now a crumbling mess, what chance did we have of escape when they took him down so easily.

"Lily, I need you to try and wake up Amber, nudge her try to rouse her awake." I watched as Lily used her elbow trying to nudge Amber awake, all it managed to do was make her move closer to the edge and closer to falling. I shook my head at Lily to stop, and she did. I could hear Amber's heartbeat, but it was so faint, I knew she was only just clinging on to life. Looking at my hands, I tried to wriggle them free, but it was no use. I actually wished; I could shift it would come in handy right about now to escape these restraints. Wendy shifting her head and groaning pulled my attention to her.

"Wendy, you're awake, are you okay?" She lifted her head, and I could see the full extent of her injuries, her eyes were swollen shut, her lips bruised and bloody, her hair sticking to her face from the dried blood from the gash on her head. "Mitch, Mitch, where are you?" She muttered.

"Wendy, it's Aria, I need you to look at me, I'm on your right side." She moved her head, it rolled more to the side then moved. She was weak.

"Aria, where is Mitch? Why isn't he here?" She was disorientated that much I knew.

"We are in some lab," I told her. I didn't want to tell her, I felt Mitch's teether snap, I knew when she came too, she would realise and feel he was gone. I felt him leave this life just as the first explosion went off outside the bunker doors. Felt his life be snuffed out.

"Wendy, what do you remember?" She slurred her words and muttered something that didn't make sense before going unconscious again. I put my head back against the wall. We were screwed. I was losing feeling in my limbs from the restraints. Looking at my hands again, I stretched my fingers and realised they were only a few centimetres off David's. Then an idea popped into my head, one that might actually work.

David was drooling on the floor, but I needed him awake. Just when I went to call out to him, the door opened again. This time another man walked in, he had a shaved head and bulging eyes, he wasn't dressed like the others, in their lab coats instead, he wore a white singlet with jeans, and I could see his tribal tattoos that ran up both his arms from his wrist to his shoulder. He looked towards the table.

"Stay away from them, don't fucking touch them!" I yelled pulling on my restraints. David hearing me yell, looked up and started struggling as well to get free. He walked towards the table Lily and Amber were at. He lifted Amber's head by her hair and sneered as he let go, her head hitting the table with a thud. Lily started screaming as he grabbed her, before undoing the cuffs holding her to the table. He then pulled her to her feet, and she stumbled, trying to free herself.

"Let her go, she is just a child." The man grabbed her arm and started taking her towards the door.

David and I both screaming at him.

"Let her go, where are you taking her?" I screamed tears building in my eyes, panic setting in. The man opened the door. Pushing her through the door she fell forward, she got up and tried to run, but another man grabbed her, we watched on in horror as he held her. Another man brought in a mesh cage, he opened it and shoved her inside. Her fingers clutching the mesh as she called for us. She couldn't even stand the cage was fit for a dog, not a person. Kade walked over with a syringe in his hand, walking directly towards her, Lily backed into the corner of the cage trying to get away from him screaming and crying. My heart tearing into pieces at seeing her so frightened and defenceless.

David screamed for them to stop, but they ignored our pleas. Kade put the syringe on the end of a pole before shoving the pole through the mesh. He tried to stab her with it, but she managed to move just in time. This went on for a few seconds before he jabbed it into her thigh.

Chapter 45

Aria's POV

I WATCHED AND THOUGHT MAYBE whatever they gave her didn't work, I prayed to the Moon Goddess that whatever they injected her with was a failure. Only when I heard her scream, did my blood run cold, colder than ice. I could feel the blood leave my face and bile rose in my throat. And if that weren't enough, they then wheeled her in so we could listen to her agonised screams. She looked at me in panic, her fear radiating out of every pore in her body, making the room fill with her scent. She writhed in agony panting, as wave after wave of pain shot through her.

"Lily, focus on me, bub, focus on my voice," I called out to her, tears running like a stream down my cheeks. I watched them close the doors, leaving her screaming in pain. They sat on the other side of the glass, notepads in hand scribbling whatever garbage they were writing on to the pads. Lily looked at me, her eyes begging me to stop the pain. That's when I heard her bones start snapping and moving, morphing, her eyes changed colour half blue, half yellow.

"Make it stop, make it stop, please Aria, make it stop. Daddy please." Her voice taunting and tugging at the pieces of my heart. David, hearing her call him Daddy snapped. I could hear his shoulder break as he pulled against the restraints trying to get to her.

Blood dripping from her mouth as her face morphed. I will never forget the sound of her screams; they will forever haunt my memories burned into me forever. Her nails ripping from her nail beds, as her hands turned into paws, her claws going through the mesh, her screams getting louder as her spine rearranged itself, her clothes being torn to shreds, as she shifted right before our eyes.

Werewolves aren't meant to shift before they are teenagers, Lily wasn't meant to endure this torture for many years, and now she was forced to shift, and all I could do was watch. Her blue and yellow eyes staring back at us pleading to make it stop. When the shift finished, she was left standing in the cage, not as Lily but that of her wolf. She was magnificent, her fur was an unnatural silver with black paws that kind of looked like socks. One side of her face black and the other silver. Werewolves weren't these colours; I knew whatever they did to her changed her, Werewolves didn't shift early to give their wolf time to create a bond with their human part. Just as the shift completed, she let out a mangled scream before passing out on her side, the floor drenched with her blood.

"Lily, Lily, baby, wake up," David called to her. She didn't wake.

"She is still alive, listen; I can hear her heart beating still and hear her breathing." David listened before slumping against his restraints. I could see the scientist excitedly talking and writing notes before they walked away like they didn't just watch a child being tortured.

I looked at David, I had never seen this man cry before, and right now he was a sobbing mess. I just hoped Lily's wolf hasn't been permanently damaged from being forced to shift, and I hope this doesn't kill her. I knew only time would tell what impact this will have on her in the future assuming she has one.

The door opened again, I looked up and watched as they pulled Christine down from the wall she was braced on. "Please this is enough, you have done enough. Just let them go please" The man with the bulging eyes ignored us. Christine fell on the floor in a heap. He then did the same to Wendy. Wendy groaned when her body hit the floor. Christine, however, didn't make a sound. I would have thought she was dead if not for her irregular heart-beat. I thought it was strange how fast her heart was beating, it sounded a lot like mine. More of a fast fluttering than an actual thumping beat.

Wendy dragged herself to a sitting position, leaning heavily against the wall. Another scientist walked in with Kade, they stopped in front of her before bending down. Forcing her eyelids open with their fingers and flashing a light in her eyes. She tried to push their hands away, but she was too weak.

"Interesting, the lower concentrate of her blood did nothing to this one," Kade said to the other man.

The scientist wrote something while nodding his head. They walked to Christine and did the same. Only when they flashed the light in her eyes, they flicked between a burning ember before going back to normal when the light left.

"The higher concentrate and mutated version seem to work on her though. So, let's wake her up," They all walked out. David and I looked at each other, and Wendy reached out for Christine's hand, trying to pull her towards herself.

"David, I need you to see if you can reach my hands," David looked at our hands seeing they weren't far off touching. He stretched, his broken shoulder making a horrid noise as he pulled on it. His wrists dug into the metal braces, but it worked. He could reach just onto my wrist with his fingertips if I stretched far enough.

"What do you want me to do?"

"We need to get free before they come back, I have a bad feeling about whatever they have down to Christine." He nodded looking at her crumpled body on the floor.

"What next then?"

"I need you to yank on my arm and pull my elbow out, then I need you to snap my thumb and slit my wrists" David looked at me like I was insane. Saying it out loud, it definitely sounds crazy. But I would heal quickly, I hoped. I just needed to get my hands out, then I could manoeuvre my arm out. David, realising what I was thinking, nodded his head.

"This is going to hurt." I didn't even have time to process his words before he grabbed my hand and ripped on it, my body being pulled further through the braces, my shoulder tearing as the metal cut into it, it worked though. I felt my elbow dislocate. I held my breath to stop from yelling out. Gritting my teeth through the sudden pain. If Lily could shift, I could at least break a few bones for her.

David squeezed my fingers, not just my thumb, breaking all of them in his vice-like grip. I knew he didn't mean to break all of them, but he didn't have much choice; it was the only way to get enough strength to break my thumb. I couldn't help the shudder that ran through me, as I felt my thumb slide into my palm. I wanted to throw up. My entire right arm throbbing.

"You need to stretch Aria, cutting your wrists is going to be harder without my claws." Tears ran down my cheeks as I stretched my arm as far as it would go, but it still wasn't enough for him to reach my wrist. I could feel my mangled fingers trying to heal, so closed my hand into a fist, forcing my thumb to remain in its position. I looked at Wendy on the floor.

"Wendy, Wendy," She groaned before her head rolled to look up at me. "Can you stand?" she shook her head. "I need you to try. I need you to find something to cut my wrist with so I can get my arm out," She looked around, but the room was bare besides the steel table and the mesh cage. She slumped back against the wall.

I looked at David. "What about my hand?" He nodded and stretched out again. I did the same, my fingers slipping back into their rightful position. I groaned knowing we would need to break them again. David's nails dug into my hand right at the base before my wrist. I hissed as he dug his nails in. He was straining so hard trying to get them to break my skin when suddenly his claws jutted out and went straight through my hand. I screamed, not expecting his claws to come through. He looked startled but relieved to see he was able to slightly shift.

"Break it again." My blood was dripping on the floor. I had to be fast, I could feel my skin already trying to heal, although it was much slower than usual. David broke my fingers again and using my blood, I was able to make the braces slippery enough to get my hand all the way through, but not quick enough to pull my arm out when the door opened. I froze, leaving my hand just inside the wrist cuff.

Kade walked in before jamming a syringe into Christine's arm before quickly running out and shutting the door. He waited

eagerly by the door peering in the small window with a triumphant grin on his face.

Christine gasped loudly like someone who just took a deep
breath for the first time. Her eyes opened and they burned bright
like embers of a flame. She turned her head to the side, a growl
escaping from her. I recognised the look on her face instantly, a
look I was all too familiar with. The need to feed and Amber was
directly in front of her.

Chapter 46

Reid's POV

WE ALL FINALLY CAME to, I could feel my Pack members waking, I lifted my head in search of Zane. Only to realise I wasn't in the industrial area anymore but a bunker. I rolled to my side, my eyes landing on Abel, Aria's father. Zoe and he were going over something on the steel table across from me. I sat up, dropping my feet over the edge of the couch I was placed on.

"You're awake about fucking time. Now get up and help me find my daughter." Abel spoke, I could hear the venom in his words, and I jumped up growling. Abel turned to me his anger clearly on display not even trying to hide what he is, his eyes burning brightly, reflecting oddly under the lights.

"Maybe you can answer that, they should have taken you, not my mate!" I screamed, grabbing a hold of his shirt and flinging him back into the table. Zoe raced to his side but was too slow before he charged at me. Grabbing me around the waist, we fought, throwing punches back and forth. I noticed Zoe taking a seat out of the corner of my eye, looking annoyed. I headbutted Abel and felt his nose break on impact. He stumbled backwards. Just as he went to lunge again, Zoe spoke up.

"Enough we have to find my granddaughter and great-grand-child this shit isn't helping." We both stopped glaring at each other, both of us breathing heavily trying to catch our breath.

"I see being mated to my girl has made you stronger," he said rebreaking his nose into place. I knew he was holding back slightly. I shouldn't have had the upper hand on him, but I think he needed to blow off steam and I was the more durable target in the room.

"Where is the rest of my Pack?"

"I could only bring you; I am not a bloody donkey. How many did you want to bring back here?" He snarled. Zoe hit the table with her hand bringing our attention back to her, the Pack will have to wait.

"I have scoured the entire City trying to pick up their scent, they covered their tracks well," Abel said, annoyed at his lack of progress.

"How long have I been out?"

"Only about twelve hours," Zoe said matter of factly. Ryder wasn't happy about being out so long, they could be anywhere by now.

"I enlisted the help of some humans; a lot of people noticed the war happening on their doorstep and are also scouring everywhere trying to find a lead."

"Humans?"

"Yes Reid, they aren't stupid. They know what happens in their City they just choose to turn a blind eye to it, but now I have spoken to some, human or not these monsters killed innocent children they won't stand for that, they are going to help move yours and those of David's Pack that are injured to the stadium, they are willing to help if needed, we just need to find them first." Zoe added.

I nodded. It felt strange knowing they have turned a blind eye. I knew a few high up members of the city knew of our existence but never in a million years would I have thought the entire City knew, times were definitely changing. We had a war on our hands and could really use the extra reinforcements, maybe this is a good thing them knowing.

"So, what do you know? So far?"

"Not much I just got off the phone and was about to tell Abel what I know, but then you woke up, and I couldn't get a word in with you two trying to kill each other" Abel turned to her giving her his attention. He lent back on the table, and I folded my arms across my chest, waiting to listen as well. Now realising our mistake, we weren't going to get anywhere fighting amongst ourselves.

"Well, he didn't have much, an old friend heard about what happened and called me. Apparently, the Hunters dispersed years ago, but everyone was called back with the promise of immortality if they helped catch the Hybrid. Apparently, their numbers have grown massively and that a man by the Name of Kade Barclay is now running things. He said he noticed some of the original labs had been undergoing refurbishment, that he has been watching them for a while keeping tabs on them, he is on his way to help try locate them." I nodded and looked at Abel. He looked livid and his face changing to a crimson colour with his anger. Like a kettle about to boil over.

"Did you say Kade Barclay?" he asked.

"Yes, why? Have you heard of him?" Abel nodded deep in thought.

"Yes, but he is human. I don't know how he could still be alive." My eyebrows furrowed, and I felt Ryder press against my skin listening in.

"What do you mean, he should be dead?"

"He is human, and the only Kade Barclay I know was alive in the eighteenth century, it would be impossible."

"Could be someone else with the same name," I suggested he nodded but didn't look like he believed that.

"Say it is this Kade, how do you know him?"

"He captured me when I was younger, him and a group of Hunters noticed I wasn't aging figured out what I was and hunted me down, I was placed on a ship brought here to some underground labs, he was a mad scientist, crazy smart for the times and had a few small breakthroughs in medical science. After he caught me, he started looking for ways to prolong life and create immortality. As far as I knew it never worked, he also tried to replicate my Hybrid gene. He became obsessed with becoming like me. He used to test my blood on other werewolves. He even managed to capture a Vampire, using them like guinea pigs trying to mutate their genes and make them like me. All of them died from his science, and after a while, I managed to escape when they were moving me to a different compound, they sent off litres of my blood to a French scientist. He claimed he found a way to change the DNA and mutate it. I haven't seen him since I left the country. I returned a hundred years later forgetting about him and assuming he died."

That was one hell of a story, was it possible he did find a way to create immortality? Ryder was thinking the same thing.

"When will your friend get here?" I asked, looking at the clock, it was already the middle of the night.

"He should be here soon, he isn't far from here," Zoe stated. We both nodded our heads.

Not even ten minutes later we heard a knock on the door upstairs, Zoe looked to the TV screen above the bunker entrance, a man was waiting at the door with an armful of papers.

"That's him, I will go let him in. Wait here and don't kill each other." She gave us both a pointed look, and I chuckled. We were past that now, our little dispute was forgotten.

I walked over and looked at the documents on the table which were actually the City's blueprints. Every building, including mine, had underground tunnels. Something to look at in the future would be destroying those tunnels or at least blocking access from underground. I noticed one of the tunnels leading into the City ran along the boundary lines between both mine and David's Packs.

I pointed to it, and Abel nodded. "Yeah, I'm fairly sure that's how they got in without being noticed. If you follow that tunnel, it leads to nowhere though, only to the city library and cuts off halfway through in the other direction, if these maps are still correct. It could have changed by now, I think these maps are outdated, they belonged to Joe," Definitely something we needed to check out, we were going to have to go into the tunnels and see where they lead.

Chapter 47

Aria's POV

W ENDY LOOKED UP AT the noise that ripped from Christine. Christine climbed to her feet, having not noticed Wendy's crumpled form lying beside her, her eye's only on her prey. That prey was Amber, her own daughter. I struggled with my restraints, my hand slipping out from the wrist cuff, leaving only my elbow now stuck in the second cuff along that arm.

David, noticing the crazed look, started calling out to her, fighting to release himself, anything to distract her from hunting her own defenceless daughter, who was unconscious and unaware of the danger she was in, from her own mother. Wendy grabbed Christine's leg, but her bloodlust had completely taken over her. She didn't even look down at the tug on her leg, her eyes solely focused on that of her daughter.

"Wendy, you have to stop her, I can't get free." I screamed. My bone in my upper arm snapping under the pressure I was exerting trying to break free. My bone breaking through the flesh just above where my elbow should be. I screamed from the horrendous snap, my nerves in my arm feeling like I just tore straight through them. My arm bending, I was able to slip out of the cuff, my right arm dangling at a weird angle, blood running down my arm and dripping on the floor. I could already feel my arm shifting back into place and the wound healing as I endured the pain of my bones rearranging.

Christine, smelling my blood, turned and looked in my direction. The first thing I noticed were her amber eyes, except the pupil was blood red. I don't know what they gave her, but it was clear to me whatever it was, it wasn't just my blood. Whatever they did altered her DNA. Right now, I was staring back at the perfect predator. No recognition on her face that I am her friend, her Luna. I realised in that moment whatever was left of Christine was gone.

Wendy staggered to her feet between us, but Christine's eyes never left mine. She was hunting, and I was her prey. Wendy lunged forward falling into Christine's body and knocking her on the floor before landing heavily on top of her. Wendy was sweating profusely, and I could tell she was exerting what little energy she had left trying to stop her. They wrestled on the ground, Wendy trying to pin her down, but she was no match for her. Christine threw her off, Wendy smacked into the steel table her head smacking the side of the cage Lily was trapped in.

Amber groaned and shifted in her seat, dazedly looking up. Her groan, a distraction to Christine as her eyes snapped to that of her daughter.

"Mum?" Amber said, her voice a murmur as she tried to work out what was going on. David started screaming, trying to get the attention off her own daughter. I saw his braces starting to pull from the wall when his shin bone snapped, trying to get his leg free.

I struggled with my other arm, breaking my left hand before sliding it out of the wrist cuff. I was close, I just needed to free my other arm.

Christine lunged directly over the table at Amber. Amber's scream jolted Wendy to her feet just in time for Wendy to grab her around the waist. Adrenaline must have been the only thing that got her to move so fast because Wendy was there fighting her own best friend to stop her from destroying the one person she loved most in this world. Wendy slammed Christine into the wall next to me before Christine kicked her in the stomach, making her double over.

I saw the look in her eye, nothing was going to stop her from killing all of us once she was done with Amber. The hunger in her eyes proved there was nothing left of her to save. Tears poured down my face as she lunged forward. I moved, my hip dislocating as I threw my entire body toward her, my hand punching straight through her chest. I felt my hand smash through her ribs and sternum, her blood coating my arm before I felt the beating of her heart in my hand.

She stopped and looked down at my arm that was in her chest cavity. My fingers wrapped around her heart before squeezing. An agonised look crossing her features as I ripped her heart from her body. She stood upright for a second, still staring at the hole in her chest before her body collapsed in a heap on the floor.

"Please forgive me, Zane!" I screamed his name as I felt her link to me snap, my heart felt like it had been squeezed with hers and ripped away, as her teether to me snapped. Her life gone, and at my hands. Wendy screamed her voice piercing my ears and pulling at my soul. She threw herself at Amber trying to cover her eyes from seeing her mother's death. Wendy was too late though, everything happening so fast. I knew she saw me; her Luna and her mother's friend just rip the life out of her.

"I had no choice." My voice breaking at the realisation, my entire body crying out for her, crying for Amber, crying for the heartache I know I just caused Zane. But most of all, crying out for Reid, who I know would have also felt what I just did.

Amber was hysterically screaming out for her mother, trying to break free from the cage of Wendy's arms, as she held her trying to shield her from what I had done.

I killed one of my best friends, I know Christine would have wanted me to if it meant saving Amber, but that doesn't stop the hurt I have caused and feel. I knew I just destroyed and traumatised her daughter, destroyed her mate. But what choice did I have? I had to choose. It was either Christine or her daughter, and I know deep down I made the right choice, the choice she would have wanted.

"You had no choice Ari," David spoke next to me. One of his legs was free, but his arms still braced to the wall. His claws extended, and I knew whatever they gave him was wearing off, I also knew because I could feel it slowly disappearing from my bloodstream.

We need to get out of our restraints before they readminister another dose. I looked at Amber apologetically, sobs wracking her entire body. The bleeding in her mouth had stopped, but the gash on her head was still deep and not healing. I ripped my arm from the last brace. I could feel the skin tearing from my body like I was being degloved, but I didn't care I was mad, my anger numbing the pain. I would heal quickly, I just needed out of the restraints. I won't let them hurt anyone else.

My body fell forward smacking into the concrete floor, I felt my shins snap from the unnatural way my body was lying on the ground while they were still braced to the wall. Wendy let go of Amber and helped lift me up, she struggled under my weight. I was able to slide one leg out, having to twist my ankle to release myself. I felt my leg heal just as the door opened. Men rushing inside. I placed my leg on the ground, and Wendy went into defence mode, holding them back. I broke my ankle and manoeuvred my other leg out just in time, for them to run back out of the room sealing it shut. I looked up when I heard an exhaust fan start, I knew instantly they were trying to gas us out with Wolfsbane. After a few seconds Wendy started coughing. "Cover your mouth with your shirt." Both Amber and Wendy covered their mouths dropping onto the floor. The room started to fill with white smoke, I turned to David and started ripping on his restraints, they started pulling from the wall with his help he was able to get free, falling on the floor next to my feet. I couldn't see out the windows, the fog making it increasingly difficult to see.

I started choking on the fumes, my lungs filling with its toxic gas. I dropped to the floor, covering my face with my shirt.

We just had to hold out longer, wait for the gas to be turned off. I heard Lily in the cage coughing and looked up to see her naked inside the cage, the wolfsbane must have forced her wolf to change back. She coughed and choked, gasping for air. But she had nothing to shield her face. I crawled toward the cage before tearing a piece of my shirt and passing it to her through the mesh, poking it inside with my fingers. She looked up at me panicked. And I gasped to see her eyes had remained the same as that of her wolf, half blue and half orange glowing like embers of a flame.

Chapter 48

Reid's POV

ZOE'S FRIEND WAS EXTREMELY useful, I could tell years of being a Hunter himself had him still wary of Abel and myself. I could also tell; he was trying his best to conceal his discomfort. Hunters are raised in families who have generations of Hunters following in the footsteps of their forefathers. I didn't expect him to drop everything he has been raised to believe. I could tell he had only just come around to the idea that not all of us were bad, that didn't make him more comfortable though, so Abel and I let Zoe do most of the talking. This was her area of expertise even though she retired decades ago.

Abel and I were organising what was left of both Packs into scout teams, which was easy over the mind link for me, but David's Pack discovered Abel didn't need to be a Pack member. Being half Lycan allowed him to communicate with David's Pack members, he was able to contact Michael for me. I wondered why Aria never talked about the fact she could mind link any wolf. I also learned that Michael lost his mate in the war, Elizabeth. My Pack took the biggest blow; we lost two hundred and nine Pack members; David's side only lost seventy-one members. The Crescent Pack, another neighbouring Pack outside the city, was on their way over to give us a lending hand. I was grateful, but we didn't have the best relationship with them. We were currently waiting for the Crescent Pack Alpha to arrive before we made our move.

Abel also was able to verify Kade was, in fact, the same man from his younger years. We were still trying to figure out how the heck he had managed to prolong his life. Johnathan the Hunter that was helping had taken plenty of surveillance footage of trucks coming in and out of the city heading towards the area where the tunnels cut off one of those photos were of Kade. We knew now they must have built a headquarters just outside the city. Our scouts at the moment were verifying that's where the tunnels lead to.

Right now, we were waiting for people to start arriving. When we heard the familiar ding of the diner bells ringing, I knew instantly it was the Alpha from the Crescent Pack. I looked at the screen above the bunker door. I looked at Abel, and he nodded. I walked upstairs.

Walking upstairs, I came to find four enforcers and the Alpha Trent and his young son. Who looked to be thirteen? I thought he was insane for bringing his son until I remembered my brother and I were taught by our father the same way with hands-on experience.

"Alpha Trent, thanks for coming," I said, holding my hand out. Alpha Trent was a giant of man, his arms flexing as he shook my hand. He had shoulder-length blonde hair that was tied at the back of his neck and dark, almost black eyes. Anyone else would be intimidated just by the look of him, but I felt no such things.

They were the third biggest Pack, but after our loss, our numbers were pretty much the same as theirs now.

"Alpha Reid, nice to finally put a face to the name, this is my son Damien." His son put his hand out, and I quickly shook it giving him a nod.

"If you want to follow me, I will show you downstairs, please be mindful there are two retired Hunters so I would appreciate if you didn't kill my mate's grandmother or her friend, they are helping us locate my mate and our missing Pack members" He nodded once, but I was a little concerned still. It was unheard of to have Hunters working alongside the very thing they hunted.

I was halfway down the stairs when I felt it, a wave of emotion hit me. I grabbed onto the handrail and doubled over. Zane would be here any second, and if I feel this bad, he would be ten times worse. Forcing myself back up the stairs, I shoved past everyone.

"Alpha Reid, what's going on?" I looked back at them. Trent looked up at me alarmed.

"I need to get to my Beta," I gasped out, forcing my legs to keep moving up the stairs. I had just walked out to the diner's dining area when I saw Zane's car run straight into a telegraph pole out the front. The howl that resonated through the air chilled me to the bone. I ran to open the door just in time for Zane's wolf to break through the door of the car, ripping it clean off. His howls agonised as he threw himself at the ground.

I ran towards him, Zane had no control left, his wolf taking over as I felt Christine's teether to us break, her life slipping from us. Zane's agonised screams resonating through my head at the loss of his mate. And our Beta female. I hesitantly walked over to him; his wolf was whining, completely devastated.

"Zander," I called to Zane's wolf, he lifted his head at the command of his Alpha, he took a step towards me, teeth bared,

I knew he wouldn't attack me. I knew his wolf well; he made a noise that sounded strangled. "You need to give Zane control."

His wolf whined and then howled, I could hear how broken he was, I could feel it. I looked back towards the diner. Alpha Trent and Abel were watching a knowing look on their faces. I didn't have to explain anything. The sounds he was making told everyone what broke him. But right now, I needed him to focus, move through the pain he still had to find his daughter.

I put my hand on his head. "Zander, give Zane control, we still need to find your pup, your little girl buddy come on." He whined before I watched him shift, Alpha Trent walked out with a towel Zoe had given him. I threw it over his naked body. Tears running down his face as sobs wracked his body. I had never seen him like this, my strong best friend, now broken. Alpha Trent helped me get him up and inside the diner.

We placed him on a chair, Abel came out with a change of clothes and handed them to him. He took them with one hand. His eyes looking at us were empty and hollow. It was like looking into the eyes of my father, nothing left, just an empty vessel.

After a few more minutes of silence, he pulled himself together and stood up pulling the pants up before doubling over again. I turned around horrified praying to the goddess it wasn't Amber, but then I felt it too. My breathing becoming harder, my skin burning, my eyes watering. Something was terribly wrong. I could hear Trent yelling at his men to do something, anything. He wasn't prepared to deal with this, none of us were when we realised we were all linked to Aria the way we were. I didn't even have a chance to warn him before both Zane, and I passed out. The pain becoming too much. If this keeps up, we were never going to have a chance to find them. My last thought was trying to mind link Aria.

"Keep fighting, stay alive, so we can find you."

Aria's POV

I tried to fight it, tried to hold my breath, but the wolfsbane burning my flesh had me screaming only to inhale its toxic gas. Just as I passed out. Reid's voice popped into my head, he sounded weak and in pain.

"Keep fighting, stay alive so we can find you." His words giving me comfort as I succumbed to the darkness.

When I came too, I was strapped to a gurney. I turned my head to the side to see Lily in the cage. She was awake and observing everyone walking around the room. I rolled my head to the other side to see Wendy strapped down along with David. Amber was missing. I tried to ask Lily where she was, but my voice was completely gone. I must have breathed in more than I thought. Lily was covered in burns, the skin on her face all blistered. Her hands blistered, but I was surprised to see she was awake.

The only conclusion I could come to was that her wolf kept her alive, I just hoped Amber was still alive. Wolfsbane was extremely potent, and I am surprised by the amount that has been used on us repeatedly that we were all still alive. I was immune to death, but the rest of them, they weren't. I heard Wendy awaken beside me. She looked over at me panicking when she realised we were strapped to tables like some science experiment. Whatever was coming next, I knew it wasn't going to be good.

I tried to look around. We were in the same room only the table was gone and, in its place, the three gurneys we were placed on.

"Where's Amber?" asked Wendy. I shook my head, not knowing when Lily spoke.

"They took her," I looked at Lily, her blue and gold eyes gleaming back at me, but she didn't look scared or sad. She looked angry. I wasn't sure if I was looking at Lily or her wolf, it was hard to tell the difference with her eyes remaining like that. Her voice did sound different though older then the six-year-old girl she is.

The door opened and in walked Kade. A woman walking in with him. Her red hair tied tightly in a bun on top of her head, glasses perched on the end of her nose, she was around my age. She carried a small case in her hands and a clipboard.

"Start with the Hybrid," he said, looking towards me and pointing. She nodded her head and walked over, standing beside me. I wondered how she could justify doing whatever it was she was about to do, to women and children; did she feel nothing towards us. I couldn't imagine watching a child and other woman being tortured, I wondered how she sleeps at night. Peacefully or restless? Do her sins weigh heavily on her? She opened the box pulling out two syringes one filled with a green liquid. The other was empty. She jabbed the empty syringe in my arm before drawing blood. Her eyes met mine, and hers quickly darted away guiltily, yes, I knew she didn't have a clear conscience and that her sleep haunted her. I could smell her fear and something else. Guilt.

When she pulled the syringe out, she handed it to Kane before Picking up the syringe with the green liquid in it.

"What is that?" I asked my voice croaky, praying to god whatever they were about to give me wouldn't hurt my baby. I don't know why I turned so maternal all of a sudden, but as soon as she neared my arm panic for my baby kicked in, fear consumed me but not for me but for the baby growing inside me. I squirmed trying to get free.

"Oh, it's a mutation of your father's blood, I have been saving it waiting to catch another Hybrid, I want to see if I can make you shift" Shift? Hybrids couldn't shift, was he insane? I had no doubts he had a few screws loose. Just as she stabbed it in my arm, Wendy blurted out the one thing I was hoping to hide from them.

"Stop, she is pregnant, use me," The woman looked up concerned, her finger hovering above the plunger that could kill my baby. I was too scared to move in case I accidentally injected myself. Kade walked over, lifting up my shirt, revealing my bump. He pulled a stethoscope from his pocket and pressed it against the centre of my stomach and listened. I knew what he could hear, the slow thumping of its heartbeat. He looked up, surprised. He nodded at her. "Remove it." The woman looked relieved. She pulled it from my arm, and I relaxed. My fear dissipating but only momentarily. "Grab a bigger syringe, I want you to inject it into the foetus." She looked appalled.

"What?"

"You heard what I said, now get a bigger needle."

"I can't, I won't do that." I watched as he grew angry, he reached over and grabbed her leaning completely over me.

"Either you do it, or I will inject you with it." She shook her head before he let her go. I started struggling against my leather cuffs. Wait leather? This will be a piece of cake. I watched as her hands shakily drew out a bigger needle, she put it in a vial drawing out the green liquid. Her hand shakily moving towards my stomach. Fucking leather, are they for real, we managed to get out of steel braces did they really believe wolfsbane would weaken me that much? Just as her hand went to jab me, Wendy started yelling at her to stop pulling against her restraints before coming to the same conclusion I did. I felt the needle press but not break the skin on my stomach before I moved, the cuff ripping from the chain that held it to the table. I grabbed her hand, her scream echoing off the glass windows.

I sat upright, just as we heard an explosion, the entire building shaking.

Chapter 49

Aria's POV

THE BLAST FROM THE explosion shattered the windows of our glass cage. Kade being thrown backwoods and into Lily's cage. I still had hold of the woman's hand, that was no longer attached to her arm as a huge shard of glass sliced her arm off, from just below her elbow. The woman is screaming trying to stem the bleeding. I tossed her hand on the ground before undoing my ankle cuffs. Complete and utter chaos ensued. Wolves coming in from everywhere ripping apart anyone they found. Wendy was in battle with a man, still weak, she couldn't put up much of a fight, and I noticed his eyes changing to that of Christine's only he seemed to have more control. Lily was unconscious in the cage, the blast must have knocked her out as her cage was damaged. Kade stood up dusting himself off, I jumped up when he moved with so much speed, I knew he wasn't just a human at least not anymore.

Running at me, I stepped out of reach before shoving the gurney between us, the only problem was that left Lily trapped in the cage on the side he was on. But clearly, I was his target as he paid no attention to her whatsoever. The table David was on was thrown on its side, and I could hear him struggling to get loose before I heard him yell.

"Aria, duck," My body dropped instantly as the table was thrown at Kade and smashing into the brick wall behind him and landing awkwardly covering Lily's cage. Kade shifted just in time and David launched himself at him shifting mid-jump, his claws and teeth sinking into his chest and neck. Kade punched David's wolf, knocking him to the side.

I ran towards him, hitting him before he could stab David with the needle he had grabbed from the floor knocking us both through the brick wall and into the main part of the building where wolves and Hunters were fighting. I groaned having the wind knocked out me, Kade elbowed me in the face and shoved me off.

His eyes changing to a fluorescent blue. What the fuck was he? I had never seen eyes like his before. He stood up, the needle still clutched in his hand, I watched horrified as his fangs protruded from his mouth and claws like a tiger came through, hair sprouting from his arms as he half shifted. Only he wasn't a wolf; he still stood on two legs, and his face remained the same besides the fangs and eyes. He had the making of a wolf yet wasn't one.

We circled each other, trying to get an advantage. Glancing around, I noticed he wasn't the only one that had partly shifted into a wolf. The man Wendy was fighting was the same. The building caught alight. I could hear what sounded like chemicals or gases blowing up bursting and sending sparks everywhere, catching whatever it touches alight.

My attention being diverted, when I see David run from the room, heading towards the new door that had been blown out on the side of the building, he had Lily in arms. I noticed Amber's limp body over his shoulder. I wondered how he found Amber as she wasn't in the same room with us. That distraction cost me, as Kade saw it as an opportunity to get the advantage as he plunged the needle into my arm.

I felt the poison enter my bloodstream and an agonised howl ripping through the room, I looked at the needle, then at Kade who had a triumphant grin, which was soon destroyed as I see Ryder launch himself from the floor above us biting down on Kade's face.

I felt the room shake but not from an explosion but from whatever it was that I was poisoned with. I wobbled on my feet as extreme vertigo washed over me. I felt drunk and stumbled around deliriously, grabbing anything I could to remain upright. Then I saw my father's face next to mine. *Where did he come from?* I drunkenly thought he caught me as I fell to the ground, my eyes looking up at the ceiling. My entire body going numb, as I am paralysed. I hear people talking before I hear my father scream at Ryder.

"Leave him, take my daughter, that bastard is mine." I heard a savage growl, my father's shirt ripping from his body like he was on steroids. His eyes blazing almost red before he left my line of vision, my head rolling to the side. My eyes searching for anything in the smoke and chaos. I could smell the lingering smell of burning plastic and feel the heat of the flames as they got nearer.

The entire building was on fire, and I couldn't move just watch as the flames got closer. "Reid," I coughed out as I started choking on the smoke that was filling the air. What had he given me, it didn't seem to do anything but paralyse me and make me feel sick?

Then I see Reid's face hovering above mine, I could tell he was naked by his bare chest.

"Let's get you out of here," he said, scooping me up, my head falling backwards before he adjusted me, so it was resting on his shoulder heavily. He turned around, looking back at my father, who was still fighting Kade. Flames were everywhere destroying the entire building; parts of the roof were falling, and Reid sang out to all the wolves and humans present.

"Humans?" I mumbled my tongue, starting to go numb.

"I will explain everything later."

"Everyone get out, the building is going to collapse." His Alpha voice rolling over me, I could feel the power behind his words as everyone ran from the building. Reid carried me outside, leaving me on the grass before running back into the burning building. All I could see was the sky, which was black with smoke, it was night-time. I couldn't move, I just lay there. I felt a hand brush my hair from my face, my eyes looking up to see David sitting next to my head, it was his hand I felt.

"Where did Reid go?"

"To help your father and Zane, they are still inside." I felt my heart rate increase, fear taking over. They were in there while I lay paralysed, not able to help. "What about Lily?"

"I'm here,," she said, grabbing my hand and leaning over the top of me.

"Amber too, she is awake as well," I listened carefully and could hear her sobbing somewhere off to my side.

I don't know how long passed but Reid and my father finally came out with Zane. I heard Amber start screaming hysterically, wailing. I heard Zane pick her up and whisper soothingly to her.

"I know baby girl, I know." Hearing them made tears fall from my eyes. I killed her, I killed my friend, killed their loved one. The guilt was eating at me, I hope they will forgive me.

"Reid?" I called out, my voice breaking. He came into my line of vision and knelt beside me, pulling me up, so I was leaning on him.

"Why can't I move?"

"It's the drug, I think your body is rejecting it."

"What was it?"

"We aren't sure, we think it was some mutated gene of your own blood, but your father got him. The Crescent Pack are helping your father move him to their cells for questioning."

The Crescent Pack, that was a name I hadn't heard in years, no one really had an alliance with them, they tended to stick to themselves. I wondered why they suddenly wanted to help.

"Let's get you home," he said, picking me up. I started to get feeling back in my legs when we got to the car, but nausea rolled over me, and Reid helped me manoeuvre, so I didn't throw up all over him, instead emptying the contents of my stomach next to the car.

"Better?"

"A little," My gums tingled and my fangs protruded.

"Where's Lily?"

"Already in the car with David. Zane has Wendy and Amber in the other car."

He pulled me into the back, so I was sitting across his lap. Lily touched my back softly with her small hand. I managed to turn my head, getting enough mobility back to turn slightly. Reid, seeing I wanted to turn to face the front, placed me on his lap, my back pressing against his chest. I felt his hand go to my stomach before going underneath my shirt and rubbing my belly. His hand felt warm on my stomach as he rubbed my belly in circles.

We drove back to our Pack house. By the time we got back, I had full movement back. Whatever he gave me must have been a dud luckily, maybe the Moon Goddess was watching over us after all.

The drive home was quiet but peaceful. It was so strange sitting in a car with David in comfortable silence. Going back to when we were still part of the Black Moon Pack, I would have laughed if someone told me Lily would have her father back wanting to parent and that we would all become a family again. Seeing it with my own eyes now, I knew things were going to be good between us, we just have to mourn those we lost first and rebuild our Packs, but I had no doubt that David was going to step up for his daughter and be the father she deserved all along.

I looked at Lily and smiled sadly. Her blue and yellow eyes looking back at me. I was so proud of her, and I knew that Lily was strong enough to endure it no matter what happens in the future, strong enough to move past what happened and any new challenges. Which I knew we would have them, because her wolf and her had been altered and I could tell it was permanent. But we would get over these obstacles too when they arise. We finally made it home, it was a sombre feeling as we all got out of the cars. Not all of us made it back and the weight of that hung heavily in the air.

Epilogue

Lily's POV
NEARLY 12 YEARS LATER

I WATCHED AS MY SISTER chased after the kids. She was an excellent mother, a little overbearing at times and always so watchful of everything they did, including me. I couldn't get anything past her. When she had her firstborn, a inlittle boy, they named him Ryker. I could tell her life was moving on for the better. When the twins came along, Arial and Lana, I was ten and decided to move back in with my father. Aria had enough on her plate with running the Pack and looking after the kids.

I often felt guilty about her being forced to raise me, but at the same time, I'm glad she did. I knew I never would have made it to adulthood without her. My father and I have now built a bond the way it should have been in the beginning, although I also class Reid as my father, giving me two.

When the twins were born, I felt a little out of place. Life moved on, yet I stayed the same, only growing older. My life has been thrown into chaos since my wolf and I never had a chance to bond, having been forced to shift so young.

For years Aria, my father, and Reid tried to help me learn how to control her, but nothing we did worked, and eventually, we gave up trying. When she had control, it was hard taking it back from her. My wolf was completely altered, and I don't think I will ever be able to let her out willingly. She can't be trusted.

I knew I was a danger to my nieces and nephew, so I made the decision to leave. It was safer that way. Aria and Reid tried to get me to stay, but I couldn't put that burden and worry on them. Aria thinks she owes it to me to fix me, but she doesn't realise she doesn't actually owe me anything, if anything, I owe her for throwing her life away for me. For everything she has done. I still occasionally stay with them. Still see them almost daily, I just hate not being at home.

Most of the wolves of my father's Pack house are older, and if I lose control, I know they can take me down if needed. I won't risk that here with the kids present. I would never forgive myself if I hurt one of them.

As I walked through the clearing towards where Aria was playing on the swings with the kids, she looked up, a smile lighting up her face. I waved heading toward them.

Ryker, seeing me, jumped off the swing mid-air running towards me despite the panicked look his mother gave him. He was eleven now and looked so much like his father with his black hair and silver eyes. The girls had black curly hair, but their mother's amber eyes. Ryker threw himself into my arms. Catching him, we tumbled backwards onto the grass.

"Aunty, Aunty," he squealed. I hugged him tight, smelling his hair. He always smelt of cinnamon. Aria comes over, standing over the pair of us looking down at the pair of us on the grass.

"Ryker, what have I said about jumping off the swings like that? You could have hurt yourself." Ryker rolled his eyes, and I smiled before giving him a wink. He was a wild child, always up to mischief. Maybe he gets that from me.

Aria held her hand out, and I grabbed it, letting her pull me to my feet. She embraced me in a hug before holding me at arm's length, her judging eyes penetrating as she gave me the once over.

"You've been partying again. You know you need to stop this, you're about to take over the Black Moon Pack. It's time to grow up, Lily."

I sighed the same lecture every fucking time. Doesn't she get sick of giving the same speech?

"Don't roll your eyes, you know I'm right. You are about to meet the new Alpha of the Crescent Pack today, and you smell like a brewery," she scolded.

"Fine, I will change, okay?" I left out the part that my father, Reid, and I had been in discussion already about me standing down. I don't want the Alpha position. I know with my wolf, I can't be Alpha. Aria doesn't know this. I think she knows something is up. We have been waiting to let her know, deciding to come out at the meeting. I knew she would pitch a fit. But we have a plan, and today she will find out about it.

"I have already met Alpha Damien, and I don't care what anyone thinks. My life, my body, I will do what I like, Aria," I argued back. She went to say something, but I beat her to it.

"But if it makes you feel any better, I will change, okay?" She looked tired, the kids and I suppose the stress of me has caused her many sleepless nights. Yet she still looked the same, no different, never aging along with Reid. Even the other Pack members aged slower than most because of the link to her.

Aria having Vampire and Lycan blood had its advantages. My sister was a pure Hybrid. The second last of her kind, her father was born from an original Vampire and a Lycan, we only found all this out when her father came back into her life when I was six, when the Hunters attacked and destroyed everything including me.

As I walked back into the Blood Moon Pack house, I made my way upstairs to Aria's room on the top floor. As I was walking up the stairs, I saw Amber, my best friend and accomplice, although I feel Zane sometimes wishes I weren't such a bad influence on his daughter with my wild ways and partying.

"Lil, are you here for the meeting?" She called out to me.

"Yep, come upstairs with me, Aria wants me to change," I said, rolling my eyes. She walked up the stairs a knowing smile on her face, she had also been scolded a few nights before for sneaking in late. Her father Zane and the Beta of the Blood Moon Pack gave us a stern talking to, then he rang my father like he was going to do anything. I only have to bat my lashes and dad was wrapped around my finger. I know he doesn't like punishing me because of my childhood, so why not play on it.

"Where's your father?" I asked nervously.

"Probably off with Wendy, doing something,," she said.

Wendy and Zane both lost their mates in the war with the Hunters. A few years later we were shocked to find out they had been granted second chance mates. Our shock getting stronger when they announced they were getting married and were each other's second chance Mates. Amber was upset at first, no one could replace her mother, but Wendy was a great stepmother and helped raise her, so eventually, she came to see it as a good thing.

When we got upstairs to Aria's room, I walked in not expecting to see Reid getting dressed.

"Shit sorry Alpha," I said as he was standing only in his black pants, hispants, his shirt still undone as he quickly buttoned it up.

"All good Lily, you know where her closet is," he said, pointing to it in the corner of the room. Aria must have warned him I was on my way up.

"You're not gonna scold me, too, are you? Because if you are, I will rock up like this," I said cheekily. Reid smiled.

"No, I'm sure Aria will give you enough shit. Are you ready for today?"

"Yep, just want to get it over with and then bail, you can deal with Aria." I stated.

"She will come around eventually. What about meeting Alpha Damien? You haven't seen him in twelve years, and I know your father had that falling out with him last year."

"That's dad's business, not mine. I don't care for this Alpha Damien. I will just be glad when I don't have to keep going to all these Alpha meetings."

He nodded. "Amber, get your father to meet me in the board-room please," he said, walking over and kissing my head in a fatherly way. Amber quickly left, obviously feeling awkward with Reid getting dressed in front of her. Not that nudity was a big thing with werewolves, and he had pants on so besides his masculine chest you couldn't really see anything.

"Get ready, the other Alphas will be here soon. I know they won't like it when they find out that my Pack will be bigger than theirs once you hand the Pack over to me, so prepare yourself." He left the room, and I walked into the closet.

One thing I loved was Aria's sense of style. I was always borrowing her clothes, it annoyed her sometimes. I rummaged through and grabbed out a pair of jeans and a shirt before throwing on one of her black leather jackets before putting my sneakers back on. Looking in the mirror, I felt I looked decent enough, and no way was I letting Aria dress me, she would have made me wear a dress. But looking in the mirror, I looked great. I was tall, not freakishly tall but taller than Aria, my long blonde hair falling in waves down my back to my waist, then there were the eyes which is what most people saw straight away, I had hoped they would go back to normal. I hated them, people always stared, not that they would ever say anything with my father's presence. Yet, they made me self-conscious, you could tell there was something wrong with me, no matter how hard I try to pretend I am okay. I know what people call me.

Unhinged. They aren't wrong, though. So, I have learnt to accept it. My half amber half sapphire eyes staring back at me are a constant reminder of what those sick Basterds did to me.

"Fuck what anyone thinks," Layla, my wolf growled in my head. She really was a hard case to crack. One minute she almost seems normal, then others she is just a savage, primal and acts out of instinct, we still don't know what's wrong with her and our bond.

"Behave, please don't embarrass me," I whispered back to her.

"Behave? You embarrass yourself, got nothing to do with me. Besides, everything will change soon." I wondered what she meant, and I could feel her pacing in the back of my mind. She never made any sense.

"Everything will make sense, make sense?" She rambled.

"What will?" I asked, annoyed.

"When we turn eighteen, yep eighteen." Clearly, she didn't know what she was talking about, so I gave up trying to get answers. I walked out heading back downstairs only to run back into Amber, who was trying to sneak off with her mate. She found her mate on her sixteenth birthday, I haven't found mine. Layla and I don't think we have one because of what happened years ago. I was often jealous that everyone else in our grade either found their mates already or had boyfriends. People steered clear of me. I'm the unhinged one, the dangerous one, keep your children away parents would say.

Even if we did have a mate, I would have to reject them. I am not mate material. No one wants a broken mate. Layla didn't agree, she thinks reckonedour mate would accept us. She also said she will kill me if I reject our mate. Like I said, she is unhinged, to kill me; she also kills herself. My wolf one minute is lucid, the next batshit crazy. I shake my head at the memory. Amber holds a finger to her lips, and I smile as she and Shaun sneak out the back no doubt to let their wolves free in the forest surrounding the property.

I make my way down the stairs when I get hit with the most intoxicating scent. Mmm, someone must be baking chocolate cookies, my mouth instantly watering. I hear voices off to the side coming from the kitchen. I quickly duck around the corner and run for the board room. I can't afford to be late; I open the door, and all eyes turn to me.

Shit, I am already late. My father has a lazy smirk on his face like he expected nothing less. Reid didn't even look in my direction at all, he knew I was on my way down. Aria was glaring. I shrunk back under that gaze before realising I'm also an Alpha technically, so I hold my chin high and walk to my seat, ignoring her boring eyes. I notice the Alpha from the Forest Pack is already here, and the Alpha Thomas from the Red Moon Pack, but the Crescent Moon Alpha was also running late. I sat in my seat. I hated the Crescent Moon Alpha. I heard he was obnoxious and liked to sleep around. I met him when we were rescued from the Hunters and haven't laid eyes on him since. Only heard the rumours about how he killed his own father and took over the Pack; apparently, he is ruthless and merciless when it comes to his Pack, which is now the biggest Pack.

I knew he would be pissed when he found out mine and Reid's Packs were merging, making ours the biggest and strongest in the country. I stared at the ceiling waiting for the last Alpha to arrive bored already. Only looking up when that intoxicating scent hit my nose again just before the door opened and in stepped the Crescent Moon Alpha.

I must admit he was hot as fuck. He froze, his eyes looking around the room before landing on mine. He looked shocked before he composed himself and walked into the room, taking the seat across from mine. My wolf was going crazy, trying to take control.

"Settle the fuck down, what's gotten into you, Layla?" She didn't answer and just kept pushing against my skin.